THE
SHORT DROP

THE
SHORT
DROP

MATTHEW
FITZSIMMONS

THOMAS & MERCER

Text copyright © 2015 Matthew FitzSimmons

Published by Thomas & Mercer, Seattle.

www.apub.com

Amazon, the Amazon logo, and Thomas & Mercer are trademarks of Amazon.com, Inc., or its affiliates.

ISBN-13: 9781503950252 (paperback)
ISBN-10: 1503950255 (paperback)
ISBN-13: 9781503950344 (hardcover)
ISBN-10: 1503950344 (hardcover)

Cover design by Rex Bonomelli

Printed in the United States of America
First edition

For Uncle Dave

There is no satisfaction in hanging a man who does not object to it.

—*George Bernard Shaw*

PART ONE
VIRGINIA

CHAPTER ONE

Gibson Vaughn sat alone at the bustling counter of the Nighthawk Diner. The breakfast rush was in full swing as customers milled about, waiting for a seat. Gibson barely registered the crescendo of knives and forks on plates or the waitress who set his food down. His eyes were fixed on the television mounted behind the counter. The news was playing the video again. It was ubiquitous, part of the American zeitgeist—dissected and analyzed over the years, referenced in film, television shows, and songs. Like most Americans, Gibson had seen it countless times, and like most Americans he couldn't look away no matter how often it aired. How could he? It was all he had left of Suzanne.

The beginning of the video was grainy and washed out. The picture stuttered and frames dropped; distorted lines rolled up the screen like waves pounding an undiscovered shore. By-products of the store manager having recorded over the same videotape again and again and again.

Shot down at an angle from behind the cash register, the footage showed the interior of the infamous service station in Breezewood, Pennsylvania. The power of the video was that it could have been anywhere. Your hometown. Your daughter. Viewed in its entirety, the silent security camera footage was a melancholic homage to America's most prominent missing girl—Suzanne Lombard. The time stamp read 10:47 p.m.

Beatrice Arnold, a college student working the night shift, was the last-known person to speak to the missing girl. At 10:47 p.m., Beatrice was perched on a stool behind the counter, reading a tattered copy of *The Second Sex*. She would be the first to recall seeing Suzanne Lombard and the first to contact the FBI once the disappearance hit the news.

At 10:48 p.m., a balding man with long, stringy blond hair entered the store. On the Internet, he'd come to be known as Riff-Raff, but the FBI identified him as Davy Oksenberg, a long-haul trucker out of Jacksonville with a history of domestic violence. Oksenberg bought beef jerky and Gatorade. He paid cash and asked for his receipt but idled at the counter, flirting with Beatrice Arnold, in no apparent hurry to get back on the road.

The first and best suspect in the case, Oksenberg had been questioned repeatedly by the FBI in the weeks and months after the disappearance. His rig was searched and searched again, but no trace of the missing girl was found. Grudgingly, the FBI cleared him, but not before Oksenberg lost his job and received dozens of death threats.

After his departure, the store fell still. An eternity ticked by . . . and then you saw her for the first time—the fourteen-year-old girl in an oversized hoodie and Phillies baseball cap, a Hello Kitty backpack slung over one shoulder. She'd been in the store the whole time, standing in the camera's blind spot. To add a layer of intrigue, no one could say for certain how Suzanne came to be in the store in the first place. Beatrice Arnold didn't remember seeing her enter, and the security tape offered no answers.

The hoodie hung off her in great, draping folds. She was a pale, fragile stalk of a girl. The media liked to contrast the black-and-white footage with colorful family photographs—the smiling blonde girl in the blue bridesmaid's dress, the smiling girl at the beach with her mother, the smiling girl reading a book and gazing out the window. They stood in bold relief to the grim-faced kid in the baseball cap, hands thrust deep in pockets, hunched low like an animal watching warily from its burrow.

Suzanne wandered up and down the aisles, but her head was cocked toward the front window. One hundred and seventy-nine seconds passed. Something out the window caught her eye, and her posture changed. A vehicle perhaps. She snatched three items off the shelves: Ring Dings, a Dr Pepper, and a box of Red Vines licorice. A combination now known eerily as the Lost Girl's Picnic. Suzanne also paid in cash, dumping crumpled dollar bills, quarters, and pennies on the counter before shoving her purchases into her backpack.

The security camera caught her eye, and for a long moment Suzanne gazed up at it—an expression frozen in time and, like Mona Lisa's smile, interpreted a thousand different ways.

Gibson stared back, as he always did, locking eyes with Suzanne, waiting for her to smile shyly at him the way she had when she wanted to tell him a secret. Waiting for her to tell him what had happened. Why she'd run away. In all the intervening years, he'd never stopped hoping for an answer. But the little girl on the security video wasn't talking.

To him or anyone else.

In a final gesture, Suzanne drew her baseball cap low over her eyes and looked away for good. At 10:56 p.m., she stepped out the door and into the night. Beatrice Arnold would tell the FBI that the girl seemed anxious and that her eyes were red as if she'd been crying. Neither Beatrice nor the couple pumping gas noticed whether she got into a vehicle. One more frustrating dead end in a case of dead ends.

The FBI failed to turn up a single substantial lead. No one ever came forward to claim the ten-million-dollar reward offered by the family and their supporters. Despite the frenzied media coverage, despite her famous father, Suzanne Lombard walked out of the gas station and vanished. Her disappearance remained an enduring American mystery alongside Jimmy Hoffa, D. B. Cooper, and Virginia Dare.

The news went to commercials, and Gibson exhaled, unaware that he'd been holding his breath. The tape always left him spent. How much longer were they going to keep showing it? There hadn't been a development in Suzanne's case for years. Today's big breaking story was that Riff-Raff had cut his hair short and earned a college degree while in prison for a felony drug bust. The Internet, in its infinite snark, rechristened him Professor Riff-Raff or Raff 2.0. Other than that it was all a maudlin rehash of what everyone already knew, which was nothing.

But the tenth anniversary of her disappearance loomed, which meant the networks would keep running their retrospectives. Keep exploiting Suzanne's memory. Keep trotting out anyone with even a passing relationship to the family or to the case. Staging their tasteless reenactments at the service station in Breezewood and using computer models to project what she might look like today.

Gibson found the mock-ups especially hard to look at. Suzanne would be twenty-four now, a college graduate. The images tempted him into imagining what her life might have been. Where she might live. Her career path—something to do with books, no doubt. He smiled at that but caught himself. It wasn't healthy. Wasn't it time to give her some peace? Give them all some peace?

"Heck of a thing," the man beside him said, staring up at the television.

"Sure is," Gibson agreed.

"I remember where I was when I heard she was missing—hotel room in Indianapolis on a business trip. Like it was yesterday. I have three daughters." The man rapped his knuckles on the wooden counter for luck. "I sat on the edge of the bed for a couple hours watching. Just terrible. Can you imagine not knowing for ten years whether your little girl is alive or dead? Hell of a thing for a family to endure. Lombard's a good man."

The last thing Gibson wanted was to get drawn into a conversation about Benjamin Lombard. He nodded to be agreeable, hoping to put a tourniquet on the subject, but the man would not be deterred that easily.

"I mean, if some sick bastard, excuse my French, can grab the daughter of the vice president—and get away with it—what hope do the rest of us have?"

"Well, he wasn't vice president then."

"Yeah, sure, but he was still a senator. That's no joke either. You don't think Lombard had juice with the feds back then?"

In fact, Gibson knew firsthand just how much influence Lombard wielded and precisely how much the man enjoyed wielding it. Vice President Benjamin Lombard was another subject he tried not to think about.

"I think he'll make a good president," the man continued. "To come back from something like this? Get the VP nod when most people would curl up in a ball. And now a run for president? That takes a strength you can't imagine."

As a two-term incumbent VP of a popular president, Lombard had been expected to nail down the nomination early—the convention in August a mere formality, a coronation more than anything else. But Anne Fleming, the governor of California, had come out of nowhere and seemed intent on playing spoiler. The two were currently polling virtually neck and neck. Lombard led in the delegate count and was still the favorite, but Fleming was making him work for it.

That the tenth anniversary of Suzanne's disappearance fell during an election year had, in a perverse way, been a boost to Benjamin Lombard's campaign. That was nothing new, though: championing Suzanne's Law through the Senate had propelled him onto the national stage in the first place. Of course, Lombard gracefully refused to discuss his daughter. The cynic would argue that there was no need, since the media couldn't help but do it for him. And, of course, there was his wife. Grace Lombard's tireless efforts on behalf of the Center for Missing and Exploited Children had been a staple of cable news outlets throughout the primaries. She was, if possible, even more popular than her powerful husband.

"If he gets the nomination, he's got my vote in November," the man said. "Doesn't even matter who the other side runs. I'm voting for him."

"I'm sure he'll appreciate that," Gibson said and reached for the ketchup. He poured a generous dollop onto one end of his plate, mixed it with a little mayo, and scrambled it into his hash browns the way his father had taught him when he was a boy. In the immortal words of Duke Vaughn, "If you don't have anything nice to say, take a big bite and chew slow."

Words to live by.

CHAPTER TWO

Jenn Charles was parked across the street from the Nighthawk in the back of a white unmarked van. She felt pretty damned conspicuous out here—put her on a forward operating base near the Pakistani border and she was right at home, but white-panel vans in Northern Virginia weren't really her style.

She checked her watch and noted the time in the log. Say what you would about Gibson Vaughn, the man gave predictable a bad name. On the upside, it made surveillance on him simple; on the downside, it got tedious quickly. The daily logs were virtually interchangeable. Vaughn's morning began at five thirty with a five-mile run. Two hundred push-ups, two hundred sit-ups, followed by a shower. Afterward, he ate the same breakfast at the same diner at the same counter stool. Every damn morning, like it was his church.

Jenn brushed a renegade strand of coal-black hair behind her ear. She needed a shower and a good night's sleep in her own bed. She could also use some sun. A pale lethargy was creeping over her after ten days in the back of a van, which was beginning to feel unpleasantly like home. It was crammed with surveillance gear that made it a tight squeeze for one. A small cot at the front allowed a team to work in shifts, but, apart from that, the van offered little in the way of amenities.

Living the dream, Charles. Living the dream.

If Vaughn stayed true to form, in twenty minutes, when the rush died down, he would move to the back of the diner to work. He was friendly with the owners, who let him use one of the back booths as a makeshift office during his job search. It had been three weeks since Vaughn had lost his job at a small, failing biotech firm, where he'd been the information technology director. He wasn't having much luck finding work, and, given his history, Jenn didn't expect that to change.

Dan Hendricks, her partner, was a top-notch surveillance man. He'd broken into Gibson's apartment a week ago and wired it in ninety minutes flat. Motion-activated infrared cameras, bugs, the works. It gave them uninterrupted video coverage of the entire apartment, and the starkness of Gibson's living conditions was informative.

After his divorce, he'd moved into a low-rent high-rise. His living room consisted of a used IKEA table and a wooden chair. No TV, no upholstered furniture, nothing. His bedroom was equally Spartan. Spartan but spotless—eight years in the Marines didn't rub off. A box spring and mattress sat on the floor beside a reading lamp on a squat end table. An unvarnished chest of drawers with a broken leg that he'd repaired. No other furniture. Interior design courtesy of Franz Kafka.

It was hard to believe that at sixteen this guy had been the most wanted hacker in America. The infamous BrnChr0m—a forerunner to the modern, politically motivated hacktivist movement. The teenager responsible for nearly taking down the then senator Benjamin Lombard. Who stole a decade's worth of the senator's e-mails and financial records and turned it all over to the *Washington Post*. Anonymously, or so BrnChr0m had thought—the FBI arrested Gibson Vaughn at his high school and led him from chemistry class in handcuffs. Jenn had taped his mug shot to one of the monitors, and she paused to study his frightened yet defiant face. Twenty-eight now, he'd led an eventful life.

The FBI's swift apprehension of a sixteen-year-old hacker made for a pretty good story. The documents that Vaughn had leaked, on the other hand, made a great one. They detailed a cynical and criminal diversion of campaign funds to banks in the Cayman Islands. They also pointed the finger squarely at Benjamin Lombard. For a time, the revelations looked to signal the end of the senator's political career, and the media went crazy for the idea that a teenager had toppled a US senator. Everyone loved a good David versus Goliath story, even if David had broken a score of federal and state laws in the process.

Jenn had been in college at the time of his arrest and remembered infuriating debates about whether the ends justified the means. Abstracted, high-minded crap that chafed her practical nature. Offended by how many of her classmates saw Vaughn as a digital Robin Hood, she'd felt more than a little vindicated when it broke that BrnChr0m had gotten it absolutely wrong.

In the end, many of the most damning documents were either doctored or outright forgeries. A crime had indeed been committed, but the FBI concluded that the culprit was not Benjamin Lombard but his former chief of staff, Duke Vaughn, who had recently taken his own life. Duke Vaughn had not only embezzled millions of dollars but covered his tracks by implicating Benjamin Lombard. It was a Shakespearean act of betrayal, and when the anonymous hacker turned out to be none other than Duke Vaughn's son . . . well, the story became a sensation and BrnChr0m became a legend.

But Gibson Vaughn hadn't gone by that alias in a long time and was a long way from legendary now.

Since Vaughn was spending his days at the diner, Hendricks had proposed wiring the diner too. Jenn vetoed the idea, but it left a sizeable gap in their eyes-on surveillance that they had to live with. At six p.m., Vaughn would go straight to the gym for an hour and a half. Home by eight, frozen dinner at the computer, lights out by eleven. Rinse and repeat. Day after day. *Christ.* She appreciated the importance of self-discipline and structure, but she'd take a merciful two in the head before she let this be her life.

Her report already noted that Vaughn's entire world was organized around providing for his ex-wife and kid. What was clear to Jenn was that the man was punishing himself. But was he trying to win the woman back or simply atoning by living a forsaken life? First he cheated on her, then turned into Saint Francis of Springfield, Virginia. Jenn couldn't figure men out in general and Gibson Vaughn in particular. He didn't spend penny one on himself, his only luxury the gym membership. Although, to be fair, that was money well spent.

Not that Vaughn was her type. Far from it. Sure, he had a rough-around-the-edges charm about him, and the way his pale-green eyes stared through people fascinated her. But she could still see the chip on his shoulder that had landed him first before a judge and then in the Marines. No matter what he'd been through, there was no excuse for the way it continued to haunt him. You couldn't allow your past to define you.

She ran her tongue over her front teeth. It was a nervous habit. It irritated her whenever she caught herself doing it, but she couldn't make herself stop. Which only irritated her more. Where was Hendricks with her coffee?

As if on cue, Hendricks appeared at the door with two coffees and a cruller. He had to have twenty-plus years on her; she guessed he was north of fifty, but it was only a guess. After working with him for two years, she still didn't know his birthday. His hair had receded to the crown and vitiligo had carved out white patches at the corners of his mouth and around the eyes that stood out sharply against his black skin.

"Still in there?"

Jenn nodded.

"Like clockwork, that boy," Hendricks said. "Regular as a bowel movement."

He handed Jenn a coffee and took a big bite of his cruller.

"They ran out of jelly doughnuts. Believe that? What kind of bakery runs out of jelly doughnuts before nine a.m.? This whole state needs a chiropractor."

Jenn contemplated mentioning Virginia was technically a commonwealth and thought better of it. Needling Hendricks only provoked him.

"Today's the day," she said instead.

"Today's the day."

"Any idea when?"

"Soon as we hear from George."

They were on standby and were finally going to make the approach to Vaughn. Their boss George Abe would handle it personally. She knew all this, of course, but steering the conversation back to business usually kept Hendricks from going off on a rant.

Usually.

Eight years in the CIA had taught her the art of working with men in close quarters. The first lesson was that men never adapted to women. It was a boys' club, and you either became one of the boys or you became a pariah. Anything regarded as feminine was considered soft. The women who thrived were the ones who cursed louder, talked more trash, and showed no sign of weakness. Eventually, you got branded "one tough bitch" and earned a grudging tolerance.

She'd earned her "tough bitch" merit badge the hard way. On some of those forward bases in Afghanistan, she'd gone weeks without seeing another woman. Out there alone, you could never be tough enough. You were always going to be the only woman for a hundred miles. She'd seen men's eyes go from hungry to hostile to predatory, and she'd learned to sleep very, very lightly. It was akin to prison, everyone sizing you up, sniffing for vulnerability. It had gotten so bad on one base that she had contemplated sleeping with the CO in the hope that his rank might shield her. But the idea of being someone's prison bitch hadn't sat well with her.

Jenn ran her tongue over her front teeth again. They felt real enough, although her tongue remained unconvinced. The dental surgeon had done good work once she'd been medevaced to Ramstein Air Base. The experience would have been even more traumatic if she'd known that it was her last real day in the CIA, but that took months to dawn on her. She missed the Agency more than her teeth.

The man who kicked them out hadn't needed a dentist. Hadn't needed much of anyone except maybe a priest. His partner had made it home, though. He was still on her to-do list, along with one or two of the higher-ups who'd turned on her when she refused to play ball. She'd wanted her attacker tried, but it would have meant disclosing a sensitive Agency operation. Lying in a hospital bed in Germany, jaw wired shut, she'd listened to one of her superiors explain the reality of her situation: "Unfortunately, it's the price of doing business in this part of the world," he told her, as though she'd been assaulted by a couple of Taliban fighters and not a pair of sergeants in the United States Army.

But it wasn't until he patted her hand like he was doing her a favor that he went on her list.

Her tongue ran across her teeth again. *Never leave accounts unsettled.* Her grandmother had taught her that.

By comparison, Dan Hendricks was an excellent partner. Twenty-two years in the Los Angeles Police Department showed in the simple, assured way he went about his business. Especially in close quarters, since he was only five foot seven and weighed maybe one thirty if you strapped a Thanksgiving turkey to him. Beyond that, he was tidy and wasn't incessantly vulgar. And best of all, he didn't need her to be a tough bitch, just good at her job. The problem, she was discovering, was that once you learned to be a tough bitch it was hard to turn it off.

Not that Hendricks couldn't take it. The man could teach a master class in bad attitude. He was, without question, the most relentlessly negative person she'd ever met, and if he knew how to smile, she couldn't testify to it. She had no doubt that being black in the

LAPD—an organization with a historically awful record of race relations—could embitter even the most resilient person. But George Abe went way back with Hendricks, and he'd assured her that her partner's negativity had nothing to do with being black in the LAPD. It was just Hendricks.

A phone rang, and they both reached for their cells. Hendricks answered his. The conversation was brief.

"Looks like that time is now," he said.

"He's here?"

"On the way. He wants you inside. There's no telling how Vaughn's going to react."

That was the truth. There was history between her boss and Gibson Vaughn.

None of it good.

CHAPTER THREE

The rush had died down enough that Gibson could hear himself think. He glanced in the back and saw the last table preparing to leave. When they were gone he would commandeer a booth and spend another frustrating day looking for a job. It was Sunday, but he took no days off from job hunting. The mortgage on the house where his ex-wife and daughter lived was due in fifteen days. Fifteen days to find a job.

At least he couldn't have asked for a better place to work. The Nighthawk Diner reminded him of home. His father had considered himself something of a diner connoisseur and passed it on to his son. To Duke Vaughn, diners meant independence and small-business owners, not franchises and corporations. The American commons, he called it. Land owned by one but to which the community holds an indisputable right. Not a romantic populist ideal, but a place where the mythology of America met its blacktop reality—for better and for worse.

His father could, and would, opine at length about the great diners around the country, but the Blue Moon on West Main in Charlottesville, Virginia, had always been home base. If Duke Vaughn had been a professor, his classroom would have been its pockmarked counter. Father-son talks over breakfast had been a hallowed Sunday morning ritual going back to when Gibson was six years old. He'd learned the birds and bees over a slice of cherry pie—and remained embarrassed to admit how many years passed before he got his father's joke.

Duke Vaughn had been royalty at the Blue Moon. Gibson never once saw his father place an order, but it came the same way every time: two eggs sunny side up, hash browns, grits, bacon, sausage, and white toast. Coffee. Orange juice. A man's breakfast, his father called it, and there was no metaphor that Duke couldn't conjure from the meal. Gibson hadn't set foot inside the Blue Moon since his father's death. His father's suicide. Call it what it was.

But after some time had passed, Gibson found he never felt at home in a new place until he located a diner that suited him. *Home on the road,* his father had called it. Gibson thought Duke would have approved of the Nighthawk and its proprietor, Toby Kalpar.

Gibson's eyes drifted to the woman at the end of the counter. Not because she was beautiful or because she was wearing a tailored business suit in a diner on a Sunday morning. It wasn't even the slight outline of a shoulder holster under her left arm—this was Virginia after all. Concealed carry was about as rare as a collar on a dog. It was the fact that although she never looked his way exactly, he could feel her attention on him, and not in a flattering way. He forced himself to look away. Two could play that game. Just a couple of strangers . . . not looking at each other.

"You drink more coffee than a busload of bad poets," Toby said, refilling his cup again.

"You should have seen me in the Corps. I about lived on coffee and Ripped Fuel. By 1800 hours you could fry an egg on my forehead."

"What in the name of God is 'Ripped Fuel'?"

"It's a supplement. For working out. Not exactly legal these days."

Toby nodded philosophically. He and his wife, Sana, had emigrated from Pakistan twenty-six years earlier and bought the diner during the recession. Their daughter had graduated from Corcoran College of

Art and Design in DC, and Toby had picked up a love of modern art from her, renaming the diner after the Edward Hopper painting. Framed copies of midcentury American artwork—Pollock, de Kooning, Rothko—hung throughout the diner. Toby himself, thin with a neatly trimmed gray beard and wire-rimmed spectacles, looked like a man who should curate a rare-books collection, not take breakfast orders. But appearances aside, Toby Kalpar had been born to run an American diner.

Toby lingered at the counter, his expression turning to one of mild embarrassment. "I am sorry to ask again, but I could use your help with the computers. I've spent two nights trying to figure it out, and I am at a loss."

Six months earlier, Gibson had offered his help after overhearing Toby complain about the Nighthawk's computers, which were a morass of malware, spyware-tracking cookies, and assorted viruses. Turned out, Toby desperately needed saving from his compulsion to click "OK" to anything that popped onto his screen.

Gibson had spent a few hours sorting Toby's system out, installing a network, antivirus software, and a restaurant software suite. They'd become friends in the process.

"No problem. Want me to take a look?"

"Not now. I do not want to take you away from your job search. That is most important."

Gibson shrugged. "I'll need a break after a couple hours. Can you survive until lunch?"

"I would be in your debt." Toby extended a hand across the counter. The two men shook. "How is Nicole? Ellie? Both well?"

Nicole was Gibson's ex-wife, Ellie his six-year-old daughter—a four-foot perpetual-motion machine of pure love, shrieks, and dirt. He felt his expression brighten at the sound of her name. Ellie was about the only thing that had that effect on him these days.

"They're both good. Real good."

"Seeing Ellie soon?"

"Hope so. Next weekend, maybe. If Nicole can stay with her sister, I'll go out and stay at the house."

Gibson's accommodations postdivorce weren't very child friendly, and Nicole didn't like the idea of Ellie staying there. Neither did he. So, periodically, Nicole would visit family, and he would spend the weekend at the house with Ellie. One of the many small kindnesses his ex-wife had done him since the end of the marriage.

"See that you do. Little girls need their fathers. Otherwise, they wind up on reality TV."

"Reality TV isn't ready for her. Trust me."

"They would need a very nimble cameraman."

"What you said."

Gibson stood and threw his messenger bag over a shoulder. The woman at the end of the counter was still there. As he passed, her eyes picked him up in the mirror behind the counter and tracked him across the diner. It was unsettling that she didn't give a damn if he knew it.

The back of the diner was empty apart from a solitary man sitting at Gibson's regular booth. The man had his back to Gibson and was jotting notes on a legal pad. There was something familiar about the man, even from behind.

The man sensed someone behind him and stood. He wasn't big, but there was a muscular athleticism to the way he moved. Thirty-five going on fifty. A whisper of gray at the temples, a strong face with only the slightest sagging along the jawline. Otherwise there was little to gauge his age. Also, the man looked unreasonably sharp. Blue jeans and an immaculate button-down so white it belonged in a commercial for bleach. Even his jeans were ironed, and the black leather cowboy boots were spit polished.

Gibson felt a bitter hand dig its nails into his heart. He knew this son of a bitch. Knew him well. George Abe, in the flesh. Smiling at him. Gibson flinched like someone had taken a swing at him, stopping inches from his face. Why was Abe smiling? The man needed to stop smiling. It looked genuine but felt like a taunt. Gibson took a step toward him, not sure what he was going to do but wanting to be ready the second he made up his mind.

He checked himself as the woman from the counter swept into his field of vision. She circled with speed and grace, keeping her distance but making him aware of her presence. What was it they said about Ginger Rogers . . . ? She did everything Fred Astaire did only backward and in heels? Her jacket was unbuttoned, and she'd pivoted to offer him her profile in case she had to draw on him. Her face remained relaxed and expressionless, but Gibson had no doubt that would change if he took another step.

George Abe hadn't moved a muscle.

"I really was hoping for a friendly chat, Gibson."

"She come to all your friendly chats?"

"Hoping, not expecting. Can you blame me?"

"Can you blame *me*?"

"No," Abe said. "I can't."

The two men stared at each other while Gibson considered Abe's response, his initial hostility replaced by a deepening curiosity.

"So what brings you by this morning? I haven't even had time to dust myself off since your boss got me canned from my job last month."

"I know. But I haven't worked for Benjamin Lombard in some time. I was . . . let go. The week after you began basic training."

"Is that a fact?" Gibson said. "You do his dirty work and then he shows you the door? There's a kind of poetry to that, you think?"

"If you like poetry."

"Well, if you're not here for him, what do you want?"

"As I said, a friendly chat."

George Abe handed him a business card. It listed a downtown DC address and phone number. Beneath his name, it read, "Director, Abe Consulting Group."

When he was a kid, Gibson had mispronounced George Abe's name until his father corrected him: "Ah-bay. More Japanese, less Lincoln." As Benjamin Lombard's head of security, George had been a fixture in Gibson's childhood. The man in the background. Polite, courteous but professionally invisible. It wasn't until Gibson's trial that he'd paid close attention to him, but by then George Abe had been neither polite nor courteous.

"Fancy," Gibson said.

"I have a job offer for you."

Gibson searched for the wherewithal to reply, curiosity segueing to disbelief. "I've got to hand it to you, George. You've got a mighty, mighty large set on you."

"Hear me out."

"I'm not interested." Gibson handed the business card back.

"How goes the job hunt?"

Gibson froze and appraised Abe coolly. "Be a tiny bit careful."

"Understood. But know I mean nothing by it except to outline the situation," Abe said. "The fact is, you are unemployed and your history will make it hard to find a job commensurate with your skill set. You need work. I have work. Work that will pay better than any job you're likely to find. If you're able to find a job at all."

"Still not interested." Gibson turned and took four steps to the door before Abe stopped him cold.

"He's not ever going to let it go. You know that, don't you?"

The bluntness of the words shook Gibson. It summed up fears that dwelt and rutted in the dark of his mind.

"Why not?" He couldn't keep the pleading tone out of his voice.

Abe looked at him pityingly. "Because you're Gibson Vaughn. Because he treated you like a son."

"Did he get me fired?"

Maybe? Probably. It doesn't matter. If I were you, I'd

hat he'll do if he becomes president. You'll be lucky

_ria."

"Haven't I paid enough?"

"It'll never be enough. There are no bygones here. His enemies? Enemies for life. And his enemies pay for life. That's how Benjamin Lombard plays the game."

"So I'm fucked."

"Unless you give him a reason to let it go."

"What reason is there?"

Abe sat back down at the booth and gestured for Gibson to join him.

"Is this the friendly chat part?"

"I think it would be in your interest to hear me out."

Gibson weighed his options: tell George Abe to go to hell, which would feel really good, or hear him out and then tell him to go to hell.

"You want a friendly chat, tell your lady friend to stand down."

Abe motioned to the woman, who rebuttoned her jacket and withdrew to the far side of the counter.

"Shall we?" Abe asked.

CHAPTER FOUR

Gibson slid into the booth opposite Abe. George Abe. George fucking Abe. He exhaled at the wonder of it. Sitting face-to-face with him after all this time. Abe was a link to his past. A link to his father. What had it been? Ten . . . no, eleven years? Not since the last day of his trial, when the judge dropped his bombshell.

Abe hadn't sat at the prosecution table, although he might as well have. Throughout the trial, he and his legal pad were fixtures in the gallery directly behind the district attorney. Abe fed the prosecution documents, huddled for private conferences, and passed notes forward at key moments. You would be forgiven if you came away with the impression that the DA took its marching orders from George Abe. Gibson certainly had.

It was months after his arrest when Gibson realized that Benjamin Lombard wasn't leaving his trial to chance. In hacking into the senator's computers, Gibson had broken both state and federal laws, but the assumption was that the federal charges would supersede local. At least until the case had been unexpectedly rerouted to the Virginia courts. The reason, though never stated, was simple: federal judgeships were lifetime appointments, while Virginia circuit judges served eight-year

cted by the Virginia Assembly. Lombard had called
Gibson's trial to a venue where he could bring to
nfluence. The DA's decision to try him as an adult
for a nonviolent first-time offense only confirmed that suspicion. So
when his trial began, Gibson assumed the judge must also be batting
for Team Lombard.

The trial was over in nine days, the verdict a foregone conclusion.
Gibson's hard drives were all the evidence the prosecution needed.
Pronounced guilty, he was returned to his cell to await sentencing. But
a few days later, his lawyer collected him and brought him before the
judge. Not to the courtroom proper but to the judge's chambers. At
the door, the judge and Gibson's lawyer exchanged an odd, complicit
glance.

"I'll take it from here, Mr. Jennings," the judge said.

His lawyer nodded, glanced sideways at his confused young client,
and left them standing in the doorway without a word. Gibson didn't
know a lot about the law, but even he knew it was irregular. When they
were alone, the judge gestured for Gibson to come inside.

"Think we should have a chat, you and me."

The judge took two glass bottles of RC Cola from a small refrigerator and popped the caps with a bottle opener attached to the wall. He
offered Gibson one and settled behind his broad mahogany desk.

The Honorable Hammond D. Birk was a mixture of cantankerous
southern gentleman and hardscrabble Virginia blue collar. He'd been a
relentless hard-ass throughout the trial—scathing when his courtroom
didn't perform up to his standards, but charming and polite in the
manner he conveyed his considerable displeasure. The lawyers on both
sides treaded carefully to avoid incurring his wrath. Sitting in the judge's
leather armchair, Gibson was afraid to so much as take a sip of his soda.

"Son," the judge began. "I'm going to make you a one-time-only
offer. There'll be no questions, no discussion, and no negotiation. When
I'm done talking, I only want to hear one of two words out of you. Yes

or no. Just one of those words, and then we're going to go out there today and wrap up this damn circus, which frankly offends me. You understand me?"

Gibson nodded silently in case answering the question aloud was a trap that would disqualify him.

"Good," the judge said. "My offer is pretty straightforward. Ten years in prison or an enlistment in the United States Marine Corps. Not that you asked, but an enlistment is five years. That's half, in case you're wondering. And you'd be doing something useful in the service with that brain of yours other than counting the weeks, months, and years until your release. So . . . ten years or an enlistment. At the end of which, I will personally expunge your record, and you may go about making your way in this petty world of ours."

The judge emptied his bottle and squinted across the desk at Gibson.

"I'm done speaking now, son. It's your turn. Take your time and think it over. Yes for Marines, no for jail. Just let me know your answer when it comes to you. And don't go letting your RC get warm. It was your father's favorite in college."

Gibson looked up at the judge, who smiled at him.

They sat a spell in silence, though in truth the decision hadn't taken any time at all. Twenty years in the service would have been a small price to pay to avoid another night in a cell. And that was just jail—real prison was an entirely different animal, and it scared Gibson to death. But he'd enjoyed sitting there with the judge, drinking RC Cola and hoping Birk might talk a little more about his father.

But the judge never had, either then or in any of the dozens of letters they'd exchanged while Gibson was in the service. The first had arrived unexpectedly on the day before his graduation from Parris Island. Only his third piece of mail since entering the Corps, the letter was a thoughtful meditation on adulthood. It had run to twenty handwritten pages; Gibson had sat on the edge of his bunk, reading it over and over. It was Family Day, which meant that most of his fellow graduates were touring the base with relatives. The letter made him feel less alone in the world. He'd written back a heartfelt thank-you. After that, they'd traded letters every few months—Gibson's terse and newsy, the judge's expansive and philosophical. Gibson wondered what the judge would advise in this situation.

"I remember the last time I saw you," Gibson told Abe. "Right after the judge said I was going to the Marines. Everyone lost their mind, but not you. I wanted to see your reaction, but you just stood up and left. Even took the time to button your suit jacket and then walked out like nothing had happened. Very smooth. Were you on your way to deliver the bad news to Lombard?"

"I was."

"I always wondered how Lombard took it, after all that work to send me up the river. Guess it didn't go over well."

"No. It did not go over well at all. But I'm glad it worked out the way it did. I've come to realize it was a mistake. I am sorry for the part I played in what happened to you."

The apology caught Gibson off guard. He felt a strange sense of gratitude simply to hear someone apologize at last. He also resented it almost immediately. Yes, it was unexpected and might feel good, but what difference did a ten-year-old apology make?

"So you were just some innocent pawn—is that what you're selling?"

"No." Abe shook his head. "I don't believe ignorance is enough. I was ignorant, but only because I allowed myself that luxury. Because I didn't ask the questions that I should have. My loyalty misled me. I knew it was wrong, but I ignored my instincts. I am far from innocent."

"So what, then?" Gibson asked. "You and Girl Friday back there track me down so you can get that off your chest? A little Sunday morning confessional? Do you feel better?"

"It does feel good. I'm surprised at just how good. But that's not why I'm here."

Toby appeared with menus and a pot of coffee. He flipped over the cup in front of Gibson and filled it. He seemed uneasy and gave Gibson a look that asked if he should do something. Gibson shook his head imperceptibly. Whatever was happening here, Gibson didn't want to involve Toby.

"I'll be back in a few minutes, gentlemen," Toby said.

When he was gone, Gibson scratched under his lip with his thumbnail and pointed a finger at Abe. "So why *are* you here?"

"I'm here for Suzanne."

He felt cold, sharp teeth brush the nape of his neck, and the hair on his arms stood up uneasily. It was the first time someone had said her name to him in years. Even his ex-wife knew better than to bring her up.

"Suzanne Lombard."

Abe nodded. "I want you to help me find out what happened to her."

"Suzanne is dead, George. That's what happened."

"Probably. Probably that's true."

"It's been ten years!" Gibson felt his voice rising out of his control. Probably? The word scalpeled its way into Gibson, anger giving way to unthinkable despair. Suzanne was dead. She had to be. It had been ten years. The alternative was so much worse; remaining alive would not be a mercy under such circumstances. No . . . if she was alive, that meant she was hidden. And if she remained hidden after all that time, then someone had gone to desperate lengths to do so. There were no happy answers as to why; only nightmare images conjured in his mind.

"Why? What's in it for you? Hoping to get back in Lombard's good graces?"

"No. He and I are through."

"Then what? Old times' sake?"

"My reasons are none of your business."

I've never answered to my satis-
profession. My job was to protect
was part of that responsibility. In
shed on my watch."

on might start to like the guy.

en desire to dig it all up? Because of

ce with me and see for yourself."

ve?" Gibson tried to read it off of him,
nfidence. Was it possible? Could Abe
that had stymied law enforcement for a
shot was Abe playing? Did it matter? If
ance of finding Suzanne, Gibson knew he
tion.

pe across the table. Gibson opened it and
ack of money inside. He didn't count it, but

gy for interrupting your breakfast, or it's a sign-
yours."

d help, I'm offering twice your former salary plus
-dollar bonus if your work produces a substantial

d out of the booth, gave the woman a nod, and left
er.

see that he had any choice but to follow.

that. If you don't want any-
ffort to find his daughter?
it over to the feds and be

ibson didn't trust him, but
nder of an old pickup.
ibson."

one."
of tears. Abe saw it and gave

u everywhere. And I saw the way
ur own sister. We all saw it." Abe
"This bad blood between you and
Suzanne?"
vered his mouth with a firm hand
he fight to maintain his composure.
w about you, but I need to know. I
to know what happened to her. I want
lured that beautiful wisp of a girl from
rious conversation with that man. The
Abe paused, tasting the violence implicit
egin to settle the books between you and
much the better."

fired you? Because of Suzanne?"

anced out the window. Gibson thought the
ghtly. When Abe spoke it was quietly, his voice

28

CHAPTER FIVE

The motorcade knifed its way through downtown Phoenix like a war-
ship crossing a concrete-and-metal ocean. More than a half block long,
its bow was formed by a wedge of motorcycle police, sirens wailing as
they plowed a path through the congested Friday-afternoon traffic. In
its wake waited cars pulled hurriedly to the curb and pedestrians who
stopped to gawk at the spectacle.

Benjamin Lombard heard and saw none of it. He sat in the back of
one of the limousines, always a different limousine, reviewing his schedule for the coming week. He was aware of his staff's anticipation but
took his time. He was accustomed to people waiting on his decision.
Their time was, in point of fact, his time. Eventually, he made several
minor corrections and thrust the itinerary back to one of his aides.

He was tired and more than a little frustrated. Over the last twenty-
five days, he'd watched Governor Anne Fleming eat further into his lead
in the polls. What had begun as an amusing sideshow was becoming a
real threat. A recent political cartoon depicted him as a hare sleeping
under a tree while Fleming, the tortoise, passed him. He'd gone from
the chosen one to the butt of jokes on late-night television. A year ago,
the first-term governor from California hadn't even been a name in

the presidential conversation. Lombard had been such a heavy favorite that even major names in the party had chosen to sit out the election. And now he was running neck and neck with a novice. His advisers dismissed Fleming and believed she would fade, but he wasn't so sure. So far she'd countered everything they'd thrown at her like an old pro and made him look foolish in the process. The big donors were starting to wake up to it. If she wasn't neutralized now, the convention in Atlanta would be a dogfight.

"Tell Douglass to scrub the Santa Fe leg," Lombard said. "I want to go straight to the airport after the fund-raiser tonight."

Leland Reed shifted in his seat. "Ah, sir, Douglass feels it's important to put in an appearance tomorrow if we want Governor Macklin's support. We won't be out here again before the convention."

Leland Reed was the vice president's chief of staff. Now in his mid-fifties, Reed had a reputation as an unflappable operative—a problem solver. He'd earned his bona fides, time and again, over a thirty-three-year career on the Hill and innumerable campaigns.

Lombard thought highly of his chief of staff. After Duke Vaughn had committed suicide, Lombard had chewed through two replacements before settling on Reed. Reed spoke his language and shared his unblinking determination, but he was no Duke Vaughn. Not that that was something to be ashamed of—Duke Vaughn had been one of a kind. Duke would have known instinctually, as Leland Reed did not, why Santa Fe was a bad idea. Duke saw the same pieces on the board as everyone else did, but he'd played the game many moves ahead. He'd taught Lombard much of what he knew about politics.

Leland Reed was relentless but needed to be pointed in the right direction. In some ways that was preferable. Lombard had grown accustomed to being the smartest person in any room, but there were times when he missed knowing that, if a problem arose, Duke was already on it.

He fixed Reed with an icy glare.

"We're not getting Macklin's endorsement. He's going to throw in with Fleming."

"But, sir, Douglass feels that Macklin is making overtures."

"Macklin was making overtures when I was ahead by ten points. But now I'm ahead by the width of your dick, and he's going to throw in with Fleming, who he's known for twenty years and will promise him things that I won't. Sure, he'll make me dance for it, but in the end he's not going to give it to me."

"Isn't it worth it since we're already out here?"

"Megan, where is Governor Fleming scheduled to be next Friday?" Lombard asked.

His aide tabbed over to a schedule on her laptop. "Arizona, sir."

"This is a waste of time, Leland. We're being strung along, so fuck Governor Macklin and fuck Douglass while you're at it."

"Sir?" Reed's voice remained even and upbeat despite the sudden spike in the vice president's temper and language.

"I'm concerned with Douglass and the way he's reading the terrain," Lombard explained patiently. "He's making decisions based on last week's polls. I need him to get out in front of Fleming. She's not going anywhere, and I'm tired of hearing him say otherwise."

"Yes, sir," Reed said. "What should I give as a reason for canceling?"

"Something vague. 'Needed in Washington' always has a nice ring. I am still the vice president. He'll figure it out."

"Yes, sir," Reed said.

"I want to sit down with Douglass, Bennett, and Guzman first thing in the morning. We're going to get some things straight. They're not the only campaign strategists in Washington."

Lombard looked out the tinted window at the blur that was Phoenix. Living in this bubble was one of the surreal aspects of the job. For the past eight years, there hadn't been a single moment where he'd been truly alone, when thirty people didn't know his exact location. To do this job, and to do it well, was to be in constant motion, surrounded by people, ideas, action. And, by God, he loved it. He'd love being president even more.

When reporters asked him why he wanted to be president, Lombard mouthed the same elegant clichés that his forebears had uttered—platitudes about service and country and having a vision for the future of the nation. It was nonsense, of course, and he doubted that they had meant it any more than he did. The truth? When else in human history could someone ascend bloodlessly to become the most powerful man in the world? It was the chance to be a civilized god, and he didn't trust anyone who aspired to less. But the difference between him and most people was that he'd been born for it. Made for it.

The motorcade roared to a halt outside the hotel, and Lombard watched the Secret Service spring into action. Two dozen car doors opened simultaneously. Agents spilled forth and spread out like marines establishing a beachhead. When they were ready, his limousine door opened and he stepped out into the sunshine, smiling broadly. Taller than all but one of the agents, he paused to survey the hotel, button his suit jacket, and wave to his supporters on the far curb, who greeted him with a burst of applause. Then he allowed himself to be ushered into the hotel.

He made a mental note to have the tall agent moved off his detail.

His flock of aides surrounded him inside the hotel and brought him up to speed on the way to his suite. While the rundown was going on, he scanned two memos and peppered them with questions. He was adept at following multiple conversations simultaneously.

"What time is the fund-raiser?" he asked.

"Eight, sir."

"Where's my speech?"

Someone handed him a fresh copy. He also took two briefing books that included the latest intelligence on a developing situation in Egypt and an update on Senate wrangling over an immigration bill.

"Leland, I want to see you in two hours. We'll talk over lunch. Otherwise, don't bother me unless there's a constitutional crisis and I'm president."

That brought a polite chuckle from the flock. The Secret Service pulled the door shut behind him.

Alone, Benjamin Lombard took off his suit and laid it out on the bed so it wouldn't pick up a crease. The air-conditioning felt good after the unrelenting Arizona heat. He wasn't sure why, but a five-star hotel had better air-conditioning than just about anywhere else on earth. He considered it the pinnacle of civilization, enabling a man to live in such godforsaken places as Phoenix, Arizona.

Standing in his dress shirt, boxers, and black socks, he let himself cool in the dark of his suite. After a few moments, he turned on the news and was greeted by a story about Anne Fleming's campaign stop in California. Benjamin saw it now; the light attendance at his stump speech this morning had brought the big picture into focus. The more he thought about it, the more he felt that tomorrow's meeting with Douglass needed to be a bloodletting. It would send a message and would reenergize and focus the troops. He wondered what it would take to coax Abigail Saldana out of semiretirement as a pundit; she wouldn't put up with this Fleming nonsense.

A staccato knock at the door broke him from his thoughts, and his good mood evaporated. The Senate itself had better be a smoking crater, or so help him God, whatever overeager staffer stood on the far side of that door would need to move to Turkey to find a job in politics.

"What?" Lombard bellowed, nearly yanking the door off its hinges.

It was Leland Reed, and he looked troubled.

"What is it?" Lombard asked again, but the fire had gone out of his voice.

"Can I come in, sir?"

Benjamin stood aside and let him into the suite. Reed didn't sit but instead did an uneasy circuit around the room like an automated vacuum cleaner patrolling for dirt. Eventually, he came to a rest by the window.

"Well, what is it? Christ, you're making me nervous."

"Sir, you know the list you asked me to keep an eye on."

Lombard knew exactly what list Reed meant. You didn't make it this far in politics without making a few enemies. More than a few. The list comprised people who might try to hurt his campaign. Everyone from political foes to former employees to a high-school girlfriend who didn't like the way they'd broken up. It wasn't that he was expecting trouble, but every campaign dug something long forgotten out of a candidate's past. There was no reason to expect this one would be any different.

"Who?" Lombard asked.

"George Abe."

"George? Really." That surprised him. He'd always considered them on reasonable terms despite how they'd parted ways. "What's George done?"

"He met Duke Vaughn's son at a diner in Virginia. They're driving into Washington as we speak."

The hairs on Lombard's neck prickled. Gibson Vaughn and George Abe. Those were two names he never expected to hear in the same sentence, and the only thing they had in common was him. That they were together could not be a coincidence.

"What were they talking about?"

"That I don't know, sir."

"Well, find out. Do we have anyone in George's outfit?"

"No, sir," Reed said.

"Well, get someone. And get Eskridge on the phone. Looks like he may need to get hands-on after all."

CHAPTER SIX

They drove in silence to DC. Gibson sat in back beside George Abe, who disappeared into his phone, answering e-mails. When Abe entered his phone's passcode, Gibson stole it out of the corner of his eye. It was force of habit. It had taken him months to perfect the skill, but he could steal a phone's passcode from across a room simply by watching the thumb move. Gibson filed it away just in case.

Numbers had always come easy. Math, science, computers had always made sense to him. It had been a tremendous asset when he'd gone to the dark side. He'd trained himself to remember sequences of numbers. He could recall anything up to sixteen digits with one pass: phone numbers, credit cards, social-security numbers—it was remarkable how often people recited vital information in public. It ranked among his less socially acceptable talents.

Up front, Abe's girl Friday sat in the passenger seat, scanning the road like she was riding point in Fallujah. He'd seen that look before in the eyes of combat veterans. The memories that wouldn't stay memories. The sights and sounds that were forever tuning up like a discordant symphony. She carried it like that—tense and watchful—as if roadside ambushes were commonplace in Northern Virginia.

Back at the Nighthawk, Abe had introduced her as Jenn Charles. She'd given him a professional handshake, but her false, trapdoor smile was a warning not to cross her. Still, Jenn was a sweetheart compared to the dour little man driving: Hendricks—no first name given. Hendricks didn't seem to like Gibson either, but, unlike with Jenn Charles, it didn't feel personal. Hendricks didn't seem to like much of anything or anyone.

Despite it being a Sunday, traffic into DC was as heavy as rush hour. It was early April and the cherry blossoms were blooming, so the roads into Georgetown were bumper to bumper with sightseers. Somehow Hendricks maneuvered them expertly through the congestion, dancing between lanes as one ground to a halt and the other accelerated. A very practical superpower, Gibson thought. On Key Bridge, Hendricks exited onto the elevated Whitehurst Freeway, which ran alongside the Potomac and emptied them onto K Street. The river sparkled all the way down to the Kennedy Center.

Gibson glanced at Abe. His words at the diner still stung—*Suzanne loved you better than anyone.* He looked out the window at the river.

Better than anyone.

Gibson had known Suzanne since they were kids, their lives linked by their fathers' bond, which ran far deeper than senator and chief of staff. Lombard had been best man at Duke's wedding, and after his mother's death, when he was three, Gibson spent more of his holidays with the Lombards than with his own family. Senator Lombard and Duke would often work late into the night and through weekends, and as a result Gibson had his own bedroom down the hall from Suzanne. When Gibson was seven, Duke had to sit him down and explain that three-year-old Suzanne was not his actual sister. Gibson had not taken the news well.

Some of his fondest childhood memories were from the Lombards' summer house at Pamsrest on the Virginia shore. Summer began each year with the annual Memorial Day party thrown for hundreds of the

Lombards' closest friends, political allies, and their families. There were always scores of kids to play with, and they were allowed to run wild while the grown-ups socialized and networked on the lawn and wide wraparound porch. Gibson would spend the day playing epic games of capture the flag that ranged all over the back of the property. An ice-cream truck made an annual appearance to the delight of the children, who had already pigged out on hamburgers, hot dogs, and potato salad. It was a kid's paradise, and he'd always looked forward to such events eagerly.

Suzanne spent the parties inside, reading in the large bay windows that dominated the back of the house. From the raised, cushioned banquettes piled high with pillows, she could look out over the property as far as the tree line. It was a waste of a beautiful day, in his opinion. At that age, he much preferred climbing trees to contemplating them. But it was Suzanne's favorite spot in the house and the first place anyone looked for her. From there she could watch the party and read her ever-present books. If she could sweet-talk her mother into delivering her lunch, she would happily pass the day reading and napping in the sunshine.

While he counted her as a sister, Gibson didn't "get" Suzanne for the longest time and treated her the way older brothers often treat little sisters—like foreign creatures. She didn't play football or baseball; she didn't like playing soldier out back in the woods; she didn't like any of the games that he liked. So he did the only sensible thing under the circumstances—he ignored her. Not out of spite but simple expedience. They had no shared language.

But Suzanne treated him the way little sisters tend to treat older brothers—with patient love and constant amazement. She met his dismissiveness with adoration, his disinterest with beamy smiles. She was never hurt or put off that he didn't return her affection, and she was always willing to give him another chance. In the end, she simply outloved him with a child's generosity—the kind that burns away as one enters adulthood, but which Suzanne had in abundance. Gibson never stood a chance, and, eventually, with persistence, she wore him down, and he learned to love her back. And somewhere along the line she stopped being Suzanne and became his sister.

His Bear.

Not content to simply be loved, Bear pestered him, for what seemed like years, to read to her. He'd read to her once when she was very little; he couldn't remember what book, only that he'd quickly lost interest. Since then she'd begged him to read to her again, usually from her reading nook as he pelted out the back door to play in the woods. He wasn't a reader in those days, so he'd always put her off.

"Gib-Son. Gib-Son!" she would call. "Come read to me!"

"Later, Bear. Okay?" was always his answer.

"Okay, Son. Bye!" she would call after him. "Later!" As though later had become an official date.

Bear always said his name as if it were two words or sometimes shortened it to "Son" if she was excited. Duke thought she sounded like an old southern gentleman: "What are you doing, Son?" It made all the adults laugh, which only encouraged her. She didn't get why it was funny, only cared that it meant everyone was paying attention to her.

Bear finally broke him down one Christmas. The senator and Duke were in crisis mode over some piece of legislation, so Gibson spent most of that holiday at the Lombards' house in Great Falls. She was seven. He was eleven. In a moment of weakness, he said yes, and she'd gone scampering off before he could start another movie. She came back with *The Fellowship of the Ring* by someone named J. R. R. Tolkien. The movies based on the series hadn't existed back then, so he didn't know anything about the book except that it was thick and hardbound.

"Bear. No chance," he said, weighing it in his hands. "It's too big."

"It's the first book of three!" She was bouncing with excitement.

"Come on . . ."

"No, it'll be good. I promise. It's an adventure," she said. "I've been saving it for you."

Grace Lombard had watched with an amused, pitying smile that told him what he already suspected—no escape for you now, young man. Gibson sighed. How bad could it be? He flipped to chapter one. What the hell was a hobbit? Whatever. He'd read for twenty minutes, Bear would get bored or fall asleep, and that would be the end of it.

"All right. Where do you want to read it?"

"Yes!" she said triumphantly and then had to think, not having planned on getting this far. "By the fireplace?"

She led him to an armchair in the living room. The fire was dying, and Bear built it up until Grace warned her not to burn down the house. Then he'd waited another ten minutes while Bear arranged everything just so. That meant piles of pillows and a throw, hot chocolate for her, a glass of Cran-Apple juice for him. She ran around the room, adjusting the lights so it wasn't too bright but not too dark either. Gibson stood in the middle of the room, wondering what he'd gotten himself into.

"Sit, sit, sit," Bear said.

He sat. "Is this okay?"

"Perfect!" Bear snuggled contentedly across his lap and put her head on his shoulder.

He gave her ten minutes before she'd be asleep.

"Are you ready?" he said, trying to sound grumpy but failing.

"Ready. Oh, wait," she said but thought better of it. "No, never mind."

"What?"

"Never mind," she said, shaking her head. "Next time."

There wasn't going to be a next time. He opened the book and got comfortable. Halfway into the first sentence, Bear stopped him.

"Son?"

He stopped. "What?"

"Thank you."

"You know there's no way I'm reading this whole thing."

"That's okay. Just as much as you feel like."

He read the first thirty pages without a pause. Bear didn't fall asleep, and it wasn't even a bad story. There was a wizard and magic, so that was pretty cool. They were still reading when the senator and Duke took a break from their strategizing. Mrs. Lombard led them to the doorway of the living room. Stealthily, like it was a safari, and they might startle the wildlife. Gibson didn't notice them until the camera flashed.

A framed copy of the picture had hung in the hall between their bedrooms, and Duke had kept one in his office at home.

After the surprise photo, Gibson had tried to quit reading, but Bear, sensing trouble, clamped her hands around his arm.

"What happens next?"

Gibson found he was curious too.

They finished *The Return of the King* two years later, and in the process, Gibson became a reader. Something else he owed Bear. Books helped him keep his sanity first in jail and then in the Marine Corps. He read whatever he could get his hands on: obscure Philip K. Dick stories, pulp Jim Thompson mysteries, Albert Camus's *The Stranger*, which he'd found revelatory at nineteen. An ancient copy of Don DeLillo's *Great Jones Street* had been a constant companion since boot camp, and he could recite the opening monologue from memory.

If he was honest, he had never allowed himself to connect the Suzanne Lombard in the security-camera footage with his Bear. In his mind, Bear was a college graduate, living in London or Vienna the way she had always daydreamed. Bear was dating some smart, shy boy who adored her and read to her on Sunday mornings. Bear had nothing at all to do with the long-missing Suzanne Lombard. It was easier to believe that fiction.

Would she like his daughter? He sometimes caught himself comparing them—the two little girls who figured so large in his life. Not one bit alike—Ellie wasn't the quiet, introspective type. She was like her dad in that regard, much preferring to climb trees than read under one. But Ellie and Bear were exactly the same when it came to loving people. They both hugged in the same fierce, uncompromising way. Yeah, Bear would have loved Ellie, and Ellie would have loved her right back.

Where did you go, Bear?

Gibson looked at George Abe and the team he'd assembled.

Would she answer at last?

CHAPTER SEVEN

As they passed McPherson Square, Jenn shifted in her seat and let George know they were back. The Range Rover pulled into the building's underground garage.

When they parked and got out, Jenn drifted to the back so she could keep an eye on Vaughn. He glanced back at her but said nothing. He was taller than she expected, but his eyes were no less intense. He'd made her in the diner, which was embarrassing enough, but the way he met her eyes when they shook hands outside the diner made her feel like a microwavable dinner. She didn't like it.

Upstairs, the offices of Abe Consulting Group were dark and quiet. The lights hummed to life automatically. It wasn't a huge space, but the atrium was immaculate and modern with high ceilings and stylish black leather furniture. Vaughn seemed impressed.

Hendricks ushered them down a corridor toward the sound of thudding, angry music. He pushed open a pair of glass doors to a conference room, and the noise spiked painfully. It was like standing on a runway as a 747 landed over your head. Jenn recognized it but didn't know the name of the band. She never did. She didn't care enough about music to waste time committing it to memory.

A bald head popped up from behind a laptop like a weary Whac-A-Mole.

"The music, Mike! Jesus!" Hendricks yelled.

The conference room went silent, and the bald head stood up. It belonged to Mike Rilling, Abe Consulting's IT director. In his early thirties, he had the jittery, bloodshot eyes and sallow skin of a man living on a potent cocktail of caffeine and junk food. The stale smell of stress clung to the room.

"Sorry, Mr. Abe. I didn't think you'd be here until this afternoon."

"It *is* this afternoon," Jenn said.

"Oh," Mike said. "I'm sorry, Mr. Abe."

"That's fine. How is it coming?" Abe asked.

Mike's mouth opened but closed without answering the question in what Jenn recognized as the international sign for *It's not coming at all, and I wish people would stop asking about it.* She'd been there and had some sympathy for him. Mike worked as hard as anyone on the team, but this was not his area of expertise. Not his fault, though overselling his ability had been. That was why Vaughn was here. If it wasn't already too late.

Ordinarily, this was their main conference room, but it had been converted into a makeshift war room. Photographs, diagrams, maps, and notes were pinned neatly to a series of wheeled bulletin boards arranged along one wall. A photograph of Suzanne Lombard sat at the top of the center bulletin board, her immediate family arrayed below her like an inverted family tree. Vaughn's eyes went straight to it, and an expression she couldn't interpret passed over his face.

Arrayed beneath the family, staff members from Lombard's Senate days, including Duke Vaughn, formed a row of their own. George's photo was up there too. Completing the gallery, two blank placeholders hung side by side. One was labeled "WR8TH"—the anonymous chat-room handle of the person or persons with whom Suzanne had communicated online prior to her disappearance. The second read "Tom B." A line connected the pair and a question mark hung between.

Abe took a seat at the head of the table. Hendricks and Vaughn followed suit while Rilling scurried around like a frantic mother hen.

"Michael. Please. Housekeeping can wait," Abe said.

"Yes, Mr. Abe. Sorry."

Abe forced himself to chuckle. "And stop apologizing for working hard."

Jenn appreciated her boss's effort, but no amount of praise was going to unwind Mike Rilling. She wasn't convinced a bottle of Xanax and a straitjacket would do the trick. Rilling was overworked, tightly wound, and committed to the belief that he was deeply, tragically underappreciated.

"Michael, this is Gibson Vaughn," George said. "He's going to consult on the Lombard case. Gibson, this is Michael Rilling, our IT director."

Rilling shook Vaughn's hand limply and shot him a canine territorial look. Gibson either missed it or played it off.

"I'm going to have Jenn bring you up to speed," Abe told Vaughn. "Fill in some of the blanks. Sometimes it's helpful to retrace familiar terrain. You'll find all of it covered in the file."

Jenn pushed a thick binder across the conference table to Vaughn. "Suzanne Lombard" was typed neatly along the binding and on its cover; inside, it contained an overview of Suzanne Lombard's disappearance and the subsequent investigation. A lot of it consisted of internal FBI documents, photographs, and memorandum, all impressively thorough. Abe might have fallen out with Benjamin Lombard, but he carried some serious weight of his own.

Vaughn regarded it warily and rubbed hard at a spot behind his ear. Every mention of Suzanne Lombard seemed to cause him to recoil and withdraw a little further inside himself. What was it? Guilt? Remorse?

Fear? Was it fear? He caught her looking at him and smiled like someone trying to be friendly to a dentist prepping him for a root canal.

An overhead projector flared to life, and a screen descended from a wall-mounted casing. A photograph of Suzanne filled the screen. There had been no shortage of photos to choose from. The Lombards were a remarkably handsome family, photographs with the inner circle de rigueur at every get-together. The one up on the screen was cropped from one of the annual Christmas parties—Suzanne sitting on the floor at the grown-ups' feet, smiling happily at the camera. Gibson Vaughn's disembodied arm hung in the air beside Suzanne. Jenn had found a few without Vaughn—there weren't many—but she'd chosen this one to gauge his reaction.

She regretted it now. The man looked seasick.

"Jenn, you have the floor," Abe said.

She started to stand, thought better of it, and ran her tongue across her teeth. "How much do you know about Suzanne Lombard's disappearance?"

"Apart from what they've been showing on the news for ten years?" Vaughn said. "Not a lot."

"Were you ever questioned?" Hendricks interrupted. "After the abduction. We couldn't find a record of it."

"No," Vaughn replied. "I was in jail at the time."

"Dan makes a good point," Jenn said. "If anything we know about Suzanne sounds wrong to you, inaccurate, speak up. You had a special relationship with her."

Vaughn frowned. "Sure, but remember, I hadn't seen her since my father died."

"Understood," Abe said. "But you never know."

Jenn cleared her throat. "If no one objects, I thought we'd start at the beginning." She paused to see if anyone did. "Okay, so as you all know, this July is the tenth anniversary of the disappearance. It was on the morning of Tuesday, July 22, that Suzanne Lombard, the daughter of Senator Benjamin Lombard of Virginia, ran away from home. Ran away from what, according to all observers, was a perfect and happy family. Does that jibe with your recollection?"

"And then some."

"In the early stages of the investigation, the police and FBI worked from the theory that Suzanne had been snatched off the road around the family beach house outside the hamlet of Pamsrest, Virginia. Grace Lombard and her daughter often spent the entire summer there while the senator commuted back and forth between Pamsrest and DC."

Pamsrest was a small community of the "everybody knows everybody" variety. Mom-and-pop stores, two ice cream parlors, a boardwalk, and an award-winning no-frills barbeque pit. A throwback to a simpler age that people got misty about but could never quite pinpoint in time—the kind of place where families felt safe enough to let their guards down.

"Definitely," Vaughn said. "The last summer I spent down there, Bear was maybe twelve? And she already had free rein to come and go as she pleased."

"Bear?" Hendricks asked.

"Sorry. I mean Suzanne. Bear was just what I called her." `

Hendricks made a note.

"Suzanne biked everywhere," Jenn continued. "That summer she had a job at the local pool and usually left in the morning and was gone all day. This was before every kid had a cell phone. It wasn't uncommon for Grace Lombard not to speak to her daughter during the day. So she didn't get really worried until almost six in the evening. It took two calls to establish that Suzanne hadn't shown up for work. Her third was to her husband in DC; Senator Lombard called the FBI. That got the ball really rolling. By morning, the town was inundated with law enforcement—local, state, and federal. By noon, the story broke nationally and Suzanne Lombard became the latest obsession of cable news."

"Pays to be white," Hendricks said.

Jenn nodded. That was inarguable. Social scientists referred to it as MWWS, or Missing White Woman Syndrome. Suzanne followed in the footsteps of Elizabeth Smart and Natalee Holloway—if you were going to go missing in America, it certainly helped to be white, female, and pretty. Throw in daughter of a US senator for good measure, and you had a recipe for America's next obsession. The press descended on Pamsrest like a plague on Egypt. TV trucks formed a gleaming shantytown in a field on the edge of town. Any resident who cared to stand still for more than a few seconds was guaranteed to wind up on TV. The story ran round the clock for months on every media outlet in the country.

"On the afternoon of the second day, Suzanne's bicycle was found two towns over in a covert of waist-high grass behind a general store. The area was canvassed multiple times, but no one remembered seeing Suzanne Lombard. Local law enforcement went to work on registered sex offenders in the region while the FBI explored the possibility that it was a politically motivated kidnapping. Of course, no ransom call ever came."

Both Abe and Hendricks shifted in their seats. She went on before they could interrupt. She wanted to get through the old before broaching the new.

"The first break in the case came on day six. A college student named Beatrice Arnold called the FBI hotline to report she'd sold Suzanne Lombard snacks at the gas station where she worked in Breezewood, Pennsylvania.

"The Breezewood tape caused a seismic shift in the investigation and completely scrambled the assumptions of law enforcement. Suzanne Lombard hadn't been snatched; she had run away. She had somehow traveled three hundred fifty miles from the Virginia shore to the Pennsylvania line without drawing attention to herself. From the surveillance tape, three unassailable facts emerged: First, Suzanne was actively trying to conceal her identity. Second, she was waiting for someone. And third, in Suzanne's mind at least, that someone was a friend.

"When it was presumed to be a kidnapping, no one had paid too much attention to Suzanne Lombard herself. She had just been an innocent girl in the wrong place at the wrong time. But when the Breezewood tape surfaced, the FBI took a bright light to the private corners of Suzanne Lombard's life. Her environment, her belongings, her social circle were all inventoried and dissected." Jenn paused. "I assume you're with me so far, yes?"

Vaughn nodded.

"Okay, this is where we get into the part of the narrative that wasn't shared with the media. So stop me if you have questions."

Vaughn nodded again.

"So who was this 'friend' she met in Breezewood, and how did she know this individual? Initial interviews with Suzanne's friends at the pool pointed to a boyfriend—a 'Tom B.'" Jenn indicated the blank photo on the board.

"She had a boyfriend?"

"Does that surprise you?"

"A little, I guess. What do we know about him?"

"Not a lot. Her friends admitted covering for her at various points so she could leave work early to meet him. Suzanne's parents were adamant there was no boyfriend, but a search of Suzanne's room turned up a stash of love letters from him hidden in a bookcase."

"And?"

"And nada. Law enforcement canvassed but failed to turn up a single Tom B. within a fifty-mile radius. They expanded the search to include variations on the name: Tom A., Tom C., Tom D., etc., but it was a dead end."

"And he never came forward?"

Jenn shook her head. "But a new lead emerged when Suzanne's laptop was searched. The hard drive had been wiped using Heavy Scrub, a program designed to erase data permanently."

"Gibson, can you explain how it works?" George asked.

Jenn looked at her boss questioningly. George knew exactly how Heavy Scrub worked. He was the one who'd explained it to her. No doubt he had a reason for asking. Dealing with George was like playing chess with a grandmaster. He made her paranoid about her paranoia.

"Ah, sure," Vaughn said. "Well, contrary to popular misconceptions, emptying a computer's 'trash' only de-allocates it. It still exists on the hard drive, but the computer now has permission to overwrite the file should space be needed. However, an 'erased' file might exist for years depending on the user's habits. Retrieving so-called erased data from a hard drive is simple. It's been the downfall of many a would-be master criminal. Hence the need for programs like Heavy Scrub, which systematically overwrites a hard drive multiple times until any existing data becomes unrecoverable. Not the sort of thing your average fourteen-year-old would know to do."

"And certainly not a teenager described as 'technologically inept' by her parents," Jenn said.

"Which she quite clearly was," Hendricks interjected. "Because while she installed and ran the program to cover her tracks, she shut the laptop's cover before it was finished—"

Vaughn's head turned sharply to Hendricks. "Which caused the computer to hibernate and stop Heavy Scrub midwipe," he completed Hendricks's sentence. "Bear botched it?"

"Correct," Jenn said. "The laptop was taken to Fort Meade, which reconstructed as much of the data as it could—which turned out to be not much. The majority was garden-variety teenager: fragments of homework, essays, e-mails, etc. But an Internet relay chat client was found on her machine that her parents didn't know anything about. And that none of her friends used."

"I remember the FBI hunting high and low for WR8TH. Is that how the FBI knew about it?" Vaughn was sitting forward in his seat now.

"Yes. Someone using the username WR8TH befriended Suzanne in a chat room. WR8TH presented himself to her as a sixteen-year-old boy and became her confidant. What emerged was that he encouraged her to run away and helped her cover her tracks."

"Did they get anywhere with it? The feds, I mean."

"No, WR8TH was a dead end. The FBI made it public, as you know, but nothing ever came of it."

"That doesn't surprise me," Vaughn said. "Internet relay chat is purposefully anonymous. No chat logs. Someone could choose a new username at each log-in. When I was getting into computers, IRC was what I used to trade tricks and strategies and code. Everyone was paranoid that the FBI had snitches lurking around in chat."

"They did," Abe said.

"So I had like twenty different usernames that I cycled through. If WR8TH was careful, it would be almost impossible to track him back to a source."

"And that's exactly what happened. Despite thousands of tips," Jenn said. "Not one of them led to the person or persons behind WR8TH. Ironically, it wasn't that the FBI couldn't find any mention of WR8TH on the Internet; quite the opposite. It turned out to be an incredibly common username online. There are hundreds of variations of it in online gaming alone."

Jenn went on to the FBI's speculative and relatively generic profile of Suzanne's abductor. Speculative because, apart from the fragments of chat recovered from Suzanne's computer, they had nothing to go on other than the circumstances of the crime.

"The assumption was, and still is, that the perp was highly organized and probably between thirty and fifty. He was too smooth, confident, and thorough to be a novice. Young offenders are impulsive and stupid.

This one was patient and cunning. Most likely, he was an experienced predator with a long history—Suzanne would not have been his first."

"How did they reach that conclusion?"

"The perp was able to pass himself off convincingly as a teenage boy, which suggested he was extremely empathetic and skilled in social situations. It's not easy to fool a teenager. The FBI doubted he had ever been arrested because pedophiles rarely vary their methods once they find one that works. Just to be sure, they scoured cold cases for his MO—nothing.

"WR8TH also knew his way around computers and how to avoid leaving a trail for law enforcement. His home, likely a freestanding house, afforded him some privacy, which also suggested he had a job and was able to function normally in public without drawing suspicion to himself.

"When the investigation went cold two years later, the prevailing theory was that the perp hadn't known who Suzanne Lombard really was. There was nothing to indicate that she had revealed her identity to him online, and it was the FBI's belief that the perp had panicked when he realized who he had abducted. There is a high probability that he killed her, dumped the body, and moved on to less dangerous quarry."

Vaughn was staring at her. Those green eyes burning right through her.

"Where's the bathroom?" he asked, standing and leaving before anyone could answer. The conference room door swung closed behind him.

"Smooth, Charles," Hendricks said and dropped his pen on the table for effect.

"Fuck you, Dan. I didn't know he was going to be such a girl about it."

Rilling got busy typing something on his computer. George cleared his throat, and they both fell silent. Hendricks laughed. She looked at him, expecting to be reprimanded. Instead, her boss was smiling at her.

"He cares about Suzanne. Even more than I'd hoped. That's good."

"Yes, sir."

"But how about we go easy on it from here on out."

Vaughn came back but not all the way into the room. He stood in the doorway, one foot in, one foot out. He'd splashed water on his face sloppily and the front of his shirt looked wet.

"Look, George," he said. "I appreciate the job offer, but if you expected me to see something and tell you who WR8TH is, I'm sorry. I hadn't seen Suzanne in a while. I wish I could help. Believe me. But I'm not going to see anything the FBI missed. I'm sorry," he said again, and looked it. "You can have your money back. I'm sorry I wasted your time."

Abe smiled. "No, Gibson. We don't expect anything of the kind."

"Then what?"

"Jenn?" Abe said.

Vaughn's eyes leapt to her.

"WR8TH has made contact," she said.

CHAPTER EIGHT

Fred Tinsley slowly spun his scotch glass on the bar and cast a malevolent eye toward his cell phone. He was waiting for a call. He didn't know when it would come or who would be calling, but none of that concerned him. Whether the call came now or four hours from now made no difference. He wasn't sure anymore that there *was* a difference.

His wristwatch claimed he had been waiting at the bar for three hours and twenty-seven minutes. Tinsley took it on faith that was the case. It was an expensive watch, purchased precisely for its world-renowned accuracy. And he relied on it, because he had long ago lost his ability to perceive the passage of time. A minute, an hour, a year—it all felt the same to him. Time is, so the great man had said, relative. Tinsley agreed wholeheartedly. Measuring one's life in terms of days was purposeless. He could still feel his heartbeat in his chest, still taste the breath from his lungs. He yet lived, and that was the only measure of time that truly mattered.

The bar was one of those upscale establishments that had more scotches than beers. The barstools didn't even wobble. Classy. Tinsley didn't care for the kind of people it attracted—busy, nattering people who congregated like flies on the stiffening corpse of their day—but he appreciated the comprehensive selection of fine scotch.

Lately, he'd become enamored of Oban 14 year—a thick, peaty scotch. Although he'd never tasted it, Tinsley liked the way the smoky flavor clung to his nostrils. It smelled like the earth. He didn't drink, but if he was required to wait in a bar, then he preferred to order something he could respect. The original distillery had been built in 1794, and to Tinsley it showed. It took patience and a painstaking attention to detail to perfect a skill. But most of all it took time.

Tinsley admired such dedication to a craft. His craft required mastery of many skills, but above all else it demanded an appreciation of time. Tinsley had made a lifetime study of the way time affected people. The way it toyed with their good judgment and perspective. Made them impatient or rash. Made them take irrational risks. Time was the great leveler, and neither money nor power held sway over its relentless march. That was precisely what made Tinsley so good at his work. Most people didn't understand that—what really went into being a sniper. The shot wasn't the hard part. The shot was ten thousand hours of practice, tens of thousands of rounds, and an encyclopedic knowledge of the environment's effect on ballistics. No, the shot was the easy part. It simply required time, and the will to spend it. The hard part was the waiting.

Time did not affect Fred Tinsley as it did most people. Most people were overawed by time. They allowed time to bully them, fearing that it was passing too fast or too slowly, sometimes both simultaneously. But not Tinsley. He was indifferent to the passage of time, and it flowed around him effortlessly.

Inside his arid, primeval brain—and Tinsley thought of himself as almost prehistoric, something unspoiled by the softening influence of progress—he could look out at the world, blink, and in the time it took for his eyes to reopen, weeks could pass. It made him immune to boredom, to doubt or need; the privations that drove ordinary men mad did not concern him. But most of all it made him a patient, cunning predator.

When he was a young man and still plied his trade with a rifle, Tinsley once spent twenty-six days in a sewer drain in Sarajevo. It was during the height of the siege. The city and the country were in chaos despite the United Nations's best efforts. His target, a particularly nihilistic lieutenant of Slobodan Milošević's, had earned a nasty reputation that stood out even among the nasty reputations of that despicable war. The string of atrocities of which his target was accused was enough to earn a "kill not capture" order and a bounty that had drawn the interests of professionals across Europe.

Unfortunately for them, the target had proven resilient and difficult to kill. Dozens of attempts on his life only served to make him extraordinarily careful and paranoid, shuttling between safe houses and constantly revising his plans. This made it impossible to predict his movements or to find a pattern, and no one had been able to get close enough to claim the bounty.

From Tinsley's perspective, his rivals had gone about hunting this man the wrong way. Why try to anticipate a man who was purposefully trying to be unpredictable? It was foolish. Instead, Tinsley had crawled through the vile sewage of the Sarajevo sewer system, eventually taking a position in a storm drain that gave him an unobstructed view of a compromised safe house that had sat empty for eighteen months. Things had gotten very hot for the target as more and more of his sanctuaries were compromised. Tinsley's stakeout wasn't based on actionable intelligence, but instead on the assumption that eventually, given enough time, the target would believe the safe house forgotten and risk using it again. Eventually, as the UN closed in on him, as the pressure built, Tinsley's target would mistake the passing of time for the passing of memory.

Tinsley lay in a burbling stream of human waste, waiting for a shot that might not ever come. The smell was the smell of death and a city unmade by war. He'd brought food and water for two months, but found it hard to keep down and lost more than twenty-five pounds during the stakeout. Unwilling to risk giving away his position, he hadn't moved from his spot and had slept with his chin resting on his balled-up fists so he didn't drown in the filth.

The conditions in the sewer were inhuman, or so the advance team that swept the area ahead of the target's arrival had assumed. It never occurred to them to look where no human could exist. But Tinsley had endured. Endured in that subterranean hell by switching himself off and going into something akin to a fugue state. Aware only of the building a hundred yards away, he allowed the time to pass in an instant, patiently waiting for his prey to pass in front of his nest.

The shot itself had been routine by comparison. A clear, bright night with only a slight breeze from the south-southwest—an amateur hunter could have made it. Tinsley was already slinking away into the darkness before the splinters of skull and viscera had settled like a fatal sleet on the face of the startled bodyguard.

Tinsley had long since moved on from the rifle. Not that he was ungrateful. The rifle had taught him his identity. Taught him there was a purpose for his particular gifts. But it was a blunt tool and drew too much attention. Attention being the true purpose of the rifle. The rifle was intended to deliver a message, a warning, its target merely an envelope to be opened. These days, there simply wasn't much call for blowing someone's head off from a thousand yards. Statement kills were no longer in vogue, outside of organized crime and parts of the world that couldn't afford him. And in any case, sniping was a young man's game. Instead, Tinsley had evolved into a highly specialized killer. One who rarely left any indication that a crime had even occurred. It required a deft touch. Most of his hits had been closed by local law enforcement either as accidental deaths or suicides. The rest were chalked up to unsolved violent crimes such as burglaries or stickups. He probably had twenty in this area alone. There was always work to be had in the nation's capital.

His phone vibrated with a text message—a series of six letters and numbers. Tinsley paid his tab and walked outside, blinking in the bright sunshine. He slipped on a pair of latex gloves while he looked for a license plate that matched the text message. A black sedan rolled to a stop beside the curb, and he got in back. The divider was up, and he sat alone. The car pulled back into traffic.

Beside him, a thick manila folder lay alongside a much thinner folder. He picked up the thicker of the two and thumbed through the file. He read slowly and carefully, cataloguing every detail in his mind. It took several hours, and the car drove patiently through the city while he worked. When he was done, Tinsley went back and lingered over the five photographs. Four men and a woman. Jennifer Auden Charles. Gibson Peyton Vaughn. Michael Rilling. Daniel Patrick Hendricks. George Leyasu Abe. Only Abe and Charles would pose any difficulty, and only if they knew he was coming. They never did.

His orders called for no immediate action. Abe's crew was hunting someone, and Tinsley was only to move if they located their target. Until then his instructions were to watch and wait.

He put it aside and opened the second folder. A familiar face greeted him. One he had not seen in many years, but it may as well have been an hour. It would be good to see her again.

Well, well . . . He hadn't expected this.

He worked his way through the second file. It didn't take long by comparison. A woman in her sixties wouldn't pose any difficulty, and the orders gave no reason to wait before attending to her. He took the monogrammed envelope as he'd been instructed, but even though the envelope had been left unsealed he gave no thought to reading its contents. It wasn't that it didn't interest him; it was that it never occurred to him that it should.

Tinsley knocked on the divider to signal he was finished and put the folder back on the seat. The car pulled over to the curb and let him out. Tinsley dropped his gloves in a nearby trash can and drifted along with the evening commuters.

CHAPTER NINE

"What do you mean he's been in contact?" Gibson asked.

"We believe we have been contacted by the person or persons known as WR8TH," Jenn said.

"How?" he asked, taking his seat back at the table. "When?"

"Sir?" Jenn turned to her boss.

"I'll take it from here. Thank you," Abe said. "Several months ago an old friend, a producer at CNN, asked me to be interviewed for a segment she was putting together on Suzanne's disappearance. A tenth-anniversary retrospective. People have been chasing my interview for years."

"You never talked to the press? Even after you were fired?"

"No, and in truth, I had no intention of breaking my silence now. I'd already turned down five or six requests from other programs. I simply saw no benefit in reopening old wounds. Out of respect for the family."

"I thought you and Lombard were finished."

"We are. However, despite his grandstanding, Benjamin is not Suzanne's only parent."

Gibson realized the truth of that statement. Grace Lombard had been a tireless advocate for missing children in the years since her daughter had disappeared. But she preferred to work quietly behind the scenes and leave the limelight to her husband. An arrangement that more than suited Benjamin Lombard. In the end, it was always about Benjamin Lombard.

"But then the hotline began to see an uptick in traffic."

"You still have a hotline? After all this time?"

"Calista absolutely insisted," Abe said.

"Calista?"

"Ah, yes, I apologize. Calista Dauplaise."

Gibson recognized the name now. She had been a regular cast member of Lombard's political theater, but in his childhood memory she was simply one of the many grown-ups that his father mentioned from time to time. He doubted that he'd spoken to her other than to say hello and good-bye.

"Calista was . . ." Abe paused and corrected himself. ". . . *is* Suzanne's godmother. An old family friend of the Lombards. She is also an investor in my company. Among other things, Abe Consulting administers and maintains the hotline on her behalf. She knew your father well."

"And she's involved in this how?"

"The reward. That was her doing. When Suzanne disappeared, Calista was distraught. She put up the ten million. She hoped it would make a big enough public splash to tempt someone to come forward."

"But no one ever did."

"Don't be ridiculous. Half the free world came forward. The hotline got tips, theories, and sightings that took years to sift through. It's been an incredible sinkhole of man-hours over the years."

"Obviously it's a long shot at this point," Jenn said. "The website stopped getting heavy traffic after year four, but you never know in cases like this. The perp might develop a conscience, can't deal with the guilt anymore. Or wind up in jail for something unrelated and brag about it to a cellmate. The chances are remote, but it happens."

"So how much traffic are we talking about?" Gibson asked.

Mike Rilling sat forward, anxious to contribute something. "Over the previous five years, the eight hundred number averaged one point eight calls per month. Discounting spam, we were seeing four point six e-mails per month. And the website was getting four hundred sixty-seven hits per month. We monitor traffic to the website and back check IP addresses on the off chance the perp gets curious and/or stupid."

"Smart. And recently?"

"Thirty-eight calls per month. Two hundred forty-eight e-mails. Thirty-thousand-plus hits to the website."

"All crap, of course," Hendricks said.

"It only takes one," Abe reminded him.

"Have you thought about doing a website redesign?" Gibson asked. Mike shook his head.

"Well, if it was me, I'd give some thought to updating it. Old websites look . . . well, they look old. They look forgotten. If you're hoping to lure him in, then you need it to look like an ongoing investigation."

"That's a good thought," Abe said. "Michael, get that ball rolling on Monday."

"And while you're at it, the FBI documents in this folder? Put some of those up too."

"Wait. Why tip our hand?" Jenn asked.

"To bait the hook. Give your guy a reason to visit the site. Don't these serial-killer types have a thing for reading about themselves? Don't they get off on that shit? Or is that just in the movies?"

Jenn nodded thoughtfully. "No, that's not just the movies." She turned to Abe. "We'd have to clear it with the Bureau. But it's a possibility."

"Agreed." Abe made a note on a legal pad with his fountain pen. "I'll call Phillip in the morning."

"I'm happy to talk website design all day, but are we getting to the part where WR8TH contacted you?"

"Getting there, yes," Abe said. "The increased traffic to the website was what made me decide to do the CNN interview. My condition for doing the interview was that it would mention the website and hotline, and our info would be in the crawler as well as linked on CNN's website. In the end, it was pretty perfunctory stuff. I was hoping to get into some depth, but they only used about three minutes. Still, I was able to confirm that the reward was still available for a credible lead that led to Suzanne. And that was it. Exchanged some pleasantries and went back to the office. Didn't even bother to watch the broadcast. But the day after it aired, we were e-mailed this. Mike?"

A new photograph appeared on the screen. A pink Hello Kitty backpack sat on a wooden table. Off the edge of the table, Gibson could see dirty linoleum tile and the base of a kitchen cabinet. The backpack showed the wear and tear of a well-loved possession. The photograph itself was old or was staged that way—the resolution wasn't as clear as modern digital cameras, but that was simple enough to fake. Clearly, the backpack was meant to be the one from the infamous Breezewood footage. If genuine, it was an astonishing lead.

"Was there a message?" Gibson asked.

Abe nodded. A blowup of an e-mail appeared on screen.

> Nice interview, George. Very moving. You should have kept her safe. How much for the backpack?

Gibson winced and shot a quick glance at Abe, who sat stoically. It was a cruel taunt, but Abe kept whatever he felt about it well hidden.

"What about the e-mail address?" Gibson asked.

"S.lombard@WR8TH.com. We traced it to a privately hosted server in the Ukraine," Mike replied. "The domain was registered to a 'V. Airy Nycetri' for an added screw-you."

Gibson rolled his eyes. No real surprise, though. The fringes of the Internet were often hosted in places like Eastern Europe, where governments had more pressing concerns than shady web hosts. Spammers, illegal gambling sites, child pornography traffickers, and hackers all used remote server farms to grant themselves a layer of anonymity. Chances were good that whoever had sent the e-mail had never been within a thousand miles of the server that generated it.

"What do you think?" Abe asked.

"Of the backpack? Not much. I could probably find three dozen on eBay before lunch. Probably just someone trolling you because they saw you on TV."

Abe nodded. "That's what we thought too."

"I assume you replied?"

Abe gestured to Rilling. A new e-mail appeared.

> For a photograph of a backpack? Nothing.
> However, our investigators are very inter-
> ested in talking to anyone with evidence in
> the case.

"And?"

"A day later, this."

Another photograph appeared on the screen. This time, Gibson rose from his seat, his mind reeling as it fought to acknowledge what it saw: the same photograph, only larger. The first image had been cropped from this one, and this photo just might be worth ten million dollars.

Suzanne Lombard.

Still the child she'd been when she ran away, sitting at an old kitchen table. The backpack sat at her left elbow. She was cupping a glass of what looked like milk and giving the camera a weary half smile. A Phillies baseball cap was pushed back high on her head.

Gibson stared dumbly at Bear.

"We all had the same reaction," Abe said.

"And you think . . ." Gibson trailed off, not knowing how to finish his thought.

"We do."

Gibson looked back and forth between George and the photo. It was unbelievable.

"We believe it's authentic," Abe said. "Likely taken the night she disappeared in Breezewood. And I would very much like to speak to the person who took it."

Gibson nodded, fury stoking itself back to life inside him. That was a conversation he very much wanted in on. Whoever this guy was, he was playing games. Playing games and using Bear as a pawn. He realized now why he was here.

"But you can't. Can you?"

Abe nodded thoughtfully.

"Let me guess. You tried to hack the e-mail server."

"Yes."

"But you fumbled it. Spooked him, and he went to ground."

Mike began to protest, but Abe cut him off. "Yes."

"And you think I'm going to find him for you."

"Can you?"

"No. I can't. It doesn't work like that, George. You burned the only lead with that e-mail stunt. If he's clever enough to have covered his tracks all this time, then how are we even going to . . . ?" Gibson drifted into silence, lost in thought. Something was wrong here.

"What is it?"

Gibson held up a hand for quiet. What was he missing? He shut his eyes to block everyone and everything out. He stood there until the answer appeared. It was exactly what he would have done. Exactly what he'd advised Abe to do.

Bait the hook.

"You ever ask yourself why he sent that first picture?" he asked.

"What do you mean?" asked Jenn.

Gibson turned to each of them in turn, grinning at the realization. "Oh, he's clever, isn't he? Folks, I do believe you've been played."

CHAPTER TEN

Gibson rubbed feeling back into his face with the heel of his hand. He took out his earbuds and stretched backward in his chair—a satisfying crack ran the length of his spine.

Better.

His phone said it was two thirty a.m.

On Friday.

It felt like a Friday. Fridays were always a little grimy and worn out—a week on its last legs. Or maybe it was just that he hadn't been home since he'd arrived at ACG on Sunday.

He'd been working for almost five straight days. Was that possible? He often lost track of time once he'd sunk his teeth into a problem, and he hadn't had a puzzle this interesting since he'd left the Marines. He felt exhilarated—answers beckoned just out of reach. He was close now. Another few hours and he'd know if his suspicion were correct.

Where are you, WR8TH? What do you know that you don't want me to find out?

He could have gone home at night, but the thought never entered his mind. He needed to be near the work when inspiration struck. Besides, there was nothing waiting at home apart from a restless bed.

Sleep was out of the question. Bear lurked behind his eyelids, patient and hopeful. Her smile jolted him awake and hurried him back to his keyboard.

The only meaningful breaks he took were his nightly video calls to Ellie. Once she was tucked in, Gibson would read to her until she got sleepy. They were halfway through *Charlotte's Web*, and Ellie was anxious about Wilbur. She loved stories with the same intensity as Suzanne. It was an obvious connection, but somehow he'd never made it before now. That he read to both of them. Well, he could forgive himself for not thinking like that. It was safer that way. But now he couldn't *not* see it, no matter how hard he worked to keep the two girls separate in his mind.

He had worked long into the night that first Sunday. Mike Rilling offered his assistance and set up a workstation for him, but Gibson politely and firmly threw him out of the conference room. He needed to be alone to think. Charles and Hendricks had been none too pleased to be shut out, but Abe got it and laid down the law.

Around three a.m. that first night, he'd hit a snag and taken a break, making a looping circuit around the empty corridors of ACG. He thought more clearly when he walked, and after a few laps, an answer began to present itself. He was on the way back to the conference room when he'd noticed a light on under an office door that had been dark the last time around. He'd stopped to listen at the door when it opened sharply. He stood eye to eye with Jenn Charles, who in her heels might have an inch on him. She'd taken off her suit jacket, but not her gun—the new office casual.

"What are you doing?"

"Sorry," he said, taking a step backward. "Didn't think anyone was here. Thought you were a burglar."

"Do you need something?"

"No. Just walking." He spun a finger in a circle. "Helps me think."

Jenn nodded noncommittally.

Gibson hesitated and then asked, "Actually, can I ask you a question? On your board . . . why is there a question mark between WR8TH and Tom B.?"

"A theory circulated that Tom B. and WR8TH were one and the same."

"If he was local, then why did she go to Pennsylvania to meet him?"

"We don't know for a fact that she met him in Pennsylvania. That's just another assumption. Maybe he took her in Pamsrest and Pennsylvania was just on his way home."

"What do you think?"

"It's plausible. Perhaps I'll get a chance to ask him to his face."

"What are you still doing here anyway? It's late."

"Working."

"At three in the morning? I don't need a babysitter."

"I have paperwork to catch up on."

"All right," he said, conceding defeat. "Well, you know where to find me."

"Yes. I do."

She stepped back, moving to close the office door.

"Where did you serve?" he asked.

She stopped, her eyes narrowed. "Don't do that."

"Do what?"

She shut the door on him, and Gibson stood there staring at it, chuckling to himself in disbelief. Okay, well, that was . . . Actually, he didn't know what to call that. There was a hard edge to Jenn Charles that he didn't understand. Probably for the best if this job only took a few days. He went back to work.

On Monday morning, when the staff began to arrive, Gibson was standing in the conference room, staring at the picture of Suzanne pinned to the board. Abe had ordered a cot to be set up in the conference room. Gibson used it to stack printouts. Someone had been dispatched to buy him a change of clothes, but the bag sat untouched alongside the cot. Food was delivered, and Gibson wolfed it down while he worked. He was on the hunt again, and every day brought him closer.

At first, Gibson became an object of much speculation among the staff. Evidently, no one outside of Abe's inner circle knew why he was there, and that piqued their interest. But by Tuesday afternoon, curiosities had waned—watching someone work at a computer ranked top five among dullest activities in the world. Periodically, Mike Rilling would stick his head in the door to ask if he needed anything. And whenever Hendricks came in to get a file, he would glower at Gibson. Jenn Charles became his most regular visitor, passing by once an hour like a guard walking a post.

When the office opened on Thursday, Gibson requested a printout of the firm's browser history for the previous month. It ran to nearly a thousand pages. He broke it up into four stacks and began sifting through it with a highlighter. Tedious work, but over the next twenty-plus hours he'd narrowed his hunt to a handful of possibilities.

Now he was sure.

Gibson checked the time—six a.m., Friday morning. George arrived around seven, so Gibson shut his eyes for an hour. For once, Bear let him be. When he woke, George was working in his office and seemed to be expecting him. Gibson told him what he had found. Abe took the bad news in stride and asked for options.

Gibson gave him three.

"Which would you recommend?"

"Option one. If you want a shot at catching WR8TH."

"Why?"

Gibson explained.

Abe stopped him several times to ask questions and when Gibson was done, sat in silence for several minutes.

"All right, I want you to lay it out to the team. Pretend I haven't heard any of this. I want to hear their unfiltered opinion."

"If that's what you want, but I'm going home first. I need to shower. I need to shave. I'd say I'm just north of toxic."

"Agreed. A car will be downstairs." Abe looked at his watch. "Be back here at four."

At home, Gibson stood in the shower until he felt like a human being again. He felt good. Really good. He knew he'd missed the work, but not how much. That his skills might help find Bear . . . *Don't get ahead of yourself,* he cautioned himself. Better not to allow that hope to take root.

But what if?

It was after five before they were all gathered back in the conference room. Hendricks and Charles were anxious to hear what he'd discovered, but Gibson took his time fussing with the computer. Finally, Abe could stand it no longer.

"So, Gibson. Enlighten us. What have you learned?"

"Okay. Well, initially I was bothered by the fact that WR8TH sent two photographs."

"So you told us on Sunday," Hendricks said.

"Right, but I mean, why bother? Why send the e-mail of the backpack at all if you have the whole photograph? It's a waste of time."

"Maybe he just likes playing games?" Jenn put in.

"Right. But what was the game? The person who sent that photo is likely the same person who took it. Agreed?"

The room nodded its consent.

"So, what are the odds of WR8TH, if it is the original WR8TH, collecting a ten-million-dollar reward? I've got a better chance of being invited to Benjamin Lombard's birthday party."

"So what, then?" Jenn asked.

"Well, if it's not the reward, then what got this guy to break cover? I mean, he got away with it clean. Law enforcement is no closer to catching him than they were ten years ago. Yet here he is, taking an enormous risk to send a highly incriminating photograph to you. What's in it for him?"

Hendricks spoke up. "He's a narcissist. The tenth-anniversary coverage got him all stirred up, and he doesn't like not getting any of the attention. The picture is a taunt. Get the focus back on him."

"That makes sense, but this didn't get him much attention, did it? Two e-mails, and he had to shut it down. If he wanted attention he would have posted the picture online. Or he could have released the photo to the media instead. Get all . . . who was that serial killer in San Francisco who wrote all the letters to the papers?"

"The Zodiac," Hendricks said.

"Right. Go all Zodiac on it. Imagine the attention he could get if he released the photograph with a bunch of cryptic biblical passages and vague threats."

"The Internet would go crazy," Hendricks admitted.

"Right, so if it's about attention, then there are better ways to get it. Agreed?"

"Agreed, but let's not forget the guy is crazy."

"Fair enough, but in my opinion this wasn't about attention at all. So I come back to why he sent two e-mails, two photographs. Unless the first photograph was a test run."

"A test of what?" Rilling asked.

"A test of whether you would open it. And when you did, and replied, he knew it was safe to send the second one. He did just what I told you to do."

"Which was?"

"He baited the hook and got you to take a big bite."

"Are you suggesting there was a virus?" asked Rilling.

"Embedded in the second photograph."

"No. No way," Rilling said. "Not possible. We've got a topflight antivirus service, and we scanned both those attachments before we opened them."

Rilling looked around the room for confirmation that what he was saying was true, but he wasn't getting much love. Abe sat back, observing his people. Charles stared at the ceiling like she'd just been told she had six months to live. Hendricks was eying Rilling like a hyena sizing up a wildebeest too dumb to stay with the herd.

"We scanned it!" Rilling protested when no one spoke.

"Let him explain," Abe said. "Gibson, walk us through what you found."

"Look. All antivirus services do is check incoming files against a definition database of known viruses and malware. And you're right, Mike, 99.999 percent of the time for 99.999 percent of the people that's good enough. But if the virus is new, if it's been written with a specific target in mind, then antivirus scans are about as useless as a four-foot fence against an eagle."

"And you're saying that's what he did?" Abe asked.

"Apparently so. It's not on file with any of the groups that track malware. I've only had a couple of days to dissect it, but it looks like a variant on Sasser. Has some Nimda DNA floating around in it too."

"English, Vaughn," Hendricks said.

"It's a well-written virus by someone who knows their trade. And he's crafty. Whoever it is learned the lessons of some of the big viruses of the last ten years and improved on them. It's not destructive so far as I can tell. So that's the good news."

"And the bad?" Jenn asked.

"It's busy downloading files from your servers."

"What!" she said. "What files?"

"Anything it wants. I assume it's targeting files pertaining to Suzanne Lombard, but it would take a cyber forensics team to know for sure. And that's not my area."

"Jesus Christ." Hendricks threw his pen against the wall.

"Again, no," Rilling said. "We monitor outgoing traffic. Everything's been normal. We haven't seen any uptick in volume, no abnormal IP address hits."

"Well, unfortunately, he was prepared for that too. It's download-ing at a rate of twelve kilobytes per second. Slow but steady. Taking its time. That volume would just blend into the background of a company this size. Right, Mike?"

Rilling nodded morosely.

"If it's been working around the clock since we opened that e-mail," Abe said, "how much could he have?"

Rilling scribbled figures on a legal pad and slid the pad across to Abe, who nodded grimly.

"Actually that's the cool thing about it. It isn't working around the clock," Gibson said. "It stops every day at five."

"Oh, does it take weekends off too?" Hendricks asked.

"Actually, yes," Gibson replied. "This is strictly a nine-to-five virus. See, it'd look strange if someone was surfing the *Washington Post* at two in the morning."

"The *Post*?" Rilling asked.

"Yeah, WR8TH is using an ad on the *Washington Post* home page as a relay point."

"That can be done?" Jenn asked.

"Sure, it's increasingly common among hackers. Corrupt an ad on a mainstream website that won't look unusual in a company's browser history and use it as a relay point to send hacked data to its intended recipient."

"Well, we need to pull the plug immediately," Hendricks said. "Shut down until we can scrub this thing from our system."

"Agreed," Jenn said. "This is a disaster."

"You could do that, but I wouldn't advise it. Not if you want to catch this guy."

Abe raised a hand to quiet the others. "Why not?"

"Because I can't see beyond the relay point. Once it passes through the ad on the *Post* website, I don't know where WR8TH's virus is sending your data. If you shut down now, then he'll know we're onto him. Then we really are dead in the water."

"So what do you suggest?"

"Business as usual."

"Let him keep stealing our clients' data?" Jenn asked. "Do you have any idea how damaging that would be?"

"It's not ideal, I know. It comes down to how bad you want this guy. So that's your call."

The room exploded in heated debate. Abe let it go on for a few minutes before holding up a hand again. His people lapsed into an uneasy silence, all watching Abe think it through.

"What do you think WR8TH wants?" he asked at last. "What's his endgame?"

Gibson shrugged. "That's an excellent question."

"So if I allow this to continue, with potentially calamitous fallout with my clients, what would be our next steps?"

"WR8TH is hunting for something. I'd recommend luring him in with something he wants. Something new about Suzanne."

"And write our own virus," Abe said.

"Exactly. He thinks he's slick, and he's already gotten away with it. He won't be expecting you to play back at him like this. But if we want him to fall for it, we need to embed our virus in something tempting."

"What about the internal FBI documents we were going to post to the revamped website?" Jenn asked. "Something that hasn't been released to the public?"

"That would probably do it," Gibson said.

"I'll need to make a call," Abe said. "How long would it take you to write a virus?"

"Already written," Gibson said.

All heads turned to stare at him.

Abe was smiling. "What will it do?"

"Well, if he goes for it, our virus will travel upstream through the corrupted ad, and when he opens the files at his end, my virus will 'phone home' with GPS coordinates and an IP address."

"If he opens the files," Hendricks said.

"If," Gibson agreed.

George glanced at Jenn Charles, and something meaningful passed between them that Gibson couldn't decipher.

"Make it happen," Abe said.

CHAPTER ELEVEN

For the next two weeks, WR8TH's virus kept to its routine—waking up at nine a.m. and systematically nibbling away at ACG's database. It was a model employee that way. Didn't take a lunch break and never called in sick.

Gibson knew from studying the code that the virus could be directed remotely and given fresh batch instructions by WR8TH. Otherwise it would just continue relentlessly on its current task forever. But so far nothing. Either WR8TH wasn't keeping close enough tabs on changes to ACG's registry to notice the new FBI documents, or he was too smart to go for the lure.

It was a well-laid trap, Gibson reassured himself. Over the last two weeks, he had uploaded a few more FBI files each morning. The idea being to make it appear to be an ongoing ACG project, converting paper files into digital records.

"Come on," Gibson whispered to his monitor. "You got away with it. You're smarter than us. We're a bunch of dummies. Help yourself. We'll never know."

When staring at his monitor and willing something to happen lost its charm, Gibson began digging through the boxes of evidence.

Curiosity led him to a thick folder labeled "Tom B." The mysterious boyfriend who had never identified himself. The folder contained a staggering amount of data for a lead that hadn't gone anywhere. Not surprising given how little the FBI actually had to go on. Besides a name, all they had was a vague physical description cobbled together from her teenage coworkers at the pool: dark complexion, stocky build, thick brown hair, bright-blue eyes. Not even an exact age, only a shared sense that Tom was "older," which left a disquieting range of possibilities.

Were WR8TH and Tom one and the same? If they weren't, then why hadn't Tom B. ever come forward? If they were, could Gibson really see Bear calling an Internet pedophile her boyfriend? Keeping his love letters? Running away with him? None of it made much sense.

Gibson flipped through the rest of the folder and put it back. You couldn't really appreciate the tedious nature of criminal investigations until you looked at the Everest of paperwork it generated. Looking through it was almost more mind-numbing than staring at his stubbornly unchanging computer screen.

He was about to quit when he stumbled across a box labeled "Family Media." Inside were CDs of photographs from Suzanne's school and family get-togethers, all neatly cataloged by date and place. He spent hours hunting in vain for the photograph of him reading to Suzanne in the armchair, but it was nowhere to be found. A CD labeled "Memorial Day, 1998" caught his eye. He couldn't remember 1998 in particular, but, curious, he slipped the CD into his laptop. He didn't have any pictures of Duke and hoped to find a few that he could show Ellie. There would come a day when he would have to tell her about her grandfather.

The disk turned out to be a gold mine. Duke seemed to be in every third picture. Unfortunately, Lombard was in most of them too, right beside his father, smiling his unctuous, fox-in-the-henhouse smile. Gibson found a couple of shots that he could crop and moved them to his hard drive. Just to be sure, though, he went back through the CDs one more time. His perseverance paid off with a photo that captured Duke the way Gibson liked to remember him—on the back porch at Pamsrest, beer in hand, grin on his face, holding court, and spinning what you could tell was one tall political tale. His audience hanging on his every word.

Gibson looked at it a long time. He missed that version of his father. He missed being able to think about Duke without bitterness, without his mind leaping to the basement—that miserable, god-awful basement where Duke stepped away from his life, stepped away from his son. It had been easier when he had Lombard to blame. When he thought Lombard had betrayed Duke and not the other way around. That had been wishful thinking. Duke Vaughn was nothing but a criminal, and rather than face the consequences, he'd gone down into the basement. It was his life, his decision to make, and Duke had made it, thinking only of himself. That was the truth, and there was nothing else to be said. Even if there had been, there was no one left to whom Gibson cared to say it.

The sad truth was, Gibson had believed in Duke blindly, and his life had been in free fall ever since. It was a terrible sensation, and he wanted it to be over. There was an old joke—it's not the fall that kills you but the abrupt stop. Well, a lucky few survived the impact, didn't they? Gibson would take his chances with the unforgiving ground. Anything was better than this, the series of rash, ill-considered decisions he'd made at the mercy of his high-velocity swan dive. There had been days since the end of his marriage when Gibson thought he understood Duke's choice. Understood, but not forgave. He couldn't imagine doing that to his daughter. To any child.

He forced himself to close the photo file, but first he made a copy. For better days . . . if they ever came. He was about to eject the disk when he spotted a thumbnail image that sparked a memory. He opened it to see a photograph of himself: He couldn't have been more than ten, and he stood in front of a small fountain, holding, at arm's length, an enormous bullfrog out to the camera. Like the frog was radioactive. The bullfrog just hung there, legs dangling indignantly, like a celebrity who'd been dragged into posing for pictures with a pushy fan.

Beside Gibson, practically attached to his hip, was Bear. Wearing an ill-fitting, saggy-bottomed bathing suit, her hair a chaotic tumble of curls, she looked up at the frog as if he'd wrestled a lion into submission. He'd forgotten all about catching that damn frog. It had taken all afternoon. They'd finally cornered it by the old well on the back of the property, where he'd chased it back and forth while Bear pointed unhelpfully from a safe distance.

Once they'd had it, they both realized chasing it was a lot more fun than actually catching it. The bullfrog agreed and peed on him to drive home the point. But the Lombards' photographer had spotted them and insisted that they take a photograph with their trophy. They'd kept the frog just long enough to take the photograph by the fountain and then released the savage beast back into the wild. Bear had stood on the edge of the well and waved until the frog disappeared into the brush.

The memory made him smile. It was one of the few times Bear left the safety of her books to go on an actual adventure. What a distance that image was from a teenager with a mystery boyfriend. From the tired girl in the Phillies cap so far from home. Hell, she wasn't even a baseball fan . . .

Gibson froze. That hat . . . Something about the Phillies cap bothered him, now that he thought about it, but he couldn't put his finger on the reason.

He made a copy of the frog photo before he ejected the disk. God how he missed that little girl. His ferocious Bear. She was all that was left of his childhood that he loved unreservedly—everything else in his memory was tainted. And someone had stolen her.

Gibson found George in his office. Gibson knocked on the open office door. George looked up and beckoned for him to enter.

"Gibson, what brings you by?"

"Are you going after him?"

"After who?"

"After WR8TH. If he uploads my virus. You're not going straight to the FBI. You're going after him yourself."

Abe's eyes went to his still-open office door. Gibson took that as a yes.

"I want in."

"Gibson . . ."

"I need to go."

"Would you shut the door," George said and waited until they had privacy. "Please believe me: I have great respect for the work you've done, and I will never question your loyalty to Suzanne. But I hired you to help us locate WR8TH. That's all. In the field, you would be a liability."

"A liability?"

"Jenn and Dan have thirty-plus years' experience between them."

"I was in the Marines. I'm not a goddamn liability."

"I'm well aware of your military record. But if we do get that far, Jenn and Dan will handle it."

"No."

"No?" George looked genuinely taken aback.

"You need me."

"I need you?"

"Yeah, you do."

Abe took a long look at him and put his pen down. "All right. Convince me."

"Seriously?" He hadn't expected to get this far.

Abe chuckled. "Yes, I'm serious. Assuming we get lucky and your virus produces a lead on WR8TH. Convince me why I should send someone with no experience out there."

"Simple. You need someone on computers. Who are you going to send? Mike Rilling? I may not have any field experience, but I'm Jason Bourne next to that guy."

"Isn't your virus supposed to give us his location?"

"It will give us *a* location. And, yeah, maybe he's cocky enough to risk his home IP, but I doubt it. Based on what we've seen so far, my money is on him being cautious as hell. Odds are, he's stealing wireless from somebody. What if it leads Jenn and Hendricks to a coffeehouse with free Wi-Fi? Would they know what to do then? Look, WR8TH isn't a person; he's a figment of the Internet. Now, if you want to find the man behind WR8TH, then you need a figment that thinks like him. This is my world, George. Let me go with them."

Abe leaned back in his chair. He sat for a few minutes, mulling it over before finally responding. "I need to sit with the idea for a few days and talk to my people. Acceptable?"

"Acceptable."

"And if the answer is still no, you'll respect my decision?"

"I'll give it a shot."

CHAPTER TWELVE

"We'll be on the ground in San Francisco in forty-five minutes, Mr. Vice President."

"Thank you, Megan," Lombard said and returned his attention to Abigail Saldana, who was reviewing the latest polling data.

A stern, brilliant woman, Saldana had stabilized his numbers and restored confidence to a floundering campaign since joining the team last month. They weren't out of the woods by any means, but they weren't bleeding support the way they had been a month ago.

The California primary was four days out and had the potential to swing the nomination one way or another. It was Fleming's turf, so there was no expectation of winning, but if he could take 30 percent in her home state, it would serve as a statement and give them momentum heading into the final primaries. It was an aggressive strategy that wasn't without risk. But Saldana felt Fleming was vulnerable at home, so they had poured time and money into California over the last month. It would all come down to Tuesday.

The vice presidency didn't come with a dedicated aircraft—Air Force Two simply referred to whichever plane the vice president was on board. It could be any one of a number of aircraft that were shared among the cabinet. The planes tended to be cozy affairs, with fewer amenities than Air Force One—a perk to which Lombard was very much looking forward. At the fore of the plane was a small office, but you couldn't seat more than three or four comfortably. Lombard preferred his people clustered together, so he spent flights midcabin, where eight could work in relative comfort at a pair of open tables.

At the table across the aisle, his wife was being quizzed on the biographical details of the key individuals on this afternoon's campaign stop. People responded to a personal connection—ask after their children by name and they never forgot it. It was an old political parlor trick, but it took practice and study. Grace Lombard glanced up and smiled wearily at him. Although she had never been a fan of the campaign trail, he had yet to hear her complain in twenty-five years. In his opinion, it was precisely her disinterest in the trappings of power that made her so appealing to voters. So many in the public eye cultivated an image of being normal and down-to-earth, but his wife was the genuine article. He knew that she helped to balance him. They made an ideal team in that way.

"Leland," he asked his chief of staff. "What are my dinner plans?"

"Senator Russell. After your speech," Reed said without looking up from his laptop.

"Push it back. See if he'd let me buy him a scotch at the hotel around eleven instead."

Reed stood with his phone and walked down the aisle to make the call. Lombard looked back across the aisle to his wife's assistant, Denise Greenspan.

"What's the name of the restaurant my wife likes so much with the view of the Bay Bridge?"

"Boulevard, sir. On the Embarcadero."

"That's it. Get us in there. Seven thirty."

"How many, sir?"

"Just two." He smiled at his wife, who blew him a kiss across the aisle.

Abigail Saldana was nodding her approval at the idea. The personal sacrifice and forced intimacy required of political campaigns was daunting. Duke Vaughn had taught Lombard that lesson. It was hard to work on them without investing in the couple at the center. Particularly to the young, idealistic staffers who did the thankless grunt work, this wasn't merely a job. This was their family, and they needed to believe in their candidate. A quiet dinner with his wife would be good for everyone's morale. The same way children were reassured by small acts of affection between their parents.

"Ben," Grace stage-whispered. "Everyone's been pushing so hard. How about we send the team out while we're at dinner?"

Lombard didn't like that idea at all, but it was Grace to a tee. Too kindhearted for her own good. Or his. Still, he laughed magnanimously like it was the best idea he'd heard in years. Actually, when he thought about it, he liked how it would work itself out. Reed and Saldana would decline, which meant their people would have to skip it. That would leave a few lower-level staffers going out for dinner on his nickel. It would look good without costing him much in terms of work—a win, coming and going.

"And that is why I married this woman," he said. "But after dinner, right back on the chain gang, everyone!"

That brought laughter all around, but his message was clear: there was work to be done. Things were turning around, and people liked working for a winner. He'd take care of them once he was in the White House, but for now a small taste of his largesse would tide them over.

One of Reed's phones was ringing, but he wasn't back from shuffling his appointment with Senator Russell. Reed's aide glanced at the number but let it ring.

"Would you get that?" said Lombard.

The aide answered the phone, asked a few questions, and covered the mouthpiece with his hand. Lombard knew immediately that he'd made a mistake.

"Sir, I have a Titus Eskridge? He has an update for you on the 'ACG situation'?"

Lombard kept his expression even and disinterested but felt his wife's gaze on him. Colonel Titus Stonewall Eskridge Jr. was the founder and CEO of Cold Harbor Inc.—a private military contractor based out of Virginia. Cold Harbor had been a major contributor to his Senate campaigns, and Lombard went way back with Eskridge. Grace could find something redeeming in most people, but she couldn't even pretend to tolerate the man. Years ago, Lombard had severed political ties with Cold Harbor at her insistence, so he would need a very compelling reason for taking his call. A reason he didn't currently have.

A career in politics might have taught him the art of the bluff—he could take a knife in the back and whistle a happy tune—but somehow Grace had always been immune to such deceptions.

"Titus Eskridge? Well, they sure do come out of the woodwork this time of year." He waved the phone away. "Give it to Leland or take a message."

"Yes, sir," said the aide.

He glanced over to his wife, but she had already turned away. He would wait for her to bring it up later. One thing was for sure—his quiet, romantic dinner had just been canceled.

CHAPTER THIRTEEN

Jenn Charles sat at her desk and went back through her report on Vaughn. It had been one thing to bring him in to consult, but now George was contemplating inserting him into her team for phase two. It was a mistake. She knew it in her gut but couldn't articulate it beyond that. She needed more to back up her hunch.

Gibson Vaughn, son of Sally and Duke Vaughn. Born and raised in Charlottesville, Virginia. His mother passed when he was three. Ovarian cancer. Hard way to go, she thought. Gibson Vaughn had been raised, if one could call it that, by his workaholic father.

Duke Vaughn had been a legend in Virginia politics. Undergraduate and master's degrees in political science were both taken at the University of Virginia. A larger-than-life personality, Duke was a born charmer who put friends and foes alike at ease. He lived for the political dogfight and found his life's calling as Benjamin Lombard's chief of staff. They made a great pair—Lombard, the stubborn, principled brawler, and Vaughn, the master of the backroom deal. Vaughn was widely credited for guiding a green and largely unknown Benjamin Lombard to the US Senate and for helping him win a second term in a landslide.

From what Jenn could tell, Duke's devotion to Lombard came at the expense of his son. The demands of the job caused Duke to spend long stretches in DC or on the road with the senator. It was a seven-days-a-week job, which meant that Duke spent most of his weekends with the Lombards.

By all accounts, the Lombards treated Gibson like family; Duke and Gibson each had their own bedroom at both the senator's home in Great Falls and his beach house at Pamsrest near the North Carolina border. However, Duke had been determined not to uproot his son from school, so during the week Gibson was often left home in Charlottesville. Duke's sister, Miranda Davis, lived nearby and would look in on Gibson. But she had a family of her own, and as Gibson grew older she didn't always get over to check on him. So, by the time he was twelve, Gibson Vaughn was effectively living on his own from Monday to Friday.

A lot of children would resent being abandoned that way, but Gibson showed no signs of bitterness or anger. On the contrary, the young Gibson Vaughn quite clearly worshipped his father and had been determined to pull his weight. Gibson kept the household going while his father was away—organized the bills, cleaned the house, did yard work, and saw to minor upkeep. In a lot of ways, Gibson Vaughn raised himself.

On the surface, he had done a good job of it. Good grades. No disciplinary record of any kind. That was if you excluded the time he was pulled over for doing forty-six in a twenty-five. Of course, it was understandable that a thirteen-year-old might not be crystal clear on speed limits. According to unofficial reports, because there was no official report, Duke and the senator had been on a fact-finding tour to the Middle East. Gibson had run out of milk. Rather than call and risk waking his aunt, the boy had done the only reasonable thing and driven himself to the supermarket.

The arresting officer's report stated that when stopped, the boy had politely asked, "Is there a problem, officer?" Gibson Vaughn had been perched atop *The Collected Writings of Thomas Jefferson* to help him see over the steering wheel. When asked where his parents were, Gibson had pled the Fifth. Afraid of embarrassing his father, he'd refused to speak until the police were able to track down his aunt.

No charges were filed, and the entire incident became a piece of Virginia lore. Partly because the police chose not to pursue charges against a thirteen-year-old, but it didn't hurt that Duke Vaughn was a close personal friend of the Charlottesville chief of police. It seemed there wasn't much of anyone in the great commonwealth of Virginia with whom Duke Vaughn hadn't been a close personal friend.

That anecdote made Jenn smile. She'd been raised by her grandmother and knew what it was like to have to be self-sufficient at a young age. It could make you or it could isolate you, harden you. She would have liked that little boy—resourceful, proud, and a little foolhardy. They'd been a lot alike once, and she could still see traces of that boy now. The problem was she didn't see enough to reassure her. Duke Vaughn's suicide had seen to that.

Duke Vaughn had driven home from Washington unexpectedly one Wednesday and hanged himself in his basement. Jenn flipped through the autopsy photographs that she'd culled from the conference room before Vaughn settled in. What kind of selfish prick hangs himself where he'll be found by his fifteen-year-old son? No note, nothing. It was unforgivable.

After his father's death, Gibson Vaughn became a completely different person—hostile, defiant, and antisocial. The impact was clear as day. He withdrew from the computer science classes he was auditing at the University of Virginia. His grades plummeted. Three fights in two months. A suspension for cursing out a teacher. He'd gone to live with his aunt full time, and Jenn's report had copies of the increasingly despairing letters Miranda Davis wrote to her sister-in-law, detailing her nephew's deteriorating behavior. How he rarely spoke anymore. Didn't eat. Wouldn't leave the house except to go to school. How he spent all day and night in his room on his computer.

It was a matter of public record what he'd done on that computer.

She knocked lightly at her boss's door. George had always encouraged her to trust her instincts and to speak her mind. It was a trait that had never served her well at the Agency, and it had taken time for her to take him at his word. She didn't come by trust easily, but George Abe had it. She would walk on broken glass for him.

He'd thrown her a lifeline after her career at the Agency had imploded. Recruited her when she thought she didn't want a job, tracked her down at home when she ignored his numerous calls and convinced her to come to work for him. To this day, she had no idea how he'd even known who she was. But he'd nursed her back into work shape and given her room to regain her confidence without feeling coddled. A good thing, because she would have quit on the spot. In retrospect, she knew she would never be able to repay that debt.

"Come."

She opened the door. George was behind his desk, reviewing the financials from the first quarter. The Rolling Stones played in the background. A live version of "Dead Flowers." She didn't pay much attention to music and hardly ever knew who was playing, but she knew this song, because George had once spent an hour extolling the virtues of Townes Van Zandt's acoustic cover during a trip to New York. The Stones were George's favorite band, and she'd grown accustomed to Jagger's lecherous caterwauling. An autographed poster of an enormous pair of lips, tongue protruding, hung framed on one wall. It was from one of the band's US tours and was one of George's prized possessions. A photograph of George beside Keith Richards hung nearby.

The far wall was a bookshelf neatly divided in two, which, in a way, summed up her boss. George descended from one of the oldest Japanese families in the United States. His ancestors had fled Japan following the

Meiji Restoration and arrived in San Francisco in 1871. They had carved out a rich and successful life for themselves, weathered internment, and rebuilt their fortunes in the 1950s. The Abes were proud both of their heritage and their adopted country. It was a family tradition to recognize the two halves in the names of their children.

George Leyasu Abe.

One half of the bookcase was devoted to books on Japanese history. George was particularly fascinated by the culture of the samurai, and dozens of books on the subject took up an entire shelf. His middle name, Leyasu, was taken from the founder of the Tokugawa shogunate in 1600, which was dissolved by the Meiji Restoration of 1868. The other half of the shelf was given over to books on American colonial history. George Washington, his namesake, was especially well represented, as were Madison and Franklin. But, and Jenn knew this for a fact, there wasn't a single book on Thomas Jefferson. George considered Jefferson disloyal and a traitor. It was a subject he could lecture upon for hours. She didn't always understand her boss, or agree with his condemnation of Jefferson, but loyalty was one subject about which they were in complete agreement. That was why she couldn't understand his decision to bring Gibson Vaughn into the next phase of this mission.

George stopped what he was doing and pointed to a chair. Jenn sat, realizing immediately that she didn't know how to broach the subject. George, as he so often did, read her mind.

"So. Gibson Vaughn."

She smiled ruefully at her transparence. Poker had never been her game.

"I just don't get it," she said. "Mike is the wrong guy, clearly, but it's not like Gibson Vaughn invented the computer. What really qualifies him for this? So he hacked a senator when he was a kid. Is that really the résumé of someone we want to be working with? I mean, this whole keeping-us-in-suspense thing. He's a prima donna, and he clearly prefers to do things his own way."

George smiled. "So you don't like him."

"Not really, which is immaterial. I don't trust him, which isn't. He's a risk. And I'm afraid . . ." She trailed off.

George leaned back. "Say what you came to say."

"I'm afraid this history between you . . . that it's blinding you. You think he's going to be grateful for this chance you're giving him. I know you believe you're cleaning the slate, and I respect that, but he's not the type. He's never going to forgive anyone anything, because it's all someone else's fault."

"He's performed well up until now."

"Yes, he has. But taking him out into the field is a whole other thing. I'm worried that if we get close to WR8TH that he'll burn us. Even if that means burning himself."

"The proverbial scorpion on the turtle's back."

"He's undependable," she said. "Respectfully, sir."

"Is that all?"

"I don't like him poking around in our computers."

"Anything else? His haircut perhaps?" George stood and fetched a bottle of mineral water from a built-in refrigerator. He sat beside Jenn and gazed off into space. He often took his time composing his thoughts and never spoke before he was ready. She knew better than to interrupt him now that she'd said her piece. It used to make her nervous, but she'd come to admire her employer's introspective nature.

"You may be right," he said at last.

The answer surprised her, but she remained silent.

"About all of it. You may be right. I have my doubts too."

"Is he really worth the risk, then?"

"How much do you know about what Vaughn did in the Marines?"

"I know he was a penetration tester. A glorified hacker."

"Not exactly."

"That's what it says in his file," she said and realized as she did that there was more to it. "But that was a cover, wasn't it?"

"It was, yes."

"What did he really do?"

"Well, let me ask you this. How do you fly two Blackhawk helicopters into a sovereign nation, brazenly violating their airspace, and set them down in the heart of one of their biggest cities without drawing attention?"

"You're talking about bin Laden. Pakistan."

"Theoretically," Abe said. "Supposing I am. Ask yourself how we managed it. Ask yourself why they didn't know we were there until they saw it on the news."

"The choppers were specially outfitted. Some kind of stealth technology."

"Partially true, but only partially. You can baffle a helicopter, to a degree, so that it runs quiet if not silent, but what about radar? You can't make a Blackhawk completely invisible to radar and certainly not to Pakistani air defense. The Pentagon canceled the program to build a stealth helicopter in '04. And stealth is not a design feature you can easily retrofit."

"So how?"

"Radar is a machine. Software translates electrical impulses so that users can see what radar sees. So rather than spending billions on stealth helicopters, wouldn't it be simpler to take control of the software? Insert code right into their system so that the software only showed them what you wanted them to see. Voila, Blackhawks that are there but not there. If you follow me."

"We did that?"

"Vaughn did that," said Abe. "Well, he was involved with the operation. It was an incredibly intricate job. Lot of moving parts. The SEALs might have pulled the trigger, but all four service branches were needed to put bin Laden in harm's way. CIA. NSA. Vaughn impressed a lot of people, if my source is correct."

"Vaughn wrote the code?" asked Jenn.

"He contributed to the code, but no, that wasn't his unique contribution."

"What was?"

"He got the Pakistanis to install it."

"He what?"

"That's what I'm told."

"Pakistan installed a virus onto their own system?"

"Apparently. He's just that persuasive, and they are not people who are easily persuaded."

"You're telling me the Activity recruited Gibson Vaughn?"

"Right out of basic."

"Holy hell."

The Activity or Intelligence Support Activity was the intelligence-gathering branch of the JSOC—the Joint Special Operations Command. The military's CIA. After the 1980 Operation Eagle Claw ended in disaster in an Iranian desert, the Armed Forces had blamed the CIA for failing to share mission-critical assets and information. The Activity had been birthed so that the military would never again have to rely on the CIA. Jenn knew the lore well; everyone in the CIA did.

The Activity was the competition.

It cherry-picked its personnel from the four military branches, and she could see how a marine like Gibson Vaughn would catch their eye. They put a premium on out-of-the-box thinkers, and sometimes you needed a thief to catch a thief. It threw her portrait of Gibson Vaughn out of focus. She was also reasonably certain that her boss wanted it that way.

"Jesus," she said. "The guy helped take down bin Laden and now he can't even get a job at Burger King."

"Well, as you said, he didn't invent the computer, and it's safer to hire someone else than cross the vice president. Scratch that. The next president."

"So you're saying I should give him a break?"

"No, I'm not. What I'm saying is that people are rarely as black and white as you sometimes make them out to be. Now, in the field there are times when snap judgments are necessary, and you excel in those situations. It's why I hired you. Your instincts are very rarely wrong, but we're not in the field yet, and you have a tendency to throw the baby out with the bathwater where people are concerned."

"Sorry, sir."

"Don't be. Something about Vaughn rubs you the wrong way. Makes your trigger finger itch. But I knew him when he was a boy, and I saw his relationship with Suzanne. You had to see it to believe the way he took care of her. She was a very special little girl, and he was a great kid too."

"But that was a long—" she began, but he put up a hand to stop her.

"I don't believe Gibson Vaughn would knowingly sabotage an effort to find her. I also think that his history with Suzanne Lombard is unique and invaluable. He may see something that no one else could. That alone makes him worth the risk to me. But perhaps you're right. Perhaps my judgment is clouded by history. That's why I want you right where you are. If he acts against us, I trust you to see it. And we'll deal with it if he does. In the meantime, I believe he gives us the best odds of seeing this issue to a positive conclusion. Am I understood?"

"Yes, sir." She stood to go.

"Jenn," George said. "Gibson Vaughn has endured a great deal in his life and served his country ably. It would be shortsighted to under-estimate him."

"Yes, sir."

"Besides, WR8TH seems disinclined to show himself, so this may all be moot."

"Yes, sir."

"And, Jenn. This isn't the CIA. Please feel free to call me George."

"Yes, sir."

CHAPTER FOURTEEN

Gibson crossed the field under the Saturday morning sun. It felt good to be outdoors again. On Thursday evening, George Abe had thrown him out of the office and warned him in no uncertain terms not to show his face until Monday. It was hard to step away; it made Gibson feel guilty. But he had another little girl who needed him, and she had a soccer game today.

He hadn't seen enough of Ellie the past few weeks. He knew it, and he hated it. But it was a necessary evil. Abe's money had paid the mortgage on the house where she and her mother lived. Where they all had lived before the divorce.

In hindsight, he and Nicole probably shouldn't have bought the house. They bought at the height of the market before the crash. It had been a stretch, financially, but at the time Gibson believed he would have his pick of jobs when he was discharged from the Marines. It wasn't an unreasonable assumption. He'd watched the private sector snap up guys from his unit as soon as their boots hit US soil. Guys with half his experience or commendations sparked bidding wars among the big defense contractors. So with his résumé, he figured he would have it made.

What he hadn't counted on, and what he hadn't understood, was what being on Benjamin Lombard's blacklist meant. Really meant. He'd job hunted for months without so much as a callback. At first he'd limited himself to the big fish, the whales of the defense industry that always needed guys with his skill set. When he finally accepted that they weren't going to hire him, he'd applied for jobs with second-tier companies. The crickets came from far and wide to sing him a sad song.

He took a job at a chain electronics store selling home computers just to keep some money coming in. He'd become bitter and defensive. It had been a bad time. He'd shut down, only surfacing to lash out at his wife and daughter. To his shame, he'd fought with Nicole about everything. Anything. And God help her if she broached the subject of selling the house. That ignited fights that lasted for days and left him in an angry, pulsating silence. Knowing he was failing. Fearing Nicole had hitched her happiness to the wrong man. Fearing that she knew it too, he read resentment in her every action.

It went on like that for months, and things were unraveling fast when his former commanding officer alerted him that Potestas, a local biotech company, was looking for an IT director and put in a good word for him. Potestas was small enough to fall beneath even Benjamin Lombard's attention. Or so he'd assumed until a month ago. The work was entry-level IT: mindless and dull. He flew through the interview process and gratefully accepted a salary offer that he would have scoffed at only a year earlier. But with a wife and daughter and a crippling mortgage, Gibson didn't dare risk making a counteroffer. Suddenly health insurance and a steady paycheck seemed like a gift from above. Job satisfaction and his dreams of spoiling his wife would just have to wait.

Ex-wife, he reminded himself. They'd been divorced for almost a year, and still he couldn't bring himself to say it.

Ex-wife.

It wasn't that he'd meant to go looking for trouble, but he hadn't put up any resistance when trouble found him. He just let it happen.

Through all those deployments in the Corps, cheating on his wife had never once crossed his mind. Ironically, it started after he got the job at Potestas. The job hadn't magically fixed the cracks that had appeared in their marriage, and he'd been too stubborn and prideful to set to fixing them. Instead, he'd gone to a happy hour with a sales rep named Leigh.

In retrospect, he saw it for what it was: a temporary refuge. Cowardice, pure and simple. Leigh liked him and was nice to him. She didn't need anything from him except a drink and a laugh. The man who had slept with Leigh was a mystery to him. Even now, it was hard to reconcile that man with who he thought he was.

To her infinite credit and his eternal gratitude, Nicole wasn't cruel or vindictive. Her lawyer was fair, and while their marriage ended, it never extended to his relationship with his daughter. Compared to the stories that he'd heard, he'd gotten very lucky. But then anyone who knew Nicole was lucky.

The hardest part was watching Nicole go dead to him. She did her grieving behind closed doors. Always had. So there had been no fights. No tears. Just a numb distance. She reached her conclusion about the marriage before she even confronted him. Everything else was a formality.

He begged for another chance, but Nicole wasn't the forgiving kind. They'd known each other since high school, and he'd never once known Nicole to bend. She gave no second chances when it came to loyalty. You were loyal or you weren't; it wasn't something you learned. If he wasn't a man she could trust, he wasn't a man she could be married to. Gibson had always loved the confidence she had in her own counsel, but it was another thing entirely being on the wrong side of it.

And just like that, he was a single, divorced father living in a bland high-rise concrete-slab apartment. Gone were six years of marriage. And in its place he had alimony payments, an hour commute to see his daughter, and a deepening suspicion that he was the dumbest son of a bitch who'd ever lived.

That was why the house mattered.

It was a good house—a sturdy, two-story Cape Cod. Far out from DC—quiet and safe. Good schools. One July, on furlough, he'd planted the row of azaleas that ran alongside the driveway. Afterward, he and Nicole sat in deck chairs, drinking beers and planning the garden until the bugs chased them inside. Ellie followed nine months later. That was the happiest Gibson had ever been, and he didn't regret buying the house, even now. Even if it was killing him trying to hold on to it. The house represented the life that he owed Nicole and Ellie. He'd rather die than see them lose it because of him.

The soccer game was just getting started as he walked up. The ball bounced toward the sideline, and a pack of girls from both teams chased after it, shrieking happily. He spotted Ellie immediately. She was on the far side of the field, bent over and staring intently at something in the grass. Gibson grinned. It was just possible that his daughter was the least talented soccer player in the history of the world. It wasn't only her utter lack of coordination and inability to judge the flight of the ball. It was her flagrant utter disregard for the rules of the game. The idea of playing a single position bored her, and she roamed the field with impunity. Without the uniform, it would have been hard to tell which team she was on.

Out on the field, Ellie began running in a tight circle with her arms out, looking up at the sky until she got dizzy and fell over in a heap.

Gibson couldn't help but smile. Half the time he didn't know what planet his little girl was from, but he loved her so much it physically hurt him that he couldn't put her to bed every night. Reading bedtime stories over a computer wasn't any way to be a father.

Ellie clambered happily to her feet and took off running across the field—a constant reminder of how much joy could be wrung out of life. Should he be embarrassed to admit his role model was his six-year-old daughter?

Out on the field, the ball bounced to Ellie, who took a mighty kick at it. It sliced hard to the right and spun fifteen yards out of bounds. Gibson took a step toward the pitch and clapped like Ellie had just won the World Cup. She stopped in her tracks to wave at her daddy while the other players thundered past her after the ball.

Up the sideline, his wife glanced over at him. *Ex-wife,* he reminded himself. Nicole was sitting with the main clump of "home" parents, who had set up a little oasis of folding chairs and coolers. Gibson made a habit of standing apart from them. Far enough away that he wouldn't crowd Nicole, but not far enough away that it looked like he was making a big deal of it. She'd made friends with several of the parents, and he was glad to cede her that territory. She nodded at him, and he returned it. She turned back to the game and didn't look his way again.

At halftime, the players gathered at opposite goals and sucked on orange slices while the coaches discussed strategies the young girls had no prayer of executing. The parents chatted among themselves or went in search of a porta-john. Nicole walked down the sideline to him. She was wearing one of the loose, flowing sundresses that she'd favored since high school. She looked gorgeous silhouetted against the sun.

"Hi," she said.

"Hi."

That much pleasantness exhausted the both of them, and they took a second to regroup. Talking to Nicole was always safer when they stuck to Ellie as a topic. A lot of bad things had transpired between them, but when it came to Ellie, they were absolutely on the same page.

"Looks like El has the MVP all sewn up this season," he said.

"I've been fielding calls from the Brazilians all game."

"Hold out for the big bucks."

"Agent to the stars."

"Did you get the money?"

"I did. Thank you. Why are you getting paid in cash, Gib?"

"It was a signing bonus."

"In cash." She was squinting at him. "Is it safe to deposit?"

"Of course it is." He felt his temper spike, but Nicole had a point. Who got paid in cash?

"What's going on?"

"Nothing. It's fine."

"It's fine? You're really going to the well with that."

"We need the money. It's fine. I promise."

"Please don't make me promises, Gib. Okay?"

It came out evenly and without any malice, but it stung, and he looked away from her. They stood silently, as if any sudden moves would be interpreted as a hostile act. These were the worst moments of his life. Standing beside the only person he'd ever been able to talk to openly, reduced to guarded, delicately worded conversations or guarded, stumbling silences.

"I'll bring the money by your place on Monday."

"Nicole."

"Gibson," she said, not giving an inch.

"Suzanne. The job. The money. It's about Suzanne."

Nicole's entire demeanor shifted at the mention of Suzanne's name. Her practiced mask of indifference split apart, and for the first time in a year, Gibson saw concern and worry in her eyes—the clouds parting for an instant.

"Suzanne." She searched his eyes for the truth. "Are you trying to find her?"

He nodded.

"Jesus."

"I wish I could tell you the whole thing. But they have me on kind of a short leash. I promise, though, the money's legit."

"No, it's all right. I don't need to know."

"Thank you."

"Are *you* all right, Gib? I mean . . . Suzanne."

"I think so."

"Ellie's got a friend's birthday party after the game. Parents are invited. Pizza and punch. I think they even hired a clown. You should come."

"I'd like that."

He turned to see what Nicole was looking at over his shoulder. Jenn Charles, in suit and heels, was walking toward him. Even from behind her sunglasses, the look on Jenn's face gave him butterflies.

"What? What happened?" he asked as she reached them.

"We got him," Jenn said.

"When? Where?"

Jenn glanced at Nicole and didn't answer.

"Am I going, at least?" he asked.

"Boss needs to talk to you. He's in the parking lot."

Gibson looked over to the cars, then back to Jenn and finally to Nicole.

"I have to go."

"Go," Nicole said.

"But Ellie—"

"She'll understand. Just make sure you call. She gets funny if she doesn't talk to you."

"I will."

He started to follow Jenn back to the parking lot, but Nicole stopped him.

"Gib."

"Yeah?"

"Good hunting."

CHAPTER FIFTEEN

George was waiting for him in a black M-Class Mercedes. A long rectangular box wrapped in bright-red paper with little white unicorns on it lay in the passenger seat.

"What's with the box?" Gibson asked.

"It's not for you."

"Well, now you're just hurting my feelings."

George chuckled and put the gift in the backseat and handed Gibson a sports jacket.

"Put that on. We've got an appointment."

"Good luck," Jenn said.

"Aren't you coming?"

She shook her head. "See you back at the office."

The sedan glided out of the parking lot in a luxurious cocoon. Gibson had never been in a car this nice, and it was easy to see the appeal. He might actually look forward to getting stuck in traffic.

"Well?" Gibson said.

"You were right."

"Where is he?"

"On Friday afternoon your virus pinged from an IP address in western Pennsylvania. A little town called Somerset."

"Why didn't anyone call me?"

"One ping and it went dormant."

"Dormant?" That wasn't supposed to happen, and several theories as to why jumped to mind. "What was I right about?"

"It was a public library."

Gibson thought it over; it made sense. Lot of bodies coming and going. It was smart and added another layer of anonymity that would be tricky to peel back. They would have to stake out the library in the hope that they could make an ID if WR8TH tried to access ACG's servers again.

At Washington Circle, they took New Hampshire to Twenty-Second, then hung a left on P Street into Georgetown. Apartment buildings gave way to brick row houses and then to large private homes cloistered by soaring elms and oaks.

Duke Vaughn had described Georgetown as the land of deep pockets and sharp teeth. His father had attended four or five work-related events here a year, but never took his son with him. *They aren't those kinds of parties,* Duke had explained. *It's hostile territory.*

Even if they're on your side? Gibson had asked his father.

Especially if they're on your side, his father had answered with a wink.

"Does that mean I'm going?"

"I'd like to keep you on," Abe said. "You've been invaluable thus far, and my guess is that your skill set may yet prove useful. Also, your relationship with Suzanne."

"So is that a yes?"

"That all depends."

"On?"

"Ms. Dauplaise asked to see you."

Gibson nodded, watching Abe. He'd been summoned for an audience with the queen. At least that's how it felt.

"I think you can help us, and I've told her exactly that. But Ms. Dauplaise prefers to make up her own mind."

George pulled up to a wrought-iron gate. A black metal sign with gold letters read, "Colline." A mass of brightly colored balloons bobbed from one of the spires, and a line of families waited to be checked through by a pair of security guards. The men all wore jackets, the women dresses. Even the children had dressed up, and all carried presents. If heaven were sponsored by Laura Ashley and Ralph Lauren, it would look something like this.

One of the security guards broke away from the line and approached the car.

"You're going to have to find street parking . . ." The guard trailed off when he recognized the driver. "Oh, hello, Mr. Abe. Are you here for the party?"

"No, Tony. Here to see Ms. Dauplaise."

"Oh, sure, go on up. But park in front of the carriage house instead of your usual spot. I'll radio to let them know. It's a little crazy up there today."

"I appreciate it."

They drove up the pebbled drive toward an imposing Federal mansion flanked by manicured gardens that sloped off in both directions. The scale of it stunned Gibson. He counted at least seven chimneys. It was a property that belonged in the English countryside, not in the middle of an American city. Another guard directed them off the main driveway, and Abe parked by a two-story garage that was bigger than Nicole's house. Seven bays with white retractable doors spanned the length of the redbrick building. The center bay stood open—inside, a beautifully maintained vintage green Bentley.

Abe saw him admiring it. "That's a '52. It belonged to Ms. Dauplaise's grandfather. He was ambassador to France under Roosevelt. Theodore, not Franklin."

"And he lived here too?"

"The Dauplaises have lived here since the 1820s. There aren't many older families in the city. The main house was designed by Charles Bulfinch and Alexandre Dauplaise after the War of 1812."

"What does 'Colline' mean?" Gibson asked.

"'The Small Hill.' It's the name Alexandre's wife gave the house when she arrived from France. Of course, Ms. Dauplaise can tell you more. She's an encyclopedia when it comes to the family history."

"Who else lives here?"

"At the moment, it is just her and her niece. The party is for Catherine's birthday."

"Two people? That's it?"

"Ms. Dauplaise has a son from a former marriage. He lives in Florida. Doesn't visit often. She also has two living sisters. One lives in San Francisco. Another is a dean at the University of Pittsburgh medical school. Her youngest sister passed during childbirth: her niece's mother. Calista adopted Catherine. Then there are about a hundred cousins of one kind or another that I can't keep up with."

They walked up to the house. Abe stopped them and turned to Gibson. He was struggling for how to put something.

"Calista . . . Ms. Dauplaise is a good woman."

"But . . . ?"

"She's hard. She doesn't do disagreement well. She's a woman who is accustomed to the sound of her own voice, if you follow me."

"What do you need me to do?"

"Let her hear it. If you want the job."

Gibson did want the job. He needed to see Somerset, Pennsylvania. Needed it. He was afraid of what they might find there, but he had to know. If tap-dancing for Calista was the price of the ticket, then dance he would. His father had made a career of handling the landed gentry. Surely some of it must have rubbed off.

As they rounded the side of the house, the sound of music and the gleeful screams of children greeted them. It was quite a scene. He guessed there were better than three hundred people on the lawn, which stretched away from the balustrade that ran the length of the long, wide terrace. Down below, a Dixieland band was in full swing beneath one of several white tents. A parquet dance floor had been assembled, and dozens of couples danced. Clowns and magicians performed tricks of all sorts for groups of children.

He thought about the birthday party that Ellie was going to this afternoon. He hoped it had a clown. Ellie would love a clown.

"How old is this kid?" Gibson asked.

"Eight."

"Eight?" he said, incredulous. "They're all here for an eight-year-old?"

"Don't be absurd. They're here for Ms. Dauplaise."

"Right. Did my dad ever come here?"

"Of course," Abe said. "He worked closely with Ms. Dauplaise. You don't get very far in Washington ignoring invitations from Calista Dauplaise."

"How did she get involved with Lombard?"

"You have it backward. Calista Dauplaise discovered Benjamin Lombard. Invented him, really. He was languishing in the Virginia General Assembly when they met. She plucked him from obscurity and polished his rough edges. Helped him make the right connections and bankrolled his run for the United States Senate."

"Mighty generous of her."

"Well, there are kings and there are kingmakers. Regardless of what populist history might argue, you rarely have one without the other."

"So she must get some kind of trophy if he gets elected president in November."

"She and the vice president are no longer on good terms."

They climbed a stone staircase to the terrace. It appeared to be the designated child-free zone. Two dozen tables shaded by umbrellas had been arranged. People milled about, drinking and socializing. Waiters in bow ties circled, refilling wine glasses and offering trays of hors d'oeuvres. Gibson was hungry and helped himself to tenderloin and horseradish on thin-sliced French bread. Abe led him to the center of the terrace, where a table larger and more elaborate than any of the others overlooked the lawn, set apart slightly from the other tables.

Abe gestured for Gibson to wait and approached a woman who was probably in her early sixties, but for whom the privilege of money had granted an extended middle age. Gibson knew without having to ask that this was Calista Dauplaise. It wasn't arrogance that she radiated. It went well beyond arrogance. It was surety—the absolute certitude that the world had been organized precisely to her liking. It lent her an elegant poise that made her companions pale by comparison. Her hair was cut in a stylish blonde bob that swept along a jawline that had clearly enjoyed the attentions of a talented plastic surgeon. Dressed all in white and trimmed in gold, she wore no jewelry whatsoever. Abe bent to whisper in her ear. She glanced past him, in Gibson's direction, her eyes sharp and piercing.

"Ladies, I apologize. Will you excuse me for a moment?" she said.

Gibson expected her to stand, but it was the rest of the table that gathered up purses and drinks and moved away. One of them, a silver-haired woman in her fifties, leaned over and whispered in Calista's ear, glancing at Gibson as she did. Calista said something in agreement, and the woman, satisfied, disappeared into the throng.

Abe waved him over. "Calista, this is Gibson Vaughn."

She smiled and extended a hand for him to shake.

"Please have a seat," she said. "Not you, George. Get yourself a drink. We'll just be a minute."

Abe excused himself, but he caught Gibson's eyes before he left. *Try not to blow this* was the unmistakable message.

"It's good to see you again, Gibson. Do you remember me?"

"I do. It's nice to see you again."

"I didn't take you away from your work, did I?"

"No."

"So you were not there for the big moment?"

It sounded like an accusation. He took a bite of tenderloin to keep from answering.

"In any event, thank you for coming at such short notice. I do apologize for all the commotion," she said, gesturing toward the party on the lawn. "I'm sure another day would have been easier, but George feels we need to move with all due speed, and I wanted to speak before things progressed."

"It's quite a party," he said.

"Yes. And such a pretty day. I regret canceling the flyby."

"The flyby?"

"Yes, the Navy has a team of jet planes that do the most wonderful tricks."

"The Blue Angels?"

"Just the same," she said.

Gibson was stunned at the idea that this woman had booked the Blue Angels for an eight-year-old's party.

"I'm having a bit of fun, of course. Are you easily taken in, Mr. Vaughn?"

"No, not usually." But something about this woman put him off his game. He felt timid in her presence, a sensation that he didn't enjoy at all. He'd once told a three-star general to pipe down in a meeting, but this woman made him feel like Oliver Twist with a cup out.

"Let us hope not." She smiled.

"Why am I here?" he asked.

"Now, don't be sore. It's important to have a sense of humor about oneself."

"Do you?"

"Have a sense of humor about myself? Absolutely. However, it is vitally important to be the one telling the jokes." She winked at him. "It makes all the difference."

"I'll keep that in mind."

"Do. My family lost the ability to laugh at itself several generations ago. You rise to a certain level of prominence, and the inclination is to view one's family with an unhealthy degree of reverence. One is lulled into believing that the family's success was not a matter of luck and hard work, but due instead to some innate superiority." She leaned in toward Gibson, as if sharing a confidence. "God's will. Good genes. Blue blood. That sort of thing. It's ludicrous, of course, but it happens with unnerving frequency. And always ends the same way. Each generation more entitled than the last. Lazier than the last. More interested in ski vacations in Gstaad than in bettering the family's fortunes. Entitlement breeds laziness, which in turn breeds decline. But of course with enough money, it is possible not to notice for decades that your family name is gathering dust. One day you awake to discover that the last member of the family to accomplish anything of note died before Kennedy. Do you know what my son does for a living?"

Gibson shook his head.

"Not a thing. He lives in a condominium in Fort Lauderdale with a woman and golfs." Her eyes widened in horror to help him realize the gravity of the situation. When he didn't appear to, she repeated it slowly. "Fort Lauderdale, Mr. Vaughn. My great uncle helped Wilson craft the Treaty of Versailles, and my son's ambition extends no further than subdivisions in the swamps of Florida. The mind boggles."

"Not a fan?"

"Of the state of Florida? No, it is evidence that perhaps air-conditioning would have been better left uninvented."

"So keep a sense of humor?"

"It has served me well." She smiled and touched the rim of her empty wineglass. A waiter appeared in an instant to refill it.

"In a way, I owe you a great debt of thanks," Calista said.

"How so?"

"That business with Benjamin that landed you in such . . . difficulty."

"I don't follow."

"Whose money do you think was embezzled? Benjamin's? Please, that man had nothing before I found him. In your ill-advised way, you helped me recognize I was betting on the wrong horse."

"I don't understand. You mean my father?"

"No, not your father. He was a lovely man, but he was just the jockey. If you'll permit the analogy."

"Lombard?"

"Indeed. He was an enterprising little thief. You upset a rotten apple cart."

"But my father . . ."

Calista looked at him pityingly. "Were you taken in by their version? That it was your father? Oh dear, no. Your father was loyal to a fault. A trait he shared with George. Duke Vaughn was merely a convenient scapegoat. The dead have no rights, or so my lawyers tell me, and rarely rise to defend themselves. Have you really gone all these years believing your father a thief?"

A surge of vertigo clouded Gibson's vision, and a high-pitched feedback in his ears pushed the party away. He staved off the urge to put his head between his knees. Instead, he interlaced his fingers as if in angry prayer and held Calista's gaze.

"Why didn't you come forward?" he asked after a long moment.

"A fair question. Because, simply put, it was not in my interests."

"It was your interests Lombard was stealing."

"Yes, and my money was returned."

"So that's it?"

"Politics is an ugly picture with a pretty frame. Much as I enjoyed Duke Vaughn, I was not about to embroil my family in a feud with Benjamin Lombard to salvage your deceased father's reputation. The cost to my own would have been irreparable."

"You let Lombard win."

"And I lived to fight another day. The lesser of two evils."

"So is that why I'm here? To assuage your and George's dirty conscience?"

"Oh, heavens no. That was all George. He's such a good man. Noble even. It's his great failing," she said with an amused smile.

"So this arrangement wasn't your idea."

"Hire the man convicted of framing Benjamin Lombard to find Suzanne? It's grotesque. Whatever choices you made were your own and have nothing whatsoever to do with me. But George, bless his heart, thinks it has symmetry. And so here we are."

"So why *are* we here?"

"To balance George's karmic scales, I suppose."

"No. Why are *we* here?" he clarified.

"Ah. Why have I invited you to my home, you mean? Because, regardless of my feelings about Benjamin, Suzanne remains very dear to me. I am her godmother. I was at her christening. I helped raise her. She was an angelic baby. Truly. One of those who never cried. She was a treasure and a wonderful young lady. As you well know. She had the appetite for life that my family has frittered away. She was brilliant, or would have grown to be. What happened to her is a tragedy."

She took a long drink from her wineglass. It was some time before she went on.

"I'm sorry. The subject is very raw to me. Even after all this time."

"I understand," he said.

"You're too kind. Mr. Vaughn, if there is even a remote chance that this photograph is genuine—and, honestly, I think it is a hoax intended to inflict anguish, reopen old wounds, the work of a sadist—but if it is authentic and this person, in fact, knows something about what happened to my goddaughter, I will move heaven and earth to find him. The person responsible for all this . . ." She paused, choosing her words carefully. "He will suffer."

The last word fell like a scythe. It reminded him of what George Abe had said about wanting to have a serious conversation with the man who took Suzanne.

"In any event, George thinks you could be of some benefit to the cause. I wanted to meet you and see for myself."

"So this is an interview?"

"Hardly. No, I'm just a curious bystander. If George says you're qualified, I'm certainly not qualified to dispute it."

"So what, then?"

"Only this. Find this man, and I will be grateful. My family is not what it once was, not that our name has entirely lost its influence, but I believe it will be great again. Do you see the small cupola beyond the hedgerow?"

She gestured to a point beyond the lawn, and he saw the domed building at the edge of the property. The hedge had to be at least fifteen feet tall, so he didn't know by what measure she thought it was small.

"It was built by my great-great-great-grandfather Alexandre Dauplaise when his wife passed away. He was buried alongside her twelve years later when he followed her. The entire family is interred there, apart from my uncle Daniel, who is buried under a white cross in Normandy. In time, I will join them, and on that date, my family's connection to this city will span three centuries. But before I do join them, I intend to see my family begin to restore its traditions of greatness and service to this country."

"No more condos in Florida?"

"Indeed. I say all this not to give you a history lesson but to assure you that my gratitude will not be inconsequential. You and your family will benefit. But should you have ideas," she said, her tone darkening, "thoughts of exploiting the situation for your own ends, making this matter public in the media, as you tried to do in the past . . . Well, I will take it very personally indeed."

"I understand."

"Good. I'm sure this conversation was entirely unnecessary."

"I'd wonder myself in your position."

Calista nodded approvingly. "I appreciate that, Mr. Vaughn. I really do."

"Aunt C! Aunt C!" a girl yelled, barreling up to the table at top speed. A pack of children followed behind but stopped at the top of the stairs as if a force field blocked their path. The girl stopped at her aunt's side, out of breath, white dress dotted with grass. Her black hair was braided down the middle, and she had pretty blue eyes. She saw Gibson and immediately became shy, pressing herself close to her aunt and whispering in her ear. Calista laughed and hugged the girl.

"Yes, of course. But no more than twenty. Let Davis know so that he can make arrangements with their parents."

The girl grinned and said thank you. She started to run back to the party, but Calista caught her by the sleeve.

"Can you say hello to our guest? This is Mr. Vaughn. This is Catherine, my niece."

"Hello." She waved.

"Hello," Gibson said.

"Properly, young lady."

She nodded at her mistake, gathered herself, and approached Gibson with her hand out. He shook it.

"So nice to meet you, Mr. Vaughn. I'm Catherine Dauplaise. Thank you for attending my birthday party."

She looked at her aunt out of the corner of her eye to see if she'd gotten it right. Calista sighed and waved her away.

"Go on, go play. And remember, no more than twenty."

"Yes, Aunt C!" Catherine yelled excitedly as she ran down the steps to the lawn.

"A work in progress," Calista said. "I'm afraid motherhood is not in my makeup. As my lackadaisical son will attest. But I do my best."

"If it's any consolation, she's better behaved than mine."

He could tell from her face that it wasn't.

"It was nice to see you again, Mr. Vaughn. Good luck in Pennsylvania."

PART TWO

SOMERSET

CHAPTER SIXTEEN

The expedition to Somerset left the next day. The parking garage beneath Abe Consulting was nearly empty, and Gibson's footsteps echoed off the concrete walls. Hendricks, smoking a cigarette, leaned against a banged-up late-model Grand Cherokee, its wheel wells mottled with rust, the side panels badly dented. It looked like someone had resculpted the rear bumper using a concrete embankment as a chisel.

"Sweet ride. Range Rover in the shop?" Gibson said.

"Ninety-thousand-dollar SUVs don't exactly blend in central Pennsylvania, Vaughn. We're trying to keep a low profile."

Gibson put up both hands. "Just a joke, man."

"Just worry about the computers, all right?" Hendricks flicked ash toward two large black duffel bags. "That's the equipment you spec'd out. Stow it in the back."

Hendricks got into the Cherokee and started the engine. Gibson unzipped the bags and took an inventory before putting them in the trunk alongside a stack of identical black bags. Hendricks was hauling along an awful lot of equipment. What *was* all this stuff?

Jenn pulled up in a Taurus that was in even worse shape than the Cherokee. The car looked like it had been driven through an alleyway a quarter inch too narrow. However, whatever cosmetic damage the Taurus had sustained didn't extend under the hood. Gibson could hear the throaty muscle of the engine as it came to a stop. Gibson shut the hatch on the Grand Cherokee and noted that it, like the Taurus, had Pennsylvania plates and a Penn State bumper sticker. He might not have a background in surveillance, but he appreciated people who paid attention to details.

The passenger door on the Taurus was locked. He rapped on the window and glanced in at Jenn. She shook her head and pointed one finger at the Cherokee. Hendricks honked.

"Are you kidding me?" Gibson mouthed.

Jenn's window dropped an inch. "See you in Somerset."

"Today," Hendricks yelled.

"I will literally pay you to open this door."

"I know what you make."

Hendricks yelled for him to hurry up. Gibson gave Jenn one last imploring glance, but she just stared stonily into the middle distance, trying her damndest to suppress a smile.

Hendricks took them out of the city on the Clara Barton Parkway, which ran along the old C&O canal. Trees canopied the roadway, and they drove with the windows down. Gibson asked if he could put on the game. Hendricks pointed to the radio.

"Do you have a team?" Gibson asked.

"Dad liked the Dodgers. Don't follow it myself."

"Was he a cop too?"

"No."

Gibson waited for Hendricks to go on, but that seemed the end of it. He reached for the radio.

"Studio engineer. Music. Did a lot of work for SST and Slash Records."

"Cool. Any groups I'd know?"

"Not unless you're into old punk bands. Black Flag?"

Gibson shook his head.

"Then you're not going to know any of them."

"So if your dad was into music, how did you end up a cop?"

"Applied to the academy. How do you think?" Hendricks flipped on the radio to mark the end of the conversation.

The Nationals were up 2–0 in the second. Duke would have loved having a ball club in DC again. When Gibson was growing up, the Orioles had been the next best thing to a home team, and Duke had taken him to ten or fifteen games a year. But if Gibson had to guess, he'd say his father preferred listening to the games on the radio. He remembered drives between Charlottesville and DC, listening to Mel Proctor and Jim Palmer call games. It was so boring. Listening to old guys on the radio describe something he couldn't see. But like so much else, it had become a comfort as he grew older. Oftentimes, he didn't even follow the game but enjoyed the soothing rhythm of it low in the background. Today was one of those times.

His conversation with Calista Dauplaise still had him reeling. If she was to be believed, then everything Gibson had thought the last ten years was based on a lie. All of his assumptions about his life had suddenly pivoted on one simple statement: Duke Vaughn wasn't a criminal. It had been Benjamin Lombard from the start. Lombard, who had embezzled millions of dollars and framed his friend to cover his ass. Gibson still hadn't recovered from the shock, couldn't fully absorb the fact that he'd been right from the beginning. But he hadn't *stayed* right. He'd bought Lombard's story about his father and, to his shame, turned on his father like everyone else.

Another thought ate at him. All these years, he'd believed that his father had killed himself out of guilt for stealing from Lombard. There'd been no note, and it was the only motive that Gibson could imagine. But if Duke Vaughn wasn't an embezzler, if he wasn't a criminal, then what had driven him to suicide? It was the question that had haunted Gibson's life long after he thought he'd answered it. The answer had left him angry and embittered, but at least it'd offered a thin, miserable sense of closure. Now he didn't even have that.

Gibson remembered the old house perfectly. The sloping front lawn that he'd spent the better part of his childhood raking or mowing. The spiraling elm. Under which Duke had tried in vain to teach his son to throw a curveball. The road-weary Volvo in the driveway that meant his father was home. The creak of the porch steps and the Adirondack chairs that Gibson never found comfortable. The front door that was never locked.

It had been wide open that day.

Gibson had called out to his father but heard no answer. The Eagles were playing on the stereo, the opening lines of "New Kid in Town." His father loved that stuff: James Taylor, Jackson Browne, Bob Marley & the Wailers, CSN&Y. His "college sunny afternoon, Frisbee music." Gibson dropped his school backpack at the foot of the stairs and walked through the house, calling again for his father. He remembered having an uneasy feeling because his dad wasn't due home until Friday, and he could count on one hand the number of times Duke Vaughn had ever been early to anything.

He checked every room twice. The backyard. Duke sometimes visited with the neighbors; he was probably just talking UVA baseball with Mr. Hooper, who worked for the university. That seemed reasonable. Still, Gibson didn't like that the front door had been wide open. He made another lap around the house and noticed the basement door was open a crack. He hadn't checked it because no one ever went down there. It was mostly storage, plus a makeshift bedroom for the rare times they had company.

He opened the door and saw the basement light was on. The acrid smell of shit hit him. He called for his father, but the basement didn't answer. Down the steps he went. Slowly. Knowing something was wrong. Four steps from the bottom, he ducked his head and peered into the basement. He saw his father's bare feet dangling in the air, pointing down at the cement floor as if he were flying away.

Another step.

It didn't look like him. The rope had pulled his father's features taut and turned them black. Gibson whispered his father's name and sat heavily on the bottom step. He hadn't cried until the police arrived and told him that he needed to come with them.

Why did you do it, Duke? You were innocent. What drove you down into the basement?

They pulled into Somerset in the late afternoon. An hour east of Pittsburgh, Somerset was a small blue-collar community of fewer than seven thousand residents. The town's historical claim to fame, such as it was, was as a rebel hotbed during the Whiskey Rebellion of 1794. More recently, it had become connected to 9/11 when Flight 93 crashed in nearby Shanksville. But it was Somerset's proximity to the Breezewood gas station—a mere fifty miles east—that mattered now.

Hendricks circled the copper-domed courthouse in the center of town and pulled over to wait for Jenn, who was ten minutes behind them. Hendricks might not be the most pleasant of traveling companions, but he was one hell of a driver. They'd hit traffic at the Maryland Line, and Gibson had pulled up traffic on his phone to look for a way around.

"Put it away," Hendricks had growled, steering them onto a wide-open Route 68 without so much as glancing at a map. The man was a human GPS.

End to end, it had been the smoothest ride Gibson could remember. Everyone believed himself to be a good driver, but Hendricks was the real deal. It was the effortless way the car flowed to a stop and accelerated so smoothly you hardly felt it. Somehow, Hendricks always had them in the lane that was moving, and it wasn't luck; if a car tapped its brakes a quarter mile ahead, Hendricks anticipated how it would ripple back through traffic and adjusted his speed or changed lanes accordingly.

Jenn pulled up a few minutes later. Since Gibson couldn't be certain how deep WR8TH had burrowed into Abe Consulting, he'd instituted a total electronic whiteout within ACG regarding their attempts to track their quarry—no e-mails, no texts, no Word documents. Michael Rilling was setting up a dedicated server for the operation that had no connection to ACG, but in the meantime everything went on legal pads and in handwritten memos, a weird adjustment for everyone except Hendricks, who seemed to prefer it.

It also meant no hotel reservations, but Hendricks knew the layout of the entire town of Somerset and rattled off the names of every motel in a three-mile radius.

"Have you ever been here before?" Gibson asked.

"Do I look like I've been here before?"

"So do you go home at night and study atlases?"

"If I'm going somewhere. Google's no substitute for knowing things. Write that down."

When Jenn pulled up, they caravanned up and picked a dumpy single-story motel that was somewhat shielded from the highway noise. Still feeling restless, Gibson opted for a run before thinking about dinner. He left his room and nodded to Hendricks, who had brought a wooden chair out of his room and was smoking lazily.

"I'll be back in an hour."

Hendricks grunted, and Gibson began an easy run out toward the street. Summer had arrived; it was still a muggy ninety degrees after six p.m. He ran south back into town, taking the lay of the land, passing the Summit Diner, a classic stainless-steel prefab diner with a red-and-green neon sign by the curb. It had been renovated, but he'd be damned if it hadn't originally been an honest-to-God Swingle Family Diner. Probably dated back to the sixties. Duke would have known for sure, but it was a collector's item in any event. Gibson knew where he would be eating his meals for the duration of their stay.

At the courthouse, he hung a right and headed west into the sun. He slowed when he saw the library and walked the rest of the way, wanting a firsthand look at it. The library had a single-page website that was little more than an electronic hours-of-operation sign. He'd found a few pictures but none that gave him a complete picture of the layout. Mostly, he was curious to get a look at what might be the base of operations of one of the FBI's most wanted.

As villainous lairs went, it was a bit of a letdown. The Carolyn Anthony Library was a pretty brick building with white-painted trim around the windows and main entrance. It was set back from the street by a neatly manicured lawn and a border of flower beds and small bushes. A bright-red fire hydrant stood on one side of the main entrance, a water fountain on the other. It was a little slice of Mayberry Americanus and, like the courthouse, felt out of place in its drab clapboard surroundings.

The drinking fountain gave little more than a trickle. Gibson managed to coax a sip out of it then circled the library. To the side and rear, a public park sloped away with park benches, picnic tables, grassy lawns, and a stone fountain at the center that threw water up in a hazy, erratic spray.

It reminded him of the photo with Suzanne and the frog. Which in turn brought to mind something that had bothered him before . . . The hat—something about that Philadelphia Phillies baseball cap. *What's the big deal?* he asked himself. She'd needed a cap to hide her face and bought a Phillies one. Settle down, Sherlock.

Still it nagged at him.

Keep your mind on the task at hand, he told himself: the layout of the library. It appeared to have three ways in and out: the main entrance, a loading dock on one side, and a side door that opened onto the park. It stood apart from its neighboring buildings, offering little excuse to loiter. That plus the size of the town meant anyone who didn't belong would quickly stand out. WR8TH would make them long before they made him.

Gibson used his cell phone to check what he already knew—the library Wi-Fi was not password protected. He walked half a block away before he completely lost the signal. Tomorrow, he'd come back with a range-tester and map out the perimeter of the Wi-Fi's signal. Already, though, it was painfully clear that WR8TH could log in to the library Wi-Fi without stepping foot in the building—practically without coming within eyeshot of it. Their job had just gotten trickier. Not impossible but much more complicated.

Well, there wasn't anything he could do about it now. He put his earbuds back in and began the run back to the motel to call Ellie before dinner.

CHAPTER SEVENTEEN

It was wall to wall at the Summit Diner, a claustrophobic little place with a blunt, utilitarian feel. Immovable black steel stools hooked out of the base of the square-topped counter. Booths crammed around the exterior wall, everyone on top of everyone else. Jenn didn't see the appeal, but Vaughn treated the place with the reverential awe that most people reserve for museums. The diner belonged in one, that was for sure. What was it with him and diners?

"Can you believe this place?" Gibson asked.

"No," Jenn said. "What the hell is a pretzel melt?" It was listed on the specials board.

Gibson grinned. "Kind of like a calzone but with a pretzel. You'll love it."

Jenn stared at him. "This is for me not letting you in the car, isn't it?"

"You'll thank me later."

"Don't wait up."

To her relief, she found salads on the menu. Hendricks ordered the meat loaf. When it came, Hendricks cut it into a dozen bite-size squares and then dipped each bite in Tabasco sauce. Gibson ordered a milkshake and a monstrosity called the Cindy Sue—a burger dripping barbecue sauce and topped with a thick onion ring. Throw in a side of fries, and it was no wonder he spent so much time at the gym; it had to be 1,500 calories. Between mouthfuls, Gibson briefed them about the challenge that surveillance of the Carolyn Anthony Library would present.

Hendricks agreed that blending in was going to be tough. "Hard truths time. This is an underused public library in a small town. New faces are going to need a damn good reason to be there."

"Well, obviously this guy hasn't avoided detection for ten years by being careless," she said, thinking out loud. "He's picked his spot well. He'll see us; we won't see him."

"Yeah, but he's also telling us something," Hendricks said.

"What's that?" Gibson asked.

"Strangers stick out. Means he isn't one. He's comfortable and confident."

"We have a bigger problem," Gibson said and explained how the Carolyn Anthony Library's public Wi-Fi required no log-in or password, ran 24-7, and was broadcasting a signal strong enough to reach the moon.

"So where does that leave us?" Jenn asked.

"Where it leaves us is our man can use the library Wi-Fi anytime, day or night, and doesn't even need to physically enter the library to do it. He can sit in his car, half a block away at two in the morning, and do his business. And we can't stop him."

"But he's only given the virus instructions during business hours," Jenn said.

"True, and no reason to believe he'll vary his tactics. I'm just saying that he can if he wants."

"If he wants," Hendricks underlined. "But it's also possible that he's had his fun and this is a dead lead."

"What's the lag time between an active intrusion to ACG's network and your sentries recognizing it and notifying you?" Jenn asked Gibson.

"Three to five seconds. Give or take. Any incoming instruction from the corrupt ad on the *Post* website's IP will trigger an alarm here. I'll get a text message, an e-mail, and a phone call."

"What about your concerns WR8TH might be monitoring ACG communications?"

"Why do you think I bypassed your network entirely?"

Jenn glanced at Hendricks. He didn't like that answer any more than she did.

"Can you route the alert to our phones as well?"

"Sure. I'll do it after dinner."

"So let me see if I understand the plan," Hendricks said. "We wait for WR8TH to access his virus and then run around like fools looking for a middle-aged pedophile with a laptop and a hard-on. Missing anything?"

"No, that's pretty much the plan," she said.

"So long as I'm clear."

"But in case he does change up his schedule, we'll sleep in shifts," Jenn said. "We need to be ready to go at all hours, but something tells me he'll stick to his schedule."

Gibson nodded his agreement. He'd gone back and sifted through ACG's network history looking for traces of WR8TH's footprints in the ACG servers. Every instance that he'd identified was at the end of the week, on a Friday afternoon.

"Which gives us all of four days to game-plan."

"I did a little research," Gibson said. "A few years ago, there were a slew of pedophiles using the Wi-Fi at Virginia public libraries. They would literally park in front of the library in the middle of the night and download child porn. So it's not a new or unique strategy."

"What are our options?" Jenn asked.

"We could do what they did and add a log-in. They also shut down their Wi-Fi after business hours, but . . ."

"Any change to the system would spook our boy."

"Right, which also means I can't interfere with the Wi-Fi's range or the bandwidth. He's shown himself to be cautious and smart. If we mess with it, he'll be in the wind."

"We could call in the cavalry. More bodies, more eyes," Hendricks said.

"Running a gargantuan surveillance operation that would almost certainly be spotted is not the answer," Jenn said. "We need a solution that doesn't depend on deploying the 101st Airborne."

"Let me work on it tonight. I may have an idea," said Gibson.

She thought about pressing him on the details but elected to heed her boss's advice and give Gibson the benefit of the doubt. When he'd finished his meat loaf, Hendricks excused himself to go scout the library. Gibson ordered a slice of blackberry pie and a scoop of vanilla ice cream. He offered her a spoon, but she declined, studying him over her coffee.

"CIA," she said.

He looked at her, not understanding.

"You asked where I served."

"Really? The way you moved on me. At the Nighthawk. Would have pegged you for military."

She felt his eyes search her face as if he were studying an equation that had produced the wrong answer.

"Parents were," she said. "Dad was a marine. Mom was Navy."

"Who was your dad with?"

"The One Eight."

"Where?"

"Lebanon."

Gibson put down his spoon. "Was he there?"

"Yeah, he was there."

She'd been two the day the truck drove onto the Marine barracks in Beirut and crashed into the lobby. The truck's only obstacles: concertina wire and sentries with unloaded rifles. Condition Four: no magazines, no chambered rounds. Not that it would have made a difference. The force of the detonation lifted the building off its foundations, and gravity slammed it back to Earth, crushing those inside. The fireball killed the rest. A good rule of thumb, Jenn had found: the brutality of a thing was directly proportional to how often the word "instantaneous" was used. Her father hadn't suffered—the most comfort that could be offered. The same could not be said of her mother.

What little Jenn remembered of her mom was hard. Beth Charles had been a small, practical woman. After her husband's funeral, she drove straight to the liquor store. Never a drinker, she settled on vodka because mouthwash masked the smell when she was on duty. She hadn't hit Jenn often. And never too hard. Only the one scar, behind her ear, but that had been an accident. Jenn remembered being really afraid only a few times. Mostly when the gun came out at night. Her mom would strip and clean it on the coffee table with the television up so loud that Jenn slept with a pillow over her head.

After the wreck, Jenn went to live with her grandmother. She ran her tongue over her teeth.

"I'm very sorry," Gibson said.

"Why did you call her Bear?"

Gibson laughed and took a bite of pie. "She was a full-body hugger. Wrap her arms around you and squeeze for all she was worth. Whenever she saw my father, she'd take a running start at him, and he'd yell, 'Bear hug, incoming!' Became kind of a thing. Suited her. Also, she was always hibernating somewhere with a book. I think I was the only one who actually called her Bear, though."

"What was she like?"

"Bear? She was my sister, you know? I mean, not my *sister* sister, but we grew up together. We didn't have a whole lot in common, but she was just good. Really good. She was one of those kids that made other parents jealous. Like why couldn't their kids be more like her? She was easy, polite. Kind to everyone. Totally unspoiled. But really stubborn too." Gibson laughed at a private memory. "When she decided something was going to be a certain way, it was a lost cause to resist. Trust me."

"When did she start to change?"

"I don't know. I was getting older. I stayed home in Charlottesville more. School and stuff. I'm not sure I even noticed at first, because she was always a quiet kid. I didn't even know she had a boyfriend. Then my father, you know . . . I didn't see the Lombards after that. I got arrested about three months after." Gibson threw down his fork and sat staring at the pie. "I've got a question. What do you know about the Phillies cap? From the Breezewood tape."

"The cap? Not a lot. Nothing special about it as far as I know. Neither of her parents identified it as something she owned. She hated baseball with a passion, so the assumption is she bought it on the road."

"Who said she hated baseball?"

"Her parents. It's in the FBI interview transcripts."

"Really? That's weird."

"Why?"

"I don't know. Just something bothers me about that cap. Probably nothing."

"Probably," she agreed. "But you have to respect a hunch. Talk me through it."

"Well, you're right about Bear not being into sports. At least that's how I remember it. But Duke and Lombard talked a lot of baseball. They were both huge Orioles fans. I think I'd remember if it got under her skin. She was kind of a heart-on-her-sleeve kind of kid, you know?"

"Well, like you said, you hadn't seen her in a while."

"Yeah," Gibson agreed without sounding terribly convinced.

At the counter, Fred Tinsley stirred cream into his coffee and looked over the menu. He wasn't hungry, but when in Rome. He couldn't hear what the two men and the woman were saying, but it made no difference. He wasn't here to eavesdrop. He just wanted a little look-see.

The little man was an ex-cop in Los Angeles, but he didn't look like much. Still, Dan Hendricks had probably been underestimated all his life. Tinsley wouldn't make that error. The other man, Vaughn, looked physically capable and had a military background, but as a computer tech of some sort. Since when did marines use keyboards? It was sad what the world was becoming.

Charles was the only one of the three with quality. She had taken lives in combat. Tinsley would appreciate killing her the most. He sipped his coffee and wondered how he would do it if actually called upon to kill them. It all depended on whether they were successful. Their lives depended on their being incompetent. It struck Tinsley as rather funny.

It really was a most unusual assignment. He would be paid in either event, so he could watch the drama unfold without a stake in the outcome. The novelty of it appealed to him, and he was curious to see how it played out. In the meantime, all he had to do was wait and watch. He was good at both those things.

And of course, he still had to pay a visit to the doctor. He had not seen her since that night ten years ago. He admired her work, so unlike his own, yet also requiring calm and professionalism under extraordinary circumstances. He respected that and looked forward to seeing her again.

The waitress came back, and he ordered a Reuben just to be done with her. He was still waiting for his food when the little man got up and left the diner. Tinsley wasn't worried about where he was going. It made no difference.

It was after two a.m. when the Cherokee pulled up in front of the motel. Hendricks had already been gone when they got back from the diner and had just returned. Gibson was sitting on his bed, trying to diagram a rudimentary solution to their library Wi-Fi problem. He listened as Hendricks went into his room and slammed the door. A few moments later it reopened, shutting more quietly this time.

Gibson put his work aside and went outside. Hendricks was sitting on the hood of the Cherokee smoking. He wore dark pants and a Windbreaker even though it was still in the mideighties. The back of the Cherokee was empty; Hendricks would be cramped with all those extra duffels stacked in his room.

"You weren't lying about the library," said Hendricks. "It's going to be a bitch trying to cover all the exits and the nearby streets with just the three of us. Never mind not being seen. And that doesn't account for shifts and sleep."

"Can Abe send more troops?"

"He could, but we run into that other problem. We stake out that library with an army and we'll stand out like Girl Scouts in Las Vegas. And local PD might not be good for a lot, but I guarantee if we set up camp at a public library that kids frequent, we are going to wind up with a Maglite shoved way, way up our ass."

"So we're screwed?"

"Not entirely. I set up perimeter cameras. They're motion-activated, but I've got coverage on all three doors. It's not ideal, but we'll get faces going in and out. If he even goes in or out. Nothing to rely on." He flicked ash into the gutter. "We sure could use some of that cyber-ninja voodoo of yours."

"Cyber-ninja voodoo?"

"Isn't that why you're here?"

"Hendricks, can I ask you a question? Did you work this kind of thing in the LAPD?"

"Did I work missing children? I had my share."

"Did you find many of them?"

Hendricks looked at him. "I answer, you going to go scurrying for the bathroom again?"

"Forget it."

"Generally, you got forty-eight hours. After that, if you do find a kid, they're not breathing."

"So do you think there's any chance Suzanne's alive?"

Hendricks lit another cigarette.

"No," he said. "No, she's been dead a long time. I think the doer didn't know who he was grabbing. I think he turned six shades of bitch when he found out he had a senator's daughter. Once he understood the magnitude of the shit he was in, he didn't waste any time in killing her and dumping the body."

Gibson groaned. A low-throated moan that he didn't realize he was making until Hendricks interrupted him.

"Hey, you asked."

"I know," Gibson said. "So what are you doing here?"

"It's my job."

"Come on."

Hendricks dropped his cigarette, slid off the hood, and crushed it out with his heel.

"It's important to the boss. So it's important to me. Plus, and this is just me talking, but I don't care for pedophiles. And I especially don't care for clever ones that think they're slick, sending taunting photographs of their victims. So what am I doing here? I'm here to put my foot on this guy's throat. That's what. And since we're on the subject, why are *you* here?"

"In case she's not."

The perpetual grimace left Hendricks's face, and he became honest and serious for a moment. "You don't want to go doing that."

"What?"

"Believing she's alive. Not for one second."

"Why not?"

"'Cause once you start, you don't stop. Hear me. Hope is a cancer. One of two things happens. Either you never learn the truth, in which case it gnaws down to the bone until there's nothing left, or worse, you do, and you go through that windshield at ninety because hope told you it was okay to make the drive without a seat belt."

"So assume the worst."

"Forty-eight hours ended a long time ago. So buckle up. All I'm saying. Find some other reason to be here." With that, Hendricks went into his room and shut the door, leaving Gibson with his thoughts.

And with Hendricks's cell phone, which the ex-cop had forgotten on the hood of the Cherokee. Gibson stared at it, calculating how long he'd have. Thirty minutes? Probably less. Was it worth the risk? Yes, he decided. Always have a plan B, even if you never needed it.

He snatched up the phone and shut himself in his room. He connected the phone to his laptop and started the program. One eye on his monitor, one ear listening for the sound of Hendricks's door opening. The worst outcome was if Hendricks came out to look for it, it wasn't there, and it magically reappeared afterward. Then Gibson would be cooked.

Twenty-seven minutes later, the phone was back where Hendricks had left it.

How was that for some cyber-ninja voodoo?

CHAPTER EIGHTEEN

It took Gibson until Tuesday night to finish his program. WR8TH hadn't put in another appearance, but his virus continued its relentless journey through the FBI memoranda and documents that Rilling kept uploading onto their servers, lest WR8TH become suspicious if the flow suddenly ceased.

Jenn stopped by Gibson's room periodically to check on his progress.

"What do you need from us?" she'd asked the first morning after he began work.

"Three hots and a cot."

"Any requests?"

"Breakfast at breakfast. Dinner at dinner. Surprise me at lunch." He handed her a Summit Diner menu. Then he ushered her out of his room, flipped the "Do Not Disturb" sign, and locked himself inside. With the shades drawn and the air-conditioning dialed down to witch's tit, it felt like a subterranean cave cut off from the outside world. He'd always thought more clearly when he was cold and bundled up.

Properly situated, he sat himself down in front of his laptop, put in his earbuds, and worked for what proved to be two straight days.

First things first. He needed the specs of the library's network. He pinged the library and ran a scan of the available ports. He felt vaguely foolish hacking a public library in central Pennsylvania. He still had a fairly heavy rep in the insular community that gave a crap about such things and doubted very much this would add to the legend of BrnChr0m. It was a bit like Al Capone extorting a kid's lemonade stand.

His scan finished and beeped, displaying its analysis. He read it with a frown. Usually you could count on rinky-dink networks like a public library to employ bottom-feeding IT personnel who were lazy or incompetent or both. Operating systems were often two generations out of date and hopelessly unpatched. Such networks were like big, friendly dogs; if you petted them they would roll right over and show you a dozen security vulnerabilities.

Unfortunately, in Gibson's continuing quest never to catch a break, he seemed to have arrived in a municipality that took its IT seriously. The library network was running a current version of Windows and, by the look of it, was freshly patched with a firewall just for good measure. Gibson sighed and sipped his coffee. It wasn't an elaborate setup, but it was professionally maintained. He'd just have to do it the hard way.

Instead of ten minutes, it took him two hours to get the specs that he needed. He liked what he saw. He knew the software and hardware inside and out, and the fact that the network was well maintained would actually make writing the program easier if he found a way to piggyback on the wireless network's infrastructure. He closed his eyes and visualized how he could exploit it. He sat there until he had it in his mind, and then a small smile creased his lips. He opened his eyes, cranked up his music, and began to write.

Programming wasn't really his strong suit; he liked the intellectual challenge and the cold logic of code, but it wasn't what made him good. Contrary to the public's misconception, hacking was not a duel between two fast-typing programming geniuses. In the movies, it was always this overdramatized, adrenaline-fueled high-wire act—hackers with guns to their heads, given sixty seconds to hack some impenetrable network. Lightning-fast keystrokes and split-second timing.

The actual penetration of a secure network was about as far from exciting as exciting got. It was slow. It was tedious. And it required patience and a painstaking attention to detail.

There were those who had an innate feel for a machine's language and could ferret out possible exploits as if they had a sixth sense. But a secure network was much more than just machines. It was also the people who operated and maintained those machines. Nine times out of ten, the easiest path into a secure computer network was not the hardware or the software, but the wetware—the people. And that was where Gibson excelled.

Gibson had always had a gift for looking at a secure network and the people who operated it, then seeing the fault lines between the two. He found the fissures between proper security procedure and the short-cuts people took because they didn't think anyone was paying attention. Ignorance, curiosity, habit, laziness, greed, stupidity—computers were only as good as the people operating them, and there was always a weak link. To Gibson, hacking computers was boring. But hacking people? Now, that was fun.

But in a pinch, he was a capable coder too. He just wasn't especially fast. So when he was finally done coding and debugging his program and ran a successful test, it was past eleven on Tuesday night. He hadn't slept but for a few hours on Sunday night, and the lack of sleep had cooked him.

Gibson ran his fingers through his hair and stuck his head out his motel room door. Hendricks greeted him and stubbed out a cigarette. The few times Gibson had left his room to clear his head, Hendricks hadn't been out smoking. He almost missed him.

"Tell her it's done," he said wearily.

"Okay."

"I'll test it tomorrow."

"Okay."

"Anything happen since yesterday?"

"Nats lost."

Gibson crawled into bed in his clothes. In a perfect world, he would have slept for eighteen hours. In the real one, he slept for six and tossed and turned for three more as his body tried and failed to sleep through all the caffeine. By nine, he was showered and shaved, gear packed. He stepped out blinking into the morning sunshine.

Hendricks and Jenn had been busy. In the last forty-eight hours, they had fine-tuned Hendricks's camera array, which now not only covered the library's entrances but also all the approaches to the library. Jenn had scouted the neighborhood for low-profile spots that provided some privacy and were still in range of the library. Hendricks had cameras trained on those too.

"Bad news is that the library's core demographic appears to be white men between forty-five and sixty," Hendricks said.

"Yeah, we've got photos of twenty-six men entering the library since Monday morning who fall within our profile's age range. We sent them back to DC. Maybe we'll get lucky."

"You think he's one of them?"

"Hendricks thinks not. I'm on the fence."

"I just don't think this guy would hang around the library reading periodicals," Hendricks said. "Doesn't fit for me. I think he does his thing, keeps a low profile, and gets out of there."

"And I think he may be so comfortable on his home turf that that's exactly what he would do," said Jenn. "But we've got so few data points on this creep that it's kind of academic. He's going to blend in unless we have a way to pick him out. Which brings us to . . ." She trailed off.

"My program," Gibson said.

"Does it work?" she asked.

"I think so. But I won't know for sure until I get it out in the field."

"Can't you test it first?" Hendricks asked.

"I have, to an extent, and it works as a simulation without crashing, but unless you want to wait while I build a dummy of the library's network, then there's no way to know for sure without just going ahead."

"How does it install?" Jenn asked.

"Thumb drive. Just need to get into the librarian's office for two minutes."

"Sounds doable. Hendricks and I will go take care of it. You hang back here, and we'll let you know when it's installed, and you can fire it up remotely and see if it works."

"Yeah, that's probably a bad idea," Gibson said.

Jenn paused, started to get angry, and stopped herself. "Why? Is it too complicated for us poor Luddites to operate?"

"No, actually it's just one mouse click."

"Then what?"

"Well, you said the library is full of guys that match our perp, right?"

"Right . . ."

"Well, what if he's one of them?"

"That's kind of the point," said Hendricks.

"I think it's a mistake to assume that he doesn't know what you both look like," Gibson said. "You need to be careful showing your faces around the library any more than you already have."

"How could he know what we look like?" Jenn asked.

"Well, he's been in ACG's database for weeks."

He watched Jenn digest his statement.

"Christ," she said. "Our employment files."

"Our photos," Hendricks said.

"Still want me to hang out in the motel?"

The Carolyn Anthony Library might be small, but the people who worked there obviously took great pride in their work. Gibson looked around, taking the lay of the land. It was well maintained, clean, bright, and inviting. It made you long to sit down and read a book. Bear would have been in heaven here. The front door opened into a small, cheerful atrium where new releases were arranged tastefully on wooden display racks.

Behind the main desk, a middle-aged woman checked books back in to the system, thick arms swaying as she worked. Her hair was cast in a brittle perm that looked like the unholy union of a microwave and caulk. She paused, greeting him with an austere nod, and went back to her task. The stacks were tight, densely packed columns of books that disappeared toward the rear of the library. To the left was a row of carrels, each with an old CRT monitor. A neatly worded sign gave instructions for requesting computer time from the librarian on duty. A wide set of stairs led down to the "Children's Section." To the right was a reading area with armchairs and footstools. All but one of the chairs were occupied by a group of retirees who looked like they were permanent fixtures.

Gibson wondered if one of them was the man they were hunting. He wanted to stare at each of them closely, study their faces. See if he could pick the man out even though he knew better than to believe that you could see that kind of evil on a man's face. The man who abducted Bear a decade ago and somehow managed to keep that secret all these years—there would be nothing about his face to give him away. He would be the last person you would suspect. After all, he didn't drag Bear into his car. She got in willingly, because she didn't see a face that frightened her. It would have only been afterward that the mask came off.

Maybe that was why hacking this Podunk library in this Podunk town felt so daunting to him. It was, by any objective measure, a simple job. But he was on edge. The man who knew Bear's fate knew this place, knew it well, and had been here within the last two weeks. He might not be here this moment, but this cozy little library was still the key to a profound secret.

And maybe Hendricks was right—that the secret had only one inevitable ending—but there would still be a modicum of justice if they managed to catch this guy. Not for Bear—there was no justice for the dead, Gibson knew. But perhaps for the living it would restore some sense of balance. No, he didn't believe that either. There was no redress for a crime of this magnitude. If Bear were dead, then finding her abductor would only serve to answer questions better left unasked. Who had taken her? Where had she been held? How had she suffered and died?

His thoughts began to turn to Ellie, but he forced them away. Under no circumstances would he allow himself to imagine his daughter in Suzanne's place.

Since blending in wasn't really an option, Gibson had taken the opposite tack—stick out painfully. He thought the ugly, mismatched sports jacket and tie and rumpled chinos were a nice combination. He looked like someone trying to make a good impression and failing miserably. Gibson had identified the librarian, Margaret Miller, and, through Google-stalking her, had found her son, Todd. Breaking into the library's office to install his program was an option, but a bad one. Far easier if Mrs. Miller invited him back there.

He looked nothing like Todd, but that was fine. He didn't need to look like him as much as visually suggest him. In most of his photos, Todd Miller looked like a bit of a dweeb. Gibson's clothes were an homage to Todd's total lack of fashion sense. Gibson also parted his hair neatly to one side in the way Todd favored.

He stood just inside the front door of the library, looking around in a panic.

"Can I help you?" she asked.

Gibson swung around and gave her his best, neediest look. *Take pity on me,* it said.

"I sure hope so. Is Mrs. Miller here?"

"I'm Mrs. Miller," she said. "What can I do for you?"

"I'm really sorry. I know this is a weird request. But someone at the gas station suggested I ask you . . ." He let his voice crack.

"Ask what? What is it?"

"Well, I have a job interview in forty-five minutes. Up at the ski resort."

"Forty-five minutes? Oh, my. You need to hurry."

"I know, ma'am. I drove up from Hagerstown this morning. It's for an assistant-manager position. My uncle knows someone up there and put in a good word for me. But, well, I overslept, and I ran out the door without my résumé. It's right on the kitchen counter," he said and gestured futilely at the imaginary kitchen counter that had callously kidnapped his résumé. "The resort was real particular too. God, my uncle set up the interview; he's going to kill me if I blow it."

He got busy staring at the floor sheepishly but watched Margaret Miller's face out of the corner of his eye for hints as to how he was doing so far. Not well by the stern look on her face.

"I'm sorry, but we don't have a public printer here. I've requested one, but it's not in our budget this year."

"Oh," he said and let himself deflate. "They said you had one in the back office."

"Well, yes, but that's only for staff use."

Come on, lady. Don't make me cry for you.

He nodded in somber understanding and clenched his jaw in a stoic restraint of manly emotion. Would a chin quiver be overkill?

"Can you think of anywhere else I can try?" he asked.

"Well, there's a print shop, but that's all the way over in . . ." Mrs. Miller looked up at the clock. "No, you'll never make it in time."

"It's okay. Maybe they won't mind that much."

Margaret Miller sighed.

"Do you have it on a disk or something?"

"Thumb drive," he said and held it out helpfully to her.

"What's it called?"

"It's just called 'résumé.' It's the only file."

She stared at it a long time. Deciding his fate.

"Follow me," she said with a sigh.

She led him back into the stacks to the librarian's office, which sat in a far back corner away from the front desk. She managed to hold her tongue for the first twenty feet, but then turned and began gently chiding him for being irresponsible. About how his uncle had stuck his neck out for him, and it was wrong to let him down like this. It almost seemed therapeutic for her, and he nodded and muttered apologetic "I knows" and "you're rights" in the appropriate places. Seemed only fair.

She unlocked her office door and paused.

"Please forgive the mess," she said.

She wasn't lying either. Her desk was buried beneath a mountain of papers that ought to have come with an avalanche warning. Books were stacked on the floor, and all of her plants required water or last rites.

The only tidy area in the office was the workstation that sat next to a rack of servers. Again, he was impressed at Somerset County's commitment to its computer infrastructure. But it sure wasn't Margaret Miller, who didn't know what or where a USB port was. Gibson had to politely point out where to plug in the thumb drive. However, she insisted on printing the document herself, which was fine. He'd embedded his virus into the résumé; as soon as she opened it, the program would install itself to the machine and then erase all record of its download. It would lie dormant until he activated it.

He watched over her shoulder as the library's virus software scanned the file and allowed it to open. She printed three copies. "Just to be on the safe side," she said.

He was counting on her not looking too closely at his résumé, which was a sample that he'd downloaded from an employment website. He'd spent ten minutes changing the details to fake businesses in Hagerstown, but it wouldn't hold up under too much scrutiny. Fortunately, she was too busy lecturing him on responsibility.

She shooed him out and wished him luck as he left the building.

CHAPTER NINETEEN

The house was set back far enough that Tinsley didn't worry about being seen. The row of tall Leyland cypresses obscured the sight lines from the street so that someone would need to come right up the front walk to spot him. Kneeling on the thick doormat that wished him a friendly forest-green "Welcome," Tinsley picked the lock quickly and efficiently. He let the door swing open and listened to what it had to say. It squeaked, just a little, at forty-five degrees. The alarm beeped questioningly.

Tinsley stepped in, shut the door, and disarmed the alarm. As the perspiration cooled on his skin, Tinsley shivered involuntarily. It felt almost chilly inside compared to the oppressive heat outside. He walked to the back of the house, where the kitchen and sitting room combined into a great room. It was late afternoon and sunlight streamed through the large picture windows. A large flat-screen television was mounted to a wall where it could be seen from both the couch and the granite-topped kitchen island. The television was flanked by large built-in bookshelves that housed an array of hardcover books. It felt as though the volumes existed to offset, and in some way apologize for, the lowbrow presence of a television. It also felt like a woman's home, although Tinsley couldn't say why.

The doctor wouldn't be home before seven. Tinsley had allowed himself plenty of time to familiarize himself with the layout—which doors were locked and unlocked, which creaked and which opened noiselessly, where the phones were located, whether he might be seen from any of the upstairs windows. He moved silently through the house, running his latex glove–covered fingers along the walls as if testing their sturdiness. He sat on the edge of her bed and thought about how she would stage it. How would a respected doctor do it? *Make me believe,* he thought. He sat that way for a long time.

When he was through, he smoothed the duvet and went back downstairs. There was a guest bedroom on the ground floor, and its door opened smoothly. He would wait there. He practiced walking the route to her bedroom. Testing the floorboards until he knew every creak. When he was satisfied, he rearmed the house security system and went into the bedroom, shutting the door behind him. He emptied his bladder carefully in the toilet. Took a piece of toilet paper and dabbed up an errant drop on the seat. Then he slipped under the guest-room bed and cleared his mind. The quiet hum of the house was pleasant.

He waited.

Tinsley felt the vibration of the garage door opening through his spine. It snapped him back to full consciousness, and he listened to what the house murmured to him. The garage door closed, and the alarm sounded again but was shut off a moment later. High heels strode toward the front of the house, and then the doorbell rang. Someone had followed her. Perhaps a friend whom she had invited home with her. But a man or a woman? She was widowed, so either was possible. He listened to her answer the door, and the sound of two women's voices speaking animatedly filled the front hall. There was laughter. They walked past his door and back toward the kitchen.

For the next several hours, Tinsley listened to the women prepare dinner and eat. Classical music muddied the sounds of their voices, but he kept careful track of where they were in the house. Each sound or smell that came to him, he analyzed and cataloged. The flush of a toilet. The clinking of silverware and glasses. The smell of garlic and olive oil. He moved them through the house on the chessboard in his mind. Mercifully for her friend, the guest bedroom never opened.

He'd only come for one.

It was after eleven before the doctor showed her guest out. They stood talking and making plans that the doctor would not keep. Her friend would find it hard to believe that the doctor would take her own life after such a lovely evening. But gradually, she would be convinced that the dinner was intended as a farewell. *But she was so cheerful, so full of life* . . . Psychiatrists would explain that suicides often become ebullient once they've made up their mind. As if a weight has been lifted. Eventually, she would accept it as the truth even if a small part of her harbored doubts. He heard a car start, and after a moment it drove away.

Tinsley listened to the familiar sounds of cleaning up after a meal. The clattering of a dishwasher being loaded. Running water. The garbage disposal. Eventually the music shut off. Footsteps. The security alarm being armed. From the crack beneath the door, he saw the lights go out, and she went up the stairs to the second floor. After ten minutes, he was certain that the doctor's dinner companion hadn't forgotten something and wouldn't be returning unexpectedly.

He slithered out from beneath the bed.

Even with the suppressor attached, the Browning Buck Mark .22 felt light in his hand. A small-caliber weapon, but it was mostly for show. If he did need it, it was effective enough at close range and virtually silent. If things took an unexpected turn, his Sig Sauer P320 made for ample backup.

Tinsley slipped out of the guest bedroom and followed the doctor upstairs. The light was on in the bedroom, but he heard her voice from the office. She was on the telephone, speaking to what sounded like her hairdresser. He stood on the landing and listened to her leave a message canceling her appointment for tomorrow. Such a tiny thing, but the kind of detail that often swayed a skeptical detective. It was very considerate of her. Once he heard her hang up the phone, he let himself into the room.

He shifted his posture, standing more erect, and let his voice take on a slight British flavor. The image of the gentleman spy was so ingrained in some Americans' imaginations that it helped them to think of him that way. Amazing what a little courtesy could get you.

"Good evening," he said.

This would go one of two ways.

She screamed and stood quickly. That was natural. The walls of the house were thick, and it wasn't loud enough to attract the neighbors' attention, so he let her get it out of her system. He held the gun up so she could see it but did not point it at her. Her mouth snapped shut, her pupils dilated, and her breathing became ragged. Her eyes flitted from his face to the gun and back to his face. Then they narrowed, recognizing him.

"It's you."

"Hello, Doctor."

"What are you doing in my house? What do you want?"

Tinsley liked her. She was smart enough to see she was cornered and that a fight would not end well for her. She was trying to reason with him. It wouldn't work, but it was her best option. He would treat her gently if she let him.

"I want for you to open your safe, Dr. Furst. Can you do that for me?"

"My safe? What do you . . ." She trailed off. "May I make a phone call? I can clear all this up."

He didn't answer. He didn't have one that she would appreciate.

"Please?" she asked again.

He gestured to the bookshelf where the safe was hidden. She stood, steadying herself on the edge of the desk, and did as he directed. The safe was behind a ceramic urn. She moved it aside and spun the dial of the safe with quick, mechanical motions. She depressed the lever, and the safe clicked open.

"Thank you, Doctor," he said. "Step back."

The only item in the safe was a thin manila folder. Inside was a single sheet of paper. The letters "UPMC" were in the top left-hand corner—University of Pittsburgh Medical Center. Below that: "DNA Test Report." Tinsley slid the sheet back into the folder without reading further.

"This is the only copy?"

"The only one."

"Good. Let's go to the bedroom, shall we? I have a message to deliver."

The doctor's eyes widened in alarm, and Tinsley saw where she misunderstood.

"No, nothing like that, Doctor. I have no intention of causing you any pain unless you are difficult. I assure you."

That was true. Painless had been an explicit instruction. He let the gun drop to his side as a gesture of good faith. She was cautious but willing to play along. Still hoping that his calm tone of voice suggested a rational, reasonable mind. He followed her into the bedroom and told her to lie down on the bed. She was becoming docile now, compliant. He stood away from her, by the window. The moon had risen.

"I was asked to tell you that there are no ill feelings. It will all be over in a few days."

"I would never have said anything to anyone," she said. Her voice brimmed with feeling. "It was just a moment of weakness."

"No, of course not. But a copy of the lab results presents too great a risk. There is too much at stake in November. You were wrong to keep it."

"I know. I'm sorry. Just when I think of that poor girl, I wonder at what we've become. What I've done." She searched his face for a sign that he understood.

He didn't know how to make that kind of face.

"It's none of my concern. I am just the messenger. But I do have a question. And I hope you'll be honest."

"Of course," she said.

"Dr. Furst, is there anything else in the house that I should know about? Anything else incriminating?"

"No, I swear. Only what was in the safe."

Tinsley nodded. He knew she was telling the truth and went through the motions of believing her. "Thank you. I appreciate that."

"So we're through?"

"Almost. I've been instructed to search your home in any event. But," he said with emphasis to let her know she was being rewarded, "I will do my best not to upset anything. Since you've been so cooperative." It was a lie but would ensure her compliance.

"Thank you," she said as if he were doing her a favor.

"I'm going to give you a mild sedative now."

"Oh?" she said, alarm creeping back into her voice.

"It's fine. As I said, I need to search the house, and I prefer not to tie you down. This will be much more comfortable. Better for your circulation. You'll be out for a few hours, and when you awake I will be gone and this whole unpleasantness will be over."

"All right," she said, working hard to believe him.

He unzipped a small leather pouch and withdrew a syringe and a vial of Luminal. Not a drug he usually used in these situations, but it was one that the doctor could get her hands on easily. It would make sense to the coroner. It was an antiepileptic, not a sedative, but had a similar effect, at least in small doses.

"How many glasses of wine did you have?"

"Two."

He adjusted the dosage slightly and placed the syringe on the nightstand.

"If you'd be so kind," he said.

"You want me to inject myself?"

"You are a doctor, Doctor."

She thought it over and took the syringe. Rolling up her sleeve, she found a vein just below her elbow. When finished, she set the syringe on the nightstand and gave him an irritated look as if to say, "Happy now?" She had gone from terrified to inconvenienced with remarkable speed.

"Please be careful with the crystal downstairs. My husband bought it in Ireland on our honeymoon. I'd hate for it to be damaged."

He assured her that he would take the utmost care.

When she was unconscious, Tinsley took another syringe from his case and gave her a second injection. Forty milliliters would be more than sufficient, given her age and weight. He sat in an armchair by the window and listened to her breathing slow and grind to a halt. He gave it a half hour then checked her vitals. Satisfied, he arranged the empty vial beside the syringe and stepped back to appraise the tableau. Something was missing.

He went downstairs to the piano and looked over the framed photographs until he found one of the doctor and her dead husband. They were holding hands, sitting with the ocean behind them. He took the picture upstairs and placed it on the bedside table where she could see it. Then he let himself out of the bedroom, shutting the door quietly as if not to disturb her.

In the office, he took the file he'd been instructed to retrieve and shut the safe. He'd been debating with himself where to leave the note and decided that the office was the right place. Her personal stationery was made of thick paper; he stood the envelope up so that the top fold tented and helped it sit prominently on the blotter. Next to it he placed the pen that had written the note.

Ordinarily, he avoided using forged letters; there were too many ways to get tripped up, but he'd been assured that no one would question this one.

Satisfied with the scene, he went back to the bedroom and took Doctor Furst's shoes off and placed them beside the bed—side by side with the toes pointing away from her. He didn't know why he felt the urge to do that, but it allowed him to leave a scene. The shoes felt final, somehow.

Tinsley let himself out quietly. It was beginning to rain; the drops were heavy and landed like little wet bodies hitting the sidewalk. Tinsley hardly registered it other than to appreciate that the street where the good doctor had lived was deserted as a result. He took off his latex gloves and slipped away into the shadows.

CHAPTER TWENTY

Early Friday morning, Jenn woke Gibson unceremoniously by flipping on the lights and clapping her hands like a drill instructor. He was pretty sure he'd locked the door.

"It's five twenty-eight," Jenn said.

That was all she'd come to say, apparently. She left the motel room door open behind her and went, he assumed, in search of baby ducks to berate. Hendricks appeared a minute later and put a large coffee on his end table.

"Morning, sunshine. Equipment check in sixty, and then she wants to review the game plan."

Twenty minutes later, Gibson's motel room looked like a low-rent command center. He'd flipped his mattress up against the wall and placed an array of laptops, monitors, and keyboards in a semicircle on the box spring. Black-and-gray cables laced it all together, and yellow stickies affixed to the monitors and keyboards helped him keep each one straight. On one set of screens, Hendricks's cameras, updating every three seconds, relayed stop-motion images of the streets surrounding the library. On another, the program Margaret Miller had so kindly installed displayed a wealth of information about the computers logged in to the library Wi-Fi.

Gibson's program wasn't overly complex, but it was brutally effective, relying on the library Wi-Fi to do most of the work for him.

There were myriad ports into a computer. All of those ports relied on a firewall to tell them whom to trust when users came knocking. A firewall was simply a big, burly bouncer who turned away anyone not on the VIP list. That was all well and good until the owner of the club, the human user, called down to the bouncer and, in effect, gave a user VIP clearance. The user was telling the bouncer to hold open the velvet rope and let them into the club, no questions asked. That was what happened whenever the user opened a web page, clicked on a link in an e-mail, or ran a program. Or joined a Wi-Fi network.

In order for a user to use Wi-Fi, the bouncer had to trust the user and open a port for him or her. Once trust was established, anything the user sent through that port was also trusted. That was because the library network had its own firewall and most users relied on default settings when setting up their computers, and default settings tended to be far too trusting where Wi-Fi networks were concerned. Bad idea in general. Really bad idea in this case, since Gibson's program was already inside the library's firewall.

As a result, Gibson's program would allow him to wander in unaccosted and gather information from most computers logged in to the library Wi-Fi. Depending on the computers' individual security settings, he might gather names, addresses, contacts, cell numbers, credit-card numbers, and outgoing IP addresses—all in a matter of seconds.

In addition, by exploiting the Wi-Fi access points scattered around the library, he could more or less triangulate users' locations. Unfortunately, there weren't enough access points to give more than a crude map, but he could tell at a glance how many users were on each floor of the library, how many in the park to the west, and if anyone was on one of the side streets within range.

As he stood to leave for Jenn's six thirty a.m. briefing, one of his monitors flashed an alert. It showed a solitary log-in coming from the park. Immediately, personal data from the device began to unspool across another monitor: Lisa Davis . . . 814 area code . . . home address . . . work address . . . e-mail . . . contacts . . . web-browser history. He smiled and toggled over to the cameras in the park. No one on a laptop; the only person in the park was a pregnant woman pushing a stroller.

Probably meant her smartphone was connecting automatically to the library network. To be certain, he dialed her number, and then on the camera monitor watched her take out her phone and, not recognizing the incoming number, send him straight to voice mail.

Sure enough, a pedestrian at the far edge of the Wi-Fi's range connected to the network for a few seconds before passing out of range. It popped up as a blip on his map and then vanished just as quickly.

Gibson frowned. Smartphones would make things messy. It was an obvious enough issue that he kicked himself for not anticipating it. Times had changed since his arrest, and he needed to catch up quickly. He was glad neither Jenn nor Hendricks was here to call him out for it.

He thought through his options, then made adjustments to his program, filtering smartphone traffic into a subdirectory. He wasn't after a phone, but he'd harvest the data and check it later. If it came to that. His fingers danced lightly over the keyboard. His handwriting might be barely legible, but he could type at nearly eighty words per minute—a child of the times. He hit "Refresh" and watched the cell signature in the park disappear. That ought to clear things up a little.

But only a little. The citizens of Somerset were clearly eager to embrace the unseasonably cool weather. After weeks of days in the upper eighties, a day in the seventies felt like a gift from God. By lunchtime, downtown Somerset bore little resemblance to the ghost town that had greeted them on Sunday. The park beside the library was packed with mothers and their young children, workers on their lunch break, and people out to enjoy the sunshine. A group of high-school girls had spread out beach blankets and were sunning themselves on the grass, which in turn had brought shirtless boys and their Frisbees. An ice-cream truck set up shop on the corner and was doing brisk trade in cones and Popsicles. As the afternoon wore on, the crowd didn't dissipate but rather swelled as people decided to play hooky from work and start their weekends early.

"How are we doing?" Jenn's voice asked through his earpiece.

His eyes wandered over to the camera aimed at the park. Jenn was sitting alone on a park bench with a good view of the area. In her employment photo, she'd worn a business suit and her hair was down. Today, she was dressed for a workout—hair pulled back tightly in a ponytail, baseball cap and oversized sunglasses obscuring her face. She sipped a water bottle looking like she was taking it easy after a run. Given the tailored suits that he was accustomed to seeing her wear, he'd taken Jenn for one of those StairMaster-obsessed women whose goal in life was spaghetti arms and a size two. But the tank top and shorts made him realize how mistaken he'd been. She was an athlete and an incredibly fit one at that. But he knew that her extreme fitness was practical; her sculpted shoulders and thighs spoke to a coiled, lethal strength.

"Looking good," he said.

She glanced toward the camera, but he couldn't read her expression behind her sunglasses and Steelers cap.

"You better be talking about the weather," she said.

"What else?"

"Uh-huh. Hendricks, status?"

Hendricks was stationed in the Cherokee a block away from the library, where he had a clear view up and down the street in front of the library.

"I've got some foot traffic into the library and park, but not a lot out. I count five, maybe six, possible matches for our profile that are inside the library. Another seven inside that fall outside our profile's parameters."

"I've got six in the park. Gibson, are we missing anyone?"

"No, that conforms to what I'm seeing too. Computer traffic has been steady, and I'm not seeing anything sneaky from the perimeter."

"And all quiet at ACG?" she asked.

Too quiet, unfortunately. The screen that displayed inbound and outbound traffic on ACG's network showed nothing out of the ordinary. And no matter how hard he glared, it seemed resolutely determined to keep on doing nothing out of the ordinary. It had led him to worry that maybe they'd tipped their hand and didn't know it.

Were they waiting for someone who would never show and was already a thousand miles away, running hard? Or what if this guy were simply taking the week off? Gibson tried to imagine waiting until next Friday to find out. And the Friday after that, and the Friday after that. Suzanne's memory weighed heavily on him each day, and it was beginning to wear him out. Hendricks had mentioned that his longest stakeout had been seven weeks. Gibson prayed that they wouldn't be out here that long.

"Gibson. All quiet at ACG?" Jenn asked again.

"Nothing so far," he said.

"All right, well, next move is his."

Although they were focusing on men who fit the FBI's profile, their cameras captured stills of everyone, man or woman, who came within a hundred yards of the library. Jenn had explained the approach to him during her briefing that morning. The woman did like a good briefing.

"In all likelihood the profile is right. A profile isn't a hunch. It's statistics, and the numbers say that whoever took Suzanne was probably a white male now in his forties or fifties."

"But . . . ," he said, feeling one coming.

"But there are always outliers. Maybe it was a woman trying to replace a lost child, or someone older or younger than we usually see in cases like this. A person of color hunting outside their ethnic group. A terrorist or some other politically motivated abductor. Truth is, the FBI had no way of eliminating any of those possibilities and neither do we."

"So play the odds, but cover our bases?"

"Play the odds. Cover our bases."

He passed the afternoon in his motel room, reviewing the surveillance footage for clear face shots, compiling them as stills and matching them, when relevant, with the compiled personal information from the computers logged in to the Wi-Fi. Every hour, he forwarded all-new photos and personal data to ACG—but not directly.

Out of fear that WR8TH had compromised ACG's corporate servers, Gibson and Mike Rilling had set up independent servers to receive all case-related communications and data. Rilling was running the faces through facial-recognition software tied into federal and state databases. Putting names with faces, essentially, and hoping to get really lucky with a criminal record. A home run would be a hit on the National Sex Offender Registry.

Gibson had the TV on mute for company and, once he'd seen the same highlights on SportsCenter three times, he switched over to the news. Benjamin Lombard's campaign was continuing to battle Governor Fleming's. Lombard had hired a new campaign manager and had performed surprisingly strongly in California, Fleming's home state. The pundits discussed the pros and cons of his new, more aggressive strategy. The vice president was in the middle of a swing through New England and was giving a speech in Boston this morning. Turnout was expected to be heavy.

Gibson wondered what would happen if they actually found Suzanne. What kind of a bump would it give Lombard's campaign? The American people were suckers for a good narrative, and the sight of a reunited family might be too much for them to resist. Would it put Lombard over the top? He wasn't sure he'd live through the irony of being Benjamin Lombard's savior.

"I need a cup of coffee," Hendricks muttered grumpily. "Don't anyone talk to me unless they spot someone wearing an 'I kidnapped Suzanne Lombard' T-shirt, all right?"

Five minutes later the next best thing arrived in the form of a tall, awkwardly thin man with a bowed back and skin that looked to be made of candle drippings. The Wax Man sat down at a worktable, took off a backpack, and laid it on the table. Then he proceeded to stare at the kids playing by the fountain like a tourist picking a lobster from a tank. There was definitely something not okay about him.

"Are you seeing this guy?" Gibson asked.

"Yeah, I've got eyes on him. He's giving me the creeps from a distance. Does he have a laptop?" Jenn asked.

"Negative. He's just sitting there like he's posing for a NAMBLA recruitment poster."

As if on cue, the Wax Man unzipped his backpack and took out a shiny silver laptop.

"He appears to be taking requests," Gibson reported. "One laptop by popular demand. See if he knows any Radiohead."

The Wax Man began typing, and Gibson watched a device connect to the Wi-Fi. In moments, his program began pulling pertinent information from the laptop's system registry.

"What do you have, Gibson?" Jenn asked.

"Meet James MacArthur Bradley. I have his home address and cellphone number."

"Good. Forward it and his picture to Washington. Let's see if Mr. Bradley has a criminal record," she said.

They watched Bradley for ten tense minutes, urging him silently to do something. Periodically, the Wax Man would pause typing and look over the top of his laptop toward the kids on the grass and lick his lips wetly.

"What's he doing?" Hendricks asked.

"Besides making my skin crawl? Not a lot," Jenn said.

"I'll second that."

"Yeah, well, him being creepy is all academic if he doesn't actually access ACG," Hendricks said.

"I wish I had good news, but no joy there," said Gibson.

Abruptly, the Wax Man shut his laptop, shoved it into his backpack, and walked briskly toward the street.

"Where the hell is he going?" Jenn asked.

"Did we spook him?"

"I don't think so," she said. "Hendricks, he's rounding the corner toward you in three, two, one . . ."

Hendricks grunted an affirmative. "Got him. Oh, yeah, I see what you mean. That is not a well guy. He's getting into a late-model Ford. Started it. Annnnnnnd, he's out of here."

"Damn it," Jenn said.

"Well, I got model and plates," Hendricks said. "But if that was our guy, then yeah, I'd say we just got made."

"And if he isn't?" Gibson asked.

"Then I guess he had somewhere to be."

"Do we go after him?"

"No," Jenn cut in. "Nothing we can do about it now. We maintain the stakeout and assume he wasn't our guy. We have enough data that we can follow up later if we need to."

With that, the three of them settled into a state of advanced, professional waiting otherwise known in the trade as excruciating boredom. By four o'clock, the park was still busy but fairly static. No one new using a Wi-Fi-enabled device had come or gone in thirty minutes. Gibson was tracking fourteen users logged in to the library's Wi-Fi. Nine outside and five inside. Outside, he had four on tablets or e-readers—two white women, a white man in his twenties, and a silver-haired African American man who had to be at least eighty. That left five outside on laptops, also a mix of genders and ethnicities, with three of particular interest.

The first was a squat, powerfully built white male in his late thirties. His computer's registry identified him as Kirby Tate. His nondescript face was completely out of proportion with his enormous shoulders and chest, and he looked like someone had Photoshopped a kid's face onto a man's body. The result wasn't pretty, but the man seemed to like the effect, since he was wearing tight khaki shorts and a tank top several sizes too small. Gibson knew the type—had served with the type—guys who would wear a tank top in a blizzard.

Tate sat at a picnic table near the fountain and divided his time between staring intently at his computer screen and staring intently at the girls on their blankets. The man's sunglasses couldn't mask the admiring way his head followed the young girls' movements.

The second was a Hispanic male in his forties, Daniel Espinosa. Balding, gray at the temple, and the right age, but pedophiles tended to hunt within their ethnic group. It didn't eliminate him, but it didn't move him to the top of the list either. He had a friendly, open face and was chatting with a couple sharing his park table.

The third man was Lawrence Kenney. He was in his early fifties and looked like he'd purchased his crisp khakis, sweater vest, and unapologetic, sweeping comb-over from the same anal-retentive superstore. The man looked like the proverbial mild-mannered accountant pecking away at his laptop, but he made Gibson uneasy. He couldn't put his finger on why. Perhaps it was the way the accountant sat among people but felt palpably apart from them. A woman pushing a baby carriage brushed past the accountant, who stiffened. His eyes trailed after her, fixing a simmering glare on her back that made the hair on Gibson's arms stand up. Did goose bumps qualify as probable cause in Pennsylvania?

Hopefully, Rilling could match names with faces and run background checks on all of them. Until then, they would have to rely on old-fashioned police work and intuition.

Jenn and Hendricks set to debating and dissecting their pool of subjects. Listening to them, two things were clear to Gibson. One, they knew what they were talking about. Two, he didn't, and the conversation quickly eclipsed his ability to follow. His knowledge of serial offenders stemmed largely from *The Silence of the Lambs* and Patricia Cornwell novels. What he did know was computers and the people who used them. He wondered if the same techniques that were used to profile killers and rapists could be applied to hackers. If he extrapolated backward from the signature of the ACG hack—to whom did it lead?

He supposed his money was on the accountant. The coding on the virus was clean, precise, and required attention to detail. At least going by wardrobe, the accountant was the best match. It was thin, though. He knew plenty of programmers who were slobs. He figured he was out of his league, discarded the theory, and went back to work sorting through the batch of driver's license photographs that Mike Rilling had sent him from DC. Over the next hour, he mapped out their locations as best he could.

By a quarter to five, Gibson wasn't asleep, but he wasn't entirely alert either. Sitting cross-legged on the floor, he was resting his chin on his knuckles and staring at the monitor displaying ACG's server data. He felt like a guy waiting for a plane that was perpetually delayed. So he was slow to react when his phone vibrated on the floor between his knees. On the third buzz, he looked down at his phone, saw the text message, and immediately snapped back up to the monitor. Adrenaline slammed through him. A red bar had popped up with an alert message. The virus on ACG's servers was receiving new instructions.

"Did either of you just get a text message?" Hendricks asked.

"Yeah, I got it. Gibson, what's happening?" There was an edge to Jenn's voice—excitement fused with a predator's hunger.

"The virus is active. WR8TH is talking to it."

"From the library?" Jenn asked.

"Hold one," he said, scanning the list of outbound library Internet traffic. *Come on, baby. Come on.* He ran his finger down the screen. And there it was. Big, beautiful, and guilty. Someone on the library Wi-Fi was communicating with the corrupt ad server that was the virus's anonymous relay station. It was an impossible coincidence and could mean only one thing.

"Son of a bitch is here," he said. Mostly to himself, but he'd left comms open and the response came back with urgency.

"Where?" Jenn demanded.

"He's outside. He's in the park," Gibson said.

He looked at the video feed from the park. Their guy was down there. Suzanne Lombard's kidnapper, and likely murderer, was sitting in plain sight, catching some rays.

"Which one?" Jenn demanded.

He matched the IP address to a machine and read through his notes until he found the driver's license photo. He looked from the name back to the monitor until he spotted their man.

"Got you," Gibson said with a smile.

CHAPTER TWENTY-ONE

Tinsley sat on the wooden crate he was using as a makeshift stool. He'd been there since before dawn and had watched the sun come up over the library. He was waiting for it to happen . . . or not. He was indifferent.

Earlier in the week, he had scoped out a small, unoccupied office to hole up in. From the second-story window where he sat, Tinsley had an unobstructed view of the library and adjacent park. At that hour, the library and park were deserted, but Tinsley wanted time for the emptiness to saturate his retinas and burn the landscape into his mind's eye. Later, as it filled with bodies, each object would stand out clearly to his brain like a blemish on a pristine original.

The leasing agent who showed him the property had complained that Tinsley was the first nibble in more than a month. Tinsley took that as a good omen and broke in later that night. He'd been using it as a base of operations, but there was no trace or sign that anyone had been there. He wanted to leave this town without causing so much as a ripple in its surface. Tinsley had no intention at this time of killing the leasing agent, but he'd taken the man's card in case things took a turn.

Tinsley blinked and the noonday sun greeted him.

Tinsley blinked and the sun dipped toward the far horizon.

His expensive watch told him he had been sitting at the window for twelve hours. His eyes continued to track the hazy movements of the shapes in the park. Nothing of importance had changed. The woman was still on the park bench. The thin, irritable man was still in his car. The third was nowhere to be seen, but Tinsley was confident that Vaughn was back at the motel. Probably typing away on one of his little computers. Type, type, type.

It was ironic in its way—the hunters unaware that they themselves were hunted. And that if they found their quarry it would mean their deaths. It did not impress him, but he did pause to wonder: Would he know if he was being hunted? Was he not arrogant to assume he alone had the edge? The thought made him grin. That would be an intricate play indeed. Set a killer on a killer; tie up all the loose ends. Doubtful but not beyond the realm of possibility. He would recalibrate his senses to be alert to such a betrayal.

In a way he longed for it. This job was proving mundane, and the prospect of killing them didn't spark anything in him. Hendricks would be nothing. Jenn Charles would need careful attention, but that was all. Tinsley had a history with Gibson Vaughn, but even that did not rouse his spirits overly.

Not that it seemed a likely prospect at this point. Friday was sup- posedly a pivotal day for them, and so far they appeared to be coming up empty. He should urinate and eat something. He didn't feel a need to do either, but he trusted the watch to tell him when it was time.

Tinsley's cell vibrated. He read the text message with cold curios- ity. It was happening. He looked back down into the park. The woman was gone from the park bench. His mind found her shape moving up toward the fountain. She circled around the main cluster of people at the tables near the library and stopped to fill her water bottle at a water fountain. The bitter man's shape was still in the car, but Tinsley could see him talking animatedly into a cell.

He was curious to see the face of the other person he had been sent to kill—the one who had eluded him all those years ago. That was, after all, his primary target. The old unfinished business that had brought him back here. Either he had killed the wrong man ten years ago, or else there had been an accomplice who had been overlooked. Time, as it always did, had given this man the false confidence to show himself again. Tinsley would balance that ledger soon.

These others would just be collateral.

———————

They were just fucking with him now. The vice president could feel it. Lombard looked at his watch with a sharp snap of his wrist. Six forty-seven p.m. He'd been twiddling his goddamn thumbs in his ceremonial office off the Senate floor for nearly seven hours.

All for a toothless immigration bill that had been languishing in the Senate since early spring. And now, miraculously, days before the crucial California primary, the Senate had gotten its act together for an up-or-down vote. The majority whip, anticipating a tie, had informed Lombard that, as vice president, he'd be needed in Washington to break the deadlock.

The majority leader had assured him that the vote would happen first thing, so Lombard had flown in first thing and arrived at the Capitol at eleven thirty for a noon vote. With the time change, he would have been back in Dallas by midafternoon for several campaign appearances. Instead, he'd endured an unexpected filibuster, a nongermane amendment, and a failed cloture vote. Each one timed exactly when the roll-call vote on the final bill appeared imminent. His worry now was that they would stretch the vote until tomorrow, which would put him back in Dallas on Saturday afternoon at the earliest.

This was no coincidence or accident. That much was obvious. Lombard knew from experience how the game was played here in the

Senate, and he could imagine the minority leader laughing at him from his office. *Well, enjoy it while you can,* Lombard thought. The unofficial agenda of his first term had been amended in the last few hours to include unseating that prick.

He checked his watch again. Although he wouldn't admit it to anyone, the campaign was in good hands and could take care of itself for a day without him. Fleming was on the ropes and, if his polling data were worth what he'd paid for it, then the nomination would be his next week.

No, it was this developing situation in Pennsylvania that was giving him heartburn. A cryptic message from Eskridge an hour ago indicated Gibson Vaughn might actually have found the man who took his daughter. It was unfathomable, and ordinarily Lombard could compartmentalize, but he'd been unable to focus on anything else. He wanted to know what was happening, and he wanted to know now.

Instead he was trapped here, surrounded by ears he didn't entirely trust, and with no way to call securely for an update. For the first time in eight years, being vice president of the United States was damn inconvenient—all the power in the world but powerless to influence the search for his own daughter. He checked his watch and wound it for good measure.

"Mr. Vice President?" A young aide stood in the doorway of the vice president's office.

"Yes? Are they ready finally?"

The aide looked unhappily at the floor.

"What now?" Lombard demanded.

"Another amendment, sir."

He felt his blood pressure rising. "How long?"

"Ninety minutes . . . maybe two hours?"

Lombard looked at his watch. There went getting back to Dallas for the speech. He needed to talk to Reed and start making arrangements for Saturday.

"Close the door."

The aide stepped gratefully back out into the hall. Lombard sat at his desk and picked up the phone, then put it back in the cradle. He sat staring at it grimly for a long while.

CHAPTER TWENTY-TWO

Gibson pulled the Taurus over to the side of the road. Traffic whipped by close enough to shake the car. He sat there, hands on the wheel, and listened to the engine idle. He was thirty miles out of Somerset. That ought to be enough. Would they have followed him? He glanced in the rearview mirror again. Nothing. It wasn't all that comforting. He wouldn't see Hendricks unless Hendricks wanted to be seen.

It had been an eventful thirty-six hours. WR8TH had turned out to be Kirby Tate, the wannabe bodybuilder. Gibson's program had done its job perfectly and drawn a straight line between the corrupted ad server and Tate's computer. While Rilling had run Tate's name through state and federal databases, Hendricks and Jenn had tailed Tate to his residence. By the next morning, they were 90 percent sure they had the right guy, and by Saturday afternoon, when Rilling forwarded Tate's file to Jenn and Hendricks, they were convinced. George had calls in to his contacts at the FBI to present their case against Kirby Tate.

"Our guy's got a sheet," Hendricks had said. "Did five and a half years at Frackville for false imprisonment. Must have been where he got jacked, because in his mug shot he's a skinny little bitch."

"What did he do?" Gibson asked.

"Got caught with eleven-year-old Trish Casper in his car is what he did."

"He's a registered sex offender," Jenn added.

"Oh, yeah. The girl's kid brother ID'd the car leaving a supermarket, and the mom called the cops. When the cops pulled Tate over, the girl was trussed up in his trunk. Half-naked."

"He got out a year and a half before Suzanne disappeared."

"Sad part is this monster should have gone down for felony kidnapping of a minor," Jenn said.

"A first-degree felony," Hendricks chimed in.

"So should have been twenty years."

"But local PD got overzealous during the arrest and beat the guy while he was cuffed," Hendricks said.

"Broke his arm and dislocated his shoulder. His lawyer cut a deal and got it knocked down to false imprisonment."

"A second-degree felony," Hendricks said.

"Which got him out of prison in time to take Suzanne," Gibson said, seeing the tragic way it all fit together.

"We got him," said Jenn.

Saturday night, while Hendricks sat on Tate's home, Jenn and Gibson walked over to the Summit Diner. A couple of conquering heroes. Jenn had unbuttoned the top button on her personality, and they'd laughed together like old friends and told stories about the last week like it had happened half a lifetime ago. He felt like part of the team for the first time, and they toasted over milkshakes. Jenn was warm and appreciative, and said they couldn't have done it without him. George Abe even called to thank him personally. It had felt good, really good to be part of something that mattered.

After she'd paid the check, Jenn had dropped the boom on Gibson: Abe wanted him back in Washington.

"You need to understand that your presence will jeopardize our credibility. The FBI is already going to be irritated that we didn't turn this over to them straightaway. We need to be airtight with them, and having someone like you here is only going to muddy the waters that much more."

"Someone like me."

"Someone with your history. The FBI won't understand how important Suzanne is to you. All they'll see is your history with Lombard."

Gibson wasn't buying it. He promised to stay out of the way. He would have promised anything. They were so close; he couldn't go home now.

"You hit a home run here," said Jenn. "We're in your debt, but you need to let us handle it from here. You want us to catch this guy, right?"

They'd stood in the parking lot of the diner and argued it around and around, voices and tempers rising until the manager came out and told them to knock it off. They picked up again back in Jenn's room, iterations of the same stale arguments flying back and forth. Eventually, they lapsed into an exhausted silence.

"For God's sake, let this go," Jenn told him at last. "You did good. For once in your life, recognize when you're ahead and keep it that way."

It was good advice even if it stung. Even if he had no intention of following it. Not where Bear was concerned. He would see this through to the end even if he had to do it alone. They could have their money back.

About halfway through, he'd realized that no argument would sway Jenn to his cause. He'd kept on arguing but only for show. At the appropriate point, he'd stormed out and gone back to his motel room to pack. In the morning, Jenn had tried to make peace, but he'd shrugged her off angrily. She wouldn't have bought it otherwise, and he'd needed her to believe he was going home.

He glanced in the rearview mirror again. Had he fooled them? If he had, then it was on them for believing a few kind words would get him to quit. Gibson cranked the steering wheel around, pulled a U-turn, and swung the car back toward Somerset.

Toward Bear.

Hendricks was right. Hope was a cancer.

Gibson watched Hendricks finish loading all the gear into the back of the Cherokee. The ex-cop slammed shut the hatch and lit a cigarette. After a minute, Jenn emerged from the motel manager's office, gestured at Hendricks to get a move on, and got in the passenger side. Hendricks crushed out his half-finished cigarette and got behind the wheel.

The Cherokee pulled out into traffic, and Gibson slouched low behind the wheel as it passed him on the way out of town. He'd parked a couple blocks away and watched them through a pair of binoculars that he'd found in the glove compartment. He still felt exposed. It was a car they knew, and Hendricks didn't miss much. He half expected them to pull over and drag him out. But Hendricks and Jenn cruised by without so much as a glance in his direction. He wanted to follow them, but he knew nothing about how to tail a car. Hendricks would make him in a half mile.

Gibson sat up, feeling foolish. But was he? Being foolish, that is? Something felt wrong to him. Supposedly, Jenn and Hendricks were to sit tight until Abe flew in so they could coordinate with the feds. So where were they going in such a hurry?

But that wasn't even it. It was more the way Hendricks was going about it. Not hurrying exactly, but moving with a purpose. It was the way he strode, economically, back and forth between the room and the vehicle. Not on a clock, but with no time to waste either. It reminded Gibson of marines packing for an imminent deployment—checking and double-checking the gear, taking a mental inventory. It was the latent intensity that settled on people before they stepped off into something heavy.

So where were they going? He'd been gone for what, an hour and a half, tops? And in that time Jenn and Hendricks had pulled up stakes. Their plans hadn't changed since he'd left; no, this had been the plan all along. Of that, he had no doubt.

He saw now what last night had been about. The camaraderie at the diner. Jenn had been putting on her own show. She'd tried to hack him, appealing to his insecurity and his vanity. She'd taken him out for dinner, held his hand, and whispered sweet nothings in his ear. All to get him to go back to DC peacefully.

What was the first rule to getting someone to fall in line? Figure out what they need and give them a taste. Not enough to sate them, but enough to whet their appetite. Enough that they wanted more. Needed more. Well, what did he need? Respect? Appreciation? Accomplishment? Wasn't that what Jenn had fed him last night at the diner? Buffed his ego until it shone. Played on his loyalty to Suzanne and counted on it to control him. Gibson looked in the passenger seat at the manila envelope. Inside was ten thousand dollars. In cash. A bonus from ACG for his "outstanding" work. That had certainly been meant to help the medicine go down, hadn't it?

If this had been the plan from the beginning, to send him home after they found WR8TH, the next question was why. What was it George Abe said to him the day they'd met about wanting to have a serious conversation with the man who took Suzanne? Something about giving the FBI the leftovers. Well, wouldn't it make sense to have him safely out of the way for that? Did they even care about finding Suzanne? And if not, what was it they were after?

The real question was what he was going to do about it. First things first. He drove to a UPS store, folded a thousand dollars into his hip pocket, and boxed the rest of the money. He mailed it to Nicole with a note. If this went badly, at least she would have the money. He walked out into the sunshine and jangled the car keys in his hand.

Let the games begin.

He might not be able to tail Hendricks, but he didn't really need to. When Hendricks had forgotten his phone outside his room, Gibson had taken it as an invitation to make a few personal upgrades. Hendricks's personal data was all encrypted, of course, so it wasn't easily accessible. But since Gibson didn't want or need access to the data, it had been simple enough to move it off the phone temporarily, jailbreak the phone, install a program of his own, and reload Hendricks's encrypted data back onto the device.

Gibson activated that app now using his own cell phone and waited for it to access the GPS feature on Hendricks's phone. When it finished loading, a red dot appeared on his phone's map. It moved steadily north away from the green dot that represented Gibson's location. He watched it until it stopped moving. Expanding the map with his fingers, he found an address and ran a search on it.

It was the address of a self-storage facility.

A twenty-minute drive out of Somerset, Grafton Storage sat on a dismal two-lane highway banked on both sides by a state park. It came up on his right and was the first structure he had seen in miles. Gibson slowed for a better look.

The property took up the better part of two acres and was a pretty simple operation—a tall razor wire–topped cinder-block wall that circled the property, an automated gate with a small office, and rows and rows of identical one-story warehouses with identical blue rollaway doors. What would possess someone to build a storage facility out here in the middle of nowhere was beyond him. But that probably explained why Grafton Storage was out of business and, from the look of it, had been for some time.

He drove on until he found a dirt road to pull onto and stashed his car. Walking the quarter mile back to Grafton Storage, he didn't see a single car pass by. The defunct storage business looked even more run-down up close: a battered "For Sale" sign hung slantways from the gate, and thick tufts of grass grew between the cracked asphalt. The thick chain and heavy corroded padlock that barred the gate didn't look like they'd been disturbed in a hundred years.

Was his program glitching? He closed and reloaded the app that was tracking Hendricks's location. Nope, it still showed Hendricks as inside Grafton Storage. Gibson looked at the padlock more closely. Were those flecks of steel showing through the rust where someone had worked a key into the stiff lock? When exactly did he become an expert on rusted padlocks?

He looked around. If Jenn and Hendricks really were inside, who had locked the gate behind them? It made no sense unless there was another way in. Or Hendricks had thrown his phone inside the wall to throw him off. But that would mean Hendricks knew he was being followed.

Or, or, or . . .

Gibson rubbed his forehead. There were too many options; time to whittle some of them away.

He called Hendricks's phone. It rang five or six times before Hendricks answered. Sounded mightily put out too.

Good.

"Hey," Gibson said as dumbly as he could manage.

"Hey what? Aren't I done with you? I remember you leaving. Didn't that happen? I remember that happening."

"I know. Sorry. Is Jenn there? Got a quick question."

"She has her own phone, you know? I'm not her secretary."

He started to apologize again, but Jenn came on the line, sounding only slightly less tense than her partner.

"Yeah?"

"Sorry to bug you guys, but would it be cool if I went straight home and dropped the car off at ACG in the morning?"

He could practically hear Jenn's eyes rolling, so he started into a story about wanting to catch Ellie's soccer game this afternoon. She cut him off and said it was fine.

"Is George there yet?" he asked.

"Not yet."

"Really think he's going to sleep in that shit-box motel?"

Jenn forced a laugh. It sounded hollow and joyless. She agreed that it would be funny.

"Well, take pictures for me. That I have to see."

She hung up without another word.

He stared at his phone quizzically. So Jenn and Hendricks had locked themselves inside an abandoned self-storage facility along Route Godforsaken. Putting aside the basic weirdness of that statement for a moment, how did they get in there and lock the gate behind them? He was just about to walk the perimeter and look for a second entrance when he noticed that a section of razor wire had been cut away some fifty feet from the main gate—easy enough to miss from the roadway.

He walked alongside the wall, dragging his hand along the smooth surface. In theory, the gap was wide enough for one person to cross through, but the top of the wall was ten feet high and even an experienced climber needed handholds. You would need . . . a ladder.

Something yellow in the underbrush caught his eye. He trotted over for a look and was lucky not to trip and gouge himself on the missing section of razor wire. He saw it at the last second, coiled like a snake in the tall grass, wickedly sharp, and he had to pirouette awkwardly to avoid it. He lost his balance and, backpedaling, caught his heel on something solid and went down hard on his back.

He lay there wincing until the pain faded, then sat up to look at the brand-new extension ladder he had fallen over.

What the hell is going on?

He was still contemplating that question when a length of rope flew over the wall from inside the compound. It hung a foot off the ground, swaying back and forth. Gibson stared at it stupidly for a moment. He scrambled to his feet, barely making it behind a tree before Jenn threw her leg over the top of the wall and shimmied down the rope to the ground. She called out that she was down, and the rope disappeared back over the wall.

He watched her unlock the padlock and slide back the gate. Hendricks drove the Cherokee out. Its back was empty, which meant they'd unloaded the gear inside. It made him wonder what had been in the other black duffel bags. And where Hendricks had been while he had been coding the program for the library.

Jenn relocked the gate, and Gibson watched them drive away for the second time today. He thought about going over the wall to do a bit of recon, but it might take a week to find wherever they had set up camp inside. Better to stay with them and see where that took him. He brushed himself off and walked back to the car.

CHAPTER TWENTY-THREE

The red dot led Gibson east through a series of small lower-middle-class townships, each bleaker than the last. By the time he passed through the last one, dusk had fallen, and the sky was a charcoal red in his rearview mirror. He slowed to check his phone—Hendricks's dot had been stationary for thirty minutes. Not far now.

A grim certainty had settled over him since he'd left the storage facility, and he was afraid he knew exactly where Jenn and Hendricks were headed. He hoped he was wrong, but it was the only thing that made sense of their actions. He'd know soon enough.

The houses thinned out until more than one hundred yards separated one home and the next. Out here, there was no clear demarcation between one property and the next. No fences. Just wide-open spaces that bled into each other.

The properties might be large, but the houses themselves were modest single-story ramblers or double-wides on cinder-block foundations. Satellite dishes dominated most of the yards. Not a lot out here to do at night except watch TV and surf the Internet, and it would be a long time before anyone bothered to run cable out in the sticks.

He rounded a bend and spotted the Cherokee ahead on the left. It was parked in the gravel driveway alongside an old wood-paneled station wagon. Whatever color the house had once been had long since faded and mottled into a sloppy bowl of old porridge. One of the front windows had blown out, but instead of a replacement, plastic sheeting was stapled across the opening. The gray shingle roof sagged lamely in the middle, and the whole house looked like it was one swift kick from toppling down. A brown-and-yellow couch had been dragged under an elm tree, where it moldered forlornly in the knee-high grass.

It was depressing to think what would drive someone to live out here. This was no one's first choice.

He saw no place to pull over where he wouldn't be seen, so he drove on. He didn't see anyone in the Cherokee; presumably they were in the house.

Two properties down stood an old Baptist church. The roadside sign read, "C me Wors p With s," but it looked like years since anyone had taken them up on the offer. Not even God wanted to live here. Gibson pulled in and circled around to the back, where the Taurus couldn't be seen from the road.

He took the binoculars and crouched behind a low brick wall to watch and wait. He checked his phone, but there was no cell service.

Hours passed.

It was a moonless night. A storm system rumbled to the south but passed without a drop of rain falling. There were no streetlights, so the only illumination came from the odd porch light or the faint blue of a TV flickering through a window. But the house where the Cherokee was parked was pitch black. If the lights were even on inside, he couldn't tell, because the shades were drawn. It troubled him to think what might be going on inside.

He weighed the pros and cons of sneaking up to the house. Pro: he'd get a much better idea of what was going on inside. Con: they were armed, and he wasn't. If they saw him, he wasn't sure which way it would go. It was funny. This morning all he'd been worried about was that they'd chew him out. What a difference twelve hours made.

When Jenn and Hendricks finally moved, Gibson didn't catch it until Hendricks started the SUV. The running lights came on, and through the binoculars he saw Jenn silhouetted against the SUV's dome light. She pushed a figure out of the house. A black hood covered his head, but it was a man, judging from the broad, powerfully built shoulders. His arms were bound behind his back, so she used the back of his neck to guide him as she bundled him into the backseat. Then she got into the old station wagon parked in the driveway and pulled out behind Hendricks.

Gibson slumped behind the wall. Jenn and Hendricks hadn't called in the feds. At least not yet, but he had a feeling that the feds had never been on their agenda. This wasn't about bringing WR8TH to justice. This was about revenge. That's why they had sent him home. What had Calista Dauplaise said to him in Georgetown? That the person responsible for taking Suzanne Lombard would pay. No, that wasn't the word she'd used. Calista had said he would *suffer*.

Neither George nor Calista had any loyalty to Benjamin Lombard. They'd both borne the loss of Suzanne heavily. He had heard it in their voices when they spoke of her. The vice president didn't know anything about this, and Gibson doubted that he ever would. This was between George, Calista, and the man who took Suzanne.

What had he allowed himself to be pulled into? How culpable was he? Would he be able to prove he didn't know what they had planned? Would that matter? He had hacked a public library . . . how would a creative district attorney spin breaking into a government building? Not to mention the cash payments he'd received. All of a sudden that seemed pretty damning too.

He considered his options. Call the police now. Probably what most people would do, but he wasn't quite ready to go back to jail. He could call Lombard. Tell the vice president what his old political ally and chief of security were up to. *Yeah,* Gibson thought to himself, *Lombard will shield me while he rains down vengeance on everyone else involved.*

When Jenn and Hendricks were gone, Gibson waited ten minutes and walked up the road to the house. The gravel driveway under his feet sounded like a rock band warming up for a show. The next house was a football field away, but that did little to settle his nerves.

The front door was locked, as was the back. He tried all the windows, but they were all firmly latched too. Gibson frowned. He went back around to the front and used his car keys to cut a slit in the plastic sheeting covering the broken window. He reached through and unlatched the frame and slid it open.

The house was a sty. At first he thought Jenn and Hendricks had trashed the place, but this was the work of years, not hours. He didn't want to risk turning on the lights, but he had a flashlight app on his phone that he used to survey an ocean of trash, broken furniture, and empty cardboard boxes. A stack of at least forty umbrellas. A shattered accordion. An unmounted deer's head stared blankly up at the ceiling.

The kitchen was diseased; there was no other word for it. The smell. Jesus, someone *lived* here. Gibson couldn't even bring himself to cross the threshold to the kitchen and decided he'd save it for last. The only clean area was a spare bedroom that had been converted into a gym. There was a bench press, rusty barbells, and a chin-up bar. Several crooked full-length mirrors hung side by side to create a vanity wall. Against another wall stood stacks and stacks of fitness magazines: *Muscle & Fitness, Muscular Development, Natural Muscle, Planet Muscle . . .*

Gibson hunted for anything personal, something with a name that would confirm what he already knew in the pit of his stomach. He thought maybe the fitness magazines, but they had all been bought off a newsstand. A photograph would do, but nothing hung on the walls, and it didn't feel like a framed-picture kind of home. There was nothing helpful in the bedroom. Gibson waded back to the front door and found a mountain of unopened mail.

He held letters up to his phone one at a time, looking for a name. Most were addressed to "resident" or "current occupant," but eventually he found a letter from the Pennsylvania Department of Corrections. The name was the one he expected to find: "Kirby Tate."

The sound of someone testing the front door startled him. The doorknob was only inches from his face, and he looked up in rapt fascination as it turned back and forth. He hadn't heard a car pull up the driveway. Could it be a neighbor stopping by? Did Tate have friends? More likely Jenn or Hendricks had forgotten something and come back for it. *Or for you,* a voice whispered uncharitably in his head.

He shoved the letter into a pocket and backed away from the door. With the element of surprise, he would have the advantage with one, but if both had come back, then he had no chance. He didn't feel like waiting around to find out. The glinting sound of metal on metal whispered through the silent house, but thankfully the door didn't open. He remembered a closet near the kitchen and slunk backward among the trash piles. Would they kill him? Had it gone that far?

He slipped into the closet, put his back against the wall, and slid down into a crouch. He couldn't get the door all the way shut behind him, because there was no handle on the inside. It was wet beneath his feet and smelled like piss. He put his phone in airplane mode and listened to the front door swing open.

As far as he could tell there was only one of them. Whoever "them" was. The intruder didn't call out and didn't switch on the lights. He heard the front door shut quietly. A flashlight came on, and through the crack in the door he saw the beam dance across the walls. He had been very aware of the creak of the floorboards when he had first arrived, but whoever was moving through the house either knew it exceptionally well or moved like a ghost. He could hear their footfalls, but only because every ounce of his concentration was focused on listening for them. A strobe went off. Then another and another. Pictures. Someone was moving through the house, taking pictures. Methodically taking an inventory of every room. Did that include closets?

If the door opened, he was going to hit them low and hard. Keep hitting them until they stopped moving. He was worried, though, that he would slip in the soupy mush under his feet. He moved slowly, shifting his feet, seeking a dry surface to brace against.

He didn't think he'd given himself away but was immediately aware when the pictures stopped. A silence so thick dropped over the house that it pulsed in his ears. He held his breath, senses straining. It was like two submarines playing cat and mouse in the murky depths—each listening for the other, deathly afraid to give away its position.

Minutes passed. Gibson heard those ghostlike footsteps retreat toward the front of the house. The door opened and then closed quietly. Then nothing.

He exhaled but didn't move. He waited there in the closet for what seemed a lifetime. Afraid that whoever it was might double back or, worse, that they hadn't left at all and were trying to bluff him out of the closet. He listened until his temples throbbed, but the house was dead.

Gibson slipped out of the closet. For half a second, he panicked as the deer's head played games with the shadows and took the shape of a man. He let out a little cry and shut his mouth in embarrassment.

Pull yourself together, boy.

He sank down onto a couch and rubbed his calves, cramped from squatting in the closet. He switched on his flashlight app and looked around. The couch was clearly where Kirby Tate spent most of his time. Gibson was sitting in the only bare patch, but otherwise it was stacked with dirty dishes, empty junk-food containers, and pornographic magazines. Hundreds of them. He hadn't even known they still made dirty magazines.

He chuckled silently to himself but stopped as a thought occurred to him. You know who would know? A guy with no Internet would know. There was no satellite dish in the yard. No satellite dish meant no TV and, more importantly, no access to the Internet.

Was he supposed to believe that the person responsible for hacking ACG had no Internet? He searched the house again. This time looking for anything that he would expect to find in the home of someone who was computer savvy. He found nothing. No tools. No books. No workspace. No storage media. Nothing but trash, porn, and gym equipment. If Kirby Tate was a hacker, then he was the only one Gibson had ever come across who could live without twenty-four-hour access to high-speed Internet.

You spent enough time working with computers, and the Internet became a second home. A refuge. A place to share ideas, trade snippets of code, and meet people who shared your interest in the extralegal applications of programming. Could such a person live without the Internet? He supposed it was possible. Yes, a voice countered, but was it probable? He was more certain than ever that whatever Jenn and Hendricks were planning at Grafton Storage, they had the wrong guy for it. Whatever was on Kirby Tate's laptop, it couldn't have gotten there without someone's help.

So who was helping him? Did Tate have a partner?

Gibson let himself out of the house as quietly as he could. By comparison to the house, it looked like high noon outside. He saw no one but to play it safe took a looping path back to his car. He didn't turn the headlights back on until he had put several miles between himself and Tate's house.

Tinsley stood in the dark of the house. So Vaughn was back. That was an interesting piece of information. He was supposed to be home by now. Well, apparently Vaughn had other ideas. Not that it changed anything. Actually, it saved Tinsley a trip back to Washington. All the eggs, as they say, were back in one basket.

He sat on the couch where Vaughn had been. An idea had come to the computer man. Tinsley had seen it on his face. They had been so close that Tinsley could have reached out and touched him. He could only imagine Vaughn's reaction if he had seen him. But Vaughn hadn't; they never did. It was just as well, because this was not the place for him to die. Ironically, this was one place where Vaughn was safe.

Tinsley looked at the dirty magazines that Vaughn had picked up, but whatever they had whispered to Vaughn, Tinsley could not hear it. He frowned. Why had Vaughn come back at all? He didn't like that he couldn't see it. No matter. If Kirby Tate was the man who had evaded him a decade ago, that meant Tinsley's work was almost done.

CHAPTER TWENTY-FOUR

Jenn watched Kirby Tate on a bank of monitors. It was dark in his cell, Tate a ghostly green on the screen. From bound wrists he hung, arms outstretched. She watched Tate dance on his toes, trying to keep his feet under him. When he slipped, his shoulders took the full weight of his body until he could get his feet back under him. It was exhausting. It was intended to be.

Through the walls she could feel the bass from music bombarding Tate. Some speed-metal band that believed anything less than 250 beats a minute was elevator music. It amazed her what some people listened to voluntarily. She only knew it as the playlist of CIA black-site detention facilities around the world.

She wiped sweat out of her eyes. Even with the rollaway door open, the heat of the sun baked the units like ovens. It was much worse for Tate. How far was she willing to take this if Kirby didn't fold as readily as predicted? She pushed the question away. He would break. They might have to tiptoe up to the edge, but she was sure he would break before things crossed the line. He had to.

In her time at the Agency, Jenn had sat in on more enhanced interrogations than she cared to remember. No matter how hard you thought you were, you carried each one with you. That she had believed in their necessity did nothing to help her sleep at night. The subjects had been men of principle and faith. Principles she despised. Principles that had led to unforgivable crimes. But principles nonetheless, and on some base level she could respect their devotion. Interrogating such men took time. It took time to break a devout man of his beliefs, and it was a terrible thing to witness. Worse still to be the one responsible.

Kirby Tate, on the other hand, believed only in his need. No principles other than his own ghoulish desires. A man like this was already broken. She did not expect to be here long. How much steel could there be in a man so weak he preyed on children?

She yawned and stretched. It had been a long night. She looked enviously toward Hendricks, asleep on the cot in the corner. She'd wake him in another two hours, and they'd go back to work on Tate.

Tate was a career criminal. In addition to the botched Trish Casper abduction, he had a lengthy record and had been in and out of lockup since he was fifteen. A child of the system, he would think he knew how it worked. Its rules. She'd known he would be confident about his ability to play it to his advantage. So after they had grabbed Tate at his house, they'd built the illusion in his mind that he was no longer in the United States. Leading him to believe that he was far, far from home and that no one was coming to rescue him. He had to learn early on that his concept of legality didn't apply here—no lawyers, no Miranda rights, no bargains to be struck. Only answers or pain. Answers or pain.

Creating the illusion had involved driving Tate to a little-used airstrip, boarding him onto a plane, and strapping him into a seat. Of course, the plane never left the hangar, but in Tate's mind they had flown halfway around the world.

Hendricks was a remarkably accomplished audio technician. He'd conjured an entire cockpit crew running through a preflight checklist. She and Hendricks had staged a prisoner transfer, manhandling Tate and barking instructions at him. Tate struggled and moaned under his hood but couldn't speak through the gag. Hendricks had rapped him across the head and told him to be a good boy.

Right before "takeoff," they'd gassed him. Nothing too potent. Just enough to knock him out for five minutes, and when he'd woken the plane was in the "air." It was an impressive effect, the cockpit humming like a plane in flight. Hendricks had defeated the plane's squat switch (a weight-sensitive trigger in the landing gear that told the plane it was on the ground) and pressurized the interior; Jenn had actually felt her ears pop. A "pilot" came over the speakers and gave the cabin a status update: airspeed, altitude, flight time. Hendricks had placed a large subwoofer beneath the plane, which produced a constant low-frequency tone to simulate the engines. They'd kept up a constant chatter: Jenn playing the part of the veteran, Hendricks the rookie. During the "flight," Hendricks had peppered her with questions about their destination, and Jenn painted a grim picture for Tate's benefit.

They'd let Tate soak up the performance for thirty minutes and then gassed him again. A little more this time. So that when he'd woken, groggy and disoriented, he was easily convinced that he was back on terra firma and being loaded into a car. The same car, as it happened, but with the sounds of foreign voices chattering in the background, there'd been no way for him to know that. Tate had whimpered under his hood.

By the time they had arrived at Grafton Storage, Tate *believed.* Jenn had heard it in his voice. Somewhere along the line, he'd wet himself too.

While Gibson had been occupied writing his program at the motel back in Somerset, Hendricks had converted one of the abandoned storage units into a rudimentary command center. They had cots, a hot plate, food, and water. A portable generator ran the monitors they used to watch their captive.

Kirby Tate's cell was a neighboring ten-by-thirty-foot storage unit, which Hendricks had adapted into a holding cell and interrogation room. He'd installed chain-link fencing and a padlocked door across one half of the room. A coil of barbed wire ran along the base. A straw pallet in the event Tate earned the right to sleep. A bucket for waste.

It was primitive and intended that way.

They'd hustled him out of the car and into his cell. Strung him up while he'd made hysterical clucking sounds through his gag. Went on making them while they'd changed into black jumpsuits and pulled on ski masks. By concealing their identities, they gave Tate a glimmer of hope that if he confessed, they would let him go. Even Tate was smart enough to know that if he saw their faces, he was a dead man.

Jenn had yanked off Tate's hood, and Tate's eyes bulged as he frantically looked in all directions. Hendricks did all the talking. She felt Tate would respond better to a male authority figure. Who knew what kind of humiliating relationship Tate had with adult women.

She'd been a little worried about Hendricks. He had decades of experience with traditional interrogations and possessed tremendous instincts. But this was something else entirely. She'd been coaching him for a couple weeks now, and while he got it in the abstract, it was very different in reality. She needn't have worried; Hendricks was a natural.

"You've done it now, boy," Hendricks had begun.

Tate tried to speak through the gag, but it came out as futile, clownish gurgles.

"You really thought you could get away with it? That we wouldn't find you? Bad news there, son. This is the end of the line for you. Should have gotten off this train a long time ago, and now you're a long way from home."

Jenn had yanked the gag out of his mouth.

"I want a lawyer," Tate had demanded.

Hendricks had laughed. "There are no lawyers in hell, son."

"This is illegal. I want my lawyer!"

"I am your lawyer. What do you need?"

"You can't do this," Tate had cried. "I know my rights."

"There are no rights out here, boy. Where do you think you are?"

Tate's eyes had been wide, filled with an animal panic. His mouth had worked silently like he still had the gag in it.

"Listen to me good. We know who you are. We know what you did. We all know it. We just want to hear you say it. You messed with the wrong man's child, and there's no coming back from that. You have any idea how powerful he is? How far he can reach? I suppose not, or you would have messed with some other kid, am I right? Well you're in it now, boy. What's done is done. There's only here and now left to think about. How it's going to go for you from here on out. Is it going to go long or is it going to go short? That's what you need to decide. How do I make it go short? Because, believe you me, you don't want this to go long."

"I swear to Christ, I don't know what you're talking about. I don't know what you're talking about!"

Hendricks had slapped him. Not hard, but the effect had been powerful. Tate had shut his mouth and stared up with sullen fear.

"That kind of talk right there," Hendricks had said. "That kind of talk is what makes a short thing go long."

"I swear," Tate had whined, eyes darting back and forth between them. There were no good cops here.

Hendricks had put a finger to his lips. "We're going to leave you to think about it. Long or short. It will be up to you. Tell the truth, this will be short and painless. Lie to us and you will hurt for a long, long time. Understand?"

Tate had said nothing.

"Understand?" Hendricks had bellowed.

Tate had nodded, his head lolling weakly to the side.

"Good," Hendricks had said. "So, we're going to leave you to think about it. In the meantime, my partner and I are going to go have dinner. Rest up for you. When we come back, you're going to tell us all about Suzanne Lombard. Or I'm going to make a mess of you." Hendricks had said it flatly. Matter-of-factly, like he was choosing between two light beers.

Hendricks had nodded to Jenn, and they'd left Tate dangling in his cell. Tate had yelled after them and kept yelling long after they had slammed shut the locker's rollaway door.

"Who?" he'd cried repeatedly. "I don't know no Suzanne! I don't. Who the fuck is Suzanne Lombard, man? I don't know her."

And on and on.

Jenn actually preferred the speed metal to the sound of Tate's voice. He was so compelling. So sincere and blameless. It would have made her heart ache if she hadn't seen this act many times before. An interrogation room was the greatest acting school ever devised. They clung to the lie like a life jacket. So convincing that she wondered sometimes if they actually convinced themselves of their own innocence. In the long run, it never made any difference. The only variable was how long it would take him to realize the same thing. She checked her watch and hit a button on her console. Tate's cell was engulfed in searing white light. His body recoiled, and his mouth stretched into a scream as if the light itself burned.

The music played on.

———

Jenn and Hendricks stepped out of Tate's cell and into the sunshine. Jenn pulled the rollaway door down. They stripped out of their jumpsuits and ski masks. It was foul in there, and they were both bathed in sweat. She watched Hendricks walk away in his boxers and Doc Martens to light a cigarette. In her shorts and sports bra, she was in no position to complain. They were way past social niceties.

She went back to their command post and fished four bottles of water out of a cooler. She found a spot in the shade, put her back against a wall, and slid down to the ground. When Hendricks came back, she handed him a bottle.

"What time is it?" he asked.

"Fuck the time, what day is it?"

He fished his phone out of his gear and held it up to her face.

"When did it get to be Thursday?" she asked.

They'd been working on Tate for four days now. It had been slow going, and they weren't in complete agreement about how much progress they were making. Hendricks thought it was going well. Jenn was a little surprised at how long it was taking. She'd expected Tate to cave before now. The pathetic child molester had more backbone than she'd expected. What was certain was that Tate had accepted the fact that his situation was hopeless. He had come to see Jenn and Hendricks as the gods of his life. At this point, his game was admitting to just enough to make them happy without incriminating himself—a standard intermediary step. He talked in circles, but the circle was getting smaller every day.

For the first two days, he had clung to the fairy tale that he'd never even heard of Suzanne Lombard or her abduction. It was a stupid lie, and Hendricks had leaned on Tate hard enough to get him to give it up on Tuesday. They'd made Tate tell them the whole story. Tate was, if anything, an aficionado of the Suzanne Lombard case and knew it backward and forward. But so far Tate hadn't told them anything that wasn't in the public record and swore up and down that he didn't know anything about hacking ACG.

"How much more do you want to push him today?" Hendricks asked. "He needs to eat. Sleep. Boy's borderline incoherent at this point."

Jenn nodded. Hendricks was right. They were in danger of breaking Tate, but not in a productive way. She would need to update George. He wasn't going to like it. Calista was on his back to produce results, and every day they were here increased their chances of detection. That would not be good, to put it mildly. It didn't matter one bit what Tate had done. If she and Hendricks got caught with Tate, they were all going away for a long, long time.

Hendricks's phone buzzed in his hand. He looked at it, puzzled at first, but then confused and worried.

"What is it?" she asked.

"It's Vaughn's virus."

"What about it?"

"It just went off."

Gibson lay flat on his stomach and watched Jenn and Hendricks peel off matching jumpsuits. He was on the roof of a storage unit at the far end of Grafton Storage that offered an unobstructed view of Jenn and Hendricks's little operation. He didn't know precisely what was happening to Tate, but he had a pretty good idea. The fact that it required ski masks made him a little sick. Tate was vile. No question. But that didn't justify whatever was happening down in that storage locker.

So why hadn't he called the police? The timer on his moral high ground had long since counted down. He might not be down in the trenches with Jenn and Hendricks, but at this point he was every bit as guilty. How far was he willing to let this go if it meant finding out what Tate knew? Where was the line?

He felt his phone buzz and put down his binoculars. He was expecting a call from ACG at some point. He'd called on Monday to ask if he could keep the car for an extra week, maintaining his ruse that he was back in the DC area. George's assistant had said he'd get back to Gibson, but there'd been no word since. Apparently ACG had other things on its mind.

He looked at his phone; he was half-right. It was a text, and it was from ACG, but it had nothing to do with the car. The beacon virus that he'd embedded in ACG's files had gone off.

The text was a long spool of data and ended with GPS coordinates. His original virus's instructions had been to install itself onto the hacker's machine, cover its tracks, and use the host machine's GPS to phone home. But that hadn't happened. Instead it had been downloaded and remained dormant ever since. That's why they'd resorted to staking out the library.

The original virus had been a long shot anyway, and Gibson hadn't been surprised when it hadn't gotten a hit. It would have required the subject to open ACG's files on a machine with an Internet connection. But the hacker had done what Gibson would have done, which was take the downloaded files somewhere safe and look at them on a stand-alone computer.

For it to go off while Tate was locked up confirmed Gibson's suspicions. His virus couldn't self-activate. For it to phone home now, someone would have to intentionally connect it to the Internet. It sure as hell wasn't Kirby Tate. So who? Who had just rung the dinner bell?

Gibson focused his binoculars back on Jenn and Hendricks, who were locked in a heated discussion. Hendricks was pointing angrily at the unit where they had Tate. Jenn had both hands, fingers interlocked, on top of her head in a gesture of disbelief.

Not the text message you were expecting either, was it?

Gibson tried to put the pieces together. If the virus had gone off now, then it meant that another player was involved. Tate had a partner. Someone who knew computers and had activated Gibson's virus either by mistake or on purpose. His money was on on purpose. But why?

If it was on purpose, then the partner knew Tate had been taken. Activating the virus might be a signal to lead them away from Tate. Unwilling or unable to risk a call to the police, the partner was doing the next best thing in trying to divert suspicion away from Tate and, in so doing, saving his life. Make them think they'd grabbed the wrong guy.

And give himself away? It just didn't make sense. He and Tate would have to be awful close for the partner to stick his neck out like this when he could just give them Tate and slip away. Unless Tate wasn't his partner at all but a pawn. In that case, what was WR8TH's play?

Gibson gave up trying to calculate all the permutations and went back to the binoculars. Jenn and Hendricks had settled on a plan. They squared Tate away and shut him up in his storage unit like a box of old clothes. In half an hour, the two were back in street clothes. They made their usual exit from Grafton, with Jenn going over the wall and unlocking the gate for Hendricks in the SUV.

When they were gone, Gibson dropped off the roof and jogged to where they were holding Tate. They had locked him in but hadn't locked the unit where they were staying. He found the keys on a hook just inside the rollaway door. He wondered what he would find in there. He didn't know, but he hoped there was still enough of Tate left to answer his questions.

CHAPTER TWENTY-FIVE

Hendricks took the Pennsylvania Turnpike toward Pittsburgh. Jenn paged through her notes, trying to make sense of what had happened and hoping she wouldn't rue the decision to send Gibson back to DC. She could have really used his expertise right about now. She ran her tongue across her teeth while she thought. For once, Hendricks was quiet, the possibility that Tate was the wrong guy too horrible to contemplate.

"Tate is no angel," Hendricks said.

She didn't answer and flipped to another page in her notebook.

The GPS coordinates that Vaughn's virus provided led them to North Huntingdon—an older, established suburban neighborhood outside Pittsburgh. Mature, stately trees shaded the streets, and the lawns were expanses of perfect green. Luxury vehicles were parked in every driveway.

"All this needs is a lemonade stand," Hendricks said.

The GPS coordinates led them to 1754 Orange Lane, a broad two-story Tudor with white trim. A police car was parked in front, and Hendricks kept driving. At the end of the block he pulled over to the curb, adjusted his mirror, and sat back to watch.

"This is the house?" Hendricks asked.

"If Gibson's virus is accurate." She called Rilling and had him look up the tax records on the house.

Twenty minutes later, an officer emerged from the house with a man and woman following him. The couple appeared to be in their early thirties, and even from a distance it was clear they were unhappy. The man shook hands with the officer while his wife clung to her husband's arm. They stood out on their porch until he drove away. The woman waved good-bye.

Jenn's phone buzzed. It was a text from Rilling. The house was owned by William and Katherine McKeogh. She showed it to Hendricks.

"What do you think?"

Hendricks waited until the couple went back inside, turned the car around, and parked across the street from the house.

"Only one way to find out," he said, getting out.

An elderly woman sitting on her porch put down her book and waved to Jenn. She waved back politely. Friendly neighborhood. Guards down. Welcoming. She followed Hendricks across the street and up the front steps of 1754 Orange Lane. Hendricks rang the doorbell and stepped back from the door. He shook out his neck like he was limbering up for a fight. As the woman opened the door, Hendricks put on a warm, friendly smile that Jenn had never seen.

"Can I help you?" Katherine McKeogh had a kind face and large brown eyes. Her hair was pulled back with an emerald bow.

Hendricks retrieved a business card from the breast pocket of his jacket and handed it to her.

"Sorry to bother you at home, ma'am. My name is Dan Hendricks. This is my partner, Jenn Charles. We were hoping to ask you and your husband a few questions."

"Are you detectives?" she asked, looking at his card.

"No, ma'am. ACG is a private firm. We've been contracted to consult with the local police department and evaluate their procedures."

"Oh," she said, handing the card back. "But an officer was just here."

"We're not police, ma'am. We're doing follow-ups. It's part of a countywide initiative to improve services. We were in the area and thought we'd stop in and see if we could take a report while it was fresh in your minds."

"He was very nice. I don't want to get him in any trouble."

Hendricks smiled sweetly. Jenn was starting to see why he'd had one of the highest case-closure rates in the LAPD. His transformation bordered on disturbing.

"I understand completely," Hendricks said. "This isn't really about him, or any particular officer for that matter. We're just looking for ways the county can improve and enhance their interactions with the community."

"Kate? Who is it?" A man's voice from inside the house.

"Some detectives with questions," the woman called back into the house.

"We're not detectives, ma'am."

A moment later, a tall, thin man in chinos and a polo shirt came to the door.

"What's going on?"

"Bill, these folks want to talk to us about the officer who took the report on our break-in," Mrs. McKeogh explained.

"Sir. My name is Dan Hendricks, and this is my partner, Jenn Charles." He extended a hand, which Bill McKeogh shook.

Hendricks caught Jenn's eye while he repeated his spiel about consulting with the police. Making it very clear that they were not, contrary to his wife's impression, detectives. The McKeoghs didn't strike Jenn as child-kidnapping pedophiles. They would have been in their early twenties when Suzanne disappeared.

The McKeoghs were more than happy to help. Hendricks produced a notepad and took notes as he asked a series of questions about the responding officer's demeanor, helpfulness, and attention to detail. Jenn played along, asking follow-up questions to coax the details of the break-in out of them. Like most victims of minor crime, the McKeoghs were eager to discuss it.

Mrs. McKeogh had come back from the grocery store and found the back door jimmied open. She'd called the police, and her husband at the office, which was only ten minutes away. She'd waited out front until the (very nice) officer arrived. The (very helpful) officer confirmed that the back door had been jimmied open and did a sweep of the basement and upstairs before letting them reenter the house. It didn't appear that anything had been taken, although there hadn't been time yet to look carefully. They didn't have a lot of cash or expensive jewelry in the house.

"The officer said it was probably just kids."

"Why?" Jenn asked.

"Because there was no damage inside the house," Mr. McKeogh said. "The officer told us that in most robberies speed is the main concern, so they would have ransacked the house. The officer said the house should be a disaster. Drawers dumped out, pictures thrown on the floor, looking for anything valuable. Usually there's a lot of damage, he said."

"And you're sure nothing is missing?" Hendricks asked.

"No, not for sure. We really just started checking."

"The officer gave us his card and said to call him if we realized something was gone," said Mr. McKeogh.

"May I see it?" Jenn asked.

Mr. McKeogh handed it over. Jenn copied down the officer's information and gave it back.

"What about electronics? Any computers in the house?"

"We have a stereo and a couple of TVs. My wife has a laptop, and we have a desktop set up in the family room for the kids."

"We don't want them looking at the Internet where we can't see them," Mrs. McKeogh said.

Hendricks asked, "So your computers are password protected?"

"Mine is, but the family room computer isn't. Why?" Mrs. McKeogh asked. "Do you think that's what they were after?"

"Anything's possible. You should probably check it to be safe."

Mrs. McKeogh went back into the house. She returned a minute later shaking her head. The computer appeared normal.

"Mind if I take a quick look at it?" Jenn asked.

The computer sat on a small wooden desk in the living room. It had an old CRT monitor. The tower sat on the floor beside the table, its front-access USB panel cover hanging open.

"Do you mind?" Jenn asked, indicating the keyboard.

The computer was in sleep mode. Jenn hit the space bar. The hard drive spun to life, and the monitor flickered on. Someone had opened a Word document and typed two words: "Terrance Musgrove."

The McKeoghs glanced at each other.

"Do you know him?" Jenn asked.

"No," Mr. McKeogh said. "Well, not exactly."

"We bought the house from him," Kate McKeogh said.

"From his estate," her husband corrected.

"We bought the house from the estate. It's kind of sad. I don't really know the whole story," she said.

"It was only the second house we looked at. We lowballed them, figuring they'd counter, but they took it. It was a steal to be honest. Thirty-day closing. Nothing like a motivated seller."

"Any idea why?" Jenn asked.

"It's a touchy subject in the neighborhood. No one really talks about it," said Mrs. McKeogh. "But we found out later . . . you don't like to feel you're capitalizing on someone else's misfortune. It's not the kind of thing you want to bring into your home. Bad energy."

Jenn cocked an eyebrow at them.

"He killed himself," Mr. McKeogh said.

"William," Mrs. McKeogh said in a shocked voice.

"Well, he did. In the house somewhere. Why we got such a good deal. It sat vacant while his siblings figured out what to do."

"What happened to him?" Hendricks asked.

Mr. McKeogh shrugged. "Couldn't tell you. It's not something the neighborhood likes to talk about. Just a tragedy."

"And I don't want to know," Mrs. McKeogh interjected. "It's in the past. It might have been one of the kids' bedrooms. Then what would I do?" Mrs. McKeogh shut down the computer. "There. That's better."

Jenn felt her phone vibrate. She stepped away to check it. It was an automatically generated text message from ACG saying that Vaughn's virus had gone offline. She nodded to Hendricks, who wrapped things up with the McKeoghs. They all shook hands at the front door, and Hendricks and Jenn walked down the driveway. Jenn showed Hendricks the text message.

At the end of the driveway, Jenn turned back to the couple.

"One other thing," she said. "How long have you lived in the house?"

"Nine years in April," Mrs. McKeogh said.

"And how long was the house vacant?"

"About two years," said Mr. McKeogh.

"Ah, okay. Thanks for your time." Back in their vehicle, Jenn turned to Hendricks. "Where does that rate on your strange meter?"

"What? That someone broke into a random house on gingerbread lane to download Vaughn's virus onto a kid's computer? All in broad daylight?"

"Yeah, that," she said.

"About an eleven."

"But they're not suspects. We agree on that?"

"Those two? Yeah."

"So why do it? Why here?"

"Maybe someone's playing with us. Letting us know he's too smart to be caught. Spinning us in the wrong direction."

"You think he's just showing off?"

"Well, this fits my definition of a wild goose chase."

"I don't know. That's a lot of risk. Break into a house? In this neighborhood? In broad daylight? And for what? To waste a couple hours of our time? Doesn't seem worth it."

"Maybe he's making an alibi for Tate. Possible there's two of them."

"That we know of. There's a lot you can do in a couple hours," Jenn said. "We should get back to Grafton."

"Agreed." Hendricks started the engine but left it in park. He stared at his partner. "What?"

"I'm going to talk to the neighbor."

"The old lady?" Hendricks asked. "What for?"

"I need to know what Terrance Musgrove has to do with any of this."

It was forty minutes before she got back in the car.

"Did she give you her recipe for snickerdoodles?"

Jenn held up a finger to him as she took out her phone and called George. She explained the situation to George as Hendricks listened.

When she finished, George asked her what they needed.

"An open-records check on a Terrance Musgrove." She spelled the name and gave his address here on Orange Lane. "Ten years ago, approximately."

She turned to Hendricks.

"What county are we in?"

"Westmoreland," Hendricks said.

George told her he would call ahead and smooth the way with the local police. Jenn dragged her tongue over her teeth. Either Tate had a partner, or they had the wrong guy. God help them if Tate was innocent.

CHAPTER TWENTY-SIX

Gibson slipped inside the storage unit and pulled the rollaway door down behind him. The smell of stale sweat and vomit greeted him in the blistering heat. He heard movement from behind a chain-link fence that stretched across part of the room, and cautiously approached in the gloom.

Kirby Tate was curled into a fetal position on a pile of straw. Despite the oppressive heat, he was shivering. Through narrowed eyes he watched Gibson with a feral wariness. Gibson forced a smile onto his face and held up a bottle of water that perspired in the heat.

Tate licked his cracked lips.

"Take it."

Tate shrunk back toward the wall as though Gibson were threatening him with a gun, not offering him a drink.

"Take it," he repeated. "It's all right."

Gibson opened the bottle and placed it inside the chain-link fence. It fell over and rolled in a lazy circle, spilling water on the concrete floor. Tate followed the bottle with his eyes, calculating the risk. Hunting for the trap that must be there. He scurried forward without standing up, snatched the bottle, and squatted on his haunches to gulp it down. When the water was gone, he retreated back to his straw nest.

Gibson set another bottle of water where Tate could see it.

"Still thirsty?"

Tate nodded.

"I need to ask you some questions."

Tate became still.

"I'm not going to hurt you. I won't even come in there. Just come closer so I can see you. I'll give you the water, and we'll talk a little."

Tate shifted but didn't move. Gibson tried again. Coaxing, reassuring. He put the second bottle of water inside the cell and sat on the ground outside the makeshift cell, hoping to seem less threatening.

Gradually Tate crept to the front of the cell. Gibson needed to be able to see the man's eyes. Tate took the bottle and sat cross-legged on the ground facing Gibson.

"So don't good cops get masks?" Tate said.

"Who are you working with?" Gibson asked without preamble.

"What?"

"Who's your partner?"

"I ain't got no partner, man. I ain't got no partner 'cause I ain't doing nothing. Like I told them other two motherfuckers."

"So you've been a little angel since they found that girl in your trunk?"

A strange expression crossed Tate's face. Part shame, part pride, and something else that made Gibson's skin crawl.

"Yeah, man, I'm on the up and up and up. Learned my lesson. Scared straight, you know?" Tate smiled his off-kilter version of an upstanding citizen's smile.

"And the kiddie porn on your laptop?"

Tate's smile faltered. "Man, that's nothing. Come on. Just pictures, you know? For in my head. Keeps me outta trouble."

"Just something to take the edge off, huh?"

"Yeah, man, yeah. The edge. You know . . . So my trunk stays empty." Tate winked.

Gibson choked back the urge to throw up.

"Y'all right there, man?" Tate was grinning now. Messing with him a little.

Gibson forced himself to smile. "I'm good. No, I get that. Keeping the edge off is the responsible thing to do."

"Responsible. Right. Responsible," Tate agreed.

"You're just doing it for them. To protect them."

Tate nodded vigorously. "Exactly. That's exactly what I'm doing. I don't wanna hurt nobody no more."

In Tate's mind, he was the good guy. He only looked at child pornography to prevent his bad impulses from taking over. He did it for the children.

Right.

An eternal truth of the human condition was that no one ever thought they were evil. No matter how reprehensible their actions, people always convinced themselves they were justified.

"Was that why you were at the library?"

"Yeah. He said that Fridays was the day the library wiped its servers so it was safe. No one would ever know."

"Wiped its servers?" That didn't even mean anything. No one wiped servers weekly, and certainly not a public library.

"Yeah. He's a pro."

"He?" Gibson asked. "He who?"

"Dunno, man. The guy. He, him. I got this letter a year ago. Well, it wasn't a letter. It was just like taped to my front door. Said he was an 'enthusiast' just like me. That he'd found me on the Internet on some database where you can find ex-cons that done like me. Had my picture and address. He said he was reaching out to everyone in the area to see if, maybe, we could create a little ring of 'like-minded individuals,' that's how he put it. All fancy and shit. *Like-minded individuals.*"

"For what?"

"To pool our . . . you know . . . resources."

"Trade pictures?"

"Pictures. Videos. Uh-huh."

Gibson saw it. Someone had turned the National Sex Offender Registry into a social networking site for pedophiles. The start-up from hell.

"And he told you about the library wiping its servers?"

"Yeah, he said on Fridays during the wipe that it was all anonymous, and I could download as much as I wanted and no one would ever notice."

"But only on Fridays."

"Only on Fridays. Guy had it all worked out."

"So who is this guy, Kirby?"

"Dunno, man. Never met him."

"Come on."

"No, for real. That was like rule numero uno—that everyone should be anonymous so we couldn't flip on each other if shit went south."

"But he knew who *you* were."

"What?"

"Well, he approached you. So he knows who you are."

That evidently hadn't occurred to Tate.

"Yeah, but I didn't know who he was, so . . ."

He watched Tate's stupidity collapse on itself.

"Kirby, it's only anonymous if everyone's identity is secret."

"Oh. Yeah, I guess so. But, you know, he was real cool." Tate's wheels were spinning now. "He helped me out. He wouldn't give me up."

"And yet here you are."

Tate stared at him for a long minute. Gibson made it a point not to look away. He watched the tumblers slowly fall into place in Tate's mind.

"Motherfuck," Tate spat.

The big man stood and stalked in circles around his cell, cursing. Gibson allowed Tate to blow himself out and slump back to the ground in front of him.

"What did he tell you I done? I mean, we didn't even trade all that much."

"You didn't?"

"No, man. I sent him some stuff at first, but he never had anything for me, so I quit sending."

"What about the other members of the group?"

"Weren't no other members. He kept trying to recruit some but couldn't get them to go for it. Too scared, he said. Said we was the only ones with vision. I offered to help recruit, but he said it was safer if it was just him."

"How'd you communicate with him?"

"Notes at first, like on my door. Then after I got me a computer we'd talk on there." Tate had a thought. "He told you I done the Lombard girl, didn't he? That's why you motherfuckers flew me to this hellhole. 'Cause he said I done her."

Flew? In the gloom, he hoped Tate didn't catch his flicker of puzzlement. He'd worry about a mystery flight if it came to it. In the meantime, he just rolled with it.

"That's what he told us."

"Well, it's bullshit."

"Do you have Internet at your house?"

"My house? Nah. I ain't got nothing at that shitbox."

"Why not?"

"Can't afford it, man. You know how much an ex-con child molester makes these days? Not much. People ain't exactly falling over themselves to hire me. I do odd jobs for my uncle. Day work when I can get it, but the fuckin' Mexicans like to hire their own, you know? Ain't no way I'm affording no satellite. Besides, what I need the Internet for? I mean, all I gotta do is go to the library for that, so what's the point?"

"The Internet does other things, Kirby."

"No, man. Too much reading. Fuck that. Hurts my head."

"So why are you protecting this guy?"

"I ain't protecting him. I don't know who he is. I ain't got shit to do with him."

"You hacked into ACG for him. Or did you just do that on your own?"

"Them other two was going on about that too. Man, I didn't hack shit."

"Come on, Kirby. I'm trying to help you here, but you have to give me something. At the library on Friday, you downloaded about ten megabytes of data from ACG."

"No, man, no. I was just downloading, you know, pictures and shit."

"Don't lie to me. We watched you. It was on your computer."

"Look, the only reason I bought the computer off him was to get my pictures. That's it."

Gibson stopped. "He sold you the computer?"

"Yeah, I was gonna buy a used one, but he said no, he could build me a new one. Make some tweaks to help keep me safe."

Gibson shut his eyes. Tate didn't have a mysterious benefactor, and he didn't have a partner. He had a puppet master. It was brilliant. Recruit a pedophile to a nonexistent kiddie-porn ring, custom build him a computer, and sell him some crap about Friday afternoons.

"What? What is it?" Tate asked.

Gibson ignored him. WR8TH had built himself a back door into Tate's computer and had been flying it remotely like a drone. WR8TH had downloaded data from ACG through Tate's computer, left a copy on the hard drive for them to find, and walked away clean. The real WR8TH could have been a thousand miles away, or he could have been at the next park table.

It was smooth. But Gibson still couldn't see what WR8TH's game was. It was a big chance to take ten years after you'd gotten away with it. What was so valuable that he was willing to risk capture?

What he did know was that WR8TH hadn't found it yet. Triggering Gibson's virus today proved that. It wasn't an accident, and he hadn't done it to protect Tate. Tate was a pawn. Triggering the virus meant that WR8TH still wanted to play. Gibson just needed to figure out how to play back.

He stood to go.

"Come on, man, I know you figured something out."

Gibson passed his remaining provisions through to Tate. A bottle of water, a granola bar, and an apple.

"I didn't do nothing. You know it."

Gibson turned to leave.

"*Nothing* is an awful big word."

CHAPTER TWENTY-SEVEN

Officer Patricia M. Daniels was not particularly happy to see them. She looked Jenn and Hendricks up and down and went back to hunting and pecking at her keyboard.

"Usually we handle this sort of thing by written request. Do you know that? We take the Right-to-Know Law very seriously. Very seriously," Patricia explained without looking up. "We have an Internet portal so that the general public, that would be you, can submit your request online."

"We understand that."

"There's a system, see? I get to people in order," Patricia said. "I have a stack of requests right here. And I told your Mr. Abe that. I did. But your Mr. Abe, he has to have it today. ASAP. He's so important, what does it matter if there's a g-d system or not? And I told him as much. But then he gets on with Frank," she said, gesturing back toward the sheriff's office. "And in five minutes, Frank is out here telling me I've got to drop everything and accommodate you people."

"We really do appreciate it," Jenn said.

Hendricks looked out the window.

"To serve and protect," said Patricia.

The records room was in the basement, but her desk was on the second floor. "They tried to put me down there with the records, but it's biblical dusty down there. Ain't fit for a dog," she said. "I told Frank as much. Told him he should try it and see how his asthma likes it."

Patricia fished her keys out of a drawer and eased herself out of her chair. She was no more than five feet tall and built like a Russian nesting doll, starting from a wide base and narrowing to a point. Patricia adjusted her belt and ambled toward the basement with a slow, bow-legged gait.

The basement records room was divided into rows by metallic shelving units that were stacked with labeled boxes. Patricia wasn't lying about the dust. It coated every surface. It was dark, and the fluorescent track lights, themselves coated in dust, did little to pierce the gloom.

Everything within the last five years was stored electronically, Patricia explained. There were plans to convert the remaining paper records, but the county hadn't freed up funds to hire a clerical team to do all the data entry. She unlocked the metal gate and led them down an aisle. She had a slip of paper with the record information and used it like a treasure map to find her way. Patricia ran a tight operation. Everything was boxed, labeled, and organized professionally, and she found the case file quickly.

"I worked LAPD for twenty years. This is the best records room I've ever seen," Hendricks said.

"Thank you," she said, brightening up. "Why didn't you tell me you was police?"

"Just me. She was CIA," he said by way of explanation.

"CIA? Oh. Well, we won't hold it against her," Patricia said, elbowing Hendricks in the side.

"We just appreciate all your help," Hendricks said.

"Well, I am happy to help. I had my dander up because when your Mr. Abe first called, and I heard 'suicide,' I just assumed he was talking about the Furst case. And you know I won't have such a recent case until next year sometime."

"Furst?" Hendricks asked.

"Evelyn Furst," Patricia said, and when that still didn't clear up the matter, "Doctor Evelyn Furst."

"Sorry, we're not from up here," Jenn said.

"Evelyn Furst? The dean of medicine at the University of Pittsburgh?" Patricia prodded them unsuccessfully. "Well, it's been in the news a lot. She lived up this way and commuted. Real tragedy. She was a nice lady. Did a lot of good. So when I heard 'suicide,' I just figured you were reporters looking to embarrass her. Not that you asked me, but in my opinion, it's a free country and that ought to include your life. Not that I ever would, but it's the principle."

"You said it," Hendricks said.

"Nope, just here for that one," Jenn said.

"Say, Patricia, you think I could get a copy of the Musgrove file?" Hendricks asked.

"The whole thing?"

"It would sure help me out."

Patricia looked uncertain. "I don't know. I shouldn't."

Hendricks put a hand on her arm reassuringly. "I understand," he said. "But you have my word, we'll be discreet. I'd owe you one. It would get the boss off my back. Truth be told, he can be kind of difficult."

This seemed to strike a chord with Patricia, and she grudgingly agreed but only after extracting several redundant promises from them. She led them back upstairs to make a copy of the file. She handed it over with a request.

"You need something else, you just call me direct. All right?" She handed Hendricks her card. "You're right about your boss. That Mr. Abe put Frank in a funny sort of mood."

They promised they would and said their good-byes.

"Going to call her?" Jenn asked once they were outside. "She took a shine to you."

"Sure I am. Right after you call Vaughn."

That stopped her dead in her tracks.

"What?"

"You heard me." He winked at her.

"Hey, do me a favor and stand right there. I need to get my gun out of the car."

"Yeah, I'll be sure to do that, Annie Oakley." He waved the Musgrove file at her. "So, wanna eat and read?"

Anywhere but a diner was Jenn's only caveat. A week of Vaughn's obsession with diner food had made her internal organs feel like they'd been sautéed in grease. She needed something fresh and green.

As they walked to a restaurant down the block, she imagined Vaughn sitting at that diner of his, the Nighthawk. Cash in his pocket and free and clear of this mess. It made her smile. He wouldn't have sat still for what she'd done. Big a screwup as he was, he had a stubborn morality that she admired. Especially when he saw someone was getting the short end of the stick, as maybe, just maybe, Kirby Tate was getting now. There was a time it would have bothered her too. But now she just saw Tate as the debris that inevitably surrounded this type of operation. It didn't even bother her that it didn't bother her.

At the restaurant, they spread the file out on the table and sifted through it while they ate. The story of Terrance Musgrove was a sad one. By all accounts Musgrove was a beloved member of the community—a local boy who put himself through college and then veterinary school. Jenn scanned a stack of written accounts that all told variations on Musgrove's willingness to go above and beyond the call of duty for a sick animal. His dedication had enabled him to expand his practice over the years to include four locations. There had been talk of franchising nationwide, but it hadn't gotten beyond the planning stages.

Nonetheless, he'd done well for himself, and he and his wife, Paula, had lived on Orange Road for eighteen years with their daughter, April.

The long and the short of Terrance Musgrove's life was that he was a good man. His wife was the author of two children's books and was heavily involved in local charities. His daughter went to private schools and was a competitive swimmer who had first swum at the Junior Nationals when she was eleven years old. The family took an annual ski vacation to Wyoming and had a summer place a couple hours away on Lake Erie.

Jenn put down the stack of papers and picked at her salad.

"Jesus, this is rough," Hendricks said.

"What you got?"

"So, the daughter, April. Fourteen years old. She and the mom were up at their summer place. Just the two of them."

"On Lake Erie."

"Yeah. So the kid and the mom are sitting on their dock, and the kid decides to go for a swim. So the police speculate that the kid swam straight out."

"And?"

"And got clipped by a motorboat. Bashed her head pretty good."

"Enough to kill her?"

"Enough to knock her out. She drowned. But it gets worse. Mom panics, jumps in, and swims out to save her kid but isn't the swimmer her daughter is. Drowns trying to save her."

"Musgrove have an alibi?"

"Says something about us that that was my first question too. Yeah, the doctor was in the office the entire day. About a hundred witnesses. Police sniffed around but never had any reason to pursue him as a suspect."

"And his suicide? How soon after did he do it?"

"Not for another two years. But people close to him said he struggled with depression and drinking in the aftermath. Said he got pretty bad by the end. Mood swings, personality change, his business suffered."

Jenn sat back and mulled it over in her mind.

"This is a sad story, but I still think we're on a wild goose chase here. What does a dead vet have to do with us?"

"Look at the date," Jenn said, tapping the autopsy report.

Hendricks glanced at it and shook his head. "What? That he killed himself a couple months after Suzanne disappeared? That's kind of a stretch, don't you think?"

"It would be if someone hadn't led us to his old house and typed his name into a computer."

"So what's your theory? That Musgrove becomes despondent? Loses his mind and starts talking to Suzanne on the Internet in some delusional attempt to replace his daughter; meets, seduces, and kidnaps Suzanne; and God knows what else? Realizes what he's done after it's too late and kills himself out of guilt?"

"Actually that's better than what I had."

Hendricks rolled his eyes. "Come on."

"Both girls were fourteen. Why not?"

"Well, for one, if Terrance Musgrove took Suzanne, and Terrance Musgrove is dead, then who is Kirby Tate in all this? And for two, who broke into the McKeoghs' house today?"

"Yeah, I don't know," Jenn admitted. "I feel like I'm playing poker with only three cards."

Hendricks was nodding. "Kind of hard to make a hand."

"What are we missing?" she asked no one in particular.

They paid the check and gathered up the Musgrove file. A photograph caught Jenn's eye. It was a crime-scene photograph of Musgrove's suicide. Terrance Musgrove had hanged himself. She felt a chill pass between her shoulder blades. Hendricks saw her expression change and looked at the photo questioningly.

"What is it?"

"I don't know. I need to get back to Grafton. I need my laptop. And . . ."

They looked at each other. Neither wanted to say the name Kirby Tate.

"You got it. Do you want to call George or shall I?"

"He's going to love this, isn't he?" she said.

"Not the word I would use."

CHAPTER TWENTY-EIGHT

Gibson sat at a table in the shade of the Carolyn Anthony Library. It was comforting after the storage locker. He'd also hoped returning to the scene of the crime would help him think, offer some clarity, but the library was just a library and had nothing useful to tell him. The park was quieter than last Friday, when he'd allowed himself to be conned. Allowed himself to be spun expertly and aimed at Tate.

How easily he had fallen for it.

Gibson looked at the GPS coordinates his virus had pinged back to ACG as if they might speak to him. No doubt Jenn and Hendricks had followed those coordinates, wherever they led. Perhaps they would take WR8TH unawares, but Gibson doubted it. WR8TH was much too careful. If Gibson's virus had activated, it was only because WR8TH had allowed it. But why reveal himself now? Didn't it defeat the entire purpose of setting Tate up? Unless, of course, WR8TH couldn't resist— was so arrogant that he couldn't stand not sharing his brilliance. Gibson had certainly known hackers like that. He'd been that hacker. This was exactly the kind of move he would have made . . . when he was fifteen years old.

His laptop pinged, and a small text window opened in the corner of his screen. The hairs on Gibson's arms stood up.

WR8TH: i hear ur looking for me

It was written in the shorthand Pidgin English favored in some quarters of the Internet. It sounded like teenage laziness, but Gibson made no assumptions. He knew programmers in their fifties with master's degrees who used it regularly online. There were sites where good grammar could get you banned on general principle.

GVaughn: I don't even know who this is.

WR8TH: true. but u know who im not, dont u???

GVaughn: You're not Kirby Tate.

WR8TH: whoops

Gibson could feel WR8TH laughing at him.

GVaughn: You really did a number on him.

WR8TH: dont feel bad for that trash. he got wat he deserved

GVaughn: That's pretty cold-blooded.

WR8TH: yeah not me who stuck him in a storage locker

GVaughn: You're quite the puppeteer.

WR8TH: r u all butthurt that i found yer program?

GVaughn: It served its purpose.

WR8TH: only cuz i let it

GVaughn: Why did you?

WR8TH: why didnt u go back to dc like they told u?

GVaughn: Been spying on us?

WR8TH: little bit. answer the question, why r u still here?

GVaughn: Suzanne.

WR8TH: same

Gibson stared at the last line of text for a full minute.

GVaughn: WR8TH. I assume that's who you're supposed to be? The WR8TH?

WR8TH: *blush*

GVaughn: I don't believe you. I think you're some wannabe using his old alias.

WR8TH: ur not that stupid. u know its me

GVaughn: Do I?

WR8TH: who else would have that picture???

GVaughn: It's probably a fake. Just like you.

WR8TH: stop playing games. ur wasting time

GVaughn: Maybe it's my turn to waste time. All your games kinda put me in the mood.

A long pause followed.

WR8TH: r u done?

GVaughn: For now. So it was you? You took Suzanne?

WR8TH: sort of...more complicated than that

GVaughn: What do you mean "sort of"?

WR8TH: i'm not wat they think I am

GVaughn: What do they think you are?

WR8TH: a pedophile like tate. that i
hurt her

GVaughn: And you didn't?

WR8TH: no, i loved her

GVaughn: You understand how sick you
are, right?

WR8TH: not wat u think

GVaughn: Okay, you loved her, all right.
So where is she now, Romeo?

Another long pause. Gibson was afraid he had goaded WR8TH
too far. He couldn't help it. Listening to this son of a bitch talk about
loving Bear was too much to take. But he needed to keep him talking.

GVaughn: Are you capable of feeling bad
for what happened to her?

WR8TH: every day man. every lousy day

GVaughn: So where is she? Come on. You
have us all in suspense. We've played your
little game. You've proven how clever
you are. The Tate thing was very clever.
Golf clap. But enough with the foreplay,
huh? It's main attraction time. The big
reveal. Isn't that what the point of all
this is? Some kind of creepy confession?

Unburden your soul at last?

WR8TH: u dont get it

GVaughn: Or do you just miss the attention?
Just hoping to inflict a little more pain
on the people who loved her?

WR8TH: I LOVED HER!!!!

GVaughn: Then where is she?

WR8TH: i dont know

GVaughn: Fuck you, "WR8TH."

WR8TH: swear to god. i thought they knew

GVaughn: They? Who is they?

WR8TH: abe consulting group. why u think
i hacked them???

GVaughn: You think ACG knows where
Suzanne is?

WR8TH: i did yeah

GVaughn: And now?

WR8TH: i dont know anymore

Gibson sat back and stared at the screen.

WR8TH: hey, dont look so surprised,
gibson

That got under his skin; he was sick of being toyed with. He punched at the keys.

GVaughn: Oh, you know my name. Good for
you. That must have been real hard to
figure out from all the ACG files you took.

WR8TH: u kidding? i would know u anywhere.
BrnChr0m. ur a legend. Suzanne talked
about u all the time

That rocked Gibson. Bear talking about him to her captor. That he'd been on her mind even then. He felt a great sweeping sadness. Sadness mixed with a returning anger.

GVaughn: Oh, yeah? She talk about the
good old days growing up on the shore
while you were torturing her, or whatever
sick shit you did?

WR8TH: KISS MY ASS!!! i LOVED her. she
did actually and she talked about u a
lot. how u called her Bear and read to
her

GVaughn: I don't want to hear it from
you.

WR8TH: wat u did to her dad. how mad u
made him

GVaughn: Screw him.

WR8TH: we agree on something at last haha

Gibson could not think of how to respond to that. WR8TH had
something on his mind.

WR8TH: why are u here?

GVaughn: To find out what happened to
Suzanne.

WR8TH: ur partners. are they here to
kill me?

GVaughn: I don't know.

WR8TH: want to know something funny?

GVaughn: What?

WR8TH: i trust u. pretty stupid, huh?

GVaughn: Yes.

They'd been typing back and forth faster and faster. Gibson was
striking the keys hard, and it slipped off his fingers before he thought
about it. He took his fingers off the keys and stared at the blinking cur-
sor, waiting for a response, but none came. He cursed under his breath.

```
GVaughn: Still there?
```

Nothing. Damn, damn, damn. Come back, you sick bastard.

Wait, what?

Gibson scrolled up and reread what WR8TH had typed: "don't look so surprised." *Look* so surprised? Son of a bitch could *see* him. WR8TH was here. Watching him the way they had watched Tate. And now that he thought about it, WR8TH must be on the library network too. How else had he opened a chat client on his laptop?

Gibson glanced around to see who else was in the park. He locked eyes with a tall, gangly man sitting opposite him two tables over. No more than twenty-five. *Scruffy* was the word that best described him. Long, curly blond hair launched off his head in all directions in a way that made Gibson doubt a comb was one of his earthly possessions. A failed attempt to grow a beard had resulted in long, patchy sideburns and a mustache that curled down but not far enough to reach the thick tuft under his chin. He wore a black Slipknot T-shirt—a heavy-metal band Gibson had heard more than enough in the Corps. Trendy black glasses couldn't disguise the man's wide, friendly eyes.

Eyes that held Gibson's gaze and didn't blink or look away.

```
GVaughn: WR8TH?
```

He typed it slowly, thinking it couldn't be him. The man sitting in front of him would have been a kid when Suzanne disappeared.

The man glanced down at his laptop, then looked up and nodded.

CHAPTER TWENTY-NINE

Hendricks slowed as he turned into Grafton Storage.

The gate was wide open.

Jenn saw it too. She opened the passenger door and stepped out as the Cherokee rolled toward the gate. Gun flat against her thigh, she trotted alongside the Cherokee, using the open passenger door as a shield. Someone had made short work of the padlock with bolt cutters.

"What do you think?" Jenn asked without taking her eyes off the road ahead. "Police?"

"The police wouldn't advertise like this. The gate would be shut to lure us in. This is something else."

"Agreed. We go in."

Hendricks nodded grimly. Jenn shut her door so he could maneuver more easily and fell in behind the Cherokee.

When they were inside, Jenn shut the gate behind them. On the one hand, she was trapping them inside with their uninvited guests. On the other, she was trapping their guests in with them. Guess they'd find out which soon enough.

She tapped the back of the Cherokee, and Hendricks rolled forward slowly. Jenn took an angle so she could both stay in cover and keep line of sight as they came up on intersections between storage buildings. She didn't hate that they had the late afternoon sun behind them either. It would help offset the tactical advantage of an enemy ambush.

They made their way to the storage locker housing Tate. It was slow going, but if it was a trap, it gave the best chance of spotting it. Jenn agreed with Hendricks, though. If it had been a trap, the gate would have been shut and they wouldn't have known until it was too late. The gate was a message, and as they neared Tate's cell, she saw that the rollaway door was up.

Hendricks drove past Tate's cell, and Jenn slipped off the bumper and took the near corner. Hendricks stopped thirty feet away and came back on foot, taking the far corner. He held up three fingers, and Jenn nodded. He mouthed "Three, two, one," and Jenn rolled around the corner in a crouch, gun up, scanning the room. Hendricks followed a half step behind, hard and fast, dividing the room in half.

They came to an abrupt halt, their guns falling limply to their sides. Tate's cell door was open. Tate was gone.

Jenn took a step forward and stepped in something wet. She looked down. A wide blood trail led from Tate's cell. Someone had bled out in the cell. Wherever Tate was now, he hadn't walked there.

"Well, this isn't ideal," Hendricks said, holstering his gun.

She looked at him, thinking. "Leave the camera running?"

"Yeah," Hendricks said.

"Roll it back and take a look. I'm going to call George."

"Don't you think, maybe, we should talk about what's happening here?"

"Not now. Check the tape."

"Then what?"

"We break camp and get the hell out of Dodge. Then we talk about what's happening here."

Jenn stepped out into the late afternoon sunshine and dialed George. It went to voice mail, and she hung up and dialed again. Voice mail again. She frowned. She hung up and called Abe Consulting's main line. It also went to voice mail. She checked her watch. Reception went home at five thirty; it was nearly six. Usually there was someone in the office. She tried Rilling but got his voice mail. Where was everybody? She called George back and left a perky two-word message. "Call me!" It was code to send the cavalry. Cavalry would be nice.

She heard Hendricks yelling her name. She found him by the monitors.

"You're not going to like this," Hendricks said.

"I don't like it now."

Hendricks hit "Play." It was a static shot of Tate in his cell. After a minute, the cell lit up and immediately dimmed again as the rollaway door opened and closed. Gibson Vaughn came into the frame.

"Oh, you have got to be kidding me . . ."

"I told you."

"Vaughn did this? I don't believe it."

"Just watch," Hendricks said.

Vaughn sat down by the cage. Tate eventually came and sat nearby, and the two men talked for a long while before Gibson left. She would pay good money to know what the two of them talked about, but the room was only wired for video. Hindsight was twenty-twenty.

Hendricks sped up the recording. The time stamp zipped ahead ninety minutes. In the recording, she watched the cell light up as the rollaway door opened yet again. Hendricks slowed the tape to its normal speed, and Jenn leaned forward. Tate stood up and came to the front of the cage. He seemed to be expecting someone, and his face registered first surprise and then fear. Whoever it was stayed back behind the camera. Tate began gesturing frantically, hands up in a gesture of surrender and compliance.

The first bullet caught Tate in the shoulder and exploded through his collarbone, twisting him around. Tate staggered backward, trying to right himself, but before he could regain his balance he was hit twice more and sent sprawling. Once Tate was down, the gunman kept firing. Jenn watched in horror as Tate's body was riddled with bullets. She counted at least a dozen impacts. There was a pause as the gunman reloaded and emptied a second magazine into Tate's unmoving body.

"Jesus."

A minute passed. A piece of black tape was placed over the camera. Hendricks sped up the recording again; twenty minutes passed before the tape came off. And, like a magic trick, Tate's cell was open and his body gone.

Hendricks hit "Pause," and the two of them stared at the frozen image.

"Ain't that some shit?" he said. "Think it was Vaughn? He could have broken into the McKeoghs', set off his virus to lure us out, and looped back to take care of Tate."

"No way."

"Suzanne Lombard was personal for the guy," Hendricks said. "If he thought Tate took her, you don't think he has it in him?"

"Maybe. But do I think Vaughn let himself be recorded and then came back ninety minutes later, blacked out the camera, and killed Tate? No, I do not."

Hendricks thought it over and grunted agreement. "We're going to wish this was Vaughn."

"I know."

"So who killed Tate? The real WR8TH?"

Jenn didn't have a response.

"What did George say?" Hendricks asked.

"He didn't pick up."

"Perfect. What now?"

"Break everything down. Bleach the cell and torch it. Erase all the surveillance footage."

"What if we need the footage later?"

"Risk we have to take."

CHAPTER THIRTY

George Abe pressed a button on his steering wheel and hung up the call. After a moment, a bootleg recording of the Rolling Stones live at the LA Forum '75 filled the car. Jagger was growling about a gin-soaked barroom queen. It was the Stones's first tour without Mick Taylor, and Ronnie Wood, while an able replacement, was still his own man and was putting his own mark on another man's chords. It was one of George's favorites, but he needed to think. He turned off the stereo and drove in silence.

The call with Calista had not been pleasant. She was impatient, anxious, and increasingly frustrated that things weren't proceeding more quickly in Somerset. That was part of it, but the death of her older sister had shaken her profoundly, and to say the least, Calista was not at her best.

Calista had been close to her sister, and in many ways Evelyn Furst was the last member of the family of which that could be said. Evelyn had shared Calista's passion for the family's legacy and standing in the world. Her career as a surgeon and as the long-serving dean of medicine at the University of Pittsburgh was something Calista celebrated. Evelyn had been a pioneer for women, had led the way, and to Calista that was what it meant to be a Dauplaise.

To say no one had seen it coming was an understatement. He had known Evelyn for years, and she'd seemed fine when he'd spoken to her at Catherine's birthday party. Perhaps a touch preoccupied but certainly not suicidal. Of course, it was impossible to predict how the loss of a spouse might affect a person. Evelyn's suicide note had been profound and sad.

Calista had rather dramatically taken to talking about being "alone in the world." It was hard to be alone in the world when you had thirty houseguests, as Calista did for the funeral, but Calista had always drawn a distinction between those who upheld her notions of Dauplaise values and those who absconded to Florida. Evelyn was, in Calista's mind, one of the last who'd carried the torch. A true Dauplaise. She was only interested in results and had no understanding of the time such matters required. And things in Pennsylvania had definitely become more complex.

She was also incensed that he had brought Gibson Vaughn home. She hadn't wanted him there in the first place, but now she was acting as if his absence explained why things were taking so long. She continued to voice doubts about Jenn and Dan's competence, and was pushing hard for George to take over personally in Somerset.

George understood, in principle. She was grasping at straws, trying to impose order over a situation that was still fluid. This was not her world, and looking for Suzanne this way exposed her to considerable risk. As it exposed them all. It weighed heavily on him. He had sanctioned these tactics when Kirby Tate had been an abstract. But now Tate was a person, and George had to question the morality of asking his people to go down this path. Jenn and Dan were loyal. When this was all over, George knew there would be a reckoning.

His phone buzzed—a voice mail from Jenn. She'd called twice while he'd been talking to Calista. She and Dan would have had time to digest the Musgrove file by now. George had decided against mentioning Musgrove to Calista until he knew better how it fit into the investigation. She was liable to overreact to such an unexpected curveball.

A black SUV passed him at speed and pulled in front of his car aggressively. George tapped the brakes as the SUV slowed and red-and-blue strobes erupted from its running lights. A second black SUV pulled in tight behind him, boxing him in. The lead vehicle squelched a short burst of siren and signaled for George to pull over. George followed their directions and hit a button on his steering wheel. The car asked what number to call.

"Jenn Charles," he said, pronouncing it crisply.

The phone rang as their little convoy came to a stop on the shoulder. It went to voice mail, and he spoke a single word: "Meiji."

He hung up as a tall agent in a dark suit rapped on his window. A second agent was at the passenger door. The doors of the SUV behind him were open, but neither agent had moved. George rolled down his window an inch.

"FBI. Are you George Abe?"

"Yes."

"I need you to come with us, sir."

"What's this about?"

"Pennsylvania, sir. Step out of the car, please." The agent tried the door, but it was locked. "Unlock the door, sir."

"Am I under arrest?"

"We'd prefer to avoid that if we can."

George weighed his options.

"Step out of the car, sir."

"Give me a minute," George said.

"Step out of the car, sir," the agent repeated, an undercurrent of menace in his voice now.

The agents were out of the other SUV now. George could feel things escalating quickly out of his control. He unlocked the door, and the agent opened it. George stepped out and allowed the agent to pat him down.

"He's clean," the agent said to his partner on the other side of the car.

The agent ushered him in the direction of the lead SUV. His partner crossed toward them, slipping between the bumpers of the two vehicles. George glanced down at the sizeable dent in the SUV's rear fender. The Bureau was slipping. There had been a time that a Bureau vehicle with a dent would have been off the road and in the shop in twenty-four hours. Then George caught the license plate, and his smile disappeared. It didn't have government plates, and it wasn't from DC or Virginia either. Tennessee plates . . . he'd been too busy calling Jenn to pick up on it when he'd been pulled over. The agent hadn't shown him credentials either. Whoever they were, they weren't Bureau. He'd have given a small fortune for the gun in his glove compartment, but it was a long way away now.

George slowed and patted his sports-jacket pockets as if he'd forgotten something.

"I left my phone in the car," he said and began to turn back.

"Just get in the car, sir." The man took him by the arm to turn him back.

The man expected a little resistance. George offered none and used the tug to spin back toward him. His fist caught the man under the chin. It was a hammer blow, and if it had caught the man in the throat as George intended, then it would have crushed the larynx. But George's feet had slipped slightly in the gravel, and it didn't land cleanly.

As it was, the man's head snapped back, and he let out a snarl of pain. George couldn't run, and while he might take both of these men in close quarters, the two men in the rear SUV would put him down. George went for the man's gun instead. His only chance was to draw it before the partner reached him. George found the gun's grip and pulled it clear, twisting sideways as he did to put some space between himself and the partner who was closing in on him. George tried to bring the gun up, but it snagged on the lining of the man's jacket. He wrenched it free, but the partner was on him by then.

Taser voltage exploded through George's central nervous system.

Jenn sat in the passenger seat of the Cherokee. On the dashboard lay the crime-scene photo of Terrance Musgrove's suicide. In the shock of discovering Tate's murder, she'd forgotten all about it. Wondering what Gibson Vaughn was doing back in Pennsylvania had brought it back to her.

She opened her laptop and scrolled to the background dossier on Gibson that she'd compiled before George had approached him for the job. She clicked on the folder labeled "Duke Vaughn" and flipped through it until she found the photograph. Her eyes went back and forth between the two.

"How is this possible?" she said out loud.

It was a small thing—a meaningless detail in the bottom corner of each photograph. Unremarkable unless you looked at them side by side. She'd figured that it was her memory playing tricks on her, or at best it was just a coincidental similarity. But this, this was something else. This was the same. Exactly the same. How was that possible?

She showed it to Hendricks.

"How *is* that possible?" he echoed.

She didn't know, but it tied Duke Vaughn to what was happening in Somerset. To Suzanne Lombard's abduction.

Hendricks looked at her seriously. "This stays between us until we know what it means."

"Even Vaughn?"

"Especially Vaughn."

They went back to work, because it was paralyzing to think about it too long, and they couldn't afford to be here a second longer than was necessary. That worked for a while, until the sound of Hendricks cursing rousted her. She thought she was well versed in all of Hendricks's tones, but there was an unfamiliar edge to his voice. He sounded panicked. She found him standing over their weapons bag.

"What's the matter?" she asked.

"One of them's gone."

"One of what's gone? One of the guns?"

"One of the Glocks." His voice had dropped to a near whisper. "That and two mags."

"Anything else?"

"There doesn't need to be anything else missing."

"What are you talking about?"

"He owns me. That's what I'm talking about. I couldn't figure why he took Tate's body instead of sticking it with us. But now I get it."

"Oh, shit."

"Oh, shit is right. I've fired that gun a thousand times. I hand-loaded those mags. I cleaned those guns. My prints are on every moving piece, on every shell casing."

"And he didn't leave any shell casings . . ."

"No. Not one. I double-checked. He picked them all up. Which means he can dump the body, plant the gun, and ring me up for murder any time he wants. So like I said, he owns me."

"Who?"

"Whoever it was. Gibson. WR8TH. Does it even matter?"

Hendricks looked at her expectantly like a child who just wanted a comforting word. She didn't know that she had any. They thought they'd been two steps ahead, when in actual fact they'd been well behind. She wondered what George would do in this situation. These kinds of blind-alley crises were his forte, but he was nowhere to be found. So the question really was, what would *she* do?

"That boy and I have a chat coming," he said.

"It's not Gibson."

"Convince me."

"This?" Jenn gestured at the blood still in Tate's unit. "This isn't him."

"Then why isn't he home where he belongs? Why did he lie? That bullshit about keeping the car a few extra days? He's been here the whole time," he said. "And that stunt at the McKeoghs' house with the computer. That doesn't sound like something he'd pull?"

"So you're saying Gibson tripped the virus to draw us away, circled back to have a one-on-one with Tate. In plain view of the camera, mind you. Then, came back an hour and a half later to kill Tate, this time making sure to stay out of view. And for good measure, takes the body and steals one of our guns. Does that sound likely to you?"

"Maybe not, but I surely intend to find out."

CHAPTER THIRTY-ONE

WR8TH sat down across from Gibson. The world's most-wanted pedophile, in the flesh.

Up close, WR8TH looked even younger. He could easily pass for a college student. He had a boyish energy and trouble sitting still. His deep-set brown eyes twinkled with a mischievous intelligence. But around his eyes were deeply etched worry lines, and one tuft of his hair had turned an incongruous gray. WR8TH fiddled uneasily with his glasses but let Gibson stare. He took out a pack of cigarettes, slid one halfway out of the pack, and pushed it back in.

"Better not," he said. "Mrs. M. will have me arrested. That would be funny."

"Mrs. M.?"

"Mrs. Miller." WR8TH hooked a thumb toward the library. "Friendly neighborhood librarian. Drinks her face off in her office, but God forbid I smoke a cigarette out here."

"Oh, Christ, you're her network guy," Gibson said.

"Guilty."

"Man, I knew the gear was a little too good for a little public library. You work for the county?"

"Yeah, it was hard not to overdo it."

"No, you did a good job. Fooled me."

"Thanks." WR8TH seemed genuinely pleased by the compliment. "Billy Casper," he said by way of introduction.

Gibson shook his hand mechanically, the guy's name ringing a faint bell. "How is that possible? How can you be WR8TH? I mean, you were what? Seventeen? Eighteen?"

"I was sixteen and five months."

"And five months?"

"Yeah, I'd just gotten my driver's license."

"And you're telling me, straight up, that you're the one everyone's been looking for all these years?"

"Believe me, I waited for the FBI to huff and puff and blow my world in. The first two years I was paranoid like a mother. Thought our phones were tapped. I was the most stressed-out high-school junior ever. Parents made me go to a shrink. Thought I was schizophrenic or something. I mean, WR8TH? Wraith? Casper? How hard is that to figure out? But they never did. Guess they weren't looking for an actual sixteen-year-old."

"Where is she?"

"I don't know."

"Where is she?"

"I. Don't. Know."

"If you're lying to me . . ."

"What? You'll kill me?"

"Yeah," Gibson said, surprised by the certainty of it.

Billy smiled. "Good. I wouldn't be here otherwise."

"You really took her?"

"Jeez, man, I didn't 'take' her. It wasn't like that. It's more complicated than that."

"Care to uncomplicate it?"

"Yeah, I do. Care to take a drive?"

"Where?"

"I'll show you. I'm not going to tell you, so don't ask. Can't have you telling your partners where I am."

"I thought you trusted me, and anyway, they're not my partners anymore."

"Screw you. I told you my name. Where I work. Maybe that's all you get right now." Billy flashed angry. "Maybe you show me a little reciprocity, huh? You don't know what they're capable of."

"Yeah, actually, I do."

"No, actually, you don't," Billy said.

Gibson drove them north out of Somerset. Billy seemed to relax as soon as they were away from the library.

"I have a gun. I guess I should tell you that," Billy said.

Gibson gave him a sidelong glance.

"Look, I'm not going to use it or anything. Not unless you cross me. Deal?"

"Just don't point it at me otherwise. Deal?"

"You got one? In your bag or somewhere?"

"I don't. Don't really like guns."

"What? You were in the Marines, man."

"Not by choice."

"Truth," Billy said simply. He looked out the window and smiled.

Gibson glanced over at him again. "What are you grinning about?"

"Just a relief, you know? You don't know what it's like to have to carry this kind of secret around for ten years. It eats at you. There are days you just want to bust. You don't know how many times I thought about posting her photo to Reddit. Sit back and watch everyone lose their shit." Billy pointed off to the right. "Turn here at the light."

"Why didn't you?"

"Why didn't I what?"

"Post it. Come forward anonymously."

"Because of Mr. Musgrove."

"Who the hell is Mr. Musgrove?"

"My neighbor growing up."

Gibson waited for him to elaborate, but Billy withdrew under a dark cloud of brooding.

They drove north in silence. Gibson kept prodding him, but Billy said he'd rather just show him. Billy asked if he could smoke. Gibson said it wasn't his car, but Billy cracked a window anyway and carefully blew his smoke away from him.

Whatever else Billy Casper might be—kidnapper, compulsive liar, schizophrenic—he seemed like a decent kid. Gibson could see why Bear trusted Billy enough to meet him in Breezewood. Enough to get into his car. Gibson liked Billy Casper. But that wouldn't save him if he'd done something to Bear.

They drove north for several hours. As they got close to their destination, Billy became agitated again. Gibson heard him groaning quietly under his breath, as if tectonic plates were shifting inside him, grinding against each other. Billy didn't seem aware he was doing it.

"I hate coming back here," Billy said.

They turned onto a narrow, shoulderless road that ran parallel to Lake Erie. It was wooded on both sides, but, through the trees and down long dirt roads, he could see expensive beachfront homes and the sun sparkling off the lake. It was a beautiful, peaceful part of the world—rustic but intentionally so. It amazed him that such a place existed less than an hour from Kirby Tate's house.

Most of the properties didn't have mailboxes and weren't otherwise marked. It would have been easy to get lost, but Billy knew exactly where they were.

"Okay, it's your next left. No, not this one, the next."

"What's on the left? Whose place is this?" Gibson asked.

"Mr. Musgrove's. I mean, not anymore, but it was before. It's his sister's now. She lives in Saint Louis. She was here for two weeks in June. Probably won't see her again until next year."

"And you know this how?"

"I'm her caretaker."

"How many jobs do you have?"

Gibson slowed and turned off onto a bumpy, poorly maintained dirt road. Like many of the properties, it had a chain between two wooden posts blocking the way. Billy hopped out and unlocked the chain and threw it off the road before getting back in the car. Trees rose up steeply on both sides, and there was barely enough room for the car to pass.

"You want to go easy here. There's kind of a big rock in the road." Billy pointed to a spot up ahead.

After a quarter mile they cleared the tree line and came upon a large two-story wood-framed house. A wide, appealing porch supported by white columns encircled the house. The dirt road gave way to a circular white stone driveway. An elm rose in the center of the loop. Short trimmed grass ran down both sides of the house and sloped away toward the water's edge. To the left were parking spots, but Gibson pulled up in front of the stairs leading up to the porch.

"Why are we here, Billy?"

"This is where I hid Suzanne. I think I got Mr. Musgrove killed for it."

Anguish swept over Billy Casper's face. He got out of the car and walked, head down, toward the lake. Gibson watched his shoulders buck uncontrollably; Billy was crying, sobbing, really. Gibson let him go, giving him a little space, then followed.

Billy sat on a wood pylon at the end of the dock. Gibson sat opposite him. Twice, Billy seemed to get a handle on himself, but then his mind would overturn some long-repressed memory and the tears would come again.

"I'm not actually a crier," Billy said, half laughing, half crying. He rubbed his hands over his face. "Impressive, huh?"

"It's not easy saying some things the first time."

Billy looked up at him gratefully and nodded.

"Who is Mr. Musgrove?"

"Aw, man, he was the nicest guy. You would have liked him. Talked to everyone like an equal, even kids. We used to talk about video-game design, computer science. Stuff like that. But like a grown-up, you know? He just knew a little bit about everything. Everything interested him. We were a couple of doors down from them. My parents were good friends with them. My mom jogged with Mrs. Musgrove a couple times a week. Ginny and my sister were like this." Billy crossed two fingers tightly. "I mean, before the accident."

Billy pointed out to the lake and told Gibson about how a boat had hit Ginny Musgrove, and how her mom had drowned trying to save her. How it had wrecked Terrance Musgrove—the drinking and anger that followed. A family destroyed in a matter of minutes.

"He only ever came out here one time afterward. Right after it happened, with the police. After that it was like the place didn't exist."

"Why didn't he sell it?"

"Dunno. Probably just easier to keep paying the mortgage than actually deal with it, I guess. He was such a mess afterward. But he shut it down. Cut off the phone, electricity. Everything but gas and water."

"And he hired you to take care of it for him?"

"Yeah, he had a guy at first, but it didn't work out. Threw a party down here or some shit—Mr. Musgrove fired him. So after I got my driver's license, Mr. Musgrove hired me. I wasn't really the party-throwing type, you know? He paid me to drive out once a month and make sure everything was good. Said he just couldn't do it. That's why I figured it was a good place for Suzanne to hole up. No one ever came out here but me."

"And you're still the caretaker?"

"Yeah, after he died, it was just easier for his sister to keep me on."

"How did he die?"

"Committed suicide. Like your dad."

The mention of his father stung. Billy had brought it up so naturally, so unexpectedly. The way only an old friend would. It reinforced his sense that Billy Casper believed they were connected in all this through Suzanne.

"I don't want to talk about my father."

"Oh, I'm sorry."

"It's okay. But if Mr. Musgrove committed suicide, why do you say you got him killed?"

"'Cause I don't think he did."

They walked back up to the house. Billy unlocked the back door and let them into the kitchen. It was a large, bright room the color of cantaloupe rind. There was a small island with a double sink and a dishwasher. Billy gestured toward a wooden kitchen table by the window.

"Recognize it?"

Gibson looked at the table. The picture of Bear had washed it out, but it was the same table.

"That's it?" he asked.

"That's it. It was against that wall back then. Suze was sitting right there. That chair," Billy said. "That exact chair. I took the picture the night we got here. She didn't want me to. She was so tired, man. But relieved too, you know? She hadn't been eating real well the last few weeks. She was so thin I couldn't believe it. Considering. But she was still so beautiful. I was just happy she was here, you know? We were together at last."

Gibson heard the ache in Billy's voice and tried to reconstruct the moment in his head. Bear sitting there. Exhausted. Billy excited, like a puppy dog, snapping her picture. He tested the image to see if he believed it. Had sixteen-year-old Billy Casper engineered one of the most famous disappearances in American history? Was it as simple as a couple of kids hiding out at a lake house?

"How long was she here?"

"Six months, two weeks, and a day," Billy said. "We played a lot of Settlers of Catan."

"Settlers of what?"

"Catan, man. You've never played Settlers? It's a board game. It's awesome. She loved it. She was so much better than me, though. Always kicked my butt."

It defied belief. Two kids hiding out, playing board games, while the FBI tore the country apart looking for them. But then law enforcement had made all the wrong assumptions and gone looking in all the wrong places. One thing was for certain: if Billy's story weren't true, then he was either a world-class liar or a world-class lunatic. But try as he might, Gibson couldn't pick up on a single false note.

CHAPTER THIRTY-TWO

"Mr. Musgrove's sister repainted," Billy said, "but that's about it. She packed all Mr. Musgrove's personal stuff, all the family things, and stored it up in the attic. That's why it's so creepy coming here. I mean, it's the same furniture and everything, just other people's pictures. Like their lives were just a coat of dust, and someone took a cloth and wiped it away. But that's how life is, right? You think a place belongs to you, but it doesn't. You're just biding time. And time comes someone will box up your stuff too, like you were never here. Man, I hate coming out here."

"So why do you? You could quit."

"I have to," Billy shrugged. "This is where I lost her."

That made a lot of sense to Gibson. They stood in the kitchen while Billy told a story he'd waited ten years to tell. He'd been dancing around the subject since they'd met at the library, but now it came tumbling out.

Billy Casper, a.k.a. WR8TH, had met Suzanne in a chat room. That much was true. Except he really was sixteen, and not some middle-aged pedophile as the FBI hypothesized. They'd become friends and confidants. According to Billy, they talked every night for hours. Some nights, he would fall asleep in front of the computer. Suzanne had been coy about who she was and would only say that her father was important and that if Billy helped her, it would be risky.

"Didn't even know her last name until she got here. Swear."

"Would you have helped her anyway?"

"No doubt," Billy said without hesitation. After a second to think about it, he nodded his head emphatically, agreeing with himself. "No doubt."

Once they decided to go ahead with it, they'd spent weeks plotting a route that would avoid high-security areas with a lot of cameras and watchful eyes. He'd coached her on how to avoid being noticed by the police. What to say if someone got curious as to why a fourteen-year-old was traveling alone.

"And she was almost fifteen," Billy said defensively. "I was fifteen when we started talking. We were only a year apart. So it wasn't weird, you know? We never had sex or anything. We kissed a couple times, but that was it. She was my friend."

"She was my friend too."

"I know," Billy said. "That's why you're here."

"So what was up with the Exxon station?"

"Right? Getting caught on camera? What *was* that?"

"You didn't know she was going to do it?"

"Are you kidding? Hell no. Not until it popped up on the news."

"Did you ask her about it?"

"Ask her? We had our only fight about it. She said it was an accident, but that was such utter bullshit. She knew what she was doing."

"Which was what?"

"Sending a message, man."

"To?"

"Don't ask me. All I know is it wasn't friendly. Did you see her eyes? She looked right at the camera and all but gave it the finger. I just wish she hadn't waited until she was in my backyard to do it. She put

Pennsylvania on the feds' radar. After they released the security tape, I was so sure that the couple at the pump had seen my car. Every time there was a knock at the door, I figured it was the feds come to raid my house. Put my whole family in handcuffs. Can you imagine?"

"They wouldn't knock."

"Well, the worst part was my mom was obsessed with the case," Billy said. "It was on all the time, and she watched it twenty-four-seven. I was sitting right next to my mom when it aired the first time. They showed the security tape and at the end froze on Suze's face. I had a goddamn aneurism. Spilled grape pop all over the carpet. Mom thought I was freaking because of what happened to my sister. I was all, 'Yeah, yeah, that's it.' Mom burst into tears, telling me it was all right. How it wasn't my fault. Gives me this big hug. I felt so shitty, but I didn't want her knowing I was the guy."

"What happened to your sister?"

Billy grimaced as if he'd meant to leave that part out. "Why do you think I fed you Kirby Tate?"

Gibson sat back, covering his mouth with the back of his hand. "Casper? It was your sister in his trunk? Trish Casper is your sister?"

Billy nodded, rage settling over him like a toxic shroud. "We're standing outside the supermarket, me and Trish. Waiting for Mom. She'd forgotten corn. Mom always forgot like three things. Tate, son of a bitch, walked right up and took Trish by the hand and just led her away. You know what he said to me?"

Gibson shook his head.

"He said, 'I'll bring her right back.' With a little smile like it was our little secret. And when I looked confused he says to me, 'Your mom said it was okay.' And I just stood there like an idiot and let him take her."

"Hey, you were a kid."

"Yeah, well, I'm not now. And what they say about revenge? It's true. You wait ten years; they never see you coming. It was so easy. Such a gullible prick."

"Jesus, Billy."

"Whatever, man. Fuck him. My sister still takes antianxiety meds because of what he did. She's got phobias they haven't even bothered to name yet. Can't go outdoors. Can't deal with strangers. Can't buy her own groceries. Last year, I dropped a glass in her kitchen. She wouldn't stop screaming for five minutes. She's never had a regular job." Billy's eyes became distant. "Yeah, Tate should have stayed in jail . . . where he was safe."

Gibson stared at him. Up until now he had had trouble believing that Billy Casper could be behind Suzanne's disappearance or the hack at ACG. Billy just seemed too sweet. A little simple. But now, listening to him talk about Kirby Tate, he could see it. See the anger and calculating intelligence that lurked behind Billy's friendly eyes.

"How long did you say you kept her here?"

"I didn't keep her anywhere. How many ways do I have to say it? She stayed here for six months. By choice. I would drive up on the weekends and after school if I could come up with an excuse. It was a long-ass drive, so it was hard to stay for too long. I made up a job. Fake friends. Just to mix up my lies. But mostly she was here by herself. That was hard. Knowing she was alone. But she seemed to like it. She read a lot. I think in a way she kind of needed it. Time to think. She was always happy to see me, but I never felt like she was that sad to see me go either. You know?"

Gibson nodded.

"Swear to God, I felt like I spent half my life in a car. I couldn't keep going to the same grocery store or pharmacy." Billy laughed at the memory. "I had to drive all over Pennsylvania so people didn't wonder what a sixteen-year-old was doing buying prenatal vitamins."

Gibson's hand went around Billy's throat and drove him back into the kitchen counter. The lie he'd been waiting on. "What happened to not having sex?"

"What? No, man! We never had sex," Billy coughed out as Gibson's hand tightened its grip. "She was pregnant when she got here! Why do you think she ran away?"

That was a thunderbolt that Gibson couldn't quite wrap his mind around. It was like having all your assumptions unceremoniously dumped out on the road and watching someone back a truck over them. To realize how profoundly wrong everyone had been about Suzanne. He let go of Billy and backed away.

"Sorry," Gibson said. "I need a drink."

Billy rubbed his throat but didn't move. "Probably still beer in the fridge."

Gibson found a six-pack of Iron City lager in the back. He took two and offered one to Billy. Billy wouldn't take it. Gibson opened both bottles and held one out to Billy again.

"I'm sorry," he said again.

Billy's eyes blazed and then cooled. He took the beer, and the two men stood in the kitchen, drinking in silence.

"Whose was it?"

"She said some boy back home named Tom."

"What did she tell you about him?"

"Not a lot. Just general stuff. She always changed the subject pretty quick. Honestly, I thought you were the father at first."

"Me?"

"Yeah. The way she talked about you all the time. I just figured she'd made up the boyfriend thing to protect you."

"Well, it wasn't me."

"I know. *I know.* You were already locked up. Math didn't work."

"Want to know something funny?"

"What?"

"The authorities thought you might be Tom B."

"I wish," Billy whispered under his breath.

A funereal silence fell between them.

Finally Gibson asked, "Was Bear . . . was she angry at me?"

"Are you kidding? She kept coming up with ways she could get in touch with you. I was like, are you out of your mind? He's on trial. You got the whole world hunting for you, and you want to risk sending secret messages to some dude in jail?" Billy put up his hands. "No offense."

Gibson waved him off. "None taken."

"Why would she be mad at you?"

"For going after her dad."

"Nah, man. She fucking loved you. Made me jealous. It was like . . . well, you could just see it. And anyway, she wasn't what you'd call her dad's biggest fan."

"Really?" That wasn't how Gibson remembered it at all. "Do you think Lombard knew? That she was pregnant?"

"No, I don't think so. Suze wasn't showing when she left. But I know she was real scared of what he'd do if he found out. How he'd go insane. Guy has a temper, apparently. She talked about how all he cared about was his career. What he'd make her do if he found out. About the baby. That's why she had to get away from him."

Gibson played out the story in his mind. Bear gets pregnant by her boyfriend, the mysterious Tom B., and decides to run out of fear for what Lombard would do if he found out. That much sounded plausible. But why enlist the help of Billy and not her boyfriend, Tom B.? Did Tom even know he was a father? Or was that exactly why he hadn't come forward?

"So where are they now? Where's Suzanne? Where's the baby?"

"I don't know."

"Come on, Billy. It's a hell of a story so far, but you need a better ending."

Billy went to the fridge and took another beer and drank it, his back to Gibson, without taking a breath. Gibson watched him put the empty on the counter and drink another. Then he wheeled around and glared at Gibson, fire returning to his eyes.

"Listen, if I knew what happened to Suze, do you think you'd be here now? Why would I need you if I knew? I didn't risk exposure, didn't risk my life hacking into ACG so we could share this tender moment. I did it because I don't know what happened to her, and it's *killing* me. I loved her, man, but I failed her. I couldn't take care of her like I said I would. Her baby—something wasn't right. The last month she was always uncomfortable. She tried to hide it, but there was blood. She couldn't get around, you know? I didn't know what to do for her. Leaving her alone killed me. I wanted to take her to a hospital. I begged her so many times, but she was so damn stubborn."

Billy was weeping now.

"I got her a disposable phone to call me in case of emergencies. One night I get a message." Billy stopped, trying to compose himself, his voice dropping to a near whisper. "Her voice is real soft. She says she loves me, and she's sorry. 'They promised to help me,' she says. That's it. I called back but the phone just rang and rang. Don't you get it? I couldn't help her so she called someone who could. And they came and they took her away. But wherever they took her, it wasn't home. Right? I kept expecting to see a 'missing girl reunited with family' story on the news. But ten years and nada. So, I mean, where *is* she?"

"You thought George Abe took her?"

"I thought maybe there was a chance. Thought maybe she called her dad, and he sent his henchmen to clean it up. Do damage control. Prevent her from embarrassing him. Look, I know how it sounds, but you'd be amazed at the paranoid shit I've dreamed up in the last ten years."

"That's pretty damn paranoid."

"I'll do you one better. The night Suze called me? That was the same night Mr. Musgrove 'killed himself.' After I got her message I drove out here, and she was gone. When I got back home, like five hours after leaving, my street was full of cop cars, a fire truck, and an ambulance. They were bringing Mr. Musgrove out in a bag."

"And you think it's connected?"

"I think Suze refused to rat me out. I think they assumed it was Mr. Musgrove who took her, since it was his house."

"You think Benjamin Lombard had your neighbor killed to prevent a political scandal? Come on, Billy. You've seen too many movies."

"Have I?"

"And you think this mysterious 'they' was George Abe?"

Billy shrugged.

"So you hacked ACG to see if George was hiding something?"

"It was the easiest place to start. Even I'm not crazy enough to hack the vice president."

"He wasn't the vice president then."

"I know. I'm just fucking with you. But yeah, I went after ACG. Rattle the cage to see what falls out. At least something to point me in the right direction, but George Abe doesn't know any more than anyone else. He's looking for her just like the rest of us. I should have let it go then. I mean, I knew that. Eventually they'd bring in someone who would find me."

"We didn't find you, Billy. You walked up and sat down."

"Yeah, but it was you."

"What do you mean?"

"I mean, you, you were a sign or something. I recognized you right away. Remember the day you jogged down to the library? I was there, in my car, using the library Wi-Fi. I looked up and there you were, Gibson Vaughn. BrnChr0m. The legend."

Gibson put up a hand. "Give me a break."

Billy cracked a smile to show he was being a wiseass. "I don't know . . . I saw you there, and I just had a feeling that you'd get it."

"You don't know me."

"No, but Suzanne did. She trusted you, and that's good enough for me."

"That's a big risk to take on a ten-year-old reputation."

"Maybe. But I'm just tired, man. I'm tired of hiding. Tired of being scared. One way or another, I need this to end."

"You still love her," Gibson said.

"Don't you?"

"Not the same way you do, but yeah. She's not the kind of girl you stop loving."

"Amen," Billy said. "Come on. I want to show you something."

CHAPTER THIRTY-THREE

"Meiji."

Jenn played George's voice mail for Hendricks. They looked at each other. She played it again, listening for nuance that she'd missed the first five times. There was none, but the meaning was unequivocal. It meant George was in trouble and so were they. It meant get to high ground and lie low. Don't be heroes. Don't go looking for him and don't try to make contact. Wait for his all clear.

"What do you think?" she asked.

"I think I hate Pennsylvania."

"What about George?"

"Probably loves it."

"Hendricks. What do we do?"

"What was wrong with getting out of here?"

He had a point.

It took the rest of the day and night to scour Grafton Storage of their presence. Hendricks bleached and scrubbed down the unit where they had held Tate. Jenn reinventoried their equipment in case their party crasher had taken more than just the gun.

Empty storage units rarely catch fire, so they needed to paint a believable picture. It wouldn't get much scrutiny unless the fire department was given a very good reason. Hendricks dressed the unit to look like a homeless person had been squatting in it and had foolishly tried to build a fire inside the unit. When he was satisfied, Hendricks struck the match and watched his Rube Goldberg arson project go up in flames.

Jenn was already in the SUV when he slid behind the wheel.

"I used to like Fridays," he said.

It took her a minute to do the math. "It is Friday, isn't it? What a fucking week."

"Anything more from George?"

She shook her head.

"Damn."

"There's more. You're not going to like it."

"What?"

"The phones at ACG are disconnected," she said.

"Jenn . . . That is not protocol."

"I know."

"Wait. All of them?"

"All of them."

"Our direct lines?"

"All of them."

"I don't like it."

"Told you."

Hendricks sat in silence, digesting the implications. Jenn watched him work through it. They had kidnapped a man from his home, questioned him aggressively in an abandoned storage locker, and now that man was dead. The shooter had taken the time to frame Hendricks with one of his own guns. George Abe was in sufficient trouble to hit the panic button. Oh, and sometime in the last twenty-four hours, ACG's phones had all been disconnected.

They were in uncharted territory.

There was a lot more at stake than a job now. Hendricks was going to have to decide for himself, and she was going to have to let him. She'd already made her choice.

"To go forward or to run," he said. "That is the question."

"Yes, it is."

"Running makes sense."

"Agreed."

"I'm a little old to take up running," he said. "I'd have to buy those ugly-ass shoes and those flimsy little shorts. I'm the wrong kind of black for that shit."

"You do have bony legs."

Each looked away out a window.

"So. Where to?" he asked.

"To Gibson Vaughn."

"Yeah, I've been meaning to look him up," Hendricks said. "Where is he?"

Jenn showed Hendricks on her map.

"Why do I know that address?"

"You wouldn't believe me if I told you."

"At this point, I'd believe it if you told me it was Hitler's bunker."

"It's Terrance Musgrove's old beach house."

"Perfect," Hendricks said. "But for the record, I preferred my guess."

"Yeah, me too," Jenn said.

George came to in a wooden chair, head down on a crude metal table. His wrists were handcuffed to a sturdy metal bar set into the center of the table. The surface of the table was cool on the side of his face, but he sat up grudgingly, and his chair swayed as if someone had taken a screwdriver to it, intentionally loosening the legs.

There wasn't much else to look at; the room was a standard eight-by-ten-foot cinder-block interrogation room. The brittle hum of the fluorescent lighting made George's head throb like a cruel dentist was excavating his eyeteeth. His throat was tight and dry, his back knotted and bruised. Judging by his hunger, he'd been out at least twelve hours, which would make it, what? Friday morning?

George checked himself in the wide mirror set in the wall. He didn't look too much the worse for wear. Hadn't had his ribs broken in transit. Thank you, gracious host. His tie was crooked, and it bothered him that he couldn't straighten it.

A door opened to his left. A man entered and sat opposite George. He placed a cup and a pitcher of water on the table. It was chilled and condensation stippled the sides.

George gave the man a once-over. He was a neatly trimmed drone in an off-the-rack suit. They stared at each other like two ex-friends who had awkwardly bumped into each other on a street corner. This was the part where George was supposed to yell indignantly, demand a lawyer, make bombastic threats of the "do you know who I am?" variety. He was thirsty, but he didn't ask for a drink. He had questions, but the suit was too cheap to have the answers to them.

"Can we just skip the overture? Is Titus in there?" George gestured with his head toward the mirror.

This time the drone's eyebrow contracted slightly. George looked up at the mirror.

"Titus. Is all the pageantry really necessary?"

The drone's eyes went down to the table, listening to instructions in his earpiece. He stood and left the room without a word.

George waited.

The door opened. A short, stocky man entered. He was only a few years older than George, but those years had been spent outdoors in some of the hardest places on Earth. The sun and elements had charred his skin, and the man had a face like steel wool, deep lines etched into it under a head of sparse hair the color of ash. A vivid scar ran down the man's jawline from his left ear and disappeared into the collar of his shirt. A souvenir from Tikrit. The pinky and ring fingers were missing from his left hand. Stories varied on how many times the man had been shot, and George believed Titus preferred it that way. Colonel Titus Stonewall Eskridge Jr., founder and CEO of Cold Harbor, was in the myth-making business.

"George." Titus sat in the recently vacated chair.

"Titus."

Each man regarded the other. Eskridge's ties to Lombard went back decades. George hadn't liked him then, and nothing he'd heard in the intervening years had caused him to reconsider.

Cold Harbor was a midsize private military contractor based east of Mechanicsville, Virginia. It was named for a particularly nasty one-sided battle of the Civil War that had inflicted terrible casualties on Ulysses S. Grant's forces. Never able to compete with the big boys for the major contracts, Cold Harbor did well for itself by fostering a reputation as an outfit that got the job—any job—done.

Sometimes ruthlessness trumped size.

Titus broke into a grin. "All right, I gotta know. How'd you know I was back there? You spooked my team, Obi-Wan. Was it one of my boys? Were they talking when they should have been listening?"

"No," George said. "Just a lucky guess."

"Where are my manners? You must be thirsty," Titus said and poured a cup of water. He pushed it within inches of George's fingers. "Was it one of my boys?"

"No. Surprisingly, I just don't have a lot of enemies."

"I'm not your enemy," Titus said.

"Weren't," George corrected.

"Weren't."

"Who was the largest donor to Lombard's Senate campaigns?"

Titus didn't answer.

"Who championed Cold Harbor for defense contracts over the big PMCs like Blackwater and KBR? It's not rocket science. If Lombard needs someone snatched, whom else is he going to call?"

"Guess that's what I'm here for." Titus smiled his affable good-old-boy grin. Just a couple of pals shooting the breeze. "Not bad, George. You always were a sharp guy. Not real practical but sharp. You put my boy in the hospital."

"I thought I missed."

"Nope, he's going to be talking funny for a long time. You haven't lost your touch sitting behind a desk."

"That's generous of you, but since only one of your boys is in the hospital, and I'm chained to this table, I'd say my touch is very much in question."

"I admire a man who takes stock of his failings."

Titus pushed the cup of water closer. George didn't ask for the shackles to be removed so he could drink it. Nor was he about to lap at it like some dog.

"Have you thought about what it means that Lombard called you and not the FBI?"

"Don't care," Titus shrugged. "Man's going to be president."

"In which case, you stand to make a fortune."

"Another fortune," Titus said with a crooked smile. "First one's getting lonely."

"Is he here?"

"The VP? Surrounded by Secret Service? Come on."

"Being a public servant can be inconvenient," George said.

"Never saw the appeal myself."

"What does he want?"

"He wants to be president. But right now he very much wants to know what you did with Abe Consulting Group."

"What do you mean?"

"Don't," Titus said wearily. "Don't play that game with me, George. I mean, where did it go?"

———————————

Mike Rilling had been unemployed for twelve hours. He, along with everyone at ACG, had been terminated via e-mail at eleven p.m. Thursday night. No warning. No exit interview. Nothing. A massacre—the entire company laid off without warning. His coworkers had all received the same e-mail explaining that unforeseen financial setbacks were forcing ACG to close its doors permanently.

It was a betrayal. Not of the company—Mike didn't give a damn about any of them—but of him personally. What about all their man-to-man talks about integrity, about doing things the right way? To be stepped on this way? It just proved that George Abe was as big a hypocrite as anyone.

It validated Mike's decision to funnel information to the vice president. After all, it was the man's daughter. In Mike's mind, Benjamin Lombard had a right to be kept informed. He didn't really see the need for all this secrecy. Finding the creep that snatched his daughter was a good thing. The vice president would be grateful.

Jenn Charles would be pissed. Well, she would just have to wait her turn. He had a few things to say to George Abe himself.

The ferocity of his emotions surprised him. Mike wouldn't admit it, even to himself, but he felt a certain gratitude and loyalty to George. He looked up to George. So after seven or eight beers, he'd screwed up his courage and called George to give him a piece of his mind. George hadn't answered then or any of the subsequent times Mike had called back.

Coward.

Well, George wasn't getting off that easy. Mike appreciated the severance package—it was generous—but this wasn't about the money. It was the principle of the thing. He'd been there since the start, and you didn't fire a guy after seven years. Not without some kind of explanation.

Mike rode the elevator up to their floor, his resolve wavering. Last night, he'd had a hellfire sermon prepared for Saint George Abe, but now the idea of facing his ex-boss seemed daunting. George had that unflappable calm thing down to a science, which tended to fluster Mike pretty quick.

Mike came off the elevator and walked down the hall to Abe Consulting Group. The doors were propped open with doorstops, which was unusual.

Reception was empty. Mike stopped in his tracks. Not empty as in no people. Empty as in *empty* empty. Everything was gone: couches, chairs, tables, lamps, artwork . . . everything. Right down to the carpet tacks and nameplates. Mike went room by room but found the same thing everywhere. Even George's office had been stripped bare. It was unbelievable. He'd left last night at seven p.m. and everything had been normal. And now it was as if Abe Consulting, like a band of gypsies, had pulled up stakes and moved camp in the night, leaving no trace that it had ever been here.

Mike's cell rang. He checked for the number but there was none. It wasn't blocked; the screen was just blank. These calls always freaked him out a little. As if they came from nowhere at all. A familiar voice came on the line, flinty and mechanical.

"I don't know," Mike said. "I don't. It's gone . . . Yeah, I'm standing right here. The place is empty . . . I don't know! What can I tell you? He doesn't exactly confide in me."

There was a pause at the other end. When the voice came back it rattled off instructions. Mike hung up and realized he was sweating. He was afraid to say no and wasn't sure what would happen if he did.

He wished George were here to tell him what he should do.

CHAPTER THIRTY-FOUR

Gibson slept until the morning sunlight crept across the floor and found his eyes. He rolled into a sitting position on the couch. Billy was upstairs in one of the bedrooms. They'd talked themselves out without reaching any conclusions and called it a night. His phone said it was after ten. When was the last time he'd slept this late? On a couch. But after four days in the back of a car, an old couch felt pretty damn good.

There was no doubting Billy's story. Not now.

Billy hadn't been kidding when he said the attic was a shrine to Terrance Musgrove's family. He'd shown it to Gibson last night. Rows of neatly stacked boxes lined the walls, each labeled—"Living Room Pictures," "Office 1," "Office 2," "Master Bathroom Sundries," etc. As if the Musgroves were expected back and would need easy access to their shampoo.

Billy had gone straight for a row of boxes labeled "Ginny's Room."

"Suzanne stayed in Ginny's room. It was still filled with girl's stuff, so I guess she just felt more comfortable. I thought she'd be a little creeped out, sleeping in a dead girl's bed, but she said it didn't bother her."

Billy had dug into the box, pulled the pink Hello Kitty backpack out, and handed it to him.

"Are you kidding me?" Gibson asked.

"Told you I had something to show you."

"Musgrove's sister didn't notice it?"

"A girl's backpack in a girl's bedroom? Not really. There's something to be said for hiding in plain sight."

"And it's just been here this whole time?"

"Tell me a better place for a single guy in his twenties to keep a kid's backpack?"

They'd brought it downstairs, and Billy watched while Gibson unpacked it and laid everything out on the coffee table—compact, hairbrush, a jewelry box, an old first-gen iPod, earphones, a couple of T-shirts and pairs of underwear, jeans. The hardcover edition of *The Fellowship of the Ring* that Gibson had read to her all those years ago. And a beat-up Philadelphia Phillies baseball cap.

Gibson rubbed the sleep out of his face and reached for the cap, handling it delicately, as if it were an heirloom from another era. Even more than the backpack, it gave him the chills. He flipped it over and, for what seemed like the hundredth time since last night, looked at the lining. In faded black marker were the initials "S. D. L."—Suzanne Davis Lombard. The *L* written with Suzanne's distinctive swoosh. This was her cap. The cap.

What did it mean?

Now, in the bright sunshine of morning, something struck him about the lining. Usually, sweat discolored the lining of a baseball cap over time, especially along the forehead. But Bear's looked hardly worn, despite the rest of the cap being beat to hell. The Phillies logo was scuffed and frayed. The stitching was coming loose from around the six eyelets, and the smartie—the button on top—was missing altogether. How do you do this kind of damage to a cap without wearing it?

Then there was the Polaroid picture. Billy had shown it to him last night, but it still didn't look real. Maybe he just didn't want it to be real. In the picture, Bear lay on the couch Gibson had slept on. Wrapped up in a fuzzy blue bathrobe, a book open across her belly. And it was a belly, because in the picture Bear was very pregnant. She looked tired but happier than in the picture Billy had taken the night she'd arrived. Gibson found it hard to look at for long. Seeing her pregnancy for himself made it real.

Billy shuffled sleepily downstairs and went into the kitchen for a glass of water.

"I'm going back to bed," Billy said upon his return.

"Hey. Question. You ever see Suzanne wear this thing?"

"Other than the night I picked her up? No. Never. She wasn't really a baseball cap kinda girl."

"Then any idea how it got this beat up?"

"Oh, that was Suze. She'd sit and yank the stitching out like it was her job. You ever see a dog go to town on a stuffed toy? That was Suze with that hat."

Billy left him alone with his thoughts.

Gibson furrowed his brow. *What's the story, Bear?* What was a girl who, according to her parents, hated baseball doing with a Phillies cap that they both swore she didn't own? Supposedly she'd bought the cap on the road to hide her face. That made sense, given it looked like it had never been worn. But if she only wore it that one time, why bother to write her initials into the brim? You did that to things you cared about losing.

What had Billy said about the security tape at the gas station? The way Bear had stared at the camera . . . a fuck-you to someone? Was the cap part of the message? It had been bothering Gibson for so long that he'd hoped seeing it, touching it, would jog something loose. But he was still drawing a blank.

With those questions swarming his mind, he wrestled himself to his feet, snatched up the cap and the book, and set off to raid the kitchen. There wasn't much to choose from, and he was forced to settle for two old cans of peaches. He sat on the back porch with Bear's book, the fruit, and a fork. The lake was choppy this morning, and he watched the waves drive diagonally toward the shore, thinking about Bear.

Bear on her banquette, reading. The way she drank tea like her mom, cup in both hands, blowing on it gently as she gazed out her window. He held the book to his nose, hoping for a smell that would pull him deeper into his childhood, but it was just an old book. He flipped through it and ate peaches out of the can.

From beginning to end, the margins were crammed with notes that had been written since he'd finished reading it to her. Billy had shown him the margin notes last night; he admitted he'd gotten drunk one night and vowed to read the book and her notes cover to cover in the hopes that he'd find some clue as to what happened to her. He'd given up on page fifty. It was just kid stuff, he'd said.

"Some are addressed to outer space and shit. I don't know. Too deep for me."

Gibson flipped to the beginning and started reading.

Suzanne's notes were written in a precise, microscopic hand and arranged in no particular order and with no discernible chronology. From what he could tell, they appeared to have been written over several years—in different colored inks, with some entries more faded than others. A few were actually about *The Fellowship of the Ring*, but those were distinctly in the minority. Most were snippets of song lyrics, movie quotes, lists of likes and dislikes, stray observations. It was the brightly colored musings of a precocious young girl. He could imagine Ellie doing something similar in a few years, although given her handwriting she would need much bigger margins.

He read slowly for a few pages, then, becoming restless, began turning pages quickly, letting his eyes trawl for anything significant. He flipped ahead ten pages, then twenty. Until it was just fields of ink: blue, pink, green, red. He stopped.

Orange.

It brought to mind a memory that made his stomach pitch. Something Bear had asked him long ago. He'd been in the kitchen at Pamsrest. Mrs. Lombard was making him a grilled cheese sandwich, and he was reading a comic book. Bear had appeared at his side, out of breath.

"Gib-Son. Gib-Son."

"Uh-huh," he said absently.

"Son! I need to ask you something."

He stopped reading and looked at her.

"What's going on?"

"What's your favorite color?"

He told her it was orange—because of the Orioles.

"Okay," she said with a serious face. "Orange is your color, okay?"

Like he was supposed to know what that meant.

"Yeah, okay, orange is my color."

"Don't forget," she half whispered.

How old had they been? He couldn't remember. He flipped back several pages, until he saw orange pen.

"Sun." *Son.* Orange was his color. He felt an awful welling of emotions. Regret. Guilt. Longing. He hung his head between his knees and cried. God, how he missed her.

For the next hour, he went back through the novel and read all the entries he could find written in orange ink. Most were the thoughts of a little girl.

sun, do you like grape juice? I do.

sun, I wish everyone would go home but you.

Sun, teach me to burp.

They went on like that. Some funny. Some wistful. But then, buried in the middle of the book, he found a note different from the others addressed to him—longer and in a more mature handwriting.

Sun, the funeral was today. I'm so sorry. I hope you're okay. They wouldn't let me go. I wanted to be there for you. Are we still friends? I understand if we can't be but I miss you. (389)

With something approaching dread, he flipped forward to page 389. The margins were blank except for a single note that had been written using two different orange pens, and if he wasn't mistaken, some years apart. The first half read:

Sun, sorry I ruined the game. Don't be mad at me?

Then, in the other pen, written God-knows-how-much later:

I should have told you after the game. I should have told you a hundred times. I was so angry with you for not seeing. I'm sorry. I wish I could tell you now. There's a lake here. It's not as pretty as Pamsrest, but we could go sit down by the water, and I could tell you everything. I want that more than anything. I wish you hadn't gone away. I hope you won't blame me.

He snapped the book shut. Blame her for what? A memory swam up from the depths, its hideous, reptilian spine almost breaking the surface before it swam powerfully away from him. He closed his eyes, afraid to lure it back, but knowing he must.

The game. What about it? Duke had taken him to a hundred games. Had Bear gone to one with them? Maybe? He had a hazy memory; the only thing he remembered was Bear being a huge brat the whole day, which wasn't like her at all. No, there was more. The memory surfaced, eyes pitiless and vast. They stared into him, daring him to blink.

It had been a day trip to see the Orioles. He couldn't remember whom they were playing. The Red Sox? That sounded right. Originally just him and Duke, but the senator had gotten wind of it and invited himself and Bear along. Lombard's wife was out of town, so it was just a couple of dads taking their kids to a ball game . . . with a security detail following at a discreet distance. Half family outing, half political theater. But then Bear had flipped out at the ballpark, and they'd missed most of the game.

No, that wasn't right. It had started earlier.

When Gibson really thought about it, Bear had been out of sorts for some time. Withdrawn. And she'd been an absolute nightmare on the drive to Baltimore. Hostile toward all of them. Kicking the back of the passenger seat. Glaring at anyone who looked her way. Nothing like the chirpy little girl he'd grown up with. She wouldn't answer him when he asked her what was wrong. That never happened. Duke, who could always bring a smile to her face, had gotten only sullen silence.

Gibson remembered Lombard's frustration and stubborn determination to have a good time. Duke had suggested calling it off halfway there, but the senator wasn't having it. The drive had become a pantomime of upbeat banter, and they had all felt the false, strained tension that came from putting on a happy face.

By the time they'd reached the ballpark, no one was much in the mood for baseball. Camden Yards had been bustling, so it wasn't until they'd gotten to their seats that he'd realized Bear was crying. At the time, he'd just seen a bratty kid not getting her way, but now he saw that she'd been more than upset; she'd been frightened.

I was so angry with you for not seeing.

What hadn't he seen?

As they had taken their seats, a play in the field brought the crowd to its feet. Gibson, out in the aisle, had turned to watch, and by the time he'd looked back, Bear was sobbing. Duke had knelt to comfort her, but Bear shrank away from him, wailing inconsolably.

Gibson got a sick feeling as he tried to recall what had happened next.

Lombard snatched up his daughter and carried her up to the concourse. Duke had just stood there, watching after them, his face drawn and troubled. What had happened at that ballpark? What was he missing? All these years, Gibson had believed his father had killed himself because he'd been caught embezzling from Lombard. It had been such a welcome relief when Calista Dauplaise told him that it had been Lombard himself. But it raised a new and unpleasant question: What *had* driven Duke Vaughn to suicide?

His phone vibrated. He snatched it up, happy to drive the thought away. He checked the number before answering.

"Hello, Jenn."

"Gibson. How's Virginia?"

"Beautiful. Go Hoos! You should come visit."

"I was thinking the same thing."

"Aw, miss me?"

"You've been busy."

"So have you," he said.

"We need to talk. You've put us in a bad spot."

"Did I? Did I make you complicit in the kidnapping and torture of a US citizen? 'Cause if I haven't, go fuck yourself and your bad spot."

"Tate's dead, Gibson. Someone killed him."

Gibson put the phone down on his thigh and said something profane. His ears rang. Tate was dead. That would be murder one. Did they execute people in Pennsylvania? He put the phone back to his ear.

"Someone?"

"Yeah. So like I said, we need to talk."

"Have a storage locker in mind?"

"Look, there'll be time for that later. Maybe you're right. But not now. Now, we need to share information because something's going on. And whatever it is, we're at the bottom looking up."

"I don't know, Jenn. Part of me wants to leave you and Hendricks to figure it out on your own. See what it feels like."

"I can appreciate that, but we're here. You're going to talk to us. I'd prefer it to be friendly."

"What do you mean 'here'?"

"We're at the Musgrove place. At the end of the driveway. I wanted to give you a heads-up. We're not busting in on you; we just want to talk."

Gibson was up on his feet. "I don't think that's such a good idea."

"Good idea or not, we're coming up now. Don't rabbit on us," she said and hung up.

CHAPTER THIRTY-FIVE

"Who's here?" Billy stood in the doorway behind Gibson. The gun in his hand shook. "Did you tell them where we are?"

"No. But they found us."

He stood and took a step toward Billy, and the gun came up to greet him. He stopped short, hands out and up.

"I don't know how they found us. They just want to talk."

"Talk . . . yeah, sure."

They both heard the car coming up the driveway at the same time. Billy's eyes went feral, and his head snapped around like an animal catching a scent.

"Billy, don't!"

But Billy wasn't in a listening frame of mind. He spun and ran back through the house. Gibson took off after him but veered left and sprinted around the house on the front porch, dodging furniture, staying low. Up ahead the Cherokee emerged from the trees and began to loop around the circular driveway.

Billy burst out the front door. He had the gun up and was waving it wildly at the Cherokee, which slammed to a halt. Billy made no effort to take cover, mad with fear and anger—yelling, crying for them to get back, to go away, to leave him alone. Hendricks was barking orders back at Billy to lower the gun, but it was lost in the babel of Billy's panic.

Gibson came around the corner. He had to get to Billy before someone got hurt. In a moment of slow-motion lucidity, he realized that he believed Billy. Believed the whole preposterous story. More than that, he cared about him. He couldn't bear the idea of Billy getting hurt.

Jenn and Hendricks closed the gap and were only fifteen feet from the porch. Everyone yelling. Hendricks moving to the left, trying to split Billy's attention. Billy more and more frantic. Gun pitching back and forth between his two antagonists. Spittle flew from his lips.

Gibson took two steps and drove his shoulder hard into Billy's ribs. Together they clattered over a wicker armchair. The gun came loose and skidded across the porch. Billy struggled for a moment, but Gibson was far too strong. Billy lay under him, panting.

"Just be cool, Billy. Be cool. It's going to be all right."

Billy struggled fitfully, unconvinced.

"Gibson! Throw your gun over the railing." Jenn's voice.

"I don't have a gun, you asshole. And I kind of have my hands full here; could one of you maybe give me a hand?"

Benjamin Lombard jotted notes in the margin of his acceptance speech. The convention was weeks away, and the race remained far from decided, but tinkering with the speech helped distract him from what was going on in Virginia and Pennsylvania. Son-of-a-bitch George Abe waging his own one-man crusade as usual.

Crafty little prick had somehow triggered the dismantling of his business within minutes of getting pulled over. By the time Titus's people had shown up there wasn't a screw to screw or pencil to push. Abe Consulting had been wiped clean from the face of the earth. Exactly Abe's style. As was denying it. He'd put on a convincing little performance about how he was as baffled as anyone. Even after Titus's boy put a licking on him.

Lombard glanced up at the monitor; George was still slumped over the interrogation table at Cold Harbor. Titus was an evil little pit bull of a man, there was no doubting that, but Lombard was beginning to doubt his ability to make a breakthrough in a timely fashion. If he knew anything about George it was that it would take more than a few broken ribs to get him to betray his people.

Fortunately, Lombard had a guy inside ACG who'd kept them up to speed, so they knew about the operation in Pennsylvania. Still, he wanted to be there to hear what George had to say for himself. Of course, that was impossible. Titus's whole operation was highly illegal, which meant Lombard remained stuck on the sidelines, watching his life play out on a twenty-seven-inch monitor. Goddamn George Abe. Maybe he should have called in the feds, but he didn't trust that peckerwood Brant at the Bureau to keep it quiet. Well, what was done was done, and anyway, it was almost time for George to go another round with Titus's big boy.

A knock came at his study door. Lombard shut off the monitor and called them in. A dyspeptic Leland Reed entered, holding out a phone. Benjamin didn't like that Reed carried his anxiety so plainly. A man in this line of work needed a better poker face. Lombard asked what he wanted.

"I have a Calista Dauplaise for you."

Benjamin nodded smoothly, as though expecting the call. He wasn't. He couldn't have been any more surprised if Reed had said Abraham Lincoln were on the line. *Calista Dauplaise?* What were the odds of the old witch calling him?

"Wasn't she one of your old donors from the Virginia days?" Reed asked. "She sounds ready to get back in bed with us in a big way, but says she wants to talk to you directly." Reed was wired in enough to know who she was but shrewd enough to play dumb. "Want me to put her off?"

Already during the primaries, he'd gotten feelers from unexpected donors, but this was another thing entirely. Calista wouldn't give him a dime to use the bathroom in hell. And today of all days. Just how involved with Abe Consulting was she?

Lombard snapped his fingers impatiently for Reed to give him the phone, then shooed him out.

"Hello, Calista."

"Benjamin."

"So, Leland tells me you found Jesus and want to help America elect the right man."

"Yes, I suppose that's true."

They both chuckled over that, but it would be a mistake to think she found this funny. Just as it was a mistake to think a hyena was smiling just because it showed you its teeth.

"What do you want?"

"How is George?" she asked.

"Don't know what you're talking about."

"Benjamin, you have George. And likely Mike Rilling as well."

"Those are pretty serious accusations you're throwing around."

"Shut up and listen to me closely if you ever hope to be president."

Benjamin Lombard hadn't been told to shut up since his sophomore year in college. He hadn't actually shut up when told to since he was fourteen years of age. But as soon as Calista began to speak, his mouth snapped shut and stayed that way until she was done.

———————

Hendricks handcuffed Billy to a toilet, arms wrapped around and behind the bowl like he was sweet on it. He warned him that if he made a sound, he'd jam Billy's head into it.

"You'll need a plumber to get it out."

Otherwise, for the time being, Billy was unharmed. Gibson tried arguing that none of it was necessary, but Hendricks was in no mood for half measures.

"You're about three good words from joining him."

Gibson brought a pillow from the living room for Billy to lie against. Billy accepted it silently; he hadn't spoken a word since Gibson had tackled him. He just stared pensively at the bathroom floor.

Gibson left Billy in the bathroom and joined his former colleagues in the kitchen. They sat around the table, staring at each other. It wasn't the warmest of reunions. But neither was anyone pointing a gun at him, so Gibson called it a draw. Of the two, Jenn seemed the friendlier. Hendricks, on the other hand, was hard as dried cement.

"Why'd you come back?" she asked Gibson.

"Why'd you send me away?"

"Why?" she asked again, her voice sharpening.

"I had my doubts."

"About?"

"You. And about Tate. It wasn't him."

"Yeah, well, it's too late for that now." Hendricks described how they'd returned from chasing down Gibson's virus at the Musgrove house to find the storage unit. The blood. The body missing. Hendricks glanced down the hall toward Billy. Gibson caught his look. It was clear Hendricks was weighing Billy in his mind. Trying to decide if he was the one who had killed Tate.

"It wasn't him," Gibson said.

"No? Okay, well, that leaves you."

"You think I killed Tate?"

"You gonna deny you were there?"

"No. Do you think I killed him?"

Hendricks stared at him long and hard.

"No. We don't," Jenn said. "But that doesn't leave us with many viable suspects."

"Other than our friend down the hall," Hendricks said. "Who admitted luring us away with that virus stunt at the Musgrove house. And while we're out chasing our tails at the Musgrove house, Kirby Tate gets dead. But you somehow don't think he had anything to do with it."

"It wasn't him. I'd swear on it." Gibson did his best to defend Billy and told them most of what he'd learned. How Billy had stuck his neck out to help and protect Suzanne ten years ago. They listened silently as he showed them the Hello Kitty backpack and laid out its contents on the kitchen table. Hendricks went over the baseball cap carefully. Gibson wasn't quite ready to divulge his misgivings about it. He watched Jenn pick up the book and thumb through it.

"What are all these notes?"

Gibson shrugged. "Teenage girl stuff."

"All right, well what do you actually know about this guy?" Hendricks said. "He's got the backpack and the cap. He sent ACG the photo. So I'll buy that Suzanne was here. But does Romeo in there have any proof Suzanne was pregnant?"

Gibson showed them the photo. Hendricks seemed unmoved, but Jenn stared at it while her partner kept up his interrogation.

"And does he have any proof it wasn't his?"

"No," Gibson said.

"Or that Musgrove wasn't a suicide?"

"No."

Jenn cleared her throat. Hendricks shot her a look that Gibson couldn't interpret.

"But you believe him anyway," Hendricks said. "That he helped Suzanne out of the goodness of his heart. Helped a girl pregnant by some other guy. And then *someone* came and took her away and killed his neighbor. You believe that fantasy, but you don't believe that the guy who hacked ACG, lured us out here, served up Tate for kidnapping his sister—you don't believe there's a chance he had something to do with the four quarts of blood I mopped up last night?"

"Come on, Hendricks. Does he strike you like a guy capable of gunning someone down in cold blood?"

"What does someone capable of that look like?"

"It wasn't him."

Hendricks's lip curled. "Well, it's either you or him. Him I can't prove, but you I know were there."

"So were you," Gibson shot back.

The two men stared flatly at each other, Gibson holding as still as he had ever been. It went on like that for some time. Then, just like that, Hendricks snorted and looked away.

"Does George think I did it?" Gibson asked.

Jenn and Hendricks looked at each other.

"What?"

"Tell him about Meiji?" Hendricks said.

"What the hell is Meiji?"

Jenn sat alone in the kitchen while Hendricks took a power nap in the next room. She was jealous of his ability to compartmentalize. Neither of them had slept more than an hour in the last two days, but she couldn't keep her eyes closed. There were just too many variables and too few constants. She knew there was only so long she'd be able to keep Hendricks at bay. Despite Gibson's efforts, Hendricks still liked Billy Casper for Tate's murder, and she was having trouble coming up with a competing theory that didn't involve Gibson.

Her phone rang. It was Mike Rilling.

"Mike?"

"Jenn, is that you?"

"Who else am I going to be?"

"I don't know. Things are kind of crazy, you know?"

Mike didn't sound good. He had always had a bit of the whiny child in him, but now he was like a middle-school cafeteria in Jenn's ear.

"It's going to be fine. Are you at the office? Why are the phones disconnected?"

Mike told her.

"What do you mean Abe Consulting's gone?"

"I mean it's gone. Cleaned out. Overnight." Mike described the way he'd found the offices. "Place was stripped right down to the baseboards."

"Where's George?"

"Arrested. The feds have him. It's a real mess."

So it *was* the FBI. At least now she knew why George had sounded the alarm. Did Meiji also trigger the dismantling of the offices? If so, it was news to her.

"Where are they holding him?"

"I'm not sure. Not sure George knows, to tell the truth. I just got off the phone with him."

"You talked to him?" Jenn was sitting forward now.

"Yeah, the feds let him make a call. He didn't sound good. The feds want everything we have on Suzanne Lombard by today, or they're dropping the hammer on George."

"Christ."

"He's calling me back in an hour. What do we have?"

Jenn ran her tongue over her teeth, deliberating. "You got something to write with?"

CHAPTER THIRTY-SIX

Gibson sat on the edge of the bathtub, feeding Billy tuna from a can. Hendricks refused to uncuff him, so it was slow and messy going. Billy hadn't asked to go to the bathroom yet, but Gibson wasn't optimistic about how that would go. Billy was trying to be cooperative but clearly remained afraid and angry. Being handcuffed to a toilet didn't help any with morale.

"I feel like a child," Billy said.

"Yeah, but that makes me your daddy, and I'm not cool with that."

Billy cracked a weak grin that turned serious. "Are they going to kill me?"

"They'll have to kill me first."

"Is your dying seconds before me supposed to make me feel better about being dead?"

It was Gibson's turn to grin weakly. "Thought that counts?"

His gallows humor wasn't helping.

"Man, get me out of here."

"I'm working on it."

"Yeah? Well work faster, okay? 'Cause me? I'm handcuffed to a fucking toilet."

Gibson hadn't talked to Jenn or Hendricks since their debrief this morning. Collectively they were all running on fumes, so giving each other a wide berth for a few hours seemed wise. Having Kirby Tate's murder hanging over his head wasn't doing wonders for Hendricks's disposition, and for once Gibson could empathize with him. A little. But if Hendricks laid a hand on Billy, then they would be at a crossroads. The memory of Kirby Tate's cell remained too vivid for comfort.

But so far this afternoon, Jenn and Hendricks had been occupied with Mike Rilling back in DC. Apparently, George was in federal custody, and they were trying to orchestrate a deal for his release—information for immunity.

To get away from it all, Gibson had holed up in Ginny Musgrove's bedroom, where Bear had spent much of her time. He'd sat with his back against the bedroom door and read more of the annotations in *The Fellowship of the Ring*. Looking for a smoking gun about his father but at the same time dreading finding one. Was Duke the one that Bear had run away from? Was that why he'd ended his life? Gibson didn't know if he could survive the truth.

Gibson studied Billy's face. His boyish eyes, the premature crow's-feet, the tuft of gray hair amid his unkempt blond rat's nest. No one was perfect, but when it came to Suzanne, Billy Casper was as close as a person got. He'd stuck his neck out for her and then done it again. The risk he had taken to find her. This absurd long shot he had played by hacking ACG. Gibson had no parallel in his own life, and it was humbling.

"Can I ask you a question?"

"Shoot," Billy said, resting his head on the pillow.

"How long did you and Suzanne talk online?"

"Almost a year."

"When did she start talking about running away?"

"Right from the beginning, man."

"Why?"

"Because of the baby. I told you."

"No. You said she wasn't showing when she got here. That meant she was only a couple months pregnant. So why did she want to run away before that?"

Billy said he didn't know, hadn't really considered it.

Gibson opened Bear's book and read the passage about the baseball game again.

"What is it?" Billy asked.

The sound of a vehicle coming down the driveway interrupted them. Gibson put the book on the sink and stood up to look out the small porthole window. Billy watched him with wide eyes.

Powerful headlights fractured the brooding dark of the woods. Gibson yelled back toward the kitchen that they had company, but Hendricks and Jenn were already on their way. Jenn was turning off lights as she went. She stuck her head in the bathroom.

"What do we have?" she asked.

"Headlights. Is this your deal with the feds?"

"No," Jenn said. "Stay with him. Call out anything you see."

She shut off the bathroom light and left them in the dark.

A huge black SUV broke the tree line, curved slightly to the left, and came to a stop. A second SUV, running dark, pulled up alongside. Together they blocked the driveway back to the main road. Like a play-by-play announcer, Gibson relayed it all out to Jenn.

In unison, both SUVs flipped on their brights, scouring the back of the house in blinding white light. Gibson had to look away, but not before he saw the blue-and-red strobes from the vehicles pulsing off the trees. So much for cutting a deal.

Over the low rumble of the idling engines, they listened to car doors open but not shut. Footsteps in the gravel. He glanced cautiously over the lip of the window frame. Two figures approached, silhouetted in the bank of headlights that cast long distorted shadows. More men were behind them by the vehicles, but he couldn't make out their number.

A voice of sandpaper and rust called out that they were FBI. There was an edge of Kentucky in his accent.

"Jenn Charles! Daniel Hendricks! Step out of the house. We have warrants for your arrest."

A lonely minute passed. He could hear Jenn and Hendricks talking in hushed tones. Billy was banging his head lightly against the toilet seat. Gibson ducked down and put his hand on the back of Billy's head to hold him still. The agent called out again, repeating his instructions.

Less warmly, if that were possible.

A hand tugged the hood off, and George Abe found himself kneeling on a dirt escarpment overlooking a valley that swept away to the south. The night sky was brilliant with stars. It amazed him how much sky you surrendered to live in a city. Why was it only in moments like these that a man noticed such things?

He rolled his head, hoping to unknot the muscles in his neck. His wrists were cuffed behind his back; his arms were zip-tied just above the elbows, which forced his shoulders back painfully. Try as he might, he couldn't find a position that took the stress off his back, and his arms were going numb.

His interrogator had had only two questions. Where were Charles and Hendricks, and what happened to Abe Consulting Group? The questions got asked a lot of different ways, but it made no difference. The first he wasn't answering. Not under any circumstances. They would kill him before he'd give up his people. As to the second, George didn't know what they were talking about. Something about his offices being shut down and dismantled. It sounded insane, probably a ruse intended to get him talking. Through the pain and blood, he strove to keep his mind sharp.

The second round of "questioning" had involved an especially brutal beating. Titus's thug had tuned him up pretty good. George's left eye felt loose in the socket, his nose definitely broken. Dried blood was caked down his chin and shirtfront. The thug was right handed, and the ribs down George's left side felt wet and pulverized beneath the muscle.

When they came back the third time, he was braced for things to take a serious turn, but instead they had thrown a hood on him and brought him here.

He'd been transported in the back of an old pickup, tossed in the bed like a side of meat and driven up this scarred and jagged road. At the top, he'd been hauled out and forced to kneel here in the dark. Frankly, he was relieved at the change of scenery. Not that he was under any illusions about his prospects improving.

Titus must have gotten what he needed some other way, which was bad news for Jenn and Dan. At least Gibson Vaughn was safely out of the way, although George wondered if that would make any difference. Benjamin was clearly playing for keeps.

A hooded figure was shoved down in the dirt beside George. The hood came off to reveal a terrified Mike Rilling. He was handcuffed but otherwise looked unharmed.

Mike got a good look at George in the moonlight. "George?"

"What are you doing here?"

Mike shook his head dumbly.

"Michael. What are you doing here? What did you tell them?"

"It's okay," Mike said uncertainly. "I took care of it."

"What did you do, Michael?"

"They just want to talk to Jenn and Dan. Resolve this peacefully."

"Do I look peaceful to you?"

Mike wouldn't meet his eyes.

"What did you tell them?" George demanded.

Mike didn't get a chance to answer. A single gunshot interrupted them and echoed across the valley. Mike toppled into the dirt and lay still. George watched blood pulse from the back of Mike's head, the final spasms of a dead heart.

George let out a snarl and struggled to his feet. His captor cracked a gun barrel across his head and stilled him with one strong hand to the shoulder. George exhaled softly and looked up at the night sky, knowing he would not hear the shot that killed him.

"Ridge, what's your status? Over," a radio squawked.

The muzzle eased off his skull.

"One for two. Over."

"Who? Over."

"Rilling. Over."

"Okay, hold there until relieved. Copy. Over."

"Roger, holding. Hard copy."

The two men left George kneeling in the dirt. He lowered his head and watched them over his shoulder. They strolled back to the pickup. They leaned against the front fender, the casual stance of experienced killers. A radio set on the hood played something that was too far away to make out clearly, but it had the choppy cadence and static of a police scanner. The two men talked in monosyllabic grunts and followed the broadcast the way other men might follow football.

After a time, another vehicle came up the road. It pulled to a stop, and a car door opened and closed. After a brief conversation, the new arrival ordered the two men to depart. George heard several crisp "Yes, sirs." It was Titus.

When the pickup was gone, the sound of its engine faded from earshot, and another car door opened and closed. Behind him, George could hear Titus talking to a woman. He looked despairingly at Mike Rilling, whose blood was already fading into the dirt. Poor fool.

The sound of footsteps made him tense. Titus appeared in front of him. He set down a folding chair and left without a word or a glance in George's direction.

"Keep it short," Titus said.

"I'll keep it however I wish, Mr. Eskridge." Calista Dauplaise sat in the chair. "Hello, George."

Jenn opened the front door a hair and slipped out onto the porch. She shielded her eyes with her hand. Damn lights were bright. Hendricks stood just inside the doorway, behind her, gun drawn.

"Down on the ground!" the agent barked. "Fingers interlocked behind your head."

"Let me see some ID," Jenn yelled back.

"Come down off the porch, ma'am, and we can talk."

"Not until I see ID."

The two agents conferred for a moment and then came forward slowly. The rear one had his suit jacket pushed back and his hand at his beltline. "A fragile situation" was what one of Jenn's instructors called these moments. And they had a nasty habit of slipping out of control over the least little thing.

The lead agent wore an ID on a chain around his neck and waved it at her as they approached. As if she could see it from here. He just wanted her attention on it and not on his partner, who was lurking off to the right and behind him. Someone fancied himself a magician. Look at this hand while the other one's busy elsewhere. If the other agent drew, Jenn's view would be obstructed, and he'd have the drop on her.

Her eyes had adjusted to the glare enough that she could make out the outlines of at least five more agents standing behind the SUV's open doors. Another agent had moved off to her left, flanking her some thirty yards away. It put him at the edge of an effective range for a handgun; he'd want to start moving up to close the distance. Unless the men at the back had rifles. In which case, if this thing went sideways, the house would be nothing but a shooting gallery, and they would wind up shredded paper targets.

A very fragile situation.

The lead agent came as far as Gibson's car, which was still parked blocking the stairs leading up to the porch. He kept it between them and held up his badge for her to see. If it was a forgery, it was a damn good one. She tapped the back of her leg once and heard Hendricks curse softly.

"Satisfied?" the agent said. "Now, are you Jenn Charles?"

She nodded.

"Is Dan Hendricks with you? Is he in the house?"

She started to nod when the glint of something metallic caught her eye. The agent's jacket had flapped open momentarily as he dropped the ID to his chest; it was his sidearm, and it was the wrong color.

Jenn glided forward, down the steps, toward the agent—drawing her weapon and moving in one liquid movement. She had it raised by the third step. The agent fumbled his draw and froze, his gun still pointing at the ground uselessly as his eyes locked on the business end of hers. They stared at each other over the hood of Gibson's car.

His partner stepped to her left, trying to get a good angle to put his gun on her. She took a step right, matching him. As it was, he would have to fire over the roof of the car, and it didn't give him a great shot. She prayed that Hendricks was backing her play and had a clear line of fire if it came to that. The agents at the SUVs brought rifles up and trained them on the house.

"Tell your boys to stay cool," she said to the lead agent. "Because you're gonna miss all the action if they don't."

He nodded and called back to them to stay where they were.

"Not the first time you've had a gun on you, is it?"

He shook his head.

"I can tell. Most guys, you point a gun at their chest, and they freak the fuck out. But not you. You're just mister ice water. I admire that. I do. So why don't you tell me who you all actually are, so this isn't the last."

"We're the FBI, ma'am. Now put that down."

"No, I like this gun. I've been shooting it, or one like it, since I was eight years old. So run that by me again."

"FBI," he said stubbornly.

"Is that a Glock 23 in your hand, *Agent?*"

The agent looked down at it. When he looked back he was nervous for the first time.

"No," she answered for him. "That looks a lot like a chrome-plated Colt 1911."

The agent nodded glumly.

"You know who carries chrome-plated 1911s? Guys with small dicks and big complexes. You know who doesn't? Bureau guys. Never have, never will. So tell me again who you are, and if you say FBI to me again, I'm going to punch a hole in that ID like it's a train ticket."

CHAPTER THIRTY-SEVEN

When George Abe was fourteen, his father began taking him to business meetings. He would sit quietly in the corner and listen. Afterward, his father would quiz him on the particulars. George was allowed to ask questions, and his father would explain his tactics. In this way, George learned the principles of negotiation and the art of reading situations. One of his father's principles was never to ask a question unless absolutely necessary.

"Wait," his father had cautioned. "Never ask a question in surprise. You will give yourself away. Wait. Think. Often the answers will be given to you."

George watched Calista, working to piece together what her presence meant. Contemplating how deep her betrayal ran. When it began. Masking both his anger and his deepening fear for his people, who he knew now were in terrible danger. He would not allow his concern to make it easier to threaten him.

"Oh, George, spare me your meditative samurai pose. We haven't the time."

"What do we have time for?"

"A few questions, perhaps."

"Ask them, then."

Calista smiled. "That's what I admire about you. You've taken Asian inscrutability and worn it like a badge of honor."

"Clearly, I still have much to learn from you."

"Yes, I suppose you do."

"At least now I know what happened to my offices."

"Yes, well, that. After consulting with my attorneys, we felt it prudent to liquidate Abe Consulting Group and write it off as a loss. For tax purposes, you see."

"I do. And I'm impressed. That must have taken some planning."

"Years of it," she said.

Years? How could that be? What exactly was Calista planning?

"So, how is Benjamin?" he asked.

Her face brightened like an actress who had forgotten her line and had just been fed her cue. "In the past few hours, Benjamin and I have come to an understanding."

"About Suzanne?"

"About a great many things," she said.

"And you think that wise?"

"Things will be different this time. He and I understand each other now."

George studied her. "What is it you want?"

"For Benjamin to be president."

"And what do you get out of it?"

"Everything my family has earned."

"And me? Do I wind up like Michael? Is that what I've earned?"

"Who on earth is Michael?"

"The man lying here!" George spat, his anger finally eclipsing his will. "The man your new partners just murdered."

Calista looked down at the body as if noticing the dead man for the first time. "That was unavoidable."

"And Jenn Charles? Dan Hendricks? Gibson Vaughn? Are their murders 'unavoidable'?"

"It's an imperfect world, George. Evelyn understood that."

Evelyn Furst? Was she that profoundly evil? "What have you done?"

Calista looked away. "Sacrifices had to be made."

"My God. Your own sister. And what about Pennsylvania? Suzanne?"

"Suzanne isn't in Pennsylvania."

For a moment, he took what she said as defeatism. That she'd given up on finding Suzanne. But that wasn't what she meant at all.

"Where is she?"

Titus came back from the truck and whispered something in Calista's ear. Calista listened but kept her eyes on George.

"I'm afraid we're out of time," she said.

"Where is she?" he yelled. "Answer me!"

"Enough!" she snapped, then took control of herself again. "That's enough. I think we're done here."

George looked up at her from his knees.

"I see. And am I your last loose end?"

"Nearly," Calista said and held out her hand. Titus handed her a radio. She turned up the volume and rested it on her knee. It was the communications channel for a Cold Harbor tactical team.

"Jenn Charles! Daniel Hendricks! Step out of the house. We have warrants for your arrest," a voice barked over the radio.

"We have a white female on the porch," a team member said.

"Is it Charles?" asked a second.

"Stand by."

George held his breath. The voices chattered back and forth.

"Positive contact. Visual confirmation. It's Charles."

Calista looked back to George.

"Very nearly."

———————

Fred Tinsley knelt on one knee deep in the woods and watched with mounting irritation the standoff develop between Charles and the seven men from the black SUVs. He'd been waiting here all day for darkness to fall before taking the house. It would have been simple. He knew its layout from the last time.

Then, as if on cue, these men had roared up, gung ho, bristling and loud. Charles didn't believe they were FBI. Tinsley didn't care one way or another. Whoever they were, they couldn't be allowed to take anyone from the house. Tinsley needed one of the three alive. Temporarily. There were questions that needed answering. Gibson Vaughn, if possible. He appeared to have leapfrogged ahead of the other two, and Tinsley wanted to know how.

Tinsley studied the battlefield. In a direct exchange of small-arms fire, he would die. That was undisputable. His Sig Sauer was a fine weapon, but it was no match for seven trained men. Five with assault rifles.

He knew, however, how to neutralize their advantage.

Rising out of the shadows, Tinsley hugged the tree line, slipping out of cover a few feet from the rear SUV. One man stood on each side of the vehicle behind an open door. The engine was running, masking Tinsley's footfalls on the white stone driveway. It helped that their focus and their rifles were trained on the confrontation with Charles.

Tinsley took the first man in a single practiced sweep of his knife. Blood splashed the window. He lowered the man to the ground into a sitting position to die.

Tinsley looked through the open doors of the SUV to the other man, who glanced back at the same instant. For a moment, they stared each other in the eye. Then the man was twisting, trying to bring his rifle to bear, but it was unwieldy in the cramped space between the door and vehicle.

Tinsley lowered the knife and asked the time.

"What?" the man asked as if he hadn't heard Tinsley correctly.

It was a strange question under the circumstances, and that strangeness slowed the man a fraction. It was enough. Tinsley shot him in the neck, the suppressor sounding a hollow rattle in the SUV's interior, and the man went down clutching the ruins of his throat.

Tinsley checked to see if the exchange had drawn unwanted attention, but all eyes remained on the standoff unfolding on the porch. It was tense, like unlit kindling. It needed a spark to make it catch. Tinsley took up the dead man's rifle and fired several bursts over Jenn Charles's head.

The effect was instantaneous.

Charles reacted first. She slid to her left, dropping as she fired twice at the man claiming to be FBI. The man tumbled backward and stayed down. His partner returned fire, but Charles disappeared behind the car. There were gunshots from the open doorway of the house, and the second man threw himself to the ground and crawled toward his fallen partner.

Automatic-weapons fire erupted from all sides. The rifles were all suppressed and, judging by the sound, loaded with subsonic ammunition. Charles was correct. These men were not the FBI.

The car Charles was hiding behind exploded in a firework of broken glass and metallic shards. Bullets crashed into the side of the house, battering the front door of the house and flinging it wide. Tinsley heard a man yell in pain.

Tinsley watched the partner of the fallen man circle the car and take his partner by the collar, dragging him back behind a large elm in the center of the circular driveway. Charles returned fire as best she could but was effectively pinned down. There was no other movement from the house. Tinsley wondered if she had sacrificed herself to buy her compatriots time to flee out the back.

That would not be ideal.

Movement drew Tinsley's eyes. The man flanking Charles had spotted him. Bullets laced past, and Tinsley threw himself into the SUV, scrambling low across the seats as the armored door absorbed a burst of rounds. The sound of the running engine stopped him. He sunk down below the dashboard, shifted it into drive, and stomped down on the accelerator. The SUV leapt forward. Rounds thudded into the engine block. White circles like cigarette burns popped in the windshield above Tinsley's head. He held the accelerator to the floor.

The SUV caught the shooter square with a meaty impact and dragged him into the woods. The SUV hit two trees simultaneously, lifting the rear axle off the ground as it wrenched to a halt.

His nose bleeding and right knee injured, Tinsley disappeared into the trees before the air bag had finished deflating.

Bullets punched holes through the walls above Gibson's head. He stumbled backward and fell to the floor behind the cover of the bathtub.

Billy was frozen, hugging the toilet like it was a life preserver. Gibson crawled over and shoved him roughly around so that the toilet was between him and the gunfire. That and the bathtub would give them some short-term protection, but he needed to get Billy out of there.

Billy begged Gibson not to leave him.

"I'll be right back," he promised.

He moved low out of the bathroom. The hallway was covered in debris and broken glass. He scuttled down the hall to the front door. Hendricks was sprawled out on the floor. It looked like the front door had cracked Hendricks in the forehead, splitting the skin from the bridge of his nose to his hairline. The wound was bleeding heavily. Gibson checked for a pulse—it felt strong and regular.

He dragged Hendricks farther from the open door and patted him down. A thick key ring was in a hip pocket. He took the keys along with Hendricks's gun and crab-walked back to the bathroom, where he fumbled through the keys, unlocked the handcuffs, and motioned for Billy to follow him.

Together, they crawled down the hallway back to Hendricks. The automatic-weapons fire had slowed, becoming more deliberate. There was a thunderous crash away from the house. A car horn rang out. It took him another moment to realize that the crash had momentarily halted the gunfire.

He gestured for Billy to drag Hendricks farther back into the house.

Gibson glanced out the door and into the dark. A round snapped past his ear. One of the SUVs had driven off into the woods. The other SUV's headlights had been shot out. He could see Jenn crouched behind the car, but no one else. Billy said something behind him.

"What?"

"Floodlights," Billy said again.

Gibson pointed to a panel of light switches above his head. Billy nodded.

Not a bad idea. He knocked on the doorframe to get Jenn's attention. They made eye contact. He showed her the gun, gestured for her to come to him, then held up three fingers. She nodded, and he counted down with his fingers. On zero, he threw all the switches at once. Powerful halogens lit up the driveway like high noon. In the glare, he saw two men back by the SUV and another behind the elm tree in the circular driveway, kneeling beside a body.

Where were the others?

As the lights came on, Jenn was up and moving swiftly. Gibson emptied Hendricks's gun in suppressing fire over her head. Jenn slid into the house, and he kicked the door shut behind her.

The men out front started shooting out the floodlights, plunging them back into darkness.

They moved deeper into the relative safety of the house, huddled around Hendricks, and regrouped. Jenn shifted and helped her partner into a sitting position, shaking him gently as he came to. She brought Hendricks up to speed while he tried to clear his head and wipe the blood out of his eyes. Gibson offered him his gun back.

Footsteps pounded up onto the porch, and something solid hit the floor in the living room. Jenn anticipated it.

"Open your mouth, cover your eyes and ears!" she ordered.

Hendricks reacted automatically. Gibson and Jenn were already curling their heads down into their knees. Gibson yelled at Billy, but he only gaped at them in confusion.

The flash-bang went off in the hallway, but Gibson still felt the change in air pressure in his skull. It was like a car alarm pressed to his ears. He could see and he could hear, if only barely. Billy had taken the brunt and curled into a writhing ball by the time the shooting started.

Gunfire rattled over the radio. Titus stood with his hands on his hips, glaring at the radio as if he could see what was happening. Calista, brow furrowed, kept asking, "What's happening? What's happening?"

No one answered her.

It was hard for George to piece together. Several Cold Harbor operatives were down. Of that much he was sure. One was screaming incoherently for his life. Bedlam. He smiled grimly to himself. Jenn Charles and Dan Hendricks had not gone gentle into that good night.

"Breach," a voice said clearly over the confusion.

Two detonations occurred simultaneously. The blood drained from Calista's face.

"Flash-bangs." Titus began pacing back and forth, cursing under his breath as the pitched battle moved inside the house.

Cold Harbor was losing.

"There's someone else here! Shoot him! Shoot him! What the . . ." The voice was swamped by a wet gurgle. Nothing coherent followed.

"Tinsley," Calista whispered to herself. "Oh, dear God."

She took out her phone and dialed frantically.

Titus snatched up the radio and demanded a sitrep from someone. "What is your status? Report! Over!"

Titus caught George's eye and didn't like what he saw. He drew his sidearm and stalked over, leveling it at George's face.

"No," Calista said.

Titus stopped and glared at Calista. "What?"

"We may need him."

"The plan was—"

"The plan was your team was competent," Calista interrupted. "Now I need a new plan."

CHAPTER THIRTY-EIGHT

It was fifty miles before Gibson eased off the accelerator, slowing to seventy miles an hour. He drove with one eye on the road ahead and one eye behind, studying the darkness for any sign that someone had followed them. His ears were still ringing.

The brim of Bear's Phillies cap was low over his eyes. His head had been the safest place for it in the confusion, but now the cap felt oddly comforting. In the chaos, he'd managed to grab it along with Bear's book. Billy's gun rested under Gibson's right thigh. Gibson still wasn't clear how he'd gotten clear without getting shot. It had been a good old-fashioned turkey shoot.

He had no idea if Jenn or Hendricks were alive. They'd been separated during the firefight, and for all he knew they were captured or dead. He didn't like leaving them, but Billy had taken one to the stomach and needed a hospital. Gibson had fireman-carried him out of the house to the car, expecting with each staggering step a bullet that never came.

He pulled the Cherokee off at an exit and found an abandoned gas station that looked as if it had been closed for years. He shut off the engine but left Hendricks's keys dangling from the ignition. Sitting in the shadow of the station's awning, he looked back the way they had come and listened to the wet rasp of Billy's breathing.

In the dim glow of the streetlights, Gibson could see Billy's face, pale and beaded with sweat. Billy coughed what looked like black tar onto his chin. Gibson wiped it away and saw that Billy's shirt and pants were soaked through with blood. Billy murmured something inchoate. He had drifted in and out of consciousness since the mad scramble back at the house but hadn't spoken a lucid word.

He had to get Billy to a hospital, but first he needed to know they hadn't been followed. The dashboard dinged noisily when he opened his door. Billy's hand shot out and grabbed him by the wrist.

"You know where you're going next?" Billy asked.

"Yeah, I have a pretty good idea."

"I knew you'd figure it out. Will you do something for me?"

"Of course."

"When you find her, will you tell her about me?"

"Hey. Don't start on a hero trip now. As soon as it's safe we're going to a hospital. You're alive, and you're going to stay that way."

"I'm glad I met you. It was good to tell someone."

"The privilege was mine, Billy. Now shut up and sit tight. I'm going to be right back."

"Okay." Billy smiled through the pain.

Pulling the hat low over his eyes, Gibson walked out to the road. He didn't see anyone, but that didn't make him feel safe. How long could he wait, though? Billy needed a surgeon.

He took out his phone. It was a risk; the phone might be how Jenn and Hendricks had tracked him to the lake house, but he saw no alternative. He powered it up—one bar. He moved across the parking lot, hunting for a better signal. He settled for three bars. Hendricks would have simply known, but Gibson needed to search for the nearest hospital. He found one eight miles from here, memorized the route, and made the call he'd been dreading. He didn't want to scare her unnecessarily, but he couldn't avoid it now.

"You wouldn't believe how hot it is here," he said when she answered.

"Say that again?" Nicole asked.

"You wouldn't believe how hot it is here."

"How hot is it?"

"One hundred and ten."

"What's the heat advisory?" she asked.

"Find shade."

She was quiet for a moment, then, "Well, try to stay cool."

"Tell her I love her."

Nicole hung up without another word.

It was their old code from when he'd been in the service. It meant there was a legitimate terrorist threat to DC, and she needed to get to safety. Calls home were monitored for key words and phrases, so a lot of guys had a way to warn family.

Nicole would take Ellie to her uncle's hunting lodge in West Virginia. She'd be on the road in less than fifteen minutes and would stay off the grid until she heard from him. He'd never had to use it while he was in the service. He was grateful now that she still respected him enough to trust him and not ask questions. Although if he survived all this, he knew he would have many to answer.

The road was still deserted in both directions, so he made another call. It was a number he hadn't dialed in over a decade; he couldn't recite it, but his fingers knew it. He just prayed it was still good.

A young boy answered. Gibson asked for his aunt. The boy set the phone down roughly and ran off, yelling "Mom."

A woman picked up. She sounded just the same.

"Hello, Miranda."

"Gibson? Is that you?"

They talked for a few minutes. He told her what he needed. She wasn't sure if she still had it but promised to look.

"If I have it, there's only one place it would be," she said.

They set a time and place to meet. He thanked her and hung up. That had gone better than he could reasonably have hoped. He tried Jenn's number, but it went straight to voice mail. He contemplated leaving a message, but he couldn't be sure her phone hadn't been taken. Instead, he hung up and pulled the SIM card and shattered his phone against the side of the gas station. If it hadn't been compromised already, it soon would be.

Anyway, there wasn't anybody left for him to call.

He walked back around to the SUV, calculating how long a drive it was to Charlottesville. He could get away with driving at night, but come dawn the bullet holes in the car would lead to unpleasant questions. The passenger door stood open; Billy was gone. Bloody footprints crossed the parking lot and disappeared at the edge of the broad field that backed the gas station. After ten yards he lost the trail. He called out to Billy in the dark. Not even the wind answered.

Gibson studied the horizon to the north but realized he couldn't be sure which direction Billy had gone. He searched the field in the dark, yelling Billy's name to the uncaring night.

He went back to the Cherokee. There comes a point when every man must choose his own way. Billy had made his choice, and Gibson hoped he could live with it.

His was Charlottesville.

CHAPTER THIRTY-NINE

When daylight came, Gibson pulled off at a motel that advertised "Clean Rooms" on a hand-painted sign. He parked in the back, away from the main road, and got a room. He paid cash for two nights, even though he only intended to be there until that evening. He put his clothes in the tub to soak the blood out of them and took a shower, stomping his clothes like an old-fashioned wine press until blood leaked out of them, swirling down the drain. He stood under the scalding water until his skin was pink like a newborn's.

He slept hard. When the need to urinate woke him, he hung his clothes to dry on the shower bar. When he woke for good, it was late afternoon. It felt like he'd been asleep for a five count, not ten hours. He took another shower to wash the sleep off and put his clothes back on. It was an improvement, but you could still see the bloodstains. He turned his shirt inside out. That helped some. Now he just looked like an idiot.

A mile down the road, he stopped at a discount clothing store in a tumbledown strip mall. He bought a pair of jeans and two shirts. He wore them out of the store and threw his old clothes in the trash. At a hardware store he bought a claw hammer. He drove on until he found a secluded turnoff. He took the hammer to the bullet holes in the side of the SUV. It looked a lot worse when he was done, but they didn't look like bullet holes.

Charlottesville had changed in the ten years he'd been gone, but at the same time it hadn't changed a bit. Not in ways that mattered. It was still first and foremost a university town. Distinctly southern and proud of its heritage and traditions, it was also young, vibrant, and easygoing—the best of both worlds, in Gibson's opinion. He drove into town on Route 29, which became Emmet Street once it crossed Route 250. The university rose up to greet him. New buildings dotted the campus, but it was familiar all the same. Part of him wanted to park and take a walk through Grounds, part of him wanted to take a detour to the White Spot for a Gus Burger, and part of him wanted to turn the car around and get out of there. It wasn't that he had made a conscious decision never to come back, but somehow he'd always found a reason to be elsewhere.

Distracted by memories, he missed his turn on University Avenue. Rather than make a U-turn, he took Jefferson Park Avenue around, picking up West Main on the far side of Grounds. School was out, and, as in the summers of his childhood, Charlottesville was slumbering, worn out by a long school year and trying to catch up on its sleep before twenty thousand students began returning in a few weeks.

The white brick exterior of the Blue Moon Diner came up on his right faster than he remembered. He pulled into the narrow parking lot that ran alongside the building and sat for a minute in the simmering dark.

He had not seen his aunt since the trial. Miranda had taken him in after his father's death, and it was fair to say he had not been a grateful child. She had been more than understanding of his tempestuous moods and bad behavior in the way that only a mother who had already raised teenage sons could be. He returned her kindness in the form of an FBI raid on her home.

During the trial, contact with his aunt was reserved and frosty. He couldn't rightly blame her, but, young and angry, he'd resented her for it anyway.

Legal bills had eaten through his father's estate, and his last correspondence with his aunt had been when the house was sold. It had taken time to find a buyer, and he was nearing graduation at Parris Island when the envelope came—plain, white, and with a check inside. There was no note, and he'd seen no cause to reply. Eventually, he'd used the money as a down payment on the house Nicole and Ellie lived in now.

He didn't know what to expect from the meeting and realized that he only had a child's memory of his aunt. He didn't know what kind of a person she was. She was just Aunt Miranda, who'd looked after him and made sure he didn't starve while Duke was out of town. Whatever else may have happened, he told himself, she had done more than most would have. He'd lost a father, but she'd lost a brother. Still, he didn't have the first idea what Duke Gibson had meant to his sister. If he was being honest, he had stayed away from Charlottesville out of the stubborn desire to avoid this very meeting.

The Blue Moon Diner wasn't the same. He shouldn't have been surprised, but he was. It had been ten years, more, and management had changed yet again. He felt a sadness for the place that surprised him.

A young white woman with tattoos down both arms touched his arm and told him to sit anywhere. He chose a booth in the front corner so he could watch the front door for Miranda.

Gibson thought the new owners had done a nice job of maintaining the feel of the place, but his father surely would have expressed disdain for most of the changes.

Duke Vaughn was progressive on a lot of fronts, but on some matters, like his diners, he was fussily old school. Take the records overflowing the windowsills, or the beer and liquor for sale. Neither belonged in the Duke Vaughn school of American diners. The chalkboard schedule of nightly singers would have surely drawn a groan. "Diners don't have singers!" he could hear his father pronouncing. And the menu, which had items like the Mountain Trout Club and the Tandoori Chicken Sandwich, would almost certainly have earned Duke Vaughn's scorn.

The club sounded pretty good. He handed the menu back to the waitress.

His thoughts turned to Billy and to Hendricks and Jenn. Were any of them alive? George Abe. Kirby Tate. Terrance Musgrove. So many lives bound together in the Gordian knot of one missing girl. But for Gibson, it came down to his father. He was under no illusion that he was safe, but it was a question he needed to answer before deciding his next move. As horrible as the truth might be, Gibson knew that the doubt would drive him insane. What had driven his father to suicide? Gibson could feel the opaque fingers of his suspicion tightening their grip.

He just prayed that his aunt had kept it.

Miranda Davis came in through the front door. Gibson stood to greet her, unsure how. His aunt solved that riddle and drew her nephew into her strong arms. He sank into her embrace, and both their eyes were wet when they parted.

The years had treated Miranda fairly. She had aged, of course, but lost none of her vitality. Her tall, thin frame, strong from years of competitive running, including six marathons, looked nearly the same. Only her hair appeared noticeably different.

"I like your hair," he said.

"Oh, I got sick of the gray. Bill thinks I look pretty as a redhead."

Bill was her husband of thirty-some years. Gibson had only ever heard him speak on two subjects: UVA sports and his lovely, lovely wife. Otherwise, he left the talking to Miranda.

"He's right. You look great."

Miranda waved the compliment away. "Well, I don't know about all that, but thank you. And, my goodness, Gibson. Look at you. A man. Lord, it's been so long." She became quiet. "Which is my fault, I know."

"No," he said with a vehemence that surprised him. "I was a shit."

"You were a child," she corrected. "I was the grown-up. I should have acted like one."

"I'm sorry," he said.

She covered his hand with hers. "I'm so glad you called."

"Me too."

"Lord but we can be a stubborn lot. Are you in town long? Bill would love to see you."

He said that he was leaving tonight. Miranda looked disappointed, and he promised that when he had time he'd like to come for a visit.

"I have a daughter." He told Miranda about Ellie, and about Nicole. Miranda asked questions, and he filled her in on his life as best he could, trying to keep the narrative upbeat. He was surprised at how much good stuff there was to tell, and at how good it felt to have someone who wanted to hear it.

"I hope to meet her someday," she said.

He promised that he would bring her to Charlottesville soon. That brought a fresh round of tears and self-recriminations. She smiled through her tears.

"Bill says I cry if the wind changes direction. I suppose that's true. Oh! I have what you asked for. I almost forgot why I was here. Such a space cadet. I found it."

She reached into her bag and lifted out a small marble bust of James Madison. She put it on the table between them. His father had bought it at a yard sale as an undergraduate at UVA. Duke called it his first "important purchase," and it had held a place of honor on his desk until the day he died.

They talked a few more minutes, Miranda all smiles, even as he walked her outside and they embraced once more.

"You look just like him, you know? Especially the eyes." In the air, her fingers traced the features of his face. "Just like him."

Back at the table, his food was waiting for him. He pushed the plate away untouched and held the statue in his hands, feeling its weight. Turning it over, he searched for the indentation in the pedestal. His thumb found it and released the panel concealing the cubbyhole in the pedestal. Originally intended for notes and the like, it was just big enough to hide a thumb drive. Still, he was a little surprised when it fell into his palm.

Duke Vaughn had kept a diary since he was an undergraduate at UVA. Always a believer in his own destiny, he claimed it would be instrumental when it came time to write his memoirs. Although Duke spoke of it often, no one had ever read a word, and so Duke Vaughn's "diary" had become something of a family legend.

Gibson had seen his father back up his computer and hide the thumb drive in the statue a million times. After his arrest, the FBI had seized his father's PC, which had contained enough incriminating evidence to destroy Duke's reputation. The computer had never been returned, and, more than likely, the thumb drive was the last remaining copy of Duke Vaughn's writing.

He plugged it into his laptop.

A single folder appeared on his screen labeled "PRIVATE." Subtle. A window appeared, prompting him for a password. When he'd first become interested in computers and encryption, his first project had been his father. The first password he'd ever hacked. His first criminal act. Second if you counted the time he'd been pulled over for speeding when he was a kid. Gibson entered the password and the window disappeared.

In the folder were more than thirty files, each named for the year in which it had been written. The earliest dated back to the late seventies. In total, they covered Duke Vaughn's life from university, through his rise in politics, up to his "suicide," running to well more than two million words. Some entries were incredibly short: "October 7, 1987—I hate canvassing for voters. I hate it," read one from a campaign trail. Others were much more serious and went on for pages. The writing became insightful and articulate. Encounters with party bigwigs, legislation Duke had been involved with, philosophical musings on politics.

Gibson opened a program that would search all the documents simultaneously for keywords. He typed in "baseball" and waited while the machine combed through his father's journals. It came back with close to two thousand matches. Gibson frowned and added "Suzanne" and "Gibson" to his search. The program did its work again and dinged to announce it had finished. A single match this time.

On the surface it was perfectly innocuous—an outing to a baseball game cut short by a difficult child. Gibson read slowly, hearing his father's voice in the words, listening for anything out of the ordinary. But it sounded merely like a man concerned for his friend's daughter. Gibson came to the part when Bear really flipped out. It matched his recollection until a part came that he didn't remember:

> I'd arranged a face-to-face with Martinez. Social. Low pressure. A chance for Ben to clear the air with the Whip after we broke ranks on the unemployment bill. It was the right call, but it's cost us. Midterms were eighteen months out, but we needed to pave over the cracks now.
>
> Hard to do the way Suzanne was behaving. Decision time. Ben wanted to postpone, but I'd worn holes in the knees of a good suit getting the meeting. It was happening. So it was agreed that I'd take Suzanne back to Virginia. George would stay with Gibson and Ben. Felt badly leaving Gibson behind, but the Whip had a son about his age. Made sense, and from what

I was told, Gibson knocked it out of the park. Kid's got a future.

Suzanne was a wreck until I got her out of the park. I kept my distance or she'd start to freak again. It was a scene. Offered to buy her a cap, and that seemed to calm her down some. Found a merchandise stand on the walk back to the car. She didn't want an Orioles cap. No Orioles. No, no, of course not. It was an O's game for Christ's sake. What else are they going to have? She started to cry again. The guy dug around in the boxes and found two Phillies caps. Wasn't sure why he had it. Bought them both—thought we could bond over it. Cap was too big for her, but it was a snapback so I cinched it all the way and it just about stayed on her head. That made her happy, and thank God she passed out in the backseat on the way home.

O's lost.

Gibson remembered that cap now. The second cap had been left in the backseat on the drive home. He'd asked Duke about it but gotten no real answer, and his father had thrown it in the trash when they got back to Charlottesville. He'd never connected it to Bear before now.

And it felt wrong. It was all so wrong. He'd found nothing definitive, but there was enough to feed his festering doubt. Gibson took the Phillies cap off and looked at it again. Billy was right. It was a message, and he had a sickening feeling it had been intended for him. Billy said she'd kept thinking up ways to make contact with him in jail.

What were you trying to tell me?

Gibson put the cap into his bag rather than back on his head. The Blue Moon was filling up. In one corner, the evening's entertainment tuned a guitar. Gibson needed to get somewhere quiet where he could comb through the rest of the diary. There had to be more.

He packed up, paid the bill, and went out the side door to the parking lot. It was a risk, but he needed to reach out to Jenn. Of course, his phone was lying shattered in a gas station parking lot in Pennsylvania. Older motels often still had pay phones. He needed a place where he could hole up for the night and kill two birds.

He was at the SUV, keys in the door, when the hand, strong as cold iron, went over his mouth, deftly turning and exposing his neck. The icy silver of a hypodermic needle kissed his skin like a wasp's sting.

"Quiet, now," a voice of rotting fruit whispered. "I'll take you to see your father."

CHAPTER FORTY

Duke smiled at his son and waved him over. He came to his father obediently and tried not to fidget as Duke rebuttoned his top button and straightened his tie for the third time. The Christmas party was in full swing, and even though the senator had a strict "no shop talk" policy at the annual gathering, politics was never far from anyone's lips.

A doughy beet-red man stopped to shake hands with Duke. Gibson was used to it. People were always interrupting to talk to his dad. His dad was important, and Gibson felt immense pride in the respect that everyone showed him. Yet as the two men spoke, Duke made the man feel like the center of the universe—asked after his wife and children by name and congratulated him on a recent triumph in the House. The man went away happy, and Duke turned back to his son.

"The day that man gets a call from me is the day I'm on fire, and he's got the only hose for three states."

Gibson laughed, even though he didn't really understand the joke. He just liked when his father treated him like one of the guys. An insider. Duke ran his hand through his son's hair, mussing it affectionately.

"Dad . . . ," Gibson complained and straightened it with the flat of his hand.

"Where are the rest of the kids? You don't need to hang out down here on the killing floor."

"They're all upstairs watching kids' movies," he said with disgust.

At ten, Gibson was in the midst of becoming wise beyond his years. His favorite movie was *The Godfather Part II*—not that the original was bad, but everyone knew that *Part II* was the superior film. According to his dad, John Cazale was the most underrated actor in movie history. *Only ever made five movies, but I'll stand those five against any five ever made,* Duke had told him when they'd watched it together the first time.

That fall, Gibson had landed in the principal's office for grabbing a classmate by the face, exclaiming, "I know it was you, Bobby, you broke my heart," and kissing him violently on the mouth. Duke had laughed until he'd cried and halfheartedly told his son not to do it again. Gibson pointed out that nothing had disappeared from his locker since.

"Kids' movies, huh? That sounds pretty rough."

"The worst. What's going on down here?"

"Just lining them up and knocking them down. These things are all about appearances, kiddo. Mark my words, there's nothing phonier under heaven than a DC holiday party. The only honest words you'll hear all night are the drink orders at the bar."

"So why do it?"

"Some things you just have to do. It's all about appearances. Did I say that already? Anyway, the trick is seeing what they're trying to hide. What are they trying to draw your eye away from? Figure that out, and you figure out the man. Or woman. But start with men, because they're easier. Women are more of a PhD thing."

"Got it." Gibson nodded sagely, then: "Like how?"

"All right, so take that fellow over there," Duke pointed to a tall, thin man with a face like a strip of sandpaper. He was surveying the room and nursing a beer.

"Is he someone important?"

"You tell me," Duke said.

Gibson stared at him a long time. "No."

"Why not?"

"Because no one is trying to talk to him. If he was important, he wouldn't be alone."

"Good boy." Duke chuckled. "But just him now. Can you tell just from looking at him?"

Gibson sized the man up. He wore a suit and shiny tie. He had a lapel pin and wire-rimmed glasses. His blond hair was combed back conservatively. Gibson couldn't see it.

"He looks like everyone else."

"Nobody looks like everybody else. We try but fail. The trick, Gib, is not to look at the center of a man. At the center every man looks the same. Suit, tie, lapel pin. He's wearing the uniform, and he looks good. At the center he could be the president of the United States. It's at the edge where the truth lies. It's like hair. Everyone brushes their hair so it looks good from straight on. Why? Because that's how we see it in the mirror. Straight on. We only ever see ourselves straight on, so that's the only angle we worry about."

"So I should look at his back?"

"Not literally, but yes. Look at his shoes. What do you see?"

"They're scuffed. One of the laces is broken."

"What does that tell you?"

"He wears them a lot?"

"And what does that tell you?"

Gibson thought hard. The shoes reminded him of Ben Rizolli's basketball. Ben Rizolli's dad had split when he was little, and it was just Ben and his mom. There wasn't a lot of money. Ben had had the same basketball since forever, and it went everywhere Ben went. The seams and lettering were worn away, and there was hardly any grip left on it at all. Gibson always felt bad that a kid who loved basketball couldn't afford a new one.

"He doesn't have many pairs. He probably can't afford a lot of shoes. He's hoping no one looks at his feet."

"Not bad. Do you think the senator is wearing scuffed shoes tonight?"

"No way."

"No way. That's right. Now look at my shoes."

Gibson looked down at his father's feet. Duke was wearing a pair of worn black wing tips. The leather was creased deeply above the toe. He looked up at his dad inquisitively.

"So what does that tell you about your old man?" Duke asked.

"I don't know."

"It means that no one thing reveals a man. Never be so arrogant to think you know a man from just his shoes. But . . ."

"But, it's a start?"

"It's a start," Duke said. "So what's the difference between him and me?"

"People keep talking to you."

Duke winked. "It's a start."

Gibson felt proud and nodded vigorously. He felt like he was missing something, but he was happy for his dad's attention and didn't want to spoil it by asking too many questions. He'd figure it out on his own.

"All right, kiddo. Give me an hour. I need to work a bit, but then I know a place in Georgetown that makes a killer Oreo milkshake. Deal?"

"Deal."

Three hours later, he awakened where he'd fallen asleep, curled up on a bed in one of the guestrooms beneath a fur coat.

"Wake up, son. Wake up. Wake up."

Duke scooped him up and carried him out to the car. Gibson didn't wake until the door slammed shut.

"Wake up . . ."

CHAPTER FORTY-ONE

Gibson came to at the bottom of an ocean strewn with the archaeology of his life. In the murky, dim light he could make out the rusted hulk of his father's green station wagon half submerged in a sandbank. The ruins of his childhood home leaned crazily to one side. Improbably, the white dogwood in the backyard was in full bloom. His first bicycle leaned against it. And to his right, the classroom where the FBI had cuffed him and perp-walked him out past a sea of TV cameras.

Something caught his eye up on the surface. He pushed off from the bottom and began to rise. As he broke the surface, his eyes flew open, and he took a deep, rasping breath. A naked lightbulb, like a wayward sun, swayed near his face. He blinked rapidly, trying to focus his eyes. But when he had, he wished he hadn't.

On tiptoes, Gibson teetered on a wooden stool. A rope around his neck was the only thing that kept him from falling, but the price was the cruel way it bit into his skin. He tried to grab the rope to take the pressure off his throat, but his hands were bound behind his back. Panicking, he began to thrash and nearly lost his balance. A steadying hand helped him regain his perch.

"All right, now. Settle down. Not just yet. Not just yet. Business first," said the voice from outside the diner.

The diner.

The attack came back to him. Something about his father. His heart sank, and he felt very foolish and very alone. The rope around his neck made it hard to look around, but he took the biggest breath he could muster and took stock of his surroundings.

He was in a basement. The half windows were set high up on the pale-yellow walls. It was night out. Watercolors of birds hung along the walls: hummingbirds, woodpeckers, and cardinals. An easel was set up in the corner. Some kind of painter's studio? A set of carpeted stairs led up, but up to where?

A man stepped into view. Gibson shuddered. In his confusion, he thought the man had followed him up from his unconscious. One of those benthic predators that lurks in the black depths of the ocean. But it was only a man. At least on the surface. Average height. Slight build. A pale, unremarkable face apart from a recently broken nose that was swollen and red. He was the sort of man who might check you into a hotel or sit beside you in a doctor's waiting room. At least that's what the man wanted you to see. But at the edges of the man, the camouflage began to fray.

The eyes were what gave him away. The eyes were the jaundiced yellow of a diurnal owl and motionless like the dead surface of the moon. Sunk deep in their sockets, they fixed on Gibson, seeming to see everything and nothing. He'd met some scary men in jail and even scarier men in the Marines, but this man, if he was a man at all, scared him more than any of those. This man was death come for him.

But perhaps more unsettling still were his clothes. The man was dressed like him. Not sort of like him. Not similar colors and styles, but the exact same shirt, jeans, and shoes. They looked like a couple of twins who shopped together. That meant the man had been in the clothing store with him, had followed behind him, had seen him shopping, and had picked out the same outfit. It told Gibson that his abduction had been exactingly planned. Whatever lay ahead, it was nothing good, and whatever he might think to try, this man would have already anticipated it.

"Pay attention now. Are you paying attention? We don't have much time," the man said in a mild and polite tone. It was the voice of a surgeon dumbing down a complex procedure for an irritating patient. They regarded each other silently, and then, without ceremony or warning, the man kicked the stool from under Gibson's feet. It made a keening whine across the wood floor and clattered into a far wall.

Gibson dropped no more than an inch, but the difference was profound. It was the callous inch that separated living from dying. The rope caught his weight with a jerk and tore into the flesh beneath his jaw. The tendons in his neck and shoulders felt like they were being ripped up like weeds. His legs thrashed in the air.

The man stepped forward and patted Gibson's leg gently. Gibson felt a helpless despair. A vast welling up of regret that he supposed accompanied the premature end of any life. His regret was cold and offered no comfort. Filled up with words that he wished he had spoken and the faces he wished he had spoken them to.

He expected to lose consciousness quickly. That was how it worked in the movies. A few moments of helpless struggling before the rope wrung the life out of its victim. Instead, he hung there struggling and listening to the leathery scratch of his breathing and the pounding of the blood in his temples.

"This is the short drop," the man said. "You'll notice that, unlike the standard drop or the long drop, your neck is not broken. Which may seem like a blessing now, but in the end you will wish it had been a longer drop and a shorter wait. But that's the good news and bad news of the short drop. You live longer, but . . . you live longer. Most people think they'd always want to live longer, but twenty minutes at the end of a rope is a long time to die. A long time to regret things that cannot be changed and that no longer matter."

The man wrapped his arms around Gibson's legs and lifted him up, supporting his weight. The stool slid under his feet, and Gibson danced on it weakly.

"So that we understand each other," the man said. "I think it helps a man in your position to understand the punishment beforehand. The punishment for not satisfying me. How do you satisfy me, you ask? Well. I have a question for you. Only one, but it's an important one. I will ask it until I am satisfied by the answer. Until I am satisfied . . . the short drop. Do you understand?"

"Yes."

The man held up his father's thumb drive.

"Did you make a copy? Upload it before you left the diner?"

"If I tell you, will you let me go?"

The stool fell away again. He dropped. Pain lanced down his back and shoulders. He hung there a long time, longer than before. Eventually, the man's arms lifted him again until his feet felt the stool slide under his feet. He felt smaller, as if a part of what he was had been torn away. The man gave him time to collect what little was left of his wits. Out of the corner of his eye, he saw his father sitting barefoot on the bottom of the stairs, gazing sadly at his son. Gibson blinked, and the apparition was gone, but he knew where he was. He was home.

"Oh," the man said. "Welcome home. I wasn't sure if you'd recognize it. It's changed in the last decade. I liked it better with the red paint."

"Fuck you," Gibson tried to scream. It came out as no more than a whisper.

"I enjoyed meeting your father." The man took out a knife and unfolded a long, unforgiving blade. "We had a good talk in this room. Two men coming to an understanding." The man smiled faintly at the memory. "But to answer your question, I will not let you go if you tell me what I need to know. Not under any circumstance. Your life is not something you can barter for. I know that is a hard thing to hear, but honesty is best. However, I will tell you what I am willing to offer you."

"Go to hell."

"Upstairs, there's a couple. Linda and Mark Tompkins. Linda paints the delightful pictures you see here. At the moment, what they know is that a masked, distraught man broke into their home and bound them. A man dressed as you are dressed. The man was sobbing. Hysterical. He said he was sorry. That he didn't want to hurt them. He told them that this had been his house once. When the Tompkinses are discovered tomorrow, they will identify you as their assailant. The police will conclude, reasonably, that in a fit of despair following your divorce and the loss of your job and family, you broke into your childhood home and followed in your father's footsteps."

"That's what you're offering me?"

"Yes."

"And if I don't answer?"

"If you don't answer, I will push the chair away. When you are dead I will go upstairs and I will butcher Linda and Mark Tompkins. I will make the man watch his wife die. I can make it last a long time."

Gibson heard kinetic excitement in the man's voice. He hid it well, but Gibson read joy on his face, or whatever passed for joy in someone like that.

"Why? They've done nothing."

"Neither have you," the man pointed out. "Unfortunately for them, events have placed them in our path just as events have placed you in mine. And through no fault of their own, their lives now hang in the balance. So to speak."

"So?" Gibson said. "I don't know them. Never met them. What the hell does who you kill have to do with me? That's on you, not me."

It was a bluff. He tried to make it a good one.

"True, true. It is 'on me.' Your conscience is clean. But it is not your conscience that should concern you." The man shrugged. "Shouldn't you be thinking about Ellie?"

At the mention of his daughter's name, Gibson went rigid with fear. "What about her?"

"Well . . . how will it affect her? Your crime, I mean," the man said. "Think how luridly it will play in the media. Imagine how you will be remembered. How Ellie will remember you. They will say that you lost your mind, but before you hung yourself, you murdered the Tompkinses—the unfortunate people who bought your father's house. They will label you a degenerate psychopath who needed to inflict his misery on innocents. The deranged end to a family tragedy that began more than a decade ago. That will be the epitaph to your life. When Ellie is grown and thinks about her father, it will be with confusion and shame. The same way you've thought about your own father. So I ask you for Linda and Mark. And for your daughter. Did you make a copy?"

Gibson opened his mouth to speak but then shut it again. Tears streamed down his face. For his father. For his daughter. For the choice he had to make now.

But he knew he was through arguing or pleading with this man. From the first moment he had stared into this man's empty eyes, Gibson had known on some level that there was no pity there and never had been. He'd be damned if he was going to waste the last minutes of his life begging. He would do something good with that time instead. He would save Linda and Mark. That would be worthwhile . . . even if her paintings were lousy.

"Did you make a copy?"

"I did not," he said.

"Why not?"

"I didn't think I had to."

The man considered that. "You did, though. That was wrong."

"Yes."

"So you did not make a copy?"

"No."

"No copies?"

"None."

It went on and on like this. The same question asked dozens of times in dozens of different ways. It was insane, but Gibson fought for the man to believe him. Expected at any moment that the stool would be kicked away again. Finally . . .

"I believe you," the man said.

Gibson stopped, exhaustion spreading through him. "Thank you," he said. He wasn't quite sure why, but he felt such gratitude, such peace, now that the man believed him. He just wanted to sleep.

The man nodded and folded his knife. He gathered his things to go, looking around to make sure he hadn't forgotten anything. When he was done, he returned to look at Gibson.

"Where is Suzanne?" Gibson asked.

"I don't know."

"Why did you kill my father?"

The man looked at him with curiosity. "Does it matter?"

"Suzanne was pregnant. The baby. Was it my father's?"

"Is that what you really want to know? Will it give you peace?"

Gibson didn't know. "Please."

The man considered for a moment. He reached into a pocket and withdrew a sheet of paper from his pocket and unfolded it, careful so as not to accidentally see what it said.

"Whatever it says, whatever you learn, do not tell me, do not show it in your face. Remember the people upstairs."

Gibson nodded and the man held it up for him to see. It took a great effort to focus his eyes and understand what he was reading. The paper was a paternity test. Three columns: "Suzanne Lombard,"

"Child," "Father (Alleged)." Beneath were rows of paired numbers that Gibson didn't understand. And at the bottom:

> The alleged father is not excluded as the biological
> father of the tested child. Based on testing obtained
> from analyses of the DNA loci listed, the probability
> of paternity is 99.9998%.

But it was the sentence that followed, and its implications, that roared in his ears—the concussive report of dominoes, stretching back through his entire life, finally falling. Oh, Bear. Oh, God, Bear.

> Benjamin Lombard is not excluded as the biological
> father and is considered to be the father of Jane Doe.

The sounds of splintering wood and heavy footfalls came from upstairs. The man snatched the paper away. Gibson met his eyes. Whatever mask he wore to blend in among people ripped loose momentarily; beneath lay something abhorrent. Something ancient and infinitely cruel that people comforted themselves by believing had long ago become extinct, but which this man had coaxed back into life.

"Gibson!" a woman's voice called out.

Jenn?

He tried to call out to her, but the stool went flying across the wood floor and suddenly he was dying all over again, hanging until consciousness slipped away.

When he came to, he lay on his back in the basement, Jenn Charles kneeling beside him.

"Did you get him?" he asked.

"Get who?" she asked. "There's no one here but us."

"Upstairs?" he asked, remembering the awful threats to the homeowners.

"They're fine. Hendricks is with them. Are you okay?"

He was laughing and crying, jagged crests of relief and despair.

"What happened here?" Jenn asked, but mercifully his mind had found the power switch, and he was not available to answer.

PART THREE
GEORGIA

CHAPTER FORTY-TWO

Gibson woke in a twin bed feeling like death's one-night stand. He went to roll on his side but simply could not. He surrendered and lay still. His body felt like it had been drawn and quartered between a pair of muscle cars. Hendricks appeared with a water bottle and helped him take a few sips. The effort exhausted him, and he slept again.

It took three days before he could swallow any of the baby food Jenn spoon-fed him, and five more before he was able to sit up on his own. When he spoke, his voice came out in a shuddering, painful rasp. Hendricks took to calling him Tom Waits and Gibson to writing things down rather than talking.

On the morning of the eighth day, being alive no longer seemed like the worst idea he'd ever had. He swung his legs off the side of the bed and gathered his strength for the Herculean task of taking a leak. He stood and pushed one leg in front of the other—an old-man shuffle. His reflection in the bathroom mirror stopped him. He *was* an old man with the damaged face of an unrepentant alcoholic. His ten-day beard couldn't hide the livid, wrenching bruise that ran across his throat from ear to ear. He ran his finger along it and thought about how close he'd come to dying.

What were they going to do now?

Gibson ran a hot shower and stood under the water a long while. Bear opened her eyes. She was in bed. It was late, and she was watching the light under the door. Watching for shadows. Scarcely breathing.

Gibson tried to shake the image from his head. It drew Bear's attention, and she looked to him now. Imploring. He wanted to ask her how Lombard had done it. Compelled her silence. But he knew—the awful emotional blackmail that her father must have used to isolate her. Control her.

But you failed, you son of a bitch. You failed. All the time, Bear had been planning her escape with Billy Casper. And then it struck Gibson—there *was* no Tom B. Bear had invented him. Created a fictional father for her unborn child in case she didn't get away. A plausible story to explain her pregnancy, to protect the child. Protect her mother. Maybe even to protect her father—so hard to beat loyalty out of children. Taking it all on herself. How could she be that strong?

He dressed gingerly, grunting through the pain of pulling on a T-shirt. His messenger bag was at the end of the bed, and he went through it to confirm that his laptop was gone, along with his father's thumb drive. But Billy's gun remained along with the Phillies cap and *The Fellowship of the Ring.* Inside he also found the picture of Bear pregnant on the couch. Pregnant with the baby of "Tom B."

A crazy thought occurred to him. He began flipping back through the pages of the book, back to the beginning. It took a minute, but he found the passage he was looking for and read the familiar words aloud:

"Now, my little fellows, where be you a-going to, puffing like a bellows? What's the matter here then? Do you know who I am? I'm Tom Bombadil. Tell me what's your trouble! Tom's in a hurry now."

Tears washed down his face, but he was smiling too. A despairing elation. In the margin, in orange pen:

I knew you would.

Gibson laughed aloud and stifled himself with a hand over his mouth. What this brave girl had done. It defied belief. His tears hadn't stopped, but he felt clearheaded for the first time in as long as he could remember. Clearheaded and angry. He wiped the tears away. He knew what came now.

He put the cap on and, holding the book tight like a catechism, shambled out to the living room. It was small and rustic and smelled like the inside of an old steamer trunk. Hendricks was asleep on a threadbare couch, but his eyes flickered open as Gibson shuffled past. A bulky old TV on a crooked stand was tuned to the news. It was a story about the imminent convention in Atlanta. Although Anne Fleming had not formally conceded, Lombard's candidacy was assured. Reportedly, the two were scheduled to meet in Atlanta about the possibility of a joint ticket.

Jenn sat at a small table by the window, several handguns and ammunition laid out before her, fieldstripping a Steyr M-A1. He was fairly sure Jenn could do it in the dark, because she never took her eyes off the tiny gap between the curtains that gave her a view of the approach.

"Done lying around?" she asked without looking up.

"Good to see you too."

She glanced his way and smiled. "You look taller."

"I don't feel it. Where are we?"

"North Carolina. Outside Greensboro."

"Greensboro?"

Jenn and Hendricks caught him up. From the chaos of the lake house shootout to the tracker sewn into his messenger bag that had led them south to Charlottesville and the Cherokee parked outside his childhood home.

"How'd you find us?" she asked.

"Hacked Hendricks's phone."

She looked almost impressed; Hendricks not so much.

"Guess that makes us even," she said.

"Guess it does."

His assailant had gone out the exterior basement steps and fled through the backyard. A neighbor must have called 911, because they'd only just got out of there before police swarmed the area. Outside Roanoke, they'd dumped their vehicles in a grocery-store parking lot and paid cash for a 1995 Ford Probe.

"Drove it right off the guy's lawn," Hendricks said. He was awake and was sitting up on the couch, stretching and yawning.

From there, they'd driven south until they found a cheap rental cabin. They'd stashed Gibson in the trunk and passed themselves off as newlyweds celebrating their first anniversary. The cabin was rented for the month of August. It was isolated. Paid up front in cash, and the landlord lived in Raleigh so was unlikely to stop by unannounced. All in all, it was about as off the grid as one could hope on short notice while transporting an injured person.

"Cell phones?" Gibson asked.

"Duct-taped to the underside of two different eighteen-wheelers," Hendricks said.

"We're on burners." Jenn held up a disposable flip phone. "So now you know our story. Mind telling us how you came to be hanging from a rope?"

"What do we have to eat? I'm starving," Gibson asked.

"Strained peas? Creamy carrots?"

"Besides baby food."

"They grow up so fast," Hendricks said.

Hendricks turned out to be a fine cook. Either that or Gibson was hungrier than he'd ever been in his life. He polished off the eggs, bacon, and hash browns and went back for seconds. And thirds. Jenn came in from the living room and stood in the doorway.

"What was in Charlottesville?" she asked.

Gibson looked at each of them. Where to begin? Without the paternity test or Duke's thumb drive, there was no proof. How could he ask them to take it on faith? Until the paternity test had been waved in his face, he'd feared that it was his father. How to convince them that Benjamin Lombard was the real enemy? Might as well start at the beginning, he decided, and opened *The Fellowship of the Ring* to show them Bear's notes. At least it was something tangible.

"What should she have told you?" Jenn asked, looking up from the book. "What happened at the game?"

He told them about the trip to the baseball game and Bear's meltdown in the stadium. "I went to Charlottesville for my dad's diary. I thought maybe it would have the rest of the story."

"Did it?"

He told them about his dad's account. The decision to take Suzanne home early. Buying the two Phillies caps.

"Duke bought the cap?" Jenn asked.

Hendricks whistled. "That's a mind-bender right there."

He explained the origin of Tom Bombadil and why she'd invented the boyfriend. "It was Lombard," Gibson said. "That was why she ran. It was Lombard's baby."

Jenn and Hendricks sat in silence, digesting his bombshell. Then Jenn glanced at her partner and they came to a silent conclusion.

"What?" Gibson asked.

"There's something we need to show you," Jenn said.

She went out and came back with her laptop and a manila folder. From the file, she handed him a crime-scene photograph of a man who had hanged himself in his garage.

Gibson studied it. "Who is it?"

"Terrance Musgrove."

"The guy who owned the lake house?"

"The same. Now I have to show you another photograph. But . . ." She paused, hesitant to go on. "It's your father."

"Duke?" Gibson asked stupidly. "Is it what I think it is?"

"I wouldn't ask, but you need to see it for yourself."

He swallowed hard and nodded. She pulled up the photograph on the laptop and turned it around for Gibson to see. For the longest time, he stared away at the edges of the photograph, hoping it would soak into his mind through his peripheral vision. Dull the impact a little. Gibson realized he was breathing fast.

He looked.

What surprised him was how much he remembered wrong. In his mind, his father had been right next to the stairs when he'd discovered him that afternoon, looming over him, close enough to touch. But in the photograph, Duke was on the far side of the room. It was a chair, not a stool, that was kicked over under his feet. His father's eyes were closed, not open.

"Why am I looking at this?" he asked, looking back and forth between the two photographs. They had everything in common that two dead men could. They were even in their socks. The shoes. Wait. He went back to the other photograph. The shoes were the same.

"The shoes?"

Jenn nodded.

He looked again. In both photographs, the shoes were placed carefully together and pointed away from the body at an angle. The same angle. A man, hanging, would naturally convulse; the rope would twist and spin. It would take time before the rope came to its final rest. The position of the shoes was an impossible coincidence.

"He killed them both."

"And now he's reappeared ten years later to kill you."

"It's insane," Gibson said.

"Out of curiosity, was the guy's nose broken?" Hendricks asked.

"Yeah. How did you know?"

"Fiftyish? White. Thin. Short brown hair, balding. Kind of nondescript?"

"Yeah, that's the guy."

Hendricks shook his head. "Same son of a bitch who shot Billy Casper. And I can't prove it, but I'd throw Kirby Tate in there too."

"It gets weirder," Jenn said. "I saw that same guy shoot one of the tactical guys in the back."

"Friendly fire?" Hendricks asked.

"Nothing friendly about it."

Hendricks chewed that over. "So Lombard gets wind that we've been in contact with WR8TH and calls in his old hitter to tie up loose ends. He's been on us from day one. Follows us to Pennsylvania, waiting to see if we find WR8TH before making his move."

"But he jumps the gun and kills Kirby Tate in the storage locker instead," Jenn said.

"Right."

"And sends in that tac team to mop us up at the lake house," Hendricks added.

"Yeah, because like a fucking idiot I gave Mike Rilling our twenty."

"You think Rilling gave us up?" Hendricks asked.

Jenn shrugged. "How long after we talked did they show up?"

"Son of a goddamn bitch."

"Who were they?" Gibson asked.

"Don't know. Lombard has ties to an outfit called Cold Harbor. I wouldn't bet against it being them."

"Then why would he send in his hitter?" Hendricks asked.

"Get him out of the way too? No reason to leave him breathing, now that it's all over."

"Lombard isn't screwing around," Hendricks said.

"Would you?" Jenn asked. "With what's at stake in Atlanta? Lombard is the chosen one at this point. If Gibson is right, and he was molesting his own daughter, got her pregnant . . . Good God, there are powerful interests with a lot riding on him winning in November. How far would you go to keep it a secret?"

"As far as Suzanne?" Gibson said.

"You think he killed his own daughter?"

"I don't know. Billy said something like that, and I thought he was crazy. But is he? Where *is* Suzanne? Her baby? If she's alive, and if Lombard's guy got to Musgrove ten years ago, then that means he got to Suzanne as well. Tell me I'm wrong. Where is Suzanne?"

Jenn put her face in her hands. Hendricks looked like he'd unlearned the art of breathing. As Gibson saw it, they only had one play left to make, and it needed to be made soon. If they weren't in Lombard's crosshairs at this very moment, they soon would be. But even if they somehow survived until the convention was over, the nomination secured, Lombard would never call off his dogs. The three of them represented too great a threat. He would hunt them. He would find them. He would kill them. It was inevitable. They simply lacked the resources to stay hidden from a man destined for the White House.

"Well, this is a hell of a ghost story, but can we prove any of it?" Hendricks asked.

"We can prove she was pregnant."

"But we can't connect it to Lombard?"

Gibson shook his head.

"So what's our move?" Jenn asked.

"We go to Atlanta."

"To the convention?" Hendricks said. "How long did you lose oxygen to your brain?"

"It's the only way," Gibson said and explained his plan. It wasn't without risk. It meant walking into the lion's den. It meant turning to the one person who might, just possibly, be innocent in all this. It meant getting to Grace Lombard and proving the unprovable—that her husband had raped her daughter and was involved with her disappearance.

When he was done, no one spoke. There was nothing to be said. One by one, Jenn and then Hendricks left the kitchen. Like boxers retreating to their corners to regroup after getting their bells rung. Gibson went to the fridge to see what else there was to eat.

A hanging did wonders for a man's appetite.

CHAPTER FORTY-THREE

When they pulled into Atlanta a week later, the city was humming and the convention in full swing. Atlanta was also, quite literally, sold out. Conventioneers were buoyant and optimistic about their man and his chances come the general election. They were feeling no pain; it was as close to Mardi Gras as politics got. The streets surrounding the convention center were a complex warren of security checkpoints and media encampments. The sidewalks, thick with pedestrians at all hours, were cumbersome to navigate. Atlanta accepted the intrusion with good old-fashioned southern hospitality. Certainly the bars and restaurants around the convention center weren't complaining.

Gibson watched Grace Lombard's personal assistant, Denise Greenspan, come around the corner toward him. History and political science double major at Hamilton College. Master's in public policy from Georgetown. The sidewalk was overflowing with conventioneers, but there was no danger of losing sight of her. At five foot eleven, she had a distinctive, gorgeous Afro with just a hint of red to it. Today it was tied back with a yellow-and-green head scarf and swayed regally above the sea of heads as she walked. She'd run cross-country and track at Hamilton, and the previous fall had finished the Marine

Corps Marathon in 3:28—an impressive pace for a first timer. Back in Washington, Denise ran with Grace most mornings, which insiders claimed was the core of their close working relationship. Denise had been with Grace for four years and by all accounts was fiercely protective of her boss.

She was also a creature of habit. Each of the last three evenings at six p.m., she had taken an hour for herself to have dinner at the same sushi restaurant some eight or nine blocks from the convention center. She favored the same table in the front window, surfing news and political blogs on her laptop while she ate.

Yesterday, Hendricks had taken the table beside her. It was a small restaurant, and the tables were narrow and packed tight together. It had made it easy to get the two fairly clear recordings of her entering her laptop password—once when she arrived, and once when she returned from the restroom. Later, Hendricks slowed the recording down and the three of them sat around a monitor going backward and forward over the tape, arguing over whether it was a K or an L. Because of the camera angle, her left hand partially obscured the right side of the keyboard. But they were reasonably certain her password was DG5kjc790GD. Or possibly DG5kjl790GD. Jenn favored DG5lhj790GD. Definitely one of those.

When Denise sat down today, it was Gibson waiting for her at the next table. He apologized and moved his bag off her seat. She smiled thanks and made herself comfortable. She set up her laptop but didn't comment on the fact they had the same computer. It was a pretty popular model after all.

Gibson went back to his work on his new laptop, which he'd bought only yesterday. Denise placed her order and proceeded to read a succession of blogs about the newly announced Lombard-Fleming ticket.

Overhead, Gibson could see Jenn's reflection in the large mirror by the door. She was at the small sushi bar with her back to him. When the waitress picked up Denise's food to take to the table, Jenn rose and went down the back hallway to the unisex bathroom. The waitress presented Denise with her food and asked them each in turn if they wanted anything else. Denise asked for a tea. Gibson asked for his check.

The past three nights, Denise had waited until her food arrived to wash her hands. Gibson held his breath until she shut her laptop and slipped out between the two tables. In the mirror, he watched her disappear around the corner. He switched laptops without looking up. Better to do something fast and with confidence than draw attention by looking around like a thief.

In his earpiece: "She's knocked. Ninety seconds."

He opened Denise's laptop and entered the first password. The log-in window shook, rejecting it. Gibson blew air up his face in frustration. Always the last one you try, he thought darkly. He tried the second . . . same thing. The third—the log-in window shook disapprovingly again.

"How are you doing out there?" Jenn asked.

"I need a minute," he muttered into his mic.

"Define a minute."

"Look it up. I'm busy."

He stared at his list of three probable passwords. The *D* and *G* were obviously her initials backward and forward. So she wasn't averse to using personal mnemonics. *D*—Denise. *G*—Greenspan. *5k*—like the race? So what were those two lowercase letters? He looked back at the three possibles they'd come up with. A lot of *j*'s, *l*'s, *h*'s and a *c*. What was she trying to spell with that alphabet soup?

He saw Jenn come out of the hallway and sit back down at the bar. *hc*—Hamilton College. *Could it be as simple as that?* he thought. He typed, "DG5khcG790GD." The computer logged him in. People loved their alma maters. He plugged in the thumb drive and began to download the file from it to her laptop. Denise Greenspan kept an immaculate desktop, so she would see the folder the first time she went to open something.

It was still downloading when Denise came out of the bathroom. He saw her in the mirror but kept his head down. What was a believable reason for being on her laptop? Other than being a thief, of course.

"Stop her," he whispered.

Jenn turned sharply and said something to Denise. Denise paused and then slowly turned her back on Gibson. The two women chatted amicably. He offered a prayer of thanks at the altar of Jenn Charles, unplugged the thumb drive, and traded the laptops back. He was packing up to pay his bill when Denise got back to her table.

"What did you say to her?" Gibson asked.

"I asked where she bought her head scarf. Said my girlfriend had similar hair, and I was looking for a gift."

They leaned forward and clinked the necks of their beer bottles over the coffee table.

"Maybe a little premature on the celebration, huh?" Hendricks was sitting by the window, looking out the gap in the curtains. They'd found a single vacant room at a motel about forty-five minutes out of Atlanta and slept in shifts, with one of them always stationed at the window.

Gibson was doing a lousy job of not staring at the burner cell phone on the coffee table between them. Was a phone the electronic equivalent of a watched pot?

Come on, Grace. Just call, already.

Hendricks snatched up the keys, saying he was hungry. He was gone thirty minutes and surprised them by bringing back food for everyone. Pretty decent Chinese. Hendricks spread the plastic dishes out on the small Formica table, and they all tucked in to eat. Hendricks only ate egg rolls. He would cut the ends off them, empty the filling out onto the table, and mix it with orange sauce. Then, laboriously, he would repack the egg rolls with a fork and finally eat them.

The phone sat in the middle of the table like a centerpiece. They talked about nothing in particular. Keeping it light. Certainly not the call they were all waiting on. For his part, Gibson kept up the pretense that he felt confident about his plan.

The contents of the message to Grace Lombard had been relatively simple. First was the photograph of Suzanne and her backpack at the kitchen table that Billy had taken all those years ago. Gibson remembered how he'd reacted to it the first time he saw it back at ACG and knew it would knock the wind out of Grace. They also included photos of Suzanne's book. The only thing they held back was the picture of Suzanne pregnant. It was his hole card, and Gibson planned to show it to Grace in person.

The final piece was a short video recording of Gibson sitting at the table with the baseball cap in front of him. Jenn had been against it. She'd wanted to send a simple letter, but he said it was the only way. She would need to see his face if they wanted any chance of a meeting.

In the video, he spoke directly to Grace.

"Hi, Mrs. Lombard, this is Gibson Vaughn. It's been a long time, but I hope you're well. You made the best sandwich I ever ate. I miss the old days at Pamsrest, and I hope the place is still standing," he said, pausing as he shifted gears. "Mrs. L., I know this is a strange way to approach you, but I believe you'll come to see that these are extraordinary circumstances. I've learned something about Suzanne, about Bear, that you need to hear. In person. I've included photographs that I believe prove the truth of what I have to say. I don't want anything. Only the opportunity to speak to you, and you alone. To tell you the truth.

"I'm going to ask you to keep this confidential until we have a chance to speak. Should you choose to involve your husband, then I guarantee that you will never know why your daughter left home or what happened to her. That may sound like a threat, but it is simply the truth."

Hendricks had called the plan insane and tried to tear it apart. He was still taking potshots at it tonight.

"Hey," Jenn said, "it's our best shot."

They'd been having variations of this argument since Greensboro. Hendricks, to say the least, had been skeptical right down the line.

"Yeah, but for all we know, she'll take the message straight to her husband. I don't care how well you knew her as a kid, Gibson. You really think she's going to keep something like this secret from him?"

"Yes, I do."

"Why?"

"Because it's Grace, and this is about Suzanne."

Hendricks groaned. "Well, be sure and tell that to the SWAT team when they get here. I'm still in favor of just going public, huh? Go to the media. Post it all over the Internet. The book. The cap. Once it's out there, then he'll have no reason to go after us."

They'd been over all this in Greensboro. But Hendricks wasn't the only one who had doubts, and sometimes it just helped to go back over things.

"That won't work," Gibson said in unison with Jenn.

"Why not?"

"You were a cop, right?" Gibson asked.

Hendricks didn't look inclined to admit to it just at the moment.

"Well, there's what you know, and then there's what you can prove. And what can we prove? The book doesn't do anything but ask questions. The hat doesn't prove Lombard is a pedophile. We go to the Internet, we're just another paranoid theory among a constellation of wacked-out conspiracy theories. It does us no good."

Hendricks grudgingly accepted the truth of what Gibson was telling him, but he wasn't happy.

"Yeah, but this is insanity. You're actually talking about walking into that hotel. It's a fortress. And it is guarded by Lombard's men. You go in there, you're a dead man."

"I think you've got it backward. That hotel is probably the safest place for me."

"How you figure that?"

"Have you seen any stories about us on the news?"

"No."

"Right, because Lombard is playing this one off the books. Secret Service isn't looking for me. It's these Cold Harbor guys, and they won't be anywhere near the hotel."

"It can't be done," Hendricks said.

"It has to be done," Jenn said. "She's the only one who will believe us. She's the only one Lombard can't silence."

"If Grace thinks I can tell her something she doesn't know about Suzanne, then she'll listen," Gibson said, hoping the statement didn't sound as wishful as it felt.

"Well, what if she knew about it? What if she's just as twisted as her husband?" Jenn had slid back to Hendricks's side of the argument.

"No, I don't believe that. I knew her. There is no way that Grace Lombard had a part in it."

"But what if she's made her peace with it and likes the prestige and power too much to give it up now? You'll just be walking into a trap."

"Maybe she has, but my father always said she was the most grounded person he'd ever met in politics."

"Jesus," Hendricks said. "Are you really going to hang your life on a twelve-year-old opinion? By a man who, no offense, kind of fatally misread his boss?"

"Look, you may be right," Gibson said. "It's probably a stupid idea. But if so, then we have nothing that'll work. And that means running. And if we run now, we run for the rest of our lives. That's what I call a stupid idea."

That quieted them all. Yes, it was a terrible plan, and it was their only option.

Hendricks chuckled. "Goddamn, Vaughn. When did your balls drop? I like the new you."

The phone rang. They stopped and stared at it. It was painful letting it ring, but that was the arrangement. After a while the phone buzzed to tell them that they had a voice mail.

Jenn took up the phone and listened to the message. When she was done, she shut it and looked up at them.

"We're on."

CHAPTER FORTY-FOUR

Denise Greenspan stood on the far street corner, looking less than thrilled. She checked her phone every thirty seconds. Down the street, Gibson watched her from the window of a coffee shop, wishing Hendricks had tried a little harder to talk him out of this.

"If she's got a tail, they're good," Jenn said through his earpiece. She was on a nearby rooftop that gave her line of sight of the intersection in both directions.

"That's very reassuring."

"I don't remember saying anything about 'reassuring' when you proposed this crazy plan."

"I figured it was implied."

"Implied? All right, well, the average life expectancy of a white American male is seventy-six point two years. So statistically, you're probably going to be fine."

"You're really bad at this."

"Look, for what it's worth, I think you're a damned good judge of character. I just hope Mrs. Lombard's still the woman you remember."

A long pause came over the earpiece.

"Any last words?" she asked.

Nothing leapt to mind. He dropped the earpiece in the trash—wasn't getting inside the hotel with it anyway—and stepped out onto the street. Time to get accustomed to dangling in the breeze. On the way across the street, he glanced up at Jenn to give her a nod, but she was gone.

Denise Greenspan stiffened when he walked up to her.

"You're that guy from the restaurant. You sat next to me."

"Sorry about that," he said.

"How'd you get my password?"

"You sit in the same seat every day. I videotaped you."

"Unreal. You take anything else?"

"No."

"As if I'm going to believe you."

"I wouldn't."

She pursed her lips. "What happened to your neck?"

"Someone tried to hang me."

"Serves me right for asking. Come on."

The bruising around his throat had faded some, and his beard was thick enough now to conceal the worst of it, but he pulled his collar up and readjusted his tie.

"Are we alone?" he asked, trying to judge her intent.

"What? Yeah, we're alone, Deep Throat. Those were your instructions. But let me tell you, I looked you up. I know what you did. What you tried to do anyway. So listen, if you're here to mess with Mrs. Lombard. In any way. I mean, if this is some con bullshit. If that picture of Suzanne is Photoshopped, and you're just out to hurt her or play on her goodwill, I will boil water on my stove, tie you down, and pour it down your lying throat. Am I clear?"

"That was vivid," he said. "Yeah. You have my word."

Her genuine irritation actually gave him hope that Grace Lombard was playing straight with him. Of course, Denise might not even know she was helping to set him up.

This was going to be tricky. What he had told Jenn and Hendricks was true—he believed Grace was someone he could trust. But obviously that trust only went one way. So if she didn't trust him, how to convince her that her husband, a man she did trust, was involved with Suzanne's disappearance? One solitary piece of actual proof sure wouldn't hurt. Proof he didn't have any longer thanks to the man in the basement. So how to get her to see the truth? He couldn't be the one to say it; he knew that. It had to come from her. Grace Lombard had to connect the dots for herself. If she felt she was being manipulated, her open mind would snap shut like a trap.

The crowds thickened as they neared the convention. Lombard's acceptance speech was scheduled for that evening, and the city hummed in anticipation.

"I listed you as media, doing an interview with Mrs. Lombard," Denise said. "Just use your real name. Show them your driver's license. You're not getting past these guys with a fake. But I'll walk you through. There won't be a problem."

Jenn had described what security would be like around the convention center, but if anything she'd undersold it. The law-enforcement presence was astounding: Atlanta PD, Secret Service, and elements of the National Guard. The convention hall and hotel had layer after layer of checkpoints. Someone might beat one, but the chances of penetrating all of them seemed nonexistent. After all his talk of this being the safest place for him, he was beginning to realize it was just that, talk.

A pair of uniforms stared hard at him as he passed by, and it was hard to muffle the paranoid voice in his head telling him to run far and to run fast.

Turned out Denise Greenspan was a good person to know. She took him around to a side entrance that was just for campaign staff. There was a line of about twenty people waiting to be checked through by security. Denise breezed right to the front, which he expected to cause a riot but didn't raise so much as an eyebrow. This was Lombard's party now, and everyone knew it.

Denise knew every Secret Service agent by name. "Hey, Charlie, I'm taking this gentleman up to interview Mrs. Lombard. Last-minute thing. He doesn't have credentials, but I put him on the list last night."

Charlie scanned a clipboard, nodded, and waved them through the metal detector, where a second agent patted Gibson down, went through his bag, checked his ID, and ran a wand over him. They handed him a temporary credential and wished him a good day.

Denise took him down a hallway to a bank of elevators. There were eight in total. The first six elevators were for general use. The two on the end were cordoned off, and Secret Service had set up yet another checkpoint.

"These two elevators are locked out," Denise explained. "One goes to the vice president's staff headquarters. The other elevator goes to Mrs. Lombard's suite. She will see you there."

"Out of curiosity, where's the vice president now?"

"He's tied up in meetings. He'll be busy right up until the speech."

"Yeah, but where?"

"One floor down."

That didn't sound nearly far enough away for comfort.

The Secret Service stopped them again, and they went through the whole procedure a second time: pat down, wand, ID check. Gibson held his breath, but his ID came back clean again. *Fortune favors the stupid,* he thought.

Nah, said the voice, *they're just taking you somewhere quiet, out of sight.*

An agent rode up with them and started the elevator with a key. A claustrophobic sweat crawled down Gibson's back, and when the elevator stopped on a middle floor, he flinched. Heart beating hard.

Calm down. Now.

"Figured Lombard for a penthouse kind of guy," he said.

"It varies," Denise said. "Not advisable to be predictable about where you stay in a hotel. Makes you vulnerable to an exterior strike on the building."

She stopped them in the hallway and made a call to say they had arrived.

"What now?"

"Now we wait."

"Here? You're kidding me, right?"

Denise shrugged. "You think it's easy to clear her entire staff and schedule without raising eyebrows? You wanted private. Private takes time."

"It's a hallway."

"Well, then, try not to make a scene."

They stood in the hallway for twenty agonizing minutes, during which Gibson learned the true meaning of paranoia. Every staffer who passed them in the hall, every sidelong glance cast his way—he tried to interpret the meaning. Hunting faces for any glimmer of recognition or intent. As the minutes ticked by, the hallway narrowed and stretched out toward infinity. A bespectacled man stopped to consult with Denise about that evening's itinerary. When they stepped away, Gibson swore he heard his name in their muted conversations.

Denise graced him with a humorless smile and led him down the hall to Room 2301, knocked once, and without waiting for a response, let him inside.

CHAPTER FORTY-FIVE

Jenn watched Denise Greenspan lead Gibson away up the street. It was a brave thing he was doing, but she wondered if he knew why he was doing it. Was it to keep them safe or to get justice for Suzanne and Duke? If he could only have one, which would he choose? Would he sacrifice them to take Lombard down? For all their sakes, she hoped it didn't come down to that.

When Gibson passed out of sight, Jenn slipped a cell phone and battery out of her pocket and turned it over and over in her hand. She'd taken it off one of the bodies at the lake house in Pennsylvania. Neither Gibson nor Hendricks knew she had it, and Hendricks would have her committed for what she was about to do. Might be right too. But the bad guys had George . . . She didn't know who they were, maybe Cold Harbor, maybe some other outfit, but they had George, and they were going to give him back.

She didn't know if he was still alive, but if he was, then the clock would be ticking the second Gibson entered that hotel. There was no telling how Lombard would react if he felt cornered.

Jenn slid the battery back into the phone and powered it up. They'd be able to track it now. If they were looking. She thought for a second and dialed Abe Consulting's disconnected main line. She called Hendricks's cell next, wherever the semi had driven it. The call went to voice mail; she left a message of dead air and hung up. Finally, she called George's cell. It was a number she hadn't dared try since the lake house; she held her breath while it rang and only exhaled when she heard George's outgoing message.

She kept it brief. "George. Had to put down some strays in Pennsylvania, but we're clear and safe. We found what we were looking for. Awaiting instructions. Four. Zero. Four."

That ought to give anyone listening something to think about. The Atlanta area code was 404. A bit obvious, but she wasn't in a subtle mood. She was banking that they wouldn't be either. They'd lost a lot of men at the lake house, and payback was a powerful motivator. She tucked the phone into an air vent and took the stairs to the sidewalk. Down the block she entered a parking garage; from its third level, she had a clear view of the main entrance to the building where she'd left the phone.

She didn't have long to wait—someone had anticipated them showing up in Atlanta.

A black SUV rolled to a stop in front of the building and sat idling at the curb. Minutes passed. They weren't storming the building, so Pennsylvania had taught the bastards something.

Good for them.

A back door opened and a man in a Windbreaker and combat boots got out and went into the lobby. There was only one reason to wear a loose-fitting Windbreaker on this still Atlanta morning.

She saw no further movement for five minutes; then two more doors opened and a pair of men walked briskly into the building after their colleague. That left only the driver.

Perfect.

Movement down on the street caught her eye. The green hood of a car nosed to a stop at the mouth of the alley beside the garage.

They'd brought backup. That was smart. She couldn't see how many were inside, but a car in an alley would be infinitely easier to take than an SUV on a sunny street. Christmas had come early.

Jenn crossed the parking garage to the rear stairwell. As she reached for the door, it opened and a man with a gym bag stepped through. She stepped aside, and their eyes met for a moment. He hid it well, but she caught the slight stutter in his stride as his brain recognized her and forgot about walking for a millisecond. He took a step past her and nodded politely, fumbling with the zipper on his gym bag. She snapped her telescoping baton down along her thigh to its full twenty-one inches.

He heard its metallic rasp and gave up on the zipper, instead swinging the bag into her. He was a big guy, and it was a heavy bag. It caught her hard in the shoulder, and she stumbled sideways, falling to one knee. He dropped the bag and took a swing at her. She blocked it with the baton as he stepped in close. With his size and weight, grappling would be a lost cause. Instead, she drove the heel of the baton into the peroneal nerve of his thigh. The leg went dead, and he staggered backward. She was up before he hit the ground, and stomped the ankle of his good leg—she heard the tendons snap as she stepped over him. The baton whistled through the air again and again until he lay motionless. She raised the baton again, adrenaline pumping, and breathed to control her fury. The sensible fear she felt before a fight had fled. Now she simply wanted a pound of flesh, and his would do. She spun the weapon in her hand and used his face to retract the baton.

While she caught her breath, Jenn zip-tied him, wrist and ankle, and dragged him behind a parked car. In the gym bag was a sleek black CZ 750—a short-barreled Czech sniper rifle that was far from standard issue for federal agents. She could see how it might come in handy and shouldered the gym bag.

The stairwell put her out at the far end of the alley behind the car. She only saw the one head, most likely the partner of the man upstairs. His elbow rested out the window. She drew a compact stun gun, pressed it to her ear like a phone, and walked up the driver side of the alley, carrying on an imaginary conversation about her crazy night.

The stun gun crackled against his neck.

The driver twitched, his mouth lolling open comically. The low voltage would only incapacitate him for a few minutes, so she zip-tied his wrists to the steering wheel. She cut his seat belt away in case he thought about getting cute on the drive, then got in beside him and pressed the barrel of her gun against his groin.

"I've had a bad week, so I'm most likely going to shoot you when this is all over," she said. "But if you're good, I'll let you pick where. Get me?"

The driver nodded and licked his lips.

"Good. Well, it's a nice morning for a drive. Head north."

He pulled out slowly from the alley and turned left. She watched the stationary SUV until it was out of sight.

"You Cold Harbor?"

The driver nodded.

"Still having trouble talking?"

He nodded again.

"That's okay. It'll give me time to describe what happens if you can't help me find George Abe."

CHAPTER FORTY-SIX

For an agonizing moment, Gibson tensed as he was led into the suite. If it was an ambush, then this would be the place to do it. He held his breath, half expecting to be greeted by a gun. But, mercifully, Grace Lombard stood alone at the window.

The bright Atlanta sun shone through her blonde hair, which fell in a wave to her shoulders, bangs swept neatly to one side—her trademark. It wasn't possible, but she looked exactly as he remembered her. Always a petite woman and never known to be dressy, she looked true to form in jeans and a plaid button-up. She appeared as if she'd just stepped off the old porch at Pamsrest. It gave him such a feeling of nostalgia, and he wanted to throw his arms around her, but Grace Lombard made no move toward him. A hug was not in the cards.

"Hello, Gibson."

"Mrs. Lombard. It's good to see you."

"Mrs. Lombard," she repeated. "You always were such a polite boy."

"Thank you for seeing me. I know it's a leap of faith."

"It is at that," she said. "I hope I was right to." She gestured for him to sit but kept her distance by the window. Her eyes looked questioningly at the bruising around his throat.

"How have you been?" she asked cautiously.

He gave her the bullet-point version of his life and finished with Ellie. "I have a daughter. She's six."

"Six?" she said. "I imagine you'd do very well with a little girl."

He found that encouraging, so he held out a picture of Ellie at the National Zoo. Grace approached, took it, and sat on a nearby armchair.

"She looks like a firecracker." The faintest caress of a smile touched her lips.

"That doesn't begin to cover it. You should see her play soccer."

"Is she good?" She handed the picture back.

"No, she's terrible, but that doesn't slow her down."

Grace laughed but stopped herself quickly.

He changed tack. "I want to thank you for the letter."

"Letter?"

"The letter you wrote me when I first went in the Marines."

"Oh, of course, yes. It seemed necessary."

"Well, it meant a lot. It helped. Hearing from you. I always meant to write back. It was just a tough time."

"It was a tough time for everyone. Not one I think of fondly. But you're welcome, Gibson. You and your father were very special to my family."

Were—past tense. There was no edge to it. Simply a statement of fact.

"Thank you, ma'am."

"Especially to Suzanne. She was devastated by everything that happened. Your father. Your . . . difficulties," she finished diplomatically.

"Yes, I'm sorry I wasn't there for her. I should have been. She deserved better."

Grace stiffened. He'd worded it clumsily so that it sounded vaguely accusatory. *Careful now,* he thought; there was only ever going to be one shot at this.

"Yes, well. Here you are now," she said. "I suppose you should explain the photograph. Where did you get it?"

"It's probably best if I start from the beginning."

"You have my undivided attention."

Gibson cleared his throat and told her the story. Told her about Abe Consulting and how they had tracked Billy Casper to Somerset, Pennsylvania. Prior to this meeting, he had considered redacting a great many things, but in the end he told her nearly everything.

Grace listened in silence while Denise hovered by the door.

When he finished describing the lake house, he took the Phillies baseball cap from his bag. He held it out to her by the brim. She held it at a distance, suspiciously.

"And what? You're telling me that this is *the* hat?"

"You tell me." He showed her the initials, and Grace studied them.

"This is her handwriting." She looked up questioningly. "And this man, Billy Casper, he gave it to you?"

"He did."

"Why wasn't he arrested? He kidnapped my daughter."

"Mrs. Lombard, Billy Casper was sixteen when Suzanne ran away."

"He was only a boy?" Grace stood and went back to the window. "How is that possible?"

He watched her carefully to see which way she was leaning: belief or denial.

"I think they were in love. Well, Billy was in love with her. I don't know about Bear."

At the mention of his old nickname for Suzanne, Grace began to weep. She didn't put a hand up to cover her eyes. She simply wept.

"There's something you're not telling me," she said at last, her almond eyes holding his gaze without modesty.

"Mrs. Lombard, when did things turn bad for Bear?"

That stopped Grace cold. "When did things start to get hard for Suzanne? Her behavior? I've asked myself that question for years; I've never been able to pinpoint it. There was no one moment. It happened over the course of several years. Little things. I thought it was just adolescence."

"Billy also gave me this." Gibson handed her the copy of *The Fellowship of the Ring*. Grace held it tightly, her head nodding at its familiarity.

"She carried this with her everywhere," she said, flipping through the pages. "After you finished reading it to her. She'd sit in the kitchen, peppering me with questions and writing in this book."

"Me too. It drove me crazy."

Grace laughed gratefully through her tears. "I looked everywhere for it. It makes sense she took it. She loved you so much."

"Do you remember Bear's nickname for me?" he asked.

"Yes," she said. "She called you 'Son.'"

He guided Grace to the page and explained the significance of the color orange. Grace read her daughter's note, and when done, she looked up questioningly.

"What baseball game?"

Gibson told her the story.

"You know, I remember that weekend," she said when he was finished. "I'd been in California for a week, visiting family, and got back the next morning. Benjamin hadn't been to bed. It was the angriest that I've ever seen him. We had such a terrible fight. And Suzanne. My God. She was a zombie for days." She looked at the cap again. "Is that where she got it? At this game?"

"My father bought it for her on the way home. To try and calm her down. You really never saw it before Breezewood?"

"Not until now. Not in person anyway. Do you know how long I stared into her eyes? Stared into that awful frozen frame of my little girl? Trying to guess what it was she was thinking? Why she ran away from me?"

"I don't think she ran away from you," he said.

"That's sweet of you to say, but she did run away." She paused and considered his words. "But not from me, you mean."

"Yes, ma'am."

"What could it possibly have to do with a baseball cap? You don't think it was an accident she was wearing it in the tape."

"No, ma'am. I think it was a message."

"A message? To whom?"

"To me."

"What does it mean?"

Gibson paused, trying to gauge the moment. At some point, he was going to have to drop the hammer on her. Was this it? He didn't want Grace to suffer, but he needed for it to hurt. It was the only way she would see. He took a breath and said it as levelly as he could.

"Bear was pregnant."

It sucked the air out of the room. Grace opened her mouth several times to speak. Her face darkened, and she stood slowly.

"I should have known better. It was a mistake to see you. Gibson, I think about the sweet little boy you were and the man you've become. I don't know how it is possible. I'll have Denise show you out."

Grace was slipping away from him as he knew she would. It was as necessary as it was cruel. She stood way out on a terrible ledge, and the fall would shatter her. Better to cast him as a liar than make the leap. But he thought he had seen a glimmer of awareness in her eyes, if only for a moment.

He held out the last picture. Bear pregnant. She snatched it from him and held it in both hands, rooted to the spot. Gibson stepped in close to her and spoke quietly.

"What it comes down to is a lie. One elegant, crafty lie. Told so convincingly that no one questioned it. Maybe I was a sweet kid like you say, and, yeah, what I am now isn't anything I'm proud of. But I know the lie from the truth now. And I'm here because you're caught up in the same lie. And it's done to you what it did to me. Caused you to make decisions and arrange your life around it. So when you're told the truth—that your daughter was pregnant, that she ran away because she was scared—you can't hear it. But that *is* the truth of the lie. And it leads to one question. Who is the father?"

"Get out!" Grace screamed.

Denise stepped between them. "Trust me, you do not want the Secret Service to come in here."

"I knew it had to be something like this," Grace choked through a torrent of tears. "Another sick attempt to humiliate my family. Is your grievance with my husband really so important to you? Suzanne adored you, Gibson. You would really ruin her reputation just to hurt him?"

"Is everything all right in there?" a man's voice asked.

It got quiet in the suite. Denise raised an eyebrow at him—*What's it going to be?*

"I'm going," Gibson said.

"Yes, we're fine, John. Thank you," Grace called out to the Secret Service agent on the other side of the door.

She held out the book to him, but he shook his head.

"It's yours. You should keep it."

"Is it even genuine?"

"You know it is."

Grace flipped the pages carelessly, holding the book at arm's length, as if it were bleeding. Then she stopped, breath caught on a jagged thorn, her hand trembling as it flattened out the pages.

"Grace?" Denise asked. "What is it?"

Grace, pale as old wheat, looked up at them.

"My favorite color is blue."

CHAPTER FORTY-SEVEN

Tinsley crouched in the bathroom and let the air-conditioning vent whisper truth to him. He'd been there a long time. Silent and still. Eyes closed. Listening to the room next door.

After the interruption in Charlottesville, it had taken some effort to track them down. They weren't fools. Once they knew they were being pursued, they had done an admirable job of covering their tracks. It wasn't until Atlanta that he'd picked up the scent again.

Calista Dauplaise was very unhappy. Understandable. The altercation at the lake house had been a bad business. Tinsley agreed wholeheartedly. Certainly, it was her prerogative to bring in a second team, but if she didn't see fit to include him in those plans, then he could not be held responsible when the overlap led to inevitable confusion.

She had not seen it that way.

Tinsley had contemplated walking away, and under other circumstances he might have done exactly that. But she was an old client, and it didn't serve his interests to make an enemy of her. But beyond that, something held him to these three people. A sense of history. Of unfinished business. It had been more than ten years since he'd entered this narrative. He felt an unexpected kinship with the son of Duke Vaughn, and it was important to see the boy through to his end.

The faint click of a light switch caught his attention. Was that humming? Singing? A TV or a man? The pipes hummed, groaned, and the inviting hiss of a shower came through the vent. Tinsley waited. The hiss changed, falling to a lower register—water on skin, not on tile. It was time.

Tinsley left his room and looked out over the parking lot. Jenn Charles and Duke Vaughn's son were gone, leaving only the bitter man. He would deal with this one now while the opportunity presented itself.

Tinsley walked the eight feet to the next door and knelt as if to tie his shoe. It was a cheap motel with cheap locks—he could pick it with a Popsicle stick. He let himself into the room and drew his gun. No more interruptions. He had missed twice, and though there were extenuating circumstances in each case, Tinsley did not feel right about it. The natural course of things had been diverted like the damming of a river. And like a dammed river, Tinsley could feel nature aching to correct itself.

Apart from the glow of the television, the room was dim. The queen beds rumpled. The bathroom door ajar. The singing or humming had stopped. Tinsley moved through the room, listening for any change. He put his back to the wall of the short hallway outside the bathroom. It occurred to him almost too late that the sound the water made was wrong. It was the sharp hiss of an empty shower—water on tile.

Tinsley brought his arms up and partially deflected the crowbar away from his head. Pain lanced through his wrists, and the crowbar scraped across the top of his head. It burned like a striking match. His gun spun across the floor. Tinsley pivoted to better defend against the next blow. It would be hard to bring a crowbar around effectively in the hallway, and it should give him time to reestablish himself on an equal footing. Unfortunately, the bitter man had the same thought. The crowbar clanged off the floor as a fist caught Tinsley on the bridge of his nose. His nose had only just begun to knit back together after Pennsylvania, and the blow ruptured it again. He tasted blood as he fell.

The bitter man forced him to the floor with several well-placed blows. Tinsley appreciated their ferocity but also their precision. Such a thing was difficult to accomplish in tandem.

The blows spun Tinsley around, and he felt a knee land heavily between his shoulder blades, the hard snap of cuffs around his wrists, and the cold circle of his own gun pressed to his temple.

"You're not as tough when someone knows you're coming."

"Is anyone?" Tinsley asked.

"Who do you work for?"

Tinsley fell silent.

"You understand you're dead if I don't get what I want," the bitter man said. "Maybe you've got some kind of code about covering for your clients. I don't really give a good goddamn. But you think on what use that reputation will be to a dead man."

Tinsley blinked through the blood. "What's a code?"

"Last chance. Who hired you? Benjamin Lombard?"

"Who?"

"Where's George Abe?"

"Who?"

"All right," Hendricks said. "Have it your way."

The bitter man dragged him into the bathroom. Tinsley understood. The tile would be easier to mop up.

"I'm going to ask you some questions. If I don't like the answers, then you're going in the bathtub. And it won't be for bath time. You understand me?"

"The tub will catch the blood when you shoot me."

"That's right."

"Pull the curtain. It will help contain the runoff."

"What are you?"

"I'm your friend."

The bitter man snorted. "My friend? You kill all your friends?"

"We weren't friends then. We had no basis for friendship."

"Oh, and now we do?"

"Things have changed. You are in the position to let me go. So I would like us to be friends. And in return I will do you a favor. One friend to another."

"You're an optimistic son of a bitch, aren't you?" the bitter man said, hauling Tinsley up to a sitting position. "Does this favor involve telling me who you work for?"

"No, this favor involves giving you the gun and shell casings that prove you killed Kirby Tate."

The bitter man sat on the toilet with the gun pointed at Tinsley's chest.

"Where is it?"

"In the trunk of a car. In a few days, if you kill me, the vehicle will be towed. The police will find your gun in my trunk. Your fingerprints. Other incriminating items," Tinsley said. "Or we can walk out together, as friends, and I can give it to you. And go our separate ways."

"And the body?"

"I didn't pack it," Tinsley said. "But the GPS coordinates where it's hidden—I have those."

"And you will leave me and my associates alone?"

"Yes."

The bitter man stared at him a long time.

"So," Tinsley said. "Friends?"

CHAPTER FORTY-EIGHT

Grace put out a hand, reaching back for the arm of the chair behind her, unable to look away from the book. Her hand hung there, forgotten, and her face flooded with a pain, profound and deep, as a thousand shards began to fall into place—the fragments of a knowledge that she hadn't known existed. But as it assembled itself from previously unconnected memories, as she stepped back and began to see not only the tail but also the entire elephant, Grace Lombard opened her mouth and let out an agonized cry.

"What is it, Mrs. Lombard?"

"Goddamn you, Gibson." She slammed the book into his chest, the book still open to the same page, and turned to Denise.

"Where is he?" she asked Denise.

Gibson held open the book, looking for writing in blue ink. He found it in the left margin:

I wish I could explain. If I go now, before he finds out, he'll be okay again. He will. I bring out something bad. That's what he always says. I just shouldn't have waited so long to leave. I was afraid. I'm sorry. Don't be sad.

Gibson looked up in horror at Grace, but she was already halfway to the door.

"Who?" Denise asked.

"My husband, Denise. Where is he?"

"Mrs. Lombard?" Denise asked, unease heavy in her voice. "What is it? Sit down for a minute. Talk to me. What's the matter?"

Grace spun back to Denise aggressively. "Stop handling me, Denise. My husband. Where is he?"

"Conference Room Three," she stammered. "Mrs. Lombard?"

But Grace was out the suite door and past the startled Secret Service agent before he could react. Half running, half walking, she plowed down the hall with a look on her face that threatened dire consequences. Staff scurried from her path like field mice from a thresher.

Denise trailed after her. Gibson trailed after Denise, who glared back at him angrily, accusingly. The Secret Service agent brought up the rear.

They caught up to Grace Lombard at the elevators. The down arrow was lit, but she pounded away at the "Down" button—a morphine drip for her uncontainable agony.

The ride was one short floor down, but it felt like a life sentence in that elevator. Such was the tension in the claustrophobic space. Denise tried to get Grace to acknowledge her; when she couldn't, she turned her anger on Gibson.

"What have you done?" Denise wrenched the book out of his hands.

He wished her luck. Whatever forces he had set in motion, it was out of his hands now. It was down to the Lombards now. He and Denise were merely bystanders.

It was standing room only in Conference Room Three. The vice president stood at the head of an enormous conference table. His jacket was off, top button unbuttoned, tie loosened, and shirtsleeves rolled up to the elbow. He looked like a man bellied up to a bar after closing a big deal, ready to tell stories and toast his victory. Instead he was holding court with his advisers, speechwriters, and press liaisons arrayed around the conference area in order of importance. It was like an old medieval throne room—proximity to power *was* power. The outer ring contained lesser celestial bodies: eager assistants, interns, and aides.

There was an upbeat feel-good vibe to the proceedings. Gibson heard it in the conference room before he saw anything—the murmur of generous, self-congratulatory laughter. There might be work yet to do, but an air of celebration had already taken hold.

The pair of agents guarding the door had been alerted that something was up. Each stood at least six foot three, with wrists thicker than Grace Lombard's legs. They stood shoulder to shoulder and struck a conciliatory, soothing tone. They never stood a chance.

"Mrs. Lombard. Can I help you with something?"

"Thomas, I'm fond of you, but get out of my way or when I'm through in there, you're next," she said. "I'm only going to tell you once."

Once was enough. The two massive agents parted. They closed ranks, blocking Denise and Gibson's way. Grace came to a halt just inside the conference room, her eyes resting heavily on her husband. Those nearest saw her and fell silent, feeling a terrible change in the atmosphere—dogs before the storm. Their silence rippled across the room. Conversations drifted off. Uncertain faces looked up expectantly until the only sound was an oblivious staffer on his cell phone, talking excitedly about television spots for Iowa. Someone elbowed him, and he turned, ashen faced, to join the mute chorus.

The room waited for her to speak, but she just went on staring at her husband. The vice president cleared his throat. He was an expert politician. He'd spent his career learning to deflect questions from reporters. He'd been described as unflappable so often it had become a cliché in the press. This was something else.

"Grace?"

"Out. Everyone," she said.

No one moved.

"Grace. What is it?" Lombard asked.

"You want to do this in front of them? Because I will."

The room's eyes flickered toward their boss. Lombard didn't like the rumble that accompanied her question. He forced a smile onto his face.

"All right, everyone," he said, a portrait of benevolence. "We're in good shape here. Let's take an early lunch. We'll reconvene at twelve thirty."

Some gathered up their things, trying not to look like they were hurrying. Others just left everything behind, anxious to be out of the terrible room. It was an awkward, tense few moments while the staff shuffled out past Grace. Lombard looked at his wife like a gambler trying to decide whether to call, fold, or possibly raise. The herd gathered in the hall, wary faces blank with questions. Some tried to pry an explanation from Denise, but she waved them off; others talked among themselves. Finally, an imposing older man with an important-sounding voice ordered them to disperse.

As the hall emptied, Gibson heard muffled, angry shouting through the thick door. The two Secret Service agents stared straight ahead and pretended they couldn't hear the war breaking out inside. He and Denise stood before the door expectantly, like Dorothy's inept cohorts hoping for an audience with the Wizard. The older suit approached Denise and demanded to know what was happening.

"I don't know."

"I'm the vice president's chief of staff. What is happening?"

"Ask him." She gestured to Gibson with her chin.

"Leland Reed," the man said and put out a hand.

Gibson looked at the hand. "A little friendly advice, Leland. Get your résumé together."

Before Reed or Denise could respond, the door flung open, and Gibson found himself face-to-face with Benjamin Lombard. God's own minute passed between them, Grace immediately behind.

"Come back here, Ben," she said. "We're a long way from done."

Gibson watched the muscles work under his face—an epic battle to resist the body's natural responses to surprise, embarrassment, and anger. It was a remarkable display of will, and Lombard was already controlling his breathing, composing himself. Composing answers to blunt his wife's questions.

What the man needed was a push in the wrong direction.

Gibson winked.

The effect was immediate and incendiary. Any pretense of composure fled the vice president, and a great purple swell of blood flooded his neck and face. Lombard pushed through the two agents, fists rising as he came toward Gibson.

All Gibson could think was *Please, please, please punch me.* He couldn't possibly be this lucky. He willed his hands to stay at his side. Defenseless would play even better. *Make it a good one, you son of a bitch. Nail your coffin shut.*

Calista Dauplaise remained seated at the end of the conference table, a look of anguish warping her imperious face. What was she doing there? But before he could answer his own question, Benjamin Lombard threw a haymaker and caught him flush on the jaw. The VP was a large man, and Gibson was out cold by the time his head bounced off the carpet.

CHAPTER FORTY-NINE

Gibson came to on the floor of Conference Room Three. He lay on his back, staring up at acoustical tile. The room was empty but not emptied. It reminded him of one of those apocalyptic zombie movies—food wrappers, paper cups, briefcases, laptop cases, all strewn about the floor. The vice president's suit jacket still hung on the back of a chair. It looked abandoned.

He had felt better. His body still carried the aftereffects of having been hung by a rope, and Lombard's punch hadn't done him any favors. He sat up slowly, somewhat surprised to discover his wrists weren't shackled. Denise Greenspan sat in an armchair, studying a stain on the carpet.

"Am I under arrest?" he asked.

Denise, preoccupied with her own thoughts, took a long time answering. "No."

"I'm free to go?"

"Yeah."

He gathered up his belongings and stood. At the door, he stopped and turned back to Denise.

"You okay?"

"No, I am not okay," she said. "How about you?"

"Head hurts. I got punched. Don't know if you saw," he said and offered her a smile.

Denise didn't return it.

"Actually, I'm a little hazy on what happened."

"What happened?" By way of an answer, Denise cupped her hands together at her waist, and then raised them up over her head. She made the rumbling sound of an explosion.

"That bad?"

"Wasn't that what you wanted?"

He nodded.

"Well, you got it. Hope you're happy."

She held out a business card. He took it. It was Grace Lombard's number.

"You have any trouble, you're to call Mrs. Lombard direct."

"Anything else?"

"Shut the door behind you." She left without another word.

Out in the hall, staffers stood in frightened clumps, whispering among themselves. They were like children who knew the grownups had been fighting but didn't understand what it was about. They watched Gibson pass but didn't speak to him.

He rode the elevator down. The gloom that had engulfed the vice president's floor had not yet made its way down to the lobby. Gibson threaded his way among cheery mobs of party fat cats, delegates, and convention staff. The good times were just getting rolling as far as they knew.

Enjoy it while you can, folks.

Ahead, a pair of bellman's carts weighed down with luggage and garment bags were being wheeled cautiously across the lobby. Calista Dauplaise followed in its wake. She was barking furiously into a phone and didn't notice him, but Gibson took an involuntary step back anyway.

What's your sin, Calista?

Gibson was so lost in his thoughts that he almost missed the girl.

Little Catherine Dauplaise lagged some thirty feet behind her aunt, lost and forgotten like a stray dog following its last sure meal. She looked scared. Unmoored. The way only a child does whose world has shifted under her feet. His heart went out to her, and then something occurred to him. He stood watching her until she was out of sight, and for some time after he continued staring after her.

———————

Hours before his scheduled acceptance speech, Benjamin Lombard resigned from the office of the vice presidency and removed himself from his party's ticket. In so doing, he became the first candidate to withdraw from a presidential ticket in the nation's history. It sent shock waves through American life that wouldn't subside for years.

Looking beleaguered and exhausted, Lombard spoke for only five minutes in a faltering voice. He disclosed that recent tests had uncovered a previously undetected life-threatening condition. It would be irresponsible to continue his pursuit of the presidency under these circumstances. The American people deserved to feel confident in their president's health. It was a heartbreaking performance.

Grace Lombard was not by his side.

Gibson watched the press conference with Jenn and Hendricks from their motel room. Initially jubilant simply to be clear of the vice president's reach, they quickly fell silent as the ramifications of Lombard's charade became clear. When it was over, Jenn shut off the television.

"It's a good story," she said.

"He's got a future in Hollywood."

"But will it hold up?" Hendricks asked.

"Of course it will. People will need it to," Gibson said.

"Why do you think his wife went along with it?" Hendricks asked Gibson as if he were the expert on all things Lombard.

"Maybe to protect Suzanne's memory?" he said. "Don't know."

"Should have protected her life." It was cold, but neither of them had the words to refute Hendricks's cruel calculus.

They found that none of them wanted much to talk about what had happened. Gibson had imagined he might feel a sense of triumph. He had dreamed of taking Lombard down since he was a teenager, but there was nothing to celebrate here. In the end, this was about a missing girl who was being systematically excluded from the conversation. It might have saved the three of them, but it had brought no justice for Bear.

They hadn't won; they'd only survived.

After all they had been through, Gibson still didn't know what had happened to Bear. But he had an idea now whom to ask. He considered telling Jenn and Hendricks about his epiphany in the hotel lobby, but to them it had only ever been a job. He didn't resent them for it, but he needed to finish it on his own.

Hendricks cracked another beer and mentioned his encounter with Kirby Tate's killer. Gibson and Jenn stared at him dumbly.

"Were you going to tell us?"

"Just did."

"Are you kidding me, Dan?" Jenn said. "Give!"

Hendricks told them the story. To Gibson it was unforgivable. Hendricks had had a gun on the man who had killed his dad but let him go to cover his own ass. The same man who had hung Gibson by the neck and stolen Duke's journals. That man was out there still. Free and untouched by all this.

Jenn was far more practical. "And you think this psychopath is going to honor your gentleman's agreement? Because why? Because you were his version of 'friends'? That's insane."

"I handled it how it had to be handled," Hendricks said. "It's not your fingerprints on the gun."

They sat there in silence while Hendricks drank his beer. When he finished, it was the signal that it was time for bed. No one had anything left to say. In the morning, Gibson woke to Jenn packing her gear. Hendricks was already gone. They said good-bye in the parking lot of the motel. She gave him a brisk hug and handed him the keys to the car.

"Where are you going to go?" he asked.

"To get George."

Gibson nodded. He hadn't realized how much she cared for her mentor.

She hugged him again. "Go home," she whispered. "For real this time. See your kid."

"Let me help you."

"I'll call you if I need you."

"If you . . . need me?"

"Exactly," she said with a grin.

"Thank you for saving my life."

"Thank you for coming back," she said. "And don't even think about hugging me again."

"You know you're going to miss me."

They laughed.

"I just might," she said.

CHAPTER FIFTY

Gibson was an hour north of Atlanta when the news came over the radio that Benjamin Lombard was dead.

Responding to a gunshot at 4:43 a.m., Secret Service found a nonresponsive Benjamin Lombard in his suite. He was transported to Emory University Hospital, where he was pronounced dead. A single gunshot to the head. All indications pointed to suicide, but no official announcement was forthcoming. To Gibson's way of thinking, a private justice had been served.

There was no mention of the vice president's shoes, but that didn't stop Gibson from wondering.

Sadly, at least according to the news, Grace Lombard had already departed for their home in Virginia. A protective narrative formed around her over the course of the drive—devoted mother and wife to whom fate had twice delivered catastrophe. The name of Jacqueline Kennedy Onassis was invoked in describing her.

Gibson found he didn't care that Lombard was dead. It surprised him at first, but he found his apathy a relief. In the end, Lombard's death righted nothing and made nothing whole.

It was a ten-hour drive to Washington; Gibson made it in just under eight. He drove hard, Billy Casper's gun wrapped in a cloth in the glove box. A reminder that it wasn't over. He'd only known Billy for a couple of days but had felt a bond. Billy had said they were connected through Suzanne without ever knowing how true that was. After this was over, he'd drive back to Pennsylvania and comb the field until he found Billy. Leaving him to lie unclaimed behind an abandoned service station didn't sit well with Gibson.

He called Nicole and told her that she could go home. Her voice was tight, and when he asked if he could talk to Ellie, Nicole said she was sleeping. Silence. He wanted desperately to fill it, to tell her what he now knew about his father. That Duke Vaughn hadn't killed himself. Hadn't abandoned him. He hadn't been able to clear his father's name with the general public, but his dad had been restored to him. It wasn't a magic potion; it didn't make him intact. Life didn't work like that. But it loosened a knot down near his heart. In the last few days, he'd been able to think about his father again, and, though tinged with melancholy, his memories of the man made him smile for the first time. If not reborn, he felt, at least, rebooted.

The moment passed, and Nicole said good-bye and hung up without waiting for him to say it back. He wondered if he would ever be able to tell anyone the truth.

There was one thing left to do. For Bear.

Traffic was heavy driving into the District. He crossed Key Bridge and steered into Georgetown down M Street. He drove with the window down. Undergrads and tourists made it slow going, and once he crossed Wisconsin Avenue he turned north into the wealthy residential neighborhood behind the shops and restaurants.

The gates to Colline were closed. Gibson pulled his car up to the intercom. A man's voice answered after a long wait, and Gibson told him who he was. The gate swung open, and he drove up to the house.

A butler in a black suit opened the door and welcomed him.

"Good evening, sir. My name is Davis. Ms. Dauplaise is expecting you."

"She is?"

"Yes. She's been waiting for . . . one of you."

"Well, I'm here."

"May I offer you anything? A drink, perhaps?"

Being invited in and offered a drink by a butler wasn't exactly how Gibson had imagined this playing out, but since he was offering . . .

"I'd take a beer."

"Very good, sir."

Davis left him alone in the entry hall filled with portraits, sculptures, and the hollow echo of disappearing footfalls. Colline was enormous in its silence.

Waiting in a hideously expensive armchair, Gibson adjusted Billy's gun, which rested uncomfortably against the small of his back. On the top step of the tall staircase at the far end of the hall, Catherine Dauplaise sat watching him. It had only been a little more than a month since she had introduced herself to him at her birthday party—it seemed many lifetimes ago. Catherine was wearing a pretty blue dress. Her hands were on her knees, chin resting on her balled-up fists.

He waved, and, after a moment, she waved back.

Davis came back with his beer wrapped in a yellow cloth napkin. Fancy.

"If you'll follow me, sir."

Davis led him through the house and out to the veranda where Gibson had first met Calista. The tables and tents from the birthday party were long gone, and Colline appeared all the more regal and expansive without the clutter. Wrought-iron furniture looked out over the property, and enormous planters blazed with every kind of flower. Somehow he'd missed the koi pond altogether. At the top of the stairs, Davis stopped and pointed to the cupola at the far end of the gardens.

"Ms. Dauplaise is just there. I apologize, but she instructed that I send you on alone. If you follow the footpath, it will take you around the hedgerow."

"Get the girl packed."

"She already is, sir."

Of course she was. "This fucking woman."

"Yes, sir."

Like so much nineteenth-century architecture in Washington, the cupola was inspired by the city's early obsession with the Greeks. Doric columns supported the domed roof and flanked a set of heavy, metal-banded doors. A low wall circled the central crypt, and several rows of identical white headstones stood symmetrically along the inside.

Calista Dauplaise sat on a green metal chair between two graves. One appeared older, fully grown over. A simple white stone cross. A heavy gray marble headstone marked the other, which was topped with freshly laid sod.

Gibson detected none of Calista's haughty imperiousness. She looked tired and aged. Her formally immaculate hair had been hastily tied up, and chaotic strands hung free. On her face was the faraway look of someone waiting for a bus that they were no longer sure would come. She clutched a handkerchief and didn't look up when he approached.

"A safe trip, I trust?" she asked.

"Benjamin Lombard is dead."

"Yes, I heard. It's regrettable that some lack the fortitude to weather life's hardships."

"Should I thank you?"

"I'm sure that won't be necessary," she said. "Won't you sit?"

There was a second chair, but he didn't want to be that close to her. Instead he circled around and leaned on the headstone of the fresh grave. It read, "Evelyn Furst." She looked at him and anger flared in her eyes, but there wasn't fuel enough to keep it burning.

"Please. A little respect. That is my sister."

"You're kidding me, right?"

"Please."

He took out the gun and rested it on the headstone. "Where is Suzanne?"

Surprise crossed Calista's face.

"Don't you know? Truly?"

"Where is she?"

"She's right here. She always has been."

He followed her eyes to the grave beside him with the simple white cross. There was no inscription. In Somerset, Hendricks had told him that Suzanne must be dead. He could still see Hendricks shaking his head at him. Hope is a cancer. Either you never learn the truth, or you do and go through that windshield at ninety because hope told you it was safe to make the drive without a seat belt.

He went through that windshield now, inertia flinging him cruelly away.

Oh, Bear, I'm sorry. I'm so sorry.

Gibson reached for the gun.

"In childbirth," Calista said. "She waited too long to contact me. She was already deep into labor when we arrived. It was complicated— a breach delivery. She'd lost so much blood. Evelyn did everything in her power, but the damage was profound. There was nothing at all we could do for her."

"So you brought her here and buried her? I thought this was only for the 'family Dauplaise.'"

"I made an exception. She was my goddaughter. I wasn't about to abandon her body in the woods like an animal. My poor girl."

"Your poor girl?" Gibson said. The gun was by his side now, the trigger cool against his finger. "Stop it. It's pitiful. This charade that you're avenging her somehow. My father came to you, didn't he?"

"He did."

"Told you his suspicions about Lombard. About Suzanne. You could have stopped it then. But you didn't. Instead you sent that man to kill my father. You let it go on and on. You killed Suzanne."

Calista shook her head. "Duke couldn't be reasoned with. He didn't understand how much was at stake. Benjamin could have been brought to his senses. If your father had only listened, none of this would have been necessary."

"Shut up," he said and raised the gun. "Not one more word."

Calista had spent years twisting her evil into a logic that excused itself. What words could he speak to it? She had made right what was unforgivably wrong, and there would never be an argument against it that she would allow. But he would kill her if she said one word more.

"Why send us after her kidnapper? Why bother? Did you need revenge that badly?"

Calista looked up at him. "Do you really want an answer?"

"Yes."

"Very well. Do you know the value of a secret? I don't mean some juicy tidbit known by a handful of insiders and gossiped about over drinks, but a real secret that would cause ruin if it were revealed. Do you know its value? Being the only one to know it. Just you and the person who fears it. Such a secret places that person's life in your hands. They will do anything for you to keep it a little longer. Anything." She stretched the word out to stress the implications. "It grants one absolute power over their lives. But only if you, and *only* you, know the truth."

"So you waited all this time. Kept his secret. Just to ruin him now?"

"Is that the limit of your imagination, Mr. Vaughn? That I waited ten years to snatch his life's ambition from him? Is that what you think you saw in Atlanta? Oh, you are a small-minded boy. I did what I've always done. What Benjamin was always too arrogant to admit he needed. I protected him."

"Protected him?"

"What do you think a secret like this getting out would do to the president of the United States? It would be the end of him; the end of his presidency. And what do you think he would have done to ensure I kept his secret? *Anything.* I didn't keep his secret to ruin him. Please. I kept Benjamin's secret so that he would achieve his destiny."

"And his presidency would have belonged to you."

"To my family," Calista corrected. "You asked why I sent you after the man who took Suzanne's photograph. I thought Terrance Musgrove closed that door long ago; I was mistaken. The photograph meant that there was someone else who knew the secret. If it were ever uncovered, my hold on Benjamin would have been erased. And I had sacrificed far too much to allow it."

"My father."

"Yes."

"Kirby Tate. Terrance Musgrove. Billy Casper."

"And Jenn Charles and Daniel Hendricks and Gibson Vaughn, had things gone to plan."

George Abe, Michael Rilling, Gibson added silently to the list.

"Does Catherine know who she really is? That she's ten, not eight?"

"She has her suspicions, but I'll leave that to you."

"What have you told her?"

"Only that her time here at Colline is at an end."

He shook his head. "You talk about the decline of your family. Lady, you are the decline of your family." He held up the gun. "This belonged to Billy Casper. He would have wanted you to have it."

"Ah. When we met, you didn't strike me as an ironist."

"When you get sent looking for a missing girl who wasn't missing . . . well, you pick it up quick."

"You intend to kill me?"

"No, I intend for you to follow Benjamin's example."

"Why on earth would I do that?"

"Imagine what will happen to your precious family name when all of this goes public."

"Please. You would have gone to the police if you had enough to charge me."

"What was it you said to me when we met? The only court that matters is the court of public opinion."

"Oh, is it to be my life for my family's reputation?"

"Yes."

"Generous, but I must decline your offer."

"It's not a bluff."

"It is a bluff. Don't be petulant. I know your penchant for revenge, but you aren't man enough to inflict that suffering on Catherine."

"Catherine? What does she have to do with it?"

"Since you remember what I say with such clarity, I'm sure you recall what I said about secrets. Their power to destroy. You may hold my secret, but it is also Catherine's secret, is it not? You cannot expose me without exposing her. And in exposing her, you'll make her a pariah. A pathetic curiosity. Never to have a normal life."

He stared at her in disgust.

"One moves the pieces one has left on the board, Mr. Vaughn. If you want me dead, it will only be by your hand. However, police response times are exceptional in this part of the city, so I do hope your affairs are in order."

He eased his finger off the trigger.

"A wise decision."

"I wish I could," he said.

"And I you," she said. "Another time, perhaps."

"Stay away from Catherine. From all of us."

"Good-bye, Mr. Vaughn."

Gibson walked back to the house. His thoughts went back to Suzanne and to his father, and he felt himself go through the windshield again. The sensation of rudderless drifting returned, and he stood still until his nausea passed. It would be back. The windshield wasn't done with him yet.

Catherine was sitting by the front door. As he neared the girl, he could see that her eyes were red and swollen from tears.

"Is it time to go?" she asked, her voice soft like falling paper.

"Yes. Do you want to come with me?"

She nodded. "Is Aunt C. coming to say good-bye?"

He shook his head. For a moment, he thought Catherine would start to cry again, but she composed herself and stood.

"Will you help me with my suitcase? It's very heavy."

It was. An entire lifetime was packed inside.

EPILOGUE

The Nighthawk Diner was busy, but they found two stools by the cash register. Gibson helped himself to a couple of menus. Toby Kalpar was busy behind the counter, and it took him a few minutes to work his way down to them. He put down ice water and looked questioningly at Gibson's throat.

"Who's your friend?" Toby asked.

"Catherine, this is my good friend Toby."

She put her hand out. "I'm very pleased to meet you, Toby."

Toby raised an eyebrow. "Not yours, obviously."

"Kid, you're making me look bad here," Gibson said, elbowing her playfully in the ribs.

Catherine giggled. She sounded just like Bear. For the first time, he saw his small companion for who she was: Bear's daughter. Bear had fought for this little girl. Given her life to keep her away from Benjamin Lombard. And in that light, it was amazing to look at Catherine now. Smiling, laughing. Bear's little girl. Healthy and safe.

When Toby came back again, they ordered a large dinner. Gibson insisted on chocolate milkshakes when Catherine admitted she'd never had one before. When the food came, she ate tentatively at first, but then gobbled down her burger and fries. She slurped her milkshake and swung her feet under the stool. After dinner, they split a piece of apple pie.

"How old am I, really?" she asked in between bites.

"You're ten."

She thought that over.

"When is my real birthday?"

"February 6."

"It's always been in May before."

"I know."

"Do you think I can have another one this year?"

"Yeah, I think so."

"It's not greedy?"

"Kiddo, it's not greedy. It'll be our secret, okay?"

"Okay." She smiled at him. "Will you come to the party?"

"If I'm invited."

She beamed. "I'll invite you."

"Then I'll be there. But I want you to have one present early."

He slid a photo across the counter to her.

"That's a big frog," she said. "Is that you?"

"It is."

"Who is she?"

"That's your mother."

She looked again, more carefully this time.

"Did you know her well?" she asked.

"Yes, I knew her very well. She was smart like you. Do you like to read?"

Catherine nodded enthusiastically.

"So did your mom. She always had a book in her hands."

"What was her favorite?"

He told her about *The Fellowship of the Ring*, about how he'd read it to Suzanne. Catherine seemed to like the story and studied the picture again as he told it to her. When he was done, he excused himself and stepped outside to make the phone call.

When they got back in the car, Catherine asked where they were going. "Home," he said. She nodded and went right to sleep. If diner food was good for one thing, it was conking out kids.

Gibson drove south, alone with his thoughts. He thought about his childhood. Memories he'd suppressed for more than a decade. Of Bear and his dad. Good memories. Next season, he would take Ellie to her first baseball game. Although he wouldn't ask her to listen to it on the radio. Not at first.

When they pulled into Pamsrest, the shops in the center of town were mostly closed. The town felt familiar, but he couldn't quite remember the way. He found a gas station that was open and stopped to ask directions. A beautiful day was becoming an equally lovely night. He looked up at the faint stars before climbing back in the car.

Catherine was awake now.

They drove along the county road until they crossed the wood bridge over a dry creek bed. The fork hooked them toward the ocean, and a little after ten they pulled up at the house. It looked just as he'd remembered it.

"Is this it?" she asked.

He nodded. "Ready to meet your grandma?"

"Do you think she'll like me?"

"Are you kidding me? She's going to love you."

Out in the dark, he heard the creak and slam of a screen door.

ACKNOWLEDGMENTS

Writing is a solitary pursuit, or so goes the familiar refrain. But for myself, the opposite proved true—in writing *The Short Drop*, I discovered that it was I who had been the solitary pursuit. I am surrounded by brilliant and loving people: family and friends—it took writing a novel for me to grasp fully how fortunate I am. It is to my shame that I am so late in learning that lesson, but I am grateful that in most cases it was not learned too late. I must begin with Mike Tyner, who provided the grist for Gibson Vaughn and who made me look considerably smarter than, in fact, I am; I continue to be amazed and alarmed at the breadth of your knowledge. Eric Schwerin and Gerald Smith gave me shelter from the storm that first difficult year; I am sorry I was not better company, but in retrospect that appears, selfishly, to have been for the best. Steve Feldhaus, who has always set the highest bar, was an irreplaceable conspirator; it would be a far different book without your peerless clarity. David and Linda Gibson opened their home at Blue Run Farm with boundless hospitality when I needed to get out of the city; the best pages of this book were written there. Lori Feathers made the introduction of a lifetime in David Hale Smith, who has already proven to be a home run of a man and an agent; it was the lunch that changed my life. Alan Turkus of Thomas & Mercer—your belief in *The Short Drop* made this next chapter in my life possible; I am deeply grateful for your guidance and passion. The brilliant Ed Stackler taught me invaluable lessons about editing while also making the process feel like working with an old friend. And to the readers who lent me a gentle shoulder on which to bang my head against stubborn characters and tangled plot points—Nathan Hughes, Karen Hooper, Allie Heiman, Christine Lopez, Brian Orzechowski, Giovanna Baffico, Tom Hughes, Michelle Mutert, David Kongstvedt, Drew Hughes, Daisy Weill, Ali FitzSimmons, Kit Manougian, Rennie O'Connor, Vanessa Brimner—your generosity astounds me. Lastly, I must thank my parents—I began with a cliché, and so I think I will end with one: this book would not exist without your love, support, and wisdom. This is not a figurative platitude but an honest and literal truth.

ABOUT THE AUTHOR

Matthew FitzSimmons was born in Illinois and grew up in London, England. He now lives in Washington, DC, where he taught English literature and theater at a private high school for over a decade. *The Short Drop* is his first novel.